MW00466572

TERMINATED

ALSO BY SIMON WOOD

ACCIDENTS WAITING TO HAPPEN
DRAGGED INTO DARKNESS
WORKING STIFFS
PAYING THE PIPER
WE ALL FALL DOWN
ASKING FOR TROUBLE
THE FALL GUY
DID NOT FINISH
HOT SEAT

As Simon Janus
THE SCRUBS
ROAD RASH

TERMINATED

Ashish,

Business & writing go together always!! :)

[signature]

SIMON
WOOD

f THOMAS & MERCER

The characters and events portrayed in this book are fictitious. Any similarity to real persons, living or dead, is coincidental and not intended by the author.

Text copyright © 2010 Simon Wood
All rights reserved.
Printed in the United States of America.
No part of this book may be reproduced, or stored in a retrieval system, or transmitted in any form or by any means, electronic, mechanical, photo-copying, recording, or otherwise, without express written permission of the publisher.

Published by Thomas & Mercer
P.O. Box 400818
Las Vegas, NV 89140

ISBN-13: 9781612184036
ISBN-10: 1612184030

Dedication

For Julie. Thanks for the idea.

CHAPTER ONE

"You're enjoying this, aren't you?"

Gwen tasted Tarbell's bitterness from across her desk. She'd made a mistake. She'd feared Tarbell's performance review would turn adversarial, or to be more exact, that Tarbell himself would turn adversarial. Now she'd incited him. She knew it wouldn't take much to set him off, and she blamed herself for this unpleasant turn of events. She thought if she cataloged his positive traits before his shortcomings, it wouldn't sound so bad. A spoonful of sugar to make the medicine go down and all that. Now she saw the glaring error of her approach. It looked to him as if she'd built him up only to slap him down. She should have given it to him straight. No doubt the direct approach would have still drawn his ire, but it also would have gotten the issue out in the open earlier.

"Steve, it's not like that."

"Stephen. Only my friends call me Steve."

Gwen trod carefully. She couldn't be seen kowtowing to Tarbell on this point. If she began calling him Stephen and it got around the water cooler that he had insisted on it, it would make her look weak. She'd never had Tarbell's respect, but she couldn't afford to lose the respect of her other subordinates. At the same time, she had to respect his wishes. For now, she wouldn't call him anything.

"This isn't personal."

He leaned back in his seat, crossed his arms and legs, and twisted his mouth into a sneer. "Isn't it?"

"No, it's not. I have to follow strict criteria for performance evaluations. I couldn't make it personal even if I wanted to."

"Bullshit."

The expletive split the air like a gunshot. Gwen glanced outside her office. The outburst hadn't caught anyone's ear.

"Steve, that's enough."

"Stephen," he corrected.

It was on the tip of her tongue to tell him to grow up, but she bit the remark back. She'd only be perpetuating his juvenile behavior. This review was on the verge of getting away from her. If she followed Tarbell down this road, it would speak more to her poor management skills than to his shortcomings. She paused to give them both a moment to cool off.

Tarbell uncurled his long-limbed body, leaned forward, and pressed a fist down on the edge of the desk. Gwen fought the urge to back away.

"Why don't we cut the crap and be honest for a second. We both know why you're doing this. You want me out because you know I should have gotten the promotion instead of you. I have more experience and seniority. What do you have? Nothing, but they still gave you the job. Call it affirmative action or sexual equality or equal opportunity employment, but you only got the job because you're a woman. I should be sitting in that seat, not you. I should be telling you that you've failed to meet the standards expected of this company. Christ. What a joke."

There it was. One of them had finally said it. Tarbell's attitude had never been great, but Gwen could pretty much track his performance deterioration from the day she'd gotten the promotion to manager of Quality Assurance six months ago. They'd both gone for the position, along with four outside candidates. Despite Tarbell's experience and years with the company, they'd chosen Gwen. It wasn't just because of Tarbell's reputation for being a short-tempered workaholic. Gwen had made an instant impact at Pace Pharmaceuticals since her arrival eighteen months earlier. She'd grasped the firm's concepts quickly and patched holes in the systems that management knew existed but had been unable to fix. Tarbell relished interdepartmental battles, whereas she was a team player. These elements won her the promotion.

"What's it like to be sitting where you are based solely on possessing a vagina?"

Christ, this guy was a first-class asshole. She deserved her promotion. She squashed the knee-jerk need to defend herself and bottled her disgust.

"I think this evaluation is at an end."

Tarbell leaned back in his chair with a smug expression plastered across his face. The son of a bitch felt he'd won a round in some prizefight that didn't exist. Gwen saw no value in pointing this out to him. It would have no effect. As much as it would be a big managerial feather in her cap if she turned Tarbell around, succeeding where others had failed, it wasn't worth it. The guy would keep acting out until he gave Pace cause enough to fire him.

Gwen slid a copy of Tarbell's evaluation across the desk. "You've received a failure to meet expectations, resulting in a number of items that you must complete to remove the substandard rating. You're welcome to challenge the rating, but you have to file your complaint with Human Resources by next Wednesday."

Tarbell made no effort to take the evaluation. He seemed content to bask in his smug condescension, staring at Gwen in disgust.

"Is there anything else you'd like to say?"

Tarbell shrugged and grabbed the evaluation. "You're a class act, Gwen," he said on his way out.

Gwen remained stoic until he passed out of view of her office window, then released a breath. *Damn that man*, she thought. She shouldn't have let him get to her, but he was so infuriating. At least it was over. Done. It was his problem to solve, not hers, and she let the stress of the encounter bleed out of her. She was breathing hard and felt sweat cooling against her skin under her arms and down her back. She needed to freshen up. She still had two more evaluations this afternoon.

She made a beeline to the restroom. Thankfully, it was empty. She could do without any chitchat. She slipped off her suit jacket and frowned at the sweat rings that had turned her white blouse transparent.

"Shit," she murmured.

She locked herself into a stall and dabbed under her arms with a wad of toilet paper. She'd have to keep her jacket on for the rest of the afternoon, but it was a small penalty under the circumstances. She gave her makeup the once-over. It helped bring out her brown eyes. Her dark hair was rediscovering its natural curl. Paul liked it, but she didn't and spent way too much money keeping it straight. She ran a brush through her hair to rein in the errant strands. The makeover helped her look refreshed and unaffected by Tarbell's tantrum.

The remainder of the afternoon passed swiftly and without incident. Her two remaining evaluations helped settle her. Lauren and David received excellent reviews and were in and out of her office in less than an hour. Swift and efficient. A little too swift and efficient. She finished up David's evaluation just after three thirty, leaving Tarbell ninety minutes to retaliate against her for his perceived injustice.

But the retaliation didn't come. Tarbell passed her office twice, never making eye contact, and it didn't look like he had shared his evaluation results with anyone either. No one gave her any sideways looks. For all his slurs and insults, maybe she'd gotten through to him. Acting like an ass in the workplace wasn't acceptable, and if he expected to keep his job, he had to change his ways. Score one to her

The evaluations screwed with her day and put her behind. By four o'clock, she realized that even if she worked without interruption, she wasn't going to catch up by five. She could either pull a late one or come in early. She was leaning toward coming in early the next day, just to put this shitty day behind her, but she found a good rhythm reviewing deviation reports and decided to finish them. She left a message on the machine at home for Paul to expect her home late.

Five o'clock came and the usual exodus ensued, with almost everyone making their way to the parking lot. As the office emptied and the whoosh of the ventilation system replaced the chatter of the cube farm, she realized her mistake. Tarbell worked late every night. They'd end up alone with each other, which would give him the perfect opportunity to ring the bell for round two. But when she went to the copy room to collect a report, she found that he'd already left. No doubt he was eager to cross today off the calendar, too. His car was gone from the parking lot, which confirmed his oddly early departure. She was somewhat pleased with herself. She'd survived her first major managerial test and confirmed as much when Deborah Langan from Human Resources looked in on her way out.

"How was Steve?"

"True to form."

Deborah laughed. "That good, huh?"

Gwen smiled.

"At least you don't have to do this for another year. See you in the morning."

Gwen stayed until seven before calling it a day. Besides the security guard at reception, she was last to leave. As she pushed the door open, the rain rushed to meet her. It had been coming down hard for the last hour, and the temperature seemed to have plummeted into the forties. Just yesterday, it had been sunny and

5

seventy degrees, but the Bay Area weather changed quickly like that in the fall. Of course, she'd left her umbrella on the backseat of her car.

She sprinted as hard as she could in her heels across the parking lot. She'd landed a near-perfect parking spot behind the trash enclosure, which kept her sprint short. She had her keys out of her purse and deactivated the alarm the moment she rounded the corner and her Subaru came into view. She grabbed the door handle and tugged it open, but it slammed shut again as an unseen force behind her crushed her body against the car.

She was seized by confusion, until a knife blade jammed up against her throat brought events into sharp focus. Someone had leaped out from behind the Dumpster and slammed her into the side of her car. He'd sandwiched her between his body and the Subaru. The impact, besides driving the air from her lungs, had forced her onto her toes, making it impossible to push back. He snaked an arm around her chest and grabbed the Subaru's roof rack to keep her pinned in place. It was an unnecessary move. The blade's tip pressing hard into the soft underside of her chin kept her in check. She could kick and scream, but unless someone put a gun to this asshole's head, she couldn't beat an upward stab. She let the tension out of her body to let him know she wouldn't be giving him any trouble. He was welcome to the car and the contents of her purse.

"It's OK," she said. "I'm not resisting. I'm not resisting." She hoped her words would come out strong and calm, but fear inserted a tremor.

Just to show who was boss, he shoved against her to reestablish his hold on her. The rain coating the car soaked through her blouse. Its chill forced an involuntary shiver.

Her assailant read something into the shiver and chuckled. She recognized the sound. She examined the white-knuckled hand grasping the roof rack.

"Steve?"

"I told you, only my friends call me Steve."

Anger boiled up inside Gwen, but the knife at her throat kept it from spilling over. This was no longer a workplace war of words. She felt Tarbell's intent in every one of his taut muscles.

"What do you want, Stephen?"

"Respect at last. Who knew it took a knife to get it?"

He'd snapped. She'd pushed him over the edge. She dreaded reasking her question, but it couldn't go unanswered.

"What do you want, Stephen?"

He said nothing. Raindrops splashed down on her face. The puddle at her feet seeped into her open-toed sandals, and the tips of her toes ground into the rough asphalt.

"Is this all it takes to get some satisfaction—a knife?" He jerked the knife just enough to draw blood. Nothing extreme, just a pinprick.

"Stephen, please take the knife away."

He constricted her with his body, crushing her against her car. She felt her ribs flex against the unyielding metal door pillar.

"Giving the orders again. You can't resist, can you?" There was a singsong quality to his voice. The son of bitch was enjoying this.

"OK, you're in charge," Gwen said, trying to sound calm.

"Have you submitted my evaluation to Human Resources?"

"No."

"Good, I want you to change it. You're going to say I'm an exemplary employee and all that managerial bullshit. Make me sound great. Deal?"

He was crazy. Had to be. He was assaulting her with a deadly weapon and for what—a positive evaluation? He had to know he couldn't get away with it.

He jabbed her with the knife again. "Deal?" he insisted.

She didn't answer.

"Just know that if you don't do what I tell you, you're going to have an intimate encounter with Mr. Sharpie here. You got that?"

"Yes."

"So you'll do it?"

The reply he wanted wouldn't come. It wasn't right. It wasn't fair. This was twenty-first-century America. People didn't succeed in the workplace by using a weapon. But Stephen Tarbell had tonight. It disgusted her to comply.

"Yes, I'll do it."

"Good, Gwen, good," he cooed. "You've got until Friday."

He released his hold on her. Without the pressure of his body holding her, she staggered back, lost her balance, and dropped to the ground, landing roughly in a puddle. Her skirt had ridden up, exposing more leg than she wanted the world to see. She pulled herself into a fetal position and sobbed hard with the rain beating down on her. When she finally looked up, Stephen Tarbell was gone.

CHAPTER TWO

Gwen sat behind the wheel of her car, just staring at the world through the rain-splashed windshield, taking none of it in. Her mind kept snagging on Tarbell and the knife. She couldn't move forward. She couldn't move back. The incident continually replayed in her mind.

She wasn't sure how much time had passed since Tarbell disappeared into the night. It could have been hours; it could have been minutes. She eyed the dashboard clock. Thirty minutes had passed.

Her cell had rung a couple of times, maybe three. A little red light pulsed to let her know there were messages. No doubt it was Paul wondering where she'd gotten to. She should call him to let him know what happened. Yes, she should, but she wasn't ready to tell anyone, even Paul.

A muffled voice called out. Panic jerked her from her thoughts. It was Tarbell. He'd come back to finish the job. She couldn't file an evaluation if she was already dead. Her heart beating rabbit-fast, she searched the blurred world outside her car. It wasn't Tarbell but the security guard approaching in her rearview mirror.

She jammed the key in the ignition and fired up the engine. The guard, a man whose name she could never remember, waved and called out again. She played dumb, as if she hadn't heard or seen a soul. She jerked the selector into drive and accelerated away. The guard gave up on his pursuit before she reached the parking lot's exit.

She joined Harbor Bay Parkway and headed home to the north side of Alameda. To the other motorists, she must have seemed like a slow driver, but she didn't care. She knew that she was in a state of shock. Her hands and feet were half a beat out of time with her reactions, as if she was operating the car under water.

The car's interior misted up within moments of hitting the road, thanks to her drenched condition. The defroster failed to dispel the humidity inside the car, so she powered down the window. Rain poured through the open window along with the roar of jets flying into Oakland International Airport as she drove past a runway enclosed by a cyclone fence.

The traffic signal ahead turned red. A dilemma approached. Left took her off Bay Farm Island toward home. Straight ahead didn't. Paul would be putting Kirsten to bed in a few minutes. She'd go home when Kirsten was asleep and she had calmed down. She jerked the car out of the left turn lane and went straight, following the road that cut alongside the airport.

Questions revolved inside her head. Would Tarbell make good on his threat? He was obviously capable of sticking a knife under her chin, but was he capable of using it? She touched the place where the tip had pricked her flesh. She thought about him lying in wait for her inside the trash enclosure. Had he been waiting in the rain the entire time? What kind of person sat huddled in the rain? Her answer caused a shiver. A crazy person.

She had a simple decision to make. Comply with Tarbell's decision or go to the cops. It was a decision that wasn't coming easily.

Gwen drove around in circles—aimlessly taking one street, then another, with little in mind other than putting off the inevitable—going home. It was after eight. If she stayed out much longer, Paul would begin calling around and when he got no success there, he'd call the police. No police. Not yet. Not until she'd come to a decision. But time had run out. She turned the car around and drove home.

She pulled into her garage and took a moment to compose herself. She half expected Paul to open the connecting door to the house with Kirsten in his arms. She dreaded the scenario. One sight of her angelic three-year-old's face and she would come apart at the seams.

She climbed from the car and crossed the garage. On the ground next to the recycling can sat a wadded ball of paper—one of Paul's free throws that hadn't made the grade. She uncurled the paper and groaned when she read the letter. It was an I'm-sorry-to-inform-you letter from a prospective employer. Paul had been out of work for the last year since the downturn in the housing market. Builders didn't need construction supervisors when no one was buying houses. She winced. Paul had been convinced he'd get this job. He had to be devastated. He missed working, and they both missed the money. They'd economized where possible. The main saving came from not having to pay daycare fees with Paul home all day. Surviving on one income had been the reason she'd gone for the promotion. The salary bump kept them afloat.

She thought about cause and effect. If the housing boom hadn't fallen flat, Paul would still be working. If Paul was employed, she wouldn't have gone for the promotion. If she wasn't the boss, Tarbell wouldn't have put a knife to her throat.

What a day to bring this mess home, she thought and let herself in.

Paul was removing her dinner from the oven, twice warmed by the look of it. He set the casserole dish down on the stovetop.

"I was getting worried, babe," he said without looking at her. "You said were going to be late, but I didn't think you meant this late. Did you get my messages?" He turned to face her. "Jesus, what the hell happened to you? You're soaked."

11

"I had an accident."

"Are you OK?" He threw down the potholders and rushed over to her. "Was it the car?"

"No, it wasn't that kind of accident." She brushed him aside. "I want to get out of these things. I'll tell you once I've changed."

She closed the bedroom door and peeled off her clothes. Reaching for her robe, she caught sight of her reflection in the mirror, including the scar. Cold and wet, her skin tone looked especially pale, making the disfigurement stand out even more. It wasn't much to look at now. It was no more than an inch across, an angled line low on the left side of her belly. It was a nasty memento from another man who'd attacked her a lifetime ago. The sight of it filled her head with the violence of the past and the present. She pulled on her robe and swiftly covered the ugliness.

She'd just grabbed a towel from the bathroom and wrapped it around her wet hair when Paul opened the door. There was no avoiding him. She'd hoped for a little more time to compose herself, but his desperate expression told her that he needed to hear what happened. "I was attacked."

This simple fact slammed into Paul as hard as Tarbell had slammed into her. He looked disoriented for a moment before closing the door and engulfing her in an embrace. His contact brought no comfort. Instead, she felt smothered. It reminded her too much of Tarbell pressing her against the car, but she didn't push Paul away. She didn't want to scare him.

"Were you mugged?"

"No."

Paul's body stiffened. If she'd been attacked and not mugged, it left only one other possibility. He pulled away from her and fixed her with a stare.

"No, I wasn't raped."

He didn't say anything.

"It wasn't like that."

"What was it like?"

"I was threatened with a knife."

"Christ."

He sat her down on the edge of the bed, kneeling before her. He handled her with so much care. She was lucky to have him. She loved him so much. Tears welled up, but she willed them not to flow. She needed to keep it together while she told him everything.

"Did you call the police?"

She shook her head.

He grabbed the cordless phone on the nightstand. "The bastard won't get away with it."

She clamped her hand over the phone's keypad. "No."

"What do you mean 'no'? Someone assaulted you with a knife. People like that need to be taken off the streets. We're going to the cops."

"No," she repeated.

He lowered the phone. "What's going on, Gwen?"

"I know the attacker. It's someone from work."

"It doesn't matter if it's someone from work or a complete stranger. We have to report it."

"No."

He put the phone on the bed. "I need a reason not to call the police, Gwen, so you'd better give me one."

She told him what had happened, the performance evaluation blowup, then the rain-soaked threat in the parking lot. She watched as her account revealed Paul's layers of emotion, one replaced by the next in quick succession. Shock gave way to horror then finally to rage. His hands tightened into white-knuckled balls, and he worked his jaw back and forth, the muscles and tendons flexing with the movement. By the time she finished telling him what had happened, he seemed to vibrate with restrained hate. Tall and angular, he looked so much like Tarbell it scared her.

"I'll get him."

"No."

"Yes."

He jumped to his feet, and Gwen leaped up after him. She snagged his wrist and put herself between him and the door. He stopped in front of her.

"Get out of my way," he said as calmly as he could manage.

"What do you think you're doing, Paul?"

"I'm going to find the piece of shit and dish out some payback."

"Don't be stupid. If you touch him, the cops will arrest you and you'll go to jail, leaving me and Kirsten alone. Is that what you want?"

"Goddamn it, Gwen," he said and backed away from her.

Gwen breathed a little easier. There were other reasons she didn't want Paul confronting her attacker. Tarbell had proved he was more than just a hothead. He'd shown a malicious side of himself that Paul didn't possess. He was more likely to harm Paul than Paul was to harm him.

Paul grabbed the phone off the bed. "Call the cops before I go and do something stupid."

"Mom. Dad," Kirsten called from outside the door.

There was a tentative and nervous note to their daughter's voice. They'd made it a point never to argue in front of her. Paul had grown up between warring parents and didn't want to pass the experience on to his children.

"Shit," he murmured.

Gwen opened the door. Kirsten stood on the other side with a teddy bear in hand. Just getting out of her toddler stage, she still had a habit of throwing her arms out to her parents when she wanted comfort. Gwen scooped her daughter up.

"Too loud," she said.

"I know. Something happened that upset us."

Paul came over and stroked Kirsten's tousled hair. "I'm sorry, kiddo."

"What's wrong?"

Gwen carried Kirsten back to her room. "Silly stuff. Nothing we can't sort out."

"Mommy, I missed you at bedtime."

"I'm sorry. Blame the silly stuff. It got in the way."

"I don't like silly stuff."

"No one does," Paul said and followed Gwen and Kirsten into the girl's bedroom.

Gwen noticed that the fight went out of Paul as he kissed Kirsten good night. It made sense. She was the perfect symbol of what he'd lose going after Tarbell. When Kirsten drifted back to sleep, Paul took Gwen's hand and led her out of their daughter's room.

"You have to call someone, Gwen." He kept his voice to a whisper in the hallway. "Don't let this son of a bitch get away with it."

He was right. She couldn't ignore this. She hadn't been attacked by a stranger but by a coworker. She'd have to face Tarbell in the morning and every morning after that. She couldn't pretend nothing had happened. The problem wouldn't go away until she made it disappear.

"I'll call Pace. They should handle this."

Paul drew her to him. She felt protected in his embrace this time. "Good."

She dug her work cell phone out of her purse and dialed Deborah Langan's number.

"Hey, Gwen, I'm a little tied up at the moment. Can I call you back in the morning?"

She sat down on the sofa. Paul sat next to her. "This can't wait."

"What's wrong?"

Pressure built in Gwen's chest and kept building. It squeezed her heart and stifled her breathing. Relief was simple and she took it.

"Stephen Tarbell attacked me tonight. He held a knife to my throat and told me to change his performance evaluation or he'd cut me."

Gwen sagged after the words were out. Paul slipped an arm around her and she leaned into him.

"My God. When?"

"When I left tonight. He attacked me in the parking lot."

"Did anyone see this happen?"

"No."

"Have you spoken to the police?"

"No. I wanted to tell you first."

"OK. I want you to hold tight for the next half hour. I need to call someone. He'll get in touch. Can you do that?"

"Sure."

"Good. I'm sorry, Gwen. We'll get through this."

Deborah hung up, and Gwen tossed the cell on the coffee table. She felt better for getting the story out but was drained to the core. She no longer felt hungry, tired, or upset, just empty.

"You did the right thing, babe," Paul said.

Telling. Not telling. Neither option felt right. Either way, it was painful for Gwen, and she knew that feeling wasn't going to go away for some time to come.

"What did they say?"

"They're rallying the troops. Someone's calling back."

"I'll get you some dinner."

She poked at the meal Paul brought her until her phone rang.

"Hello, Mrs. Farris, my name is Robert Ingram from Private Security International. I'm a consultant for Pace Pharmaceuticals. I handle violence in the workplace claims, and I'll be handling your problem. Deborah Langan contacted me about an incident with Stephen Tarbell."

Ingram spoke with an officious cop-like cadence, but there was a calming quality to his voice Gwen liked and needed to hear. It soothed away the stress knots in her neck that the evening's events had triggered.

"I need to work fast, and I need your help. Are you up for answering some questions?"

"Yes."

Ingram wanted to know the what, where, when, why and how. She gave him everything except the why. He'd have to get that from Tarbell.

Paul stayed with her, although listening to her recount the assault had to be torture for him. She took his hand and held it to her chest to help him through it.

"You haven't spoken to the police?"

"No."

"Can I ask you to hold off for the moment?"

"I'm not sure I want to involve them at all."

"Avoiding the cops may not be an option," said Ingram.

"I know," Gwen said with a sigh.

"Can I ask why you don't want police involvement?"

"I just want this over," said Gwen. "I don't want my family dragged into this. I have a young daughter. She doesn't have to learn about these things."

"I see," Ingram said, but it didn't sound like he did.

"Now I'd like to ask you the same question," Gwen said. "Why don't you want me to contact the police?"

"My objective is to protect you and everyone at Pace Pharmaceuticals from a possible violent threat. While police involvement will take care of the issue in the short term, it'll do nothing in the long term. It could give rise to retaliation and we don't want that. I need the next few hours to build a case against Mr. Tarbell"—Ingram said Tarbell's name with considerable disdain—"to dispose of him in short order."

Gwen didn't know who Ingram was and what he did, but she felt safe. She felt walls rise up around her and her family that Tarbell couldn't penetrate.

"What do I do now?"

"Carry on as normal."

"Should I go into the office tomorrow?"

"Yes. At this point, I want Tarbell to believe he's won. Submit his evaluation as requested. If he asks, tell him you've done as instructed."

"I'm not sure I can do that."

"I need you to, Gwen. It's vitally important. You won't be in any danger. My team will see to that."

"Team?"

"I need you to meet with me at my office tomorrow. I'll explain everything then. Just be rest assured that you're in no danger. I won't allow it."

Gwen no longer felt as secure as she did a moment ago.

"Just go into the office like you normally would. Don't engage or antagonize him. Just be yourself."

That was easier said than done.

CHAPTER THREE

Gwen had been soaking in the tub for ten minutes when Paul came in with a cup of tea. He set it down on the ledge and sat on the toilet. She guessed his pressuring wasn't about to let up.

"Why'd he do it?" There was no malice or underlying theme in his question.

"Jealousy. Inferiority complex. I don't know."

"How did he think he would get away with it?"

The same thought had been rattling around inside her head. He had to know she'd report the attack. He hadn't made some idle threat. He'd threatened to kill her.

"All I can think is that he believes the power of his threat will keep me from doing something about it."

She let the idea seep from her mind and concentrated on relaxing her body in the hot water. It was the first time she'd felt warm since leaving the office.

"Why don't you want to go to the cops? Is it because of before, because of him?"

"Paul, don't."

"You stood up for yourself. You put him behind bars. Do the same to this bastard."

She'd put Desmond Parker in jail for her abduction, assault, and attempted murder. Jail should have been her justice for his cruelty. It wasn't. Prison could never nullify the fear she'd felt or erase the sensation of his steak knife entering her stomach. The police and justice system couldn't repair the damage Parker had done to her, but she'd survived it. Compared to Parker's gorilla-like build, Tarbell was a fly, an irritating buzzing insect. She'd survive this thing. She'd been through worse.

"Drop it," she demanded, then softly, "please."

"I can't. I need to understand."

"You don't know what it was like when Parker attacked me. I was on trial as much as he was. The police investigation dissected my life, looking for flaws, and that was an open-and-shut case with physical evidence, testimony, and a knife left in my stomach. Parker's defense lawyer dug for dirt. But that was fine. I put up with it. There was just me to worry about. Not this time. I have you and Kirsten to think about."

"It doesn't matter. We're behind you."

"It does matter. Our life will become a circus. People will take sides. You might not think it'll hurt us, but it will. No one will treat us the same and worse than that, we won't treat each other the same."

"It won't happen."

"I love you, Paul, but believe me when I say you don't know what you're talking about. We will change. We have already and the cops will make it worse. Stephen Tarbell isn't worth it, so let me handle this my way, please."

Paul dropped to his knees at the side of the bath. She sat up and let him embrace her. He held her tight and this time, she couldn't hold back the tears.

"I'll support any decision you make."

"Thank you."

"Just don't shut me out."

"I won't."

He pulled away from her. His T-shirt was soaked and covered in bubbles. "OK, I'll leave you in peace."

"No, don't," she said and held the sponge out to him.

Paul ran the sponge down her back and over her legs. His tenderness was something she hadn't realized she needed. She held her hair up while he rinsed her off. He wrapped her in a fresh towel and kissed her.

"I'll change my shirt," he said and left her alone.

She found him lying on the bed staring up at the ceiling. She snuggled up next to him and stretched an arm across his chest.

"I saw the letter by the recycling can. I'm sorry."

He shrugged. "Yeah, well, what are you going to do? It seems petty compared to the rest of the day."

"Do you have anything else lined up?"

"Nah. I'll check with the headhunters tomorrow and make some calls. Maybe something new will come up."

"It will. We've had our quota of bad luck."

• • •

Gwen sat at the kitchen table watching her daughter eat her breakfast. Like most three-year-olds, Kirsten met the day with enthusiasm. She didn't seem to remember her rude nighttime awakening and easily put the night's upset behind her. Gwen hoped she could do the same. It was going to be a long and difficult day.

"Do you want me to come in with you?" Paul asked.

"Ingram said to act like nothing had happened. If I bring you, then Tarbell will know I haven't kept my word."

Paul frowned then nodded.

"I'll be OK. Pace will make sure Tarbell doesn't do anything."

She kissed him before grabbing her purse on the way out.

The drive across Alameda to Bay Farm Island, where Pace Pharmaceuticals had its operations, was a short one. Normally, commuter traffic across town made the short drive feel longer, but not today. For once, she wanted the commute to drag and make her day at the office a short one. She should call in sick and screw Ingram's instructions.

Pulling into Pace's parking lot, she scanned the cars for Tarbell's Toyota and didn't see it. She had no desire to be cornered by him. She parked away from the trash enclosure with an unobstructed view of the reception area. She wouldn't be caught off guard again.

She exchanged hellos with the other early arrivals. She didn't feel nervous until she entered the building. She felt as if she'd entered some creature's lair. The sensation worsened the closer she got to her department. A single incident had turned her turf into someone else's, but Tarbell wouldn't hold sway long. She passed his cubicle and her heart almost stopped even though he wasn't even there.

"Son of a bitch," she murmured, entering her office.

She sat at her desk, flicked on her PC, and tried to calm down. She had an image to portray, not only to Tarbell but to all her coworkers. It had to be business as usual. This facade would satisfy Tarbell. She couldn't afford to give him any inkling that she'd called someone last night.

People filtered in and took their seats at their desks. Gwen went cold when someone greeted Tarbell as he walked in.

This was the moment she'd been dreading most. How would he handle their first encounter? With a smirk? With an act of cruelty? It wouldn't surprise her if he sent her the knife from last night through the internal mail as a nasty little reminder, or left some voice mail or e-mail filled with innuendo. When she checked, no surprises welcomed her.

The view from her office didn't stretch as far as Tarbell's cubicle. She couldn't see him, but she could hear him. He laughed at a joke and chatted as though nothing had happened. He was in no hurry to confront her. No doubt ignoring her was a tactic to prolong her torture. He'd want her to hide in her office afraid of the monster that lurked outside her door. Well, screw him. She wouldn't be treated like this. She grabbed a report off her desk as an excuse to run over to the copy room.

"Morning, everyone," she said on her way past.

"Morning, Gwen," her staff said, including Tarbell.

She wanted to strangle the son of a bitch for his coolness.

She copied the report and stormed back to her office. She threw herself in her seat, so blinded by frustration that she didn't realize Tarbell had come in behind her. His body blocked the doorway.

"Could I have a moment?" he asked.

This was it. Ingram had promised her Tarbell wouldn't harm her. How was he going to protect her when he wasn't around? She should have gone to Deborah's office first thing this morning and insisted that security escort Tarbell off the premises. Instead, she'd left herself totally exposed with no protection. She eyed her only weapon, the phone on her desk. She reached for it.

"I'm supposed to call into a meeting right now. Can you come back later?"

"This'll only take a second," he said closing the door.

Seeing the door close set Gwen's pulse racing. She kept a tenuous rein on her panic.

"I just wanted to apologize for being late. No excuse. Just late. It won't happen again."

Before Gwen could object, he was gone, leaving the office door open. Tarbell amazed her. How could he have totally blocked the incident from his mind? Maybe he'd realized the line he'd crossed and was pretending nothing had happened. No, he was messing with her because he thought he could. Last night, he threatened her with physical harm. Today, he was using psychological threats. He wanted to scare her without saying a word.

She felt slightly sick. She couldn't keep this "acting normal" thing up all day. Ingram had promised her protection. Where was it? He'd told her that Pace had a duty to keep her safe. It was about time they showed her their plan. She had to talk to Deborah. Situations like this were the reason the head of Human Resources earned such a healthy salary.

She jumped up from her seat, then stopped. She needed a cover story to visit Deborah. Despite Tarbell's laissez-faire attitude, he would be watching her like a hawk. A trip to HR would set off alarm bells, but one thing would change that. She grabbed the evaluations file and headed out of her office. She didn't make a big production of it. She just passed by Tarbell's cubicle holding the file marked evaluations prominently so that he could see what she was doing. Let him think that she was complying with his demand and ride a wave of false security until the next one wiped him out. She felt his gaze burning into her back as she headed across the building. She estimated this piece of subterfuge bought her about five minutes.

Deborah welcomed Gwen into her office and closed the door. She ushered her to a seat before sitting at her desk.

"Have you heard anything from Ingram?" Gwen asked.

"No, but you have a meeting with him after work, don't you?"

"Yes, but that's a long way off. He promised me protection. Where is it?"

"Has something happened?"

"Yes. No. Stephen talked me. He didn't say anything threatening. It's just not easy to pretend nothing happened when it did."

"It's going to be OK, trust me. Ingram will have answers. He's very good."

"I'm sure he is." Deborah's reassurances sounded good but only because Gwen needed to hear them.

Deborah pointed to the cut under Gwen's chin. "Did Stephen do that?"

Gwen nodded.

"I hate to ask, but is that all he did to you?"

"No." Gwen unbuttoned her blouse and showed Deborah the bruises on her chest. "There are more on my back."

Deborah put a hand to her mouth. "Oh my God."

Gwen felt suddenly self-conscious and she quickly closed her blouse.

Gwen checked her watch. She estimated she had a couple of minutes before Tarbell would get suspicious. She handed the evaluations to Deborah. Tarbell couldn't see her returning with them.

Deborah escorted Gwen to the door. "Tell no one about this. Confidentiality is paramount. You'll be protected, but the program only works when no one knows of its presence."

Gwen nodded and left the office. What program? She knew the company's employment policy and its dismissal procedure. It was pretty much boilerplate stuff.

Someone passed her in the corridor and asked if she was OK. She forced a smile, horrified to realize that she was wearing her troubled emotions on the outside. It was going to be hard work maintaining a happy public face. She did her best to shake her harried look. "Yeah, I'm fine," she said. "Just thinking."

She passed by Tarbell's cubicle on the way to her office. She expected a smug smile or a wink, but he had his head down, business as usual.

She dropped into her seat behind her desk. Her body tingled as if every nerve ending was exposed to the air. She willed her body to calm itself and took a few deep breaths.

She picked up the phone and called Paul.

"How's it going?" he asked.

"Tough."

"I wish you'd let me be there."

"I wish I could."

"Has he said anything?"

She thought about Tarbell's closed-door visit. He was sending a message to her, but it was a message she couldn't use against him. He made no verbal or physical threat. That was the genius of intimidation. It was so damn hard to prove.

"No, he hasn't said anything."

"Maybe the son of a bitch is laying low because he's frightened by what you can do to him."

She doubted that but humored Paul. "Yeah, maybe."

"Crap. I've gotta go. The headhunter is on the other line. Call anytime. I'm here for you."

"OK. I will. Love you."

"You too. Hang in there. I hope they fire this asshole today," he said and hung up.

An unnerving thought punctured her mind. Pace could fire Tarbell, but that wouldn't protect her from retaliation. If he intended on following through with his threat, there was nothing stopping him from doing it. Paul was right. She should have gone to the police last night in spite of her misgivings. She'd let her emotions overrule her common sense. If Deborah didn't bring up police action, she would.

The day dragged after Paul's call. She lived on her nerves, unsure if Tarbell would pull another stunt and who'd protect her if he did.

She kept to herself, just getting on with her work, but her senses were on high alert. It was impossible to make sure she had someone in her office at all times, but she did her best, calling in her other employees for impromptu meetings. A witness was as good as a weapon with Tarbell around. The tension receded when Tarbell left for an off-site meeting.

She was exhausted by the time five o'clock came around. After a day of pretending, she wanted to go home, but her day was far from over. She still had her clandestine meeting with Ingram. She left with the main glut of her coworkers. She didn't want to leave alone. She'd learned that lesson.

It looked to be an unnecessary precaution. Tarbell had yet to return from his meeting, but that didn't mean anything. He'd pretended to leave yesterday and hadn't. She wasn't taking any chances this time.

She slipped behind the wheel of her Subaru without incident and joined the conga line of vehicles heading for the exit. She saw no sign of Tarbell. She picked up the freeway and headed toward San Francisco. *So far so good*, she thought, but she couldn't shake the paranoia that Tarbell was monitoring her. She switched lanes, watching for any vehicle matching her moves, but saw nothing. She had no idea if her maneuvers helped any, but she was pretty sure Tarbell wasn't following her and settled into her seat for the slow rush-hour drive into the city.

She crossed the Bay Bridge, found Ingram's address easily enough, and parked in a nearby lot. The building was home to Wells Fargo headquarters and more than two dozen other businesses. She went to the reception desk and asked for Ingram.

A minute later, a blocky-looking man in his late forties stepped off the elevator. He waved and strode over to her. "Mrs. Farris?"

Gwen nodded.

"Robert Ingram. Let's get you upstairs."

They rode the elevator alone. "I'm worried Stephen followed me here."

"He didn't," Ingram responded confidently.

"How do you know?"

"I had someone follow him. He attended the meeting and left a little after five, arriving back at Pace well after you left. You were never in any danger."

The news lifted the crushing weight Gwen had been shouldering all day. This would be over soon. She could put it behind her. She let out a sigh, which Ingram noticed.

He smiled and said, "You have nothing to worry about."

The elevator let them out, and she followed him to a business suite. She guessed he'd been in law enforcement or the military previously. He moved with a military bearing and spoke with the confidence of a person who operated with the backing of the law. The likes of Tarbell posed no threat to him. It was another reason for Gwen to breathe easily.

Ingram's offices were modest—two corner offices sandwiched a conference room overlooking the street below. A series of cubicles filled the remaining area. The place would have looked like a call center if it weren't for the firm's name etched into the glass doors entering the suite, Private Security International. It was all very understated. A plus for their clients, no doubt.

Less than half the cubicles were occupied. Everyone politely ignored Gwen, giving her anonymity. A woman dressed in a business suit that was a handful of years younger than Ingram left one of the corner offices. She smiled at Gwen but offered no greeting. Ingram showed Gwen into the conference room. Deborah was sitting at the end of the table.

Ingram closed the door, then went around the room and closed the blinds, giving them privacy from his colleagues. "In these situations, I like to keep everything private."

Deborah stood and took Gwen's hands in hers. "We're going to sort this out."

This was a surreal moment; Gwen took her seat, wishing Paul was with her.

"Before we start, can I offer anyone anything—coffee, tea, water?" Ingram asked.

Gwen shook her head.

"If you don't mind me saying, you look drained. You're probably dehydrated. Stress does that to people. You should drink some water."

It irritated Gwen how Ingram saw through her, but his genuine concern tempered her mood and she agreed to his offer. As he disappeared from the office, she wondered if she'd been that transparent to everyone at the office. She hoped not, but guessed her facade had been a weak one. Ingram returned and placed a glass and an uncapped bottle of water in front of her.

"I suppose it's time to give you the details," Deborah said.

Gwen poured the water into the glass and sipped.

"With violence in the workplace claims, it's Pace Pharmaceuticals' policy to bring in an outside consultant to investigate. Robert and his people make sure there is a rock-solid case against the accused, leaving no room for doubt or wrongful dismissal claims."

"No offense to Mr. Ingram," Gwen said, "but I don't really see the need. Stephen attacked me and threatened my life. It's pretty open and shut. He won't have any claim for wrongful dismissal."

"It doesn't matter if he has a case or not; he can cry foul and drag us and you through the courts. The whole thing will be nasty and expensive. The lawyers will tell us to settle and we will and Stephen will get away with what he's done with a tidy profit for his time. Do you want that?"

No, she didn't. She wanted Tarbell gone, expunged from her life with no evidence of his existence. The idea of Tarbell getting paid while she had to live under a constant cloud of doubt brought a sour taste to the back of her throat. She washed it away with another sip of water.

"The truth of the matter is," Ingram said, "we don't have a clear-cut case."

"What?"

"From the brief explanation Deborah gave me, there are no witnesses to the assault. Correct?"

A sinking feeling pulled at Gwen's insides. She saw where this was going. "No. No witnesses."

"That leaves us with a case of he said/she said."

"Are you saying you don't believe me?" Gwen didn't try to hide her contempt.

Deborah sat kitty-corner to Gwen and she pressed a hand on top of hers in an attempt at a comforting gesture. "No one is saying that. We believe you. I've seen what he's done to you, but we can't prove it."

"Everyone knows he's a hothead."

"So we have a man with a short fuse," Ingram said. "That doesn't mean he's capable of premeditated violence."

A short fuse? The words were an insult to Gwen after what Tarbell had done last night.

Ingram paused and exchanged an awkward glance with Deborah. This meeting was obviously not going as planned.

"I hoped to nip this situation in the bud." Ingram picked up a remote and switched on the TV at the end of the room. "Most people don't think their strategy through, and I hoped the security cameras would pick the assault up." He pressed play.

The image on the screen was split into four simultaneous images. The top left image captured a static view from inside the foyer. The top right caught the main walk from the parking lot. The bottom left took up where the second camera left off with a view of the parking lot. Unlike the first two cameras, this one panned back and forth to take in a panoramic view, but it failed to capture the entire lot. The image on the bottom right corner of the screen took up the slack. This caught the blind spots the other cameras missed.

Gwen's heart skipped when she appeared in the top left box on the screen silently saying good-bye to the security guard before disappearing from view. The second camera picked her up and recorded her progress until she passed out of view. The bottom left and right cameras caught her in their sweeps but then lost her. Gwen couldn't believe it. But sure enough, it seemed that the trash enclosure provided the perfect blind spot. The two cameras failed to pick up anything happening beyond the trash enclosure.

Precious seconds ticked by on the time code on the screen. Gwen relived those seconds—the impact, the knife, Tarbell's crushing weight, and the threat—and the cameras were blind to it all. She felt sick.

"Nothing happens now," Ingram said and pressed fast forward.

He was wrong. Plenty had happened, but all out of sight of the useless cameras.

Ingram fast-forwarded through the recording until Gwen's Subaru pulled away with the security guard chasing behind her. At no time did Tarbell appear on camera, although he'd long since run off by the time she raced away from the scene. It looked to the world as if she left the office, sat in her car for thirty minutes, then left.

"I've watched every minute of coverage from five p.m. through to you leaving, and Stephen Tarbell never features except when he left the building at two minutes after five. At no point does he return."

But he had. Gwen had bruises on her back and chest and a cut under her chin to prove it. She looked from Ingram to Deborah. They had to doubt her. Who wouldn't? She hoped to God they didn't think she was just another crazy broad in the workplace, ruining it for smart women everywhere. She couldn't read their expressions to tell whether or not they believed her.

"It happened," she said in a quiet, yet desperate voice.

"I didn't say it didn't," Ingram said and rewound the tape back. "The camera never lies, but it can be deceived. The security camera system is poorly set up. The cameras are mounted too low to the ground. If they were installed three or four feet higher, they would capture everything blocked out by the trash enclosure. And matters are made worse."

"The cameras covering the parking lot aren't synchronized," Gwen said.

It had taken her a moment to work out Tarbell's Houdini act. As her mind whirled to explain it, she stared hard at the two bottom images and spotted the flaw.

Ingram examined her and nodded approvingly. "You're correct, Mrs. Farris."

"I don't see it," Deborah said.

"These two cameras," Ingram pointed at the bottom two images, "pan left and right, but they aren't synchronized. They should be working together. As one pans left, the other should be capturing what its twin is missing. This means Stephen Tarbell knew this and secreted himself behind the trash enclosure when the cameras weren't looking his way."

"That's amazing," Deborah said.

"No," Ingram corrected. "That's devious."

"How do you know that last night wasn't a figment of my imagination?" Gwen said.

"This." Ingram got up from his seat, crouched in front of the TV and forward wound and rewound until he found the moment he was searching for, then paused the action. "Come take a look."

Gwen and Deborah crowded around the TV. Ingram pointed to the bottom right panel on the screen, tapped it, and told them to watch carefully. He hit play then stopped the action a second later.

"See it?" he asked.

Gwen shook her head.

Ingram set the recording up again and replayed it again, but in slow motion. He tapped the screen at the moment he wanted them to see. He pointed to the corner edge of the trash enclosure. Gwen spotted something appear then disappear before the camera panned out of view.

"I saw it," Deborah said, "but what was it?"

"A hand. Four fingers to be precise, grabbing the corner of the wall. I don't know whose for sure, but I will when I get the image enhanced."

Gwen let out a long sigh.

Ingram smiled. "We wouldn't be here if we didn't believe you, Mrs. Farris."

Ingram switched off the TV, and the three of them returned to their seats.

"Where do we go from here?" Gwen asked.

"We don't have any clear evidence beyond testimony, so two things: first, a complete background check that will unearth anything of this nature in his past and second, twenty-four-hour surveillance to either catch him in any move against you or other illegal activity."

"Will you go to the police with what you find?"

Ingram took too long in responding. "Do you want to go to the police?"

Now it was Gwen's turn to be slow to answer. "No."

"Then Mr. Tarbell will be shown the evidence and given the opportunity to leave Pace with the suggestion he leave the state, too. I can make you every assurance he won't make any attempt to harm you again."

Ingram's politely worded statement came with a steel-edged promise. Gwen didn't fancy being in Tarbell's shoes when Ingram and friends caught up to him. She wished she could be there when it happened, though. She tried to convince herself it was for reasons of justice and not revenge but came up short. *So what*, she thought. He'd put her through enough that he deserved to lose his job and more. She'd be content when Tarbell's cubicle turned up empty one morning.

"Deborah has mentioned your injuries to me," Ingram said. "I need to document them. For your comfort, I can have or one of my female colleagues come in and take the photos."

Gwen waved away Ingram's considerate gesture and let him photograph the cuts and bruises. He carried out the task with the sensitivity of someone who wasn't a stranger to this kind of victimization.

As Gwen dressed, he said, "Now I need to get a statement from you."

Gwen began with the confrontation during Tarbell's perfor-mance evaluation, then moved on to the assault in the parking lot. Ingram recorded her statement on a digital recorder. Not dis-tracted by having to make his own notes, he listened intently, stopping her to clarify points or ask questions. Gwen found that talking about the event helped work out the poison left there by her own fear. It didn't leave her feeling clean, but it helped her feel better about herself. She hadn't done anything wrong, and she didn't deserve to live in fear. She could go home and face Paul and tell him she'd done what she could to nail Tarbell.

Ingram played back Gwen's statement while he took notes and made sure she'd remembered everything that happened. Deborah made her own notes, no doubt in preparation to give a report to Pace's president. Pace was really pulling out the stops. It should have filled Gwen with a warm, fuzzy feeling of security, but it didn't. It was too much. Corporations didn't hire private security consultants to investigate violence in the workplace. For Bill Gates, yes, but for Gwen Farris, she didn't think so. Ingram and Deborah were conferring with each other when Gwen stopped them.

"This is too much, too expensive, to be standard policy. There's something you're not telling me."

Neither Ingram nor Deborah rushed to dispel the accusation. Ingram exchanged a look with Deborah before going back to his note taking. His message was clear. It wasn't his question to answer.

Deborah looked uncomfortable. "Yes, you're right, Gwen. There is something we're keeping from you. We're trying to prevent something from occurring that happened six years ago."

"What?"

"A murder."

CHAPTER FOUR

Luke Morgan had strangled his coworker, Laura Porter, in her Baltimore apartment. Laura's roommate found Morgan hunched over Laura's body. Morgan bolted but the police picked him up at home packing a bag before he skipped town.

Ingram outlined the tragic events to Gwen. He didn't put a gloss them, but he didn't do anything to play them down either. Laura and Morgan had worked together at Pace's research facility in Maryland. Morgan had been attracted to Laura, but already engaged, she spurned him. Morgan wouldn't take no for an answer and began harassing her at work and in her private life. She reported him to Pace and Pace warned him off, but took the matter no further, even after Morgan continued to follow her. Morgan's fascination escalated until he was following her home at nights and watching her at work. Her relationship with her fiancé broke off. Morgan took that as a sign of love, but when Laura spurned him again, he killed her. The story left Gwen cold. She liked to believe Tarbell couldn't cross the line Luke Morgan had crossed, but the knife and the hate he so clearly communicated didn't seem like good signs.

"I won't let the same happen to you," Ingram said. "No one has even come close to being hurt since my association with Pace."

"People are our assets," Deborah said. "Pace will do everything it can to protect them. Handling incidents like these is cheaper in the long run."

"Cheaper?" Gwen asked.

Deborah's expression changed as she realized she'd said the wrong thing, but also realized she couldn't duck the issue. "Laura Porter's family sued Pace for negligence and won five million in damages. That provoked a study to be conducted as to what workplace conflicts cost Pace each year in lost man hours, loss of industry knowledge, legal costs, resignations, firings, and hirings. It added up to millions every year across its US and Canadian facilities."

Deborah wasn't wrong when she called Gwen an asset. She was a dollar figure to Pace. She tried not to take it personally. She traded her knowledge for a monetary sum. It stood to reason a corporation would see her in financial terms, but it failed to make her feel any better about her position.

"I know how this sounds," Deborah continued, "but I want you to know the human value is more important to me. There's no way I'm going to allow the tragedy in Baltimore to happen here."

That note ended the meeting. Ingram and Deborah both gave their reassurances she was in safe hands before Deborah left her in Ingram's care.

"Not much fun discovering you're a dollar figure," he said, after Deborah stepped out.

"No, not really."

He smiled. "Look at it this way, you're not as easy to replace as a computer or a centrifuge."

Gwen smiled back and followed him into his office. The sun was going down over the city. The falling sun struck the city's buildings in all the right places, casting elegant shadows over the streets. She wanted to drink the moment in. It felt good to be alive, which was a stark contrast from the night before.

"Just a couple of things before you go, Mrs. Farris."

"Call me Gwen."

He nodded and handed her a card with a number on it where he could be reached twenty-four hours a day. "Don't hesitate calling me. Day or night."

"What do I do if Stephen asks about his evaluation?"

"Play along. Tell him you did as he asked."

"That's a diplomatic answer considering he held a knife against my throat."

Ingram smiled politely. "Call me as soon as he makes contact. I want it on record."

He escorted Gwen to the door. His people had all departed, leaving just the two of them.

"Be smart. Don't put yourself in any compromising positions and don't antagonize Mr. Tarbell if possible. Break up your routine." He handed her a fact sheet. "That will give you some pointers on how to stay safe."

"What if he's waiting outside to follow me home?"

Ingram pulled out his cell, dialed a number and spoke to someone briefly before hanging up. "He's still at the office. You've got nothing to worry about."

• • •

Idiots, Tarbell thought. "They think they're so smart, so clever," he said, unable to keep from verbalizing his disgust. "They don't know shit. I'm sick and tired of these morons. It's always me who has to clean up their mess."

He stopped suddenly, realizing he'd spoken out loud. Luckily, it didn't matter. He was the only one in the building working at this time of night—as usual. The management at this place was a joke. They didn't recognize his superior skills. No, they had put Gwen Farris in charge. It was all politics. Managers. What the hell were they, after all? Finger pointers. Big picture people. They directed traffic while people like him did the work and earned the money that put the bonuses in their pockets. He guessed he should view his lack of advancement as a compliment. If corporations couldn't fire you, they promoted you. They were keeping him down because he was more valuable to them where he was.

Screw being held down, he thought. He was sick of it. Someone always had their boot on his neck. First, it was in school. When it wasn't in school, it was his friends. When it wasn't his friends, it was his dad. That son of a bitch had practically waved a white flag of surrender over his childhood house, giving the go-ahead to bullies everywhere to kick the crap out of Stephen David Tarbell. Well, no more.

"It ends right now," he snarled and slammed his pen down. It bounced off his desk and landed on the floor. He picked it up and tried to get back into his work but gave up. He'd done enough for today.

He pushed himself away from his desk and got to his feet. He was buzzing. This always happened when his blood was up. His body vibrated with the current coursing through him. He couldn't drive home like this. He'd get into it with someone, and he didn't want to deal with road rage at the moment. Gwen was his focus. Not anyone else.

He wandered through the offices, checking the work on people's desks. He did this routinely. He liked to see what his coworkers were up to. *Coworkers*, he thought, *is a quaint term for fuckups*. He couldn't count the number of errors in judgment and outright mistakes he saw in his coworkers' poorly-written memos and badly-researched reports. Pace Pharmaceuticals prided itself on its superior knowledge. The board was deluding itself. They should count themselves lucky they hadn't been sued for gross negligence. They were just a hairbreadth from a thalidomide-type scandal. He'd save their butts and their bonuses. They could think what they liked about him, but he was their savior. Ungrateful sons of bitches.

He picked over Nguyen's desk to find further validation of his coworkers' ineptitude. He was a nice enough guy, Tarbell supposed, but he was getting a little sick of the foreign element within the company. The place was turning into a branch of the United Nations. He accepted that the US was built on the backs of immigrants, but Pace had too many foreigners on its books.

He found donuts in Mitch Balsam's desk. It wasn't the first time he'd found food tucked away there. He'd once found a pizza slice on a file folder. The loser weighed close to three hundred pounds and was eating himself toward a coronary.

He worked his way around the building back to his own department. The door to Gwen's office stood ajar, and he went inside. Gwen's office. It should be his office. Instead of the bitterness he usually felt here, a warm feeling filled him and a smile spread across his face. Gwen had been so scared when he'd leaped out at her last night. She'd trembled as he'd pressed the knife point under her chin. He'd put the fear of God into her. How dare she tell him his performance wasn't up to standard? She knew the consequences of that kind of talk now.

The crazy thing was the whole episode had been so spur-of-the-moment. Well, at first. He'd tried leaving work, but he was furious and he turned the car around to have it out with her, off the record. As he'd come up on the sign for Pace Pharmaceuticals, he'd changed his mind. Talk was talk. It meant nothing. Gwen had the power of Pace behind her. She needed to be taught a lesson and a harsh lesson at that. He'd driven by the building and noticed that only a couple of vehicles lingered in the parking lot. Gwen's car had been parked next to the trash enclosure. That had given him an idea.

He'd parked in the lot across the street from Pace and grabbed the utility knife from the glove compartment he carried in case of problems. He'd crossed the street but stopped when he remembered the security cameras. The landscaping had provided good cover to watch the cameras. They weren't hard to figure out and soon he'd taken up his hiding spot. He'd watched and waited. One by one the stragglers had left the office, leaving just him and Gwen. It was so poetic. So just. He felt the hand of fate in it.

As he'd waited, the never-ending rain had drenched him. This woman was ruining his career and now she was making him stand out in the rain. Yet the wait and the rain had meant nothing once he started thinking about the justice he'd receive.

It had all culminated in the perfect takedown.

And now here he was, sitting in her dark, empty office. He liked how the seat felt. He felt like the boss and although he might not have a big title at Pace, he'd just become the boss in every other way. Gwen would fold from now on. It didn't matter what he said and did, she'd comply. She had already. He'd seen her take the evaluations to Human Resources. He was pretty sure she'd folded to his demands.

He went through her desk to make sure and didn't find anything incriminating there, so he booted up her computer and logged on as Gwen. He knew several of his colleagues' passwords. They weren't hard to discover. People usually left them in desk drawers they never locked. He'd gotten Gwen's that way. He went through her e-mail and found nothing there either.

No, Gwen had done the right thing. He was sure of it. Tomorrow was Friday. He'd ask her outright, but it would only be a confirmation.

He picked up the picture frame on her desk. It pictured Gwen and her husband and daughter. It looked to be one of those crappy mall photo studio deals judging by the faux cloud background. The Farris family was snuggled together with sickening grins plastered across their faces. They looked happy, trapped in their slice of time. He guessed there weren't many smiles at home this very minute.

"Do the right thing, Gwen, and none of these people will come to any harm," he said to her image.

He put everything back in its place, even setting the door ajar in the same spot, and left the building. He walked over to his car. He'd taken the same parking spot that Gwen had taken yesterday. It was an inside joke he hoped he and Gwen could share. He gunned the engine and headed home.

He couldn't believe how good he felt compared to yesterday. Who knew twenty-four hours would make such a difference? It was easy to understand. He was winning for once. Life was being good to him and he liked it.

His good mood showed itself on the speedometer. He raced along and switched lanes instead of taking his foot off the gas. It became apparent he wasn't the only one enjoying the speed. A green Audi sedan bounced between lanes a few hundred yards behind him. He hadn't noticed it at first, being too lost in his thoughts. He probably wouldn't have noticed the car at all in the daylight, but its cockeyed headlight alerted him to his speed demon buddy. The headlight was knocked out of position and instead of pointing down, it pointed up and kept glinting in his rearview mirror, sporadically hitting him in the eyes with an intense blast of light.

He didn't particularly like someone aping his moves. It spoiled his fun. He could try to lose the guy, but he risked a ticket. No, he decided to be gentlemanly. *I'll let this clown overtake me and catch a ticket.*

"After you, Mr. Asshole," he said into his rearview mirror and took his foot off the gas. He waited for the mimic to blow by, but the mimic slowed. It immediately made the hairs on the back of his neck stand on end. Something was very wrong.

Tarbell lived in El Cerrito, but he pulled off two exits earlier and Mr. Headlight pulled off with him. He made a number of turns on surface streets, and Mr. Headlight took the same ones.

Tarbell cursed. It looked as if someone was following him.

CHAPTER FIVE

Gwen entered the office on Friday braced for the day's events. She'd slept little that night despite Ingram's assurances. He'd called her earlier in the morning to run through strategies for handling Tarbell. She was to let him come to her. Let him ask the questions. It made their case against him stronger. If he hadn't spoken to her by four thirty, she was to initiate contact and tell him she'd complied with his demand. Ingram doubted he'd make another surprise attack on her, but he didn't want Tarbell going home for the weekend thinking his intimidation tactics had failed. If at any time she felt in danger, she was to call him. His people were close by. When Ingram hung up, she was shaking.

"This is the day you nail him," Paul had said to her on her way out. His support felt like it was keeping her in one piece.

She wanted to get this done the moment she stepped inside the building, but her phone was already ringing before she reached her office. A labeling noncompliance sucked her into her workday, shoving her worries aside. The issue kept her up to her elbows in problems for most of the morning. She went from the labeling emergency into her usual Friday meeting, which took her through lunch.

The respite from thoughts of Tarbell was brief. He eased from the back of her mind to the forefront with a predator's stealth. The day's workload had kept her in the company of others, which was a good thing. Tarbell wouldn't try anything with so many people around her, but per Ingram's instructions, she had to make sure he believed he was free and clear. The time to talk to him was running out.

She wasn't the only one getting anxious. Ingram had called her twice on her cell asking for an update.

The meeting let out around two thirty. She returned to her office and found Tarbell missing. Time was getting away from her. It was on the tip of her tongue to ask where he was, but she kept quiet. He didn't need to know panic was setting in.

She went into the restroom and locked herself into a stall to calm down. She ran through what Ingram had told her to say. Focusing on her script extinguished her nervousness. She was ready for Tarbell.

She flushed the toilet for appearance's sake and washed her hands as she checked out her reflection in the mirror. "Stay cool and this'll work out."

She left the restroom and jumped when Tarbell called her name. He was leaning against the wall within arm's reach of the restroom door. The son of a bitch had followed her. He covered for his invasive presence by flipping through a file. To the casual observer, that was Stephen Tarbell, always too wrapped up in his job to observe social niceties. Gwen knew better.

This was it, and she was ready for him, despite her pounding heart. It was going to be a scary few minutes, but she could handle it.

Tarbell shoved himself off the wall. "I wonder if we could chat for a minute."

"Sure. What's up?"

"Not here," he said. "It's about the other day. Let's go somewhere more private."

"My office?"

Tarbell smiled. "I was thinking of somewhere more neutral."

He didn't give Gwen an option and led her in the direction of the small conference rooms. These were on the opposite side of the building on a corridor that dead ended at a fire exit. The location was off the beaten track.

He closed the door and leaned against it, cutting off Gwen's only escape route. She put as much distance between them as possible and stood by the window. Since the room was a ten by ten box, it didn't give her much of a gap. She cast a glance outside. Though she was only one floor up, the ground looked a long way down.

She said nothing. *Let him do the talking*, she thought.

"Today's the day," he said brightly.

Still, she said nothing. Her heart continued to pound, but she was keeping it together and with every passing second, her confidence grew. She wasn't the same woman she had been Wednesday night. She could handle him.

"I'm assuming you did right by me." He paused for a beat. "Otherwise, someone would have hauled me off in chains." He tossed in a grin for good measure. Gwen recoiled at the sight.

"I submitted your evaluation to Human Resources yesterday, first thing."

His grin widened. "I saw you go that way. I hope you said good things about me."

"I said your performance met company expectations."

His grin faded away. "I was expecting for something a little more than that, Gwen. I thought I was quite explicit."

His right hand slipped into his pants pocket. The move didn't intimidate her. There was no knife in his pocket. Even if there was, he wouldn't use it, not here. The rage he displayed slamming her up against her car had receded because he believed he'd gotten his way. He had no reason to do anything stupid.

"Pace doesn't care if you're a rock star or a C student. Evaluations have two grades—acceptable and not acceptable."

"Still, a little embellishment on your part would go a long way in my progression here."

"Let's not kid ourselves. You work hard, but you rub people the wrong way."

Tarbell's expression tightened into something ugly yet now familiar. "Watch your mouth, Gwen. Keep it respectful."

She'd just stepped outside Ingram's parameters without even meaning too. Her mind raced to find a way to appease Tarbell.

"I am being respectful, but I'm playing it smart too," said Gwen. "You know how people treat you around here. If I said you're a star pupil, someone would smell a rat and ask questions. Do you want people asking questions?"

Tarbell said nothing, but the tension left his face, and only irritation remained. Her tactic had worked, at least for the moment.

"As far as everyone is concerned, you're a solid employee and will be getting your raise as a result of it. Isn't that what you wanted?"

He mulled her argument over for a minute. "When does it come into effect?"

"Next month."

Tarbell nodded and reached for the door handle.

"What happens now?" she asked.

He opened the door and walked out. "Nothing," he called over his shoulder, the condescension making his voice thick. "Nothing for now."

The moment Tarbell was gone, Gwen released a breath that untied the knot in her chest. It was done. Tarbell had tripped the trap, and now it was time to lock it.

She wanted to call Ingram but held off and waited for Ingram to call her. An incoming call looked less suspicious than an outgoing one. He called at four thirty.

"Has he talked to you?"

"Yes."

"How did it go?"

"Fine."

"Well done, Gwen. I know it couldn't have been easy."

"What happens now?"

"My people will follow Tarbell's every move. He won't harm you."

"What do I do?"

"Forget all about this. You've done your part. My team will investigate and take action. Just document any further contact and call me if anything worries you. If I need anything else from you, I'll call you. Effectively, you're done."

Done. She struggled with the idea of being done, especially when her problem sat fifty feet from her.

"Have a good weekend," Ingram said and hung up.

Gwen couldn't imagine having a good weekend under the circumstances. Nothing had changed. Tarbell sat at his desk gloating over his victory. Ingram had said she'd done her part, and she wanted that to be true, but a big part of her didn't want to relinquish her grip on the investigation. She was an integral part of it. Tarbell had threatened her life. She wanted to be involved, needed to be involved, overseeing every detail until he was dealt with. She wanted to feel in control and that meant knowing what Tarbell was up to. Uncertainty came with being cut out of the loop. If the situation was handed off, she had to live in fear that he might attack her again at any time.

She blamed Desmond Parker for her attitude. All those years ago, after she'd called 911, the police took over. She'd sat back while they hunted Parker down. It hadn't been easy. Time had moved slowly when she'd been forced to take a backseat. But it wasn't like she had much of an option with a stomach wound threatening her life.

Sitting in her office, Gwen sighed at the reality that Ingram was cutting her out. In spite of her misgivings, she accepted the situation. She couldn't be the one to take action against Tarbell. She'd set him up, and Ingram would bring him down. The clock on her desk phone said it was close enough to five o'clock to call it a day. She'd take Ingram's advice and enjoy the weekend. She and Paul would take Kirsten somewhere. Life was being hard on them, and they needed to take a break from their worries. It was September and still plenty warm enough for a road trip to the beach.

She shut down her computer and said her good-byes on the way out. Tarbell made a crack about part-timers. She smiled, not at the joke, but at the surprises that Ingram was going to dish out to Tarbell down the line.

With the jump on the traffic, she made it home in minutes. The sound of the garage door closing behind her drew a line between the problems of the world and her family. She could enjoy the weekend now.

Gwen let herself in. Kirsten came charging across the kitchen, grinning and squealing. Gwen gathered her daughter up and kissed her. Kirsten wriggled in her arms and started telling her all that had happened that day.

Paul stood in the doorway between the kitchen and living room. He failed to show any of their daughter's enthusiasm at Gwen's arrival. She smiled at him to provoke a mood change, but to no avail.

"Something came for you," Paul said.

Gwen's stomach clenched. She didn't want to think what Tarbell had done now. Ingram had promised she'd be safe.

"Honey, can you give Mommy and me a minute to discuss something?"

"Can I have a cookie?" Kirsten asked.

Gwen nodded, got her one, and Kirsten went agreeably to her room.

"What's going on, Paul?"

He handed her a letter. The return address was from California's Department of Corrections and Rehabilitation. A different kind of fear swept over her and she dropped onto the sofa.

Paul sat next to her, slipping an arm around her shoulders. "I know the letter was for you, but I opened it. Was that OK?"

She nodded and removed the letter, knowing what it said without reading it. She knew this day would come eventually. Every New Year's celebration was tinged with the eventuality that one year would bring this letter. It was a notification telling her of Desmond Parker's parole hearing.

"Jerry Naylor called about it, and he wants you to call him back."

"OK," she said and tossed the letter on the coffee table.

"You all right?"

She shook her head. "I don't know. It's just shitty timing."

Paul eased her back onto the sofa. He pulled her close in a protective embrace. It was warm and comforting, but its heat failed to penetrate. She felt cold and alone.

"Just because he's up for parole doesn't mean he's going to get it."

"I'll call Jerry," she said and slipped from Paul's grasp.

"I was thinking we'd go out to dinner tonight."

"Sure. Sounds good," she said, less than enthusiastically. "Can you get Kirsten ready while I call?"

She closed the door on the spare bedroom that had become their home office. It was primarily Paul's when he worked construction projects, but she kept a small filing cabinet with important documents. One drawer was dedicated to Desmond Parker. She dug out Jerry Naylor's business card and called his cell number.

He'd been her knight in shining armor, always supportive and protective. Naylor had been the assistant DA in Yolo County who'd prosecuted Parker, but thanks to a strong record of successful prosecutions like Parker's, he'd been promoted to DA.

48

"Hi, Gwen," Naylor said, sounding like he'd just informed her that she had a terminal disease. "How's the family?"

She didn't want to be coddled. Not after this week. She got to the point. If it was bad news, she wanted it straight. "What are his chances?"

"Good, I'm afraid to say. Parker's been a model inmate. He's kept his nose clean and entered into a number of programs to improve his education and give him professional skills on the outside."

Gwen remembered Parker's skills all too well, like his ability to inflict pain and torment. Could prison really change someone like him? She hoped so. The idea of him being able to pick up from where he had left off and hurt other women was too horrible to contemplate.

"I thought he'd serve longer."

"So did I, but his sentence is fifteen to life and he's served his fifteen, so he's eligible. With all the overcrowding in prisons, the state is eager to release anyone who fits the model prisoner mold. Remember, it's only parole. One missed step and he's back inside."

What constituted a missed step? Another abduction and attempted murder? Maybe he'd perfected his skills in prison. If given another chance, he might succeed where he'd failed with her.

"He can't get to you."

Can't he? Gwen thought. Tarbell got to her easily, and he was a novice at the game. Parker was a grand master by comparison. If Parker wanted to finish what he started, he could and would.

"It might seem like a done deal, but it's not. The parole board gets to hear our side of the issue, too. You can make a written statement or even appear at the parole hearing. As the victim, your words will carry weight. Obviously, it's your choice, but I would recommend speaking at the hearing."

"I want to see him."

"You will if you decide to address the parole board."

"No, I want to see him before the hearing."

"Look, Gwen, I wouldn't recommend it."

She'd never faced Parker, not on an equal footing. The first time he'd had a knife. The second time was at the trial when she'd been on the witness stand. She wanted to face him now. If he'd changed, she wanted to see it for herself, raw, without the varnish of the parole board hearing where he'd be on his best behavior. If he'd really changed, she'd see it. If he had, should she stand in his way of a new life?

"I need to see him."

"Talk it over with your husband."

"This has nothing to do with Paul." She realized the harshness of her statement. "This all took place before I knew him. He'll try to protect me like you're doing, but both of you are outsiders. You weren't there. I have to face him and see if the monster has changed."

Naylor was quiet for a beat. "You could harm the hearing."

"I don't care."

"There's no guarantee he'll want to speak to you."

"We won't know unless you ask."

"Gwen, I don't like the position you're putting me in."

"Blame the state, not me."

Paul knocked at the door. "We're ready when you are, hon."

"I want to see him, Jerry. Make it happen."

CHAPTER SIX

Tom Petersen shifted in his seat. After three hours parked outside Stephen Tarbell's house, his butt was going to sleep. He liked the Audi. It was responsive, classy, well made and comfortable, although forced to sit in the same spot for three hours, he got to feel every Bavarian spring. It was a breed apart from the average car on the road, which made it good for surveillance. No one expects to be followed by an Audi. Something out of Detroit, yes, but not Germany.

Did anything come out of Detroit these days? he thought. GM and Ford had their plants everywhere except the Motor City. There seemed to be more foreign carmakers than domestic in the US. World economics. What a crock.

Tom's cell vibrated on the passenger seat, cutting his thoughts on globalization short. He answered the phone, careful to cover the glowing display. Tarbell lived on a good street for surveillance. It was quiet and poorly lit. The Audi was just another parked car on the street, as long as no one spotted him sitting behind the wheel. The luminous display on a phone might just blow his cover. The last thing he needed was a patrol car alerting the world to his presence.

"What are you doing, Tom?" Gonzalez asked.

"Sitting in the dark watching some prick stay in on a Friday night."

"You can see him?"

"No, but there's movement from inside." He picked up his notebook. "He came home at six thirty-seven and hasn't left the house since. Domino's delivered an hour ago. This guy is settled in for the night."

Gonzalez was his handler on this job. He'd worked with the ex-marine before. He was a little too "by the numbers" for Tom's liking, but the guy didn't fuck him around like some handlers. He always knew where he stood with Gonzalez and that was worth its weight in gold. That was what he liked about Private Security International. They were professional. They hired the best. He liked to think that was why they subcontracted him on surveillance work. He'd put in his twenty-five with the San Francisco PD, working his way up from patrol to inspector. He became a PI after he got out, working for defense lawyers. PSI came to him regularly for surveillance work, paid nice, and came with little trouble.

"Stay on top of this guy," Gonzalez said. "He threatened to slice up a woman. Tonight's the night he'll make good on his threat if he's going to. If he moves, follow him and get backup."

"Will do. No heroics here."

"I'll check in with you later," Gonzalez said and hung up.

Petersen got back to his sitting. He had another six hours of this before Reggie Glover swung by to take over the daylight shift. He preferred night work over days, even though Lynette bitched about him not being home at night. In most cases, people were less active at night, which meant less risk and less effort on his part. He was retired, for Christ's sakes. His hero days were behind him. This work bought him a time-share in Maui.

Nothing much happened for the next hour. Some kid dropped off his girl a few houses down. They made out for twenty minutes before she ran inside with a bounce in her step. A couple of dog walkers drifted by. The nearest thing to action came when a golden retriever detected his presence and wanted to check out him out, but the dog's owner, totally oblivious, jerked the dog away without noticing him sitting there. It never failed to amaze him how little the public noticed, even when it was under their noses.

He checked his watch—ten fifty-seven. He'd been on the job nearly six hours and he felt himself slipping into the floaty phase where it was an effort to keep his concentration. This was where he missed having a partner to talk shit with to keep his mind sharp. That thought was hammered home when someone jerked open the back door and slipped into the backseat. Before he could make a move, a knife was pressed hard against his throat.

"Make a move and it'll be your last," the voice snarled in the darkness.

Petersen's heart worked overtime. "I don't want any trouble."

"Too late. You've got it. Put your hands behind your back."

Petersen slipped his hands to either side of his seat. The knife never left his throat while a zip tie looped each of his wrists. There had to be a daisy chain of zip ties to counter for the width of the seat. The ties were jerked so tight that the seat back acted as a wedge, threatening to pop his shoulders from their sockets.

"Why are you following me?"

He'd been caught by the suspect. He couldn't believe it. "You've got it all wrong. I'm just waiting for a buddy to come out."

"I don't think so. You followed me home yesterday and you followed me home tonight. You really should get that misaligned headlight fixed."

Christ, he couldn't believe he'd been picked off so easily. Retirement sounded good about now.

"You're Stephen Tarbell?"

Tarbell forced the knife hard into his flesh. "Yes. You've got one more chance to tell me who you are and why you're following me."

"Take the knife away and I'll tell you."

The knife disappeared from around his neck and Petersen took his first unhindered breath.

"Cry for help and you'll be crying with a knife in your throat," Tarbell said.

For confirmation, Petersen felt the tip of the blade prick the back of his neck.

"You're being investigated."

"By whom?"

Tarbell sounded genuinely unaware of the reason for his tail. Petersen could sell him a dummy. Child support. Alimony. Any number of bullshit lies. But he didn't know enough about Tarbell. His brief was to follow this guy. Here was his work address and home address. Construct a picture from everything else he does. Petersen knew nothing about him beyond his name and the woman he'd threatened. Any lie he tried to sell the guy was bound to fail. He didn't like to think what this son of a bitch would do to him if he got the lie wrong.

"Private Security International has you under surveillance. Your employer hired them."

Tarbell jerked back on the makeshift cuffs like they were horse reins. Petersen's shoulders burned as his muscles and tendons worked against him. He bit back a cry.

"Why?"

"Why do you think?"

Tarbell was silent for a beat. "Gwen Farris?"

"Yeah."

"She told on me?" There was a childlike awe in his voice after hearing Petersen's revelation.

"Of course she did. You threatened to kill her."

There was more silence from the backseat. Tarbell hadn't expected this kind of attention and it had thrown him. Petersen willed him not to panic. Panic made the guy dangerous.

"Who is Private Security International?"

"A security firm. They carry out background checks, surveillance, and protection."

"How many people are watching me?"

"Don't know."

Tarbell jabbed him the knife in the back of Petersen's neck. "Guess."

"There's a tail on you 24-7 for two weeks. Two watchers. I have nights. A guy driving a blue Durango has days. If you stray from the beaten path, there are two two-man strike teams who will follow you on foot and vehicle. There's likely to be someone working undercover at Pace should you try anything in the office."

"Are you all working with the cops?"

"No. Just your employer."

More silence. This guy was going to do something rash. Petersen could feel it. He hated it when jobs went sideways.

"What's your name?"

"Tom Petersen."

"Driver's license?"

"I'm sitting on it."

"Registration?"

"Glove box."

Tarbell slipped from the backseat into the front passenger seat. He dug the registration document out of the glove box and read it before tossing it back. "You don't lie, Tom. I like that. I feel like we've made a connection."

He picked up Petersen's cell. It represented Petersen's only backup and it was in the hands of the enemy. Tonight had officially turned into a monumental screwup.

"You're going to leave now and not tell anyone about tonight."

"You know I can't do that."

"You underestimate yourself. You can do anything." Tarbell pressed the tip of the knife into the soft skin underneath Petersen's right eye. The pressure of the blade forced him to lose focus in that eye. "Because, if you don't agree, I'll take your eyes. Not a good look for a man who makes a living from spying on people."

"No," Petersen said, the word seeming to scrape his dry mouth.

Tarbell smiled, reached behind Petersen's seat, and slit the zip ties. Petersen groaned with the sudden rush of feeling in his shoulders. Then Tarbell was gone. He slipped from the car before Petersen could make a move to stop him; not that he would have. Tarbell wasn't a guy he was going to tangle with.

Petersen watched Tarbell walk back to his house. It wouldn't be hard to gun the engine and mow the fucker down. It was tempting, but not that tempting. He started the Audi and pulled away.

He powered down the window. Why hadn't he locked the doors? He'd practically invited Tarbell to get in the car and nab him. He was close to puking. Adrenaline didn't give him courage, just chest pains. But the rush of cool night air revived him.

"You fucking amateur, Tom," he said out loud. "Jesus Christ."

Nothing could be done now. He was off this job. His cover had been blown, so he was no good to PSI's investigation. He'd report into Gonzalez and they'd have to strategize about damage control.

He didn't take long to reach his home in Martinez. He felt old and tired pulling into his garage. Tarbell had robbed him of more than his dignity tonight. Closing the garage door, he glimpsed a car with its headlights off rolling to a halt across the street. A quickening in his heart rate told him who it was. He reopened the garage door.

Tarbell slipped from the driver's seat and leaned across the roof of his car in a neighborly fashion. He waved at Petersen like they were friends.

Petersen's .38 was in the house. There was no chance of getting it. He walked up to Tarbell and got close enough to be heard without raising his voice, but far enough to be clear of his knife.

"What do you want?"

He held out Petersen's cell. "I forgot to return this."

Petersen took the phone, but Tarbell didn't release his grip. "If anything happens to me, I know where you live and I know where to find you. Understood?"

All too well. PSI could hand the whole thing over to the cops. They'd arrest Tarbell, but he'd get bail and there'd be nothing between him and Petersen. He couldn't have that. Not with Lynette in the house.

Tarbell grinned. "It's not very nice to know you're being watched, is it?"

"No."

"I've held on to your number."

A chill ran up Petersen's back. "Why?"

"Because we're going to be phone buddies," Tarbell said with a smile. "You're going to tell your masters I've been a good boy doing good boy things, and you're going to keep me informed of the investigation. Aren't you?"

CHAPTER SEVEN

She deceived me. It was the thought that carried Tarbell to sleep and the one on his lips when he awoke. Anger accompanied the thought in the early hours of the morning. It had turned to begrudging admiration as he ate breakfast. He hadn't seen it coming. Gwen had been so convincing, not just when he'd cornered her in the meeting room, but all of Thursday. She'd acted jumpy and a second out of step with the rest of the world, which was what he'd expected. She'd looked genuinely scared when he cornered her coming out of the bathroom. If she was acting, she deserved an Oscar. But maybe she'd been jumpy because of her deception.

His admiration didn't make him want to go easy on her. No, Gwen would pay for her betrayal, and dearly. This was the second time she'd wronged him. What he'd promised to do to her in that rain-soaked parking lot wouldn't compare to what he would do now. Her treachery ignited his temper. He lashed out, casting his coffee mug across the kitchen, where it smashed on the tiled floor.

"Look what you've made me do, Gwen," he said. As he picked up the shattered pieces of mug, he realized his anger had gotten away from him again, as it had when he'd ended up threatening Gwen with the knife. It wasn't his fault. People made him angry.

Their behavior. Their attitudes. Their stupidity. Gwen had pushed him to his limit. Still, he had to get a hold of himself. Throwing things in his own kitchen? This kind of behavior wasn't acceptable, not if he wanted to keep his freedom. His anger had to be turned from indiscriminant displays of rage into precision acts of destruction that couldn't be linked back to him.

He went to the living room window and saw the blue Dodge Durango belonging to his daytime watcher. Private Security International presented a problem. Their operatives would be all over him from dawn to dusk. It made it difficult to take his revenge on Gwen, but having Petersen provided the hole in their defenses he needed. Not only did he have an inside man feeding him intelligence, but he had someone providing a bulletproof alibi. No matter what crimes he committed at night, Petersen would vouch for him and say he'd been sitting at home on the couch.

The clock was ticking, though. PSI allowed themselves two weeks to build a case against their subject before confronting them with the results. He had to destroy Gwen in that time, but give PSI no grounds for a confrontation. It was going to be tough, but doable.

There was nothing he could do now, not directly, but he could put on a show. He scrubbed the floor clean of coffee stains before backing the car out the garage and heading toward the freeway with the Durango trailing behind him. He made no effort to lose his tail. He wanted his watcher to share his boring and uneventful weekend.

He headed north across the Carquinez Bridge into the valley on I-80 and pulled off the freeway at West Sacramento. He turned into a shitty, run-down neighborhood near the Port of Sacramento and stopped in front of the familiar ranch house he came to every Saturday. Walking up to the door, he took the place in. The structure seemed to fall into deeper decay with every passing week. The roof continued to sag. The siding looked warped by one more degree. Weeds overran the small sun-baked yard. It was duty that brought him here. Nothing else. The door opened before he reached the stoop. Lupe Corrales smiled and held the door open. "Hello, Steve," she said with that ever-present smile. "You're a little late today."

"Chores," he replied, lightly irritated by her mild reprimand. "How's Dad been?"

Lupe's smiled dropped. "The same."

Lupe was a slight woman nudging fifty. How she manhandled his dad physically as well as verbally he never knew. Training, he decided. Not being a blood relative helped too. A stranger could always dismiss his father. He couldn't.

She'd changed out of her nurse's uniform and looked eager to leave. She was a full-time stay-at-home nurse, six days, seven nights. Stephen stood in for her on Saturdays.

"Anything I should know?" he asked.

"No. Business as usual. He's in the living room."

"OK, Lupe. Enjoy your day off."

Lupe threw a wave over her shoulder and disappeared in the Toyota financed by his monthly checks.

He closed the door, aware of the Durango parked across the street.

"Hey, Dad, it's me," he called out.

"In here," he barked, then more quietly, "like I'd be anywhere else."

Dennis Tarbell's world extended as far as the four walls of the living room. It provided his place to sleep, his dining room, his entertainment room, his treatment room and his bathroom most of the time. The room was by no definition palatial, but it was simply the biggest available to get all the equipment in to enable Dennis to live somewhat comfortably.

Tarbell found his father hunched over in his wheelchair with a clear plastic tube running to his nose from an oxygen bottle strapped to the wheelchair's side. Even with the oxygen's assistance, he struggled to breathe, sucking in air like it was soup.

In his prime, Dennis Tarbell had been a strong man. Where his son was gawky, the father had been muscled from a life spent working in the Richmond and Vallejo shipyards. Dennis didn't look so big these days. Forty years of smoking three packs a day had caught up with him in the form of emphysema and other smoking-related complications. His lungs rattled and wheezed every time he breathed. He looked deflated, his flesh hanging loose on his bony frame. He was a far cry from the behemoth Tarbell remembered as a frightened child.

"Come to ease your conscience?" he said.

It was an old and much used greeting. Tarbell placed it in his father's top ten slurs. It had been a couple of weeks since he'd trotted that one out.

"You want something to drink?" Tarbell said on his way to the kitchen.

"A beer."

Booze had been another of his father's crutches that his health denied him.

Tarbell opened the fridge door. "Coffee or juice?"

His father didn't answer.

Tarbell made coffee and returned to the living room with two mugs. He set one on the lap tray on the wheelchair. He set his own down on the side table next to the sofa.

"You want the TV on?" he asked.

"If I wanted the fucking TV on, I'd put it on. I ain't got much but I still got one good finger to press a button on the remote. See?" He shot Tarbell the bird to illustrate his point.

His father's acting out was his way of compensating for his body's failings. He could no longer throw a fist when his dinner was cold or backhand his son for losing a schoolyard brawl, but he could still hurl an insult and have it hit the mark every time. Tarbell put it down to lost pride. Once, his father had been breadwinner. He steered a family. His name meant something to the people who knew him. Now he elicited only pity. It couldn't be a lot of fun pissing into a pan and having your son wipe your ass when you didn't make it to the toilet in time. So he let his dad exercise his one remaining skill, his foul mouth.

He lobbed a few more taunts Tarbell's way. It looked like it was going to be a long Saturday with his father. Something had obviously pissed him off this week. Probably a doctor. Every time a doctor examined him, it resulted in having another of life's pleasures excised. First it was the smokes, followed by the booze, then his favorite foods. And his invalid status prevented him from ignoring medical advice. He was at the mercy of others. Good. Some would call that karma. Tarbell called it payback.

He ignored the slurs. Gwen's betrayal kept recurring to him like a hot spike through his thoughts. His threats should have put her in her place, but she'd gone running to her corporate mommy. He needed to up the ante and let her know what the price of disobedience was going to be.

His father's laugh jerked him from his thoughts. "You're broody today. Broody, broody, broody like a hen looking for its cock. Something's happened to you, hasn't it?"

His dad wanted a fight. Confrontations made the old man feel alive. He wouldn't be drawn in. Not today.

"Someone screwed you over, didn't they? I recognize that look of yours. You've had it since you were a kid. Some asshole knocks you down and you don't get up and fight back. Instead, you skulk away with your tail between your legs and put that face on while inside that pea brain of yours you're rewriting history where you do something about it." He shook his head in disgust. "My son, the fucking pussy."

Tarbell had the coffee mug in his hand. A faint tremor buzzed through his body as he fought to keep his temper. A bead of scalding coffee spilled over the edge and onto his hand. He ignored the pain.

But his father didn't. His eyes lit up at the sight of the tremor and the spill.

"Christ, some son of mine you are. You embarrass me. Do you know that? I have a reputation, and you don't live up to it."

Tarbell returned the coffee mug to the table.

"Look, even now, you don't even say anything to me, a fucking invalid. You're just like your mother. She wouldn't say boo to a goose."

"And whose fault is that?"

"Christ, it speaks." Dennis Tarbell raised a hand to his ear. "Do I hear the sound of balls growing? Will wonders never cease? Got a news flash for you. You left it a little fucking late to act like a man."

Rage was boiling up inside Tarbell, and he hated himself for it. His dad wanted this fight, and he was about to get it.

"So what happened? Someone call you a nasty name? Tell Papa all about it," he said in a coochie-coo voice.

It would be so easy to tell him about Gwen. He'd even earn some points with his old man for knocking a broad about. Dennis would like knowing that the apple hadn't fallen too far from the Tarbell tree. But, no, his father couldn't have Gwen. She was his plaything. If he told his dad about what he'd done and what he planned to do, he'd claim it as his own. His sleep would be thick with dreams of Gwen and what he would do to her. His father had denied him so much over the years, and now Tarbell could deny him this pleasure. A smile twisted his mouth.

"You'd be proud of me, but you don't deserve to hear the story. You haven't behaved yourself," he replied in the same babying voice.

Dennis's face contorted into a snarl, and he hurled his coffee mug at Tarbell. Twenty years ago, there would have been some real heat behind the throw, but it fell well short in distance and accuracy. It struck the ground first before bouncing against the edge of the couch. Coffee slopped against Tarbell's pant leg.

Whether the throw had been intentionally botched or not didn't matter to Tarbell. The coffee soaking into his pants severed his last ounce of restraint. He leaped off the couch and lunged for his father.

Something bordering on glee shone bright in Dennis's eyes. He'd provoked a reaction he thought he controlled. He believed Tarbell would be upset and that would be the end of it, but it wasn't like that anymore. He was different now. He grabbed the old man's wheelchair.

"Oh, look at the big man," Dennis said. "See him pick on someone who can't fight back and slap a sick old man around."

"It worked for you, didn't it? A backhand for me. A kick in the guts for Mom."

The glee turned to anger. "You two brought it upon yourselves. If you hadn't pissed me off, I would have never laid a hand on either of you."

Dennis grabbed the wheels on his wheelchair and pulled on them to steer himself away, but Tarbell held the chair firmly in place.

"Get your damn hands off my chair."

"Make me."

Dennis raised a hand to strike out. Tarbell blocked the weak attempt and slapped his father across the face. It wasn't a hard slap, but it affected both of them. It changed a lifetime of abuse. The balance had shifted. Tarbell wondered if, for the first time, his father realized he was no longer the dominant male in his world. He hoped the hell so, but regardless, he felt like the dominant male at last. It failed to make up for all the years he didn't stand up to his father or protect his mother, but it did fill him with a newfound power. Going after Gwen had opened the door, but he'd walked through it when he hit his father.

"Enjoy that, did you? Did your dick grow a couple of extra inches?"

His father was scrabbling for control. He wouldn't give it to him.

"Would you like me to scream?" Dennis contorted his face and let out a fake sob. "Would you like me to squirt out some tears? Do you expect me to beg you to stop the way you used to?"

"I don't expect you to do anything."

Dennis snorted. "You want an apology or something?"

"No. You wouldn't mean it."

"Damn right."

"You're an ungrateful son of a bitch," said Tarbell in disgust.

Dennis snorted again. He tried to puff himself up to look bigger than he was, but his body was weak. "You expect me to be indebted to you because you keep me living in this lap of luxury?"

"Something like that."

"Well, I'm not."

It was a good front, but Tarbell could see that his father was scared. He knew his body had sold him out, but until now he had still had Tarbell to lord his power over. Now that was gone.

"You need to be taught a lesson in manners and respect," Tarbell said.

Dennis laughed. Tarbell brought it to a swift end by grabbing the oxygen tube and bringing it in front of his father's face. He folded the tube back on itself. The reaction was instantaneous. His father withered without the flow of oxygen. He reached for the tubing, but Tarbell slapped his hands out of the way.

"The lesson isn't at an end yet. You need to understand your ability to continue living relies on my generosity. My money and my will keep you alive. Like oxygen, you'll only notice when it disappears."

The color drained from Dennis's face. His mouth flapped open and closed like that of a hooked trout on a riverbank as he fought to suck in air.

"I can cut you off at a moment's whim," said Tarbell. "I'll be honest with you, my whim isn't in your favor right now."

Fear burned white hot in Dennis's eyes. Tarbell had never seen his father scared. He drank the moment in until it left him giddy. At long last, his father knew what it was to be human. It was good he was learning it before his life ran out. Tarbell released the tubing.

The pressure in the line forced the kink open and life-giving oxygen flowed back to his father. After three ragged inhales, he began to recover. Tarbell patted his cheek.

"Good boy. Lesson learned, I think." He returned to the sofa and picked up his coffee mug. No tremors now. He blew at the steam still curling off the surface. "I'm the head of the family now."

CHAPTER EIGHT

Petersen sat at the bar watching the Sunday night football game and nursing a beer. This was how he'd conducted his surveillance on Tarbell since Friday night, hiding out, leaving Tarbell free to do whatever he wanted.

He was careful about his private arrangement. He relieved Reggie Glover at the scheduled time, checked in with Tarbell, gave it half an hour, then left. When it came time for Reggie to relieve him, he made sure he was in the right place for the handover. The time between, he found somewhere out of the way to kill time and file bogus surveillance reports. He chose places like this sports bar in a neighborhood where nobody from PSI would turn up. There was still a risk of being seen, but he didn't want to take the safer course of just staying at home. He just couldn't face Lynette.

His cell phone sat dormant alongside his beer glass. He kept it on for Tarbell to call if he had any instructions. It hadn't rung. That was a good thing. If Tarbell didn't call him, it meant he hadn't done anything to this woman he had it in for. In Petersen's mind, it didn't make him any less of a scumbag for not doing the right thing.

"Coward," he murmured.

"What was that?" the bartender asked.

"Can I get a Coke?"

"Sure. Do you want to see a menu too?"

"Maybe later."

The bartender nodded and went off to pour his Coke.

He couldn't keep doing this. He'd only been doing it a couple of nights and it was already driving him crazy. His mind continually churned about what he was doing or not doing, to be more exact. He'd been a cop, sworn to uphold the law. Now look at him.

Fuck Tarbell, Petersen thought, *the guy's on his own after tonight.* He was telling Ingram everything first thing Monday morning. He picked up his beer. "Here's to you, asshole."

He chugged half of his beer down. For the first time in the last couple of days, it tasted like beer and not like poison.

The sourness in his gut that had been with him since Friday dissipated, succeeding where a fistful of antacid had failed. He ordered an appetizer and took an interest in the football game playing on the flat screen.

All that ended when his cell rang partway through the second quarter. Thinking it was Tarbell, he felt his stomach clench around the beer and bar food, but the feeling passed when he saw Lynette's name displayed on the caller ID.

"Hey, what's up, babe?"

"I need you to pick me up from the emergency room."

"What happened?"

"I fell down an escalator at the mall and twisted my ankle. Nothing serious, but I need a ride."

"What the hell were you doing at the mall?"

"Tom, you're working nights and asleep during the day. I need to do something when you're not around." There was a smile in her voice. It took the tension out of his. "Can you pick me up?"

"Sure. Shouldn't be a problem. Where are you?"

"Kaiser in Vallejo."

"I need to clear it with PSI, but I should be over there within an hour. OK?"

"OK."

He hung up on his wife and called Tarbell. It sickened him that his first call was to him, but at least it kept the son of a bitch on his toes. More importantly, it neutralized him tonight, leaving it open for Petersen to confess all to Ingram in the morning.

"It's Petersen. You need to get home or tell me where you are."

"Why?"

"My wife was in an accident, and I have to pick her up from the hospital."

"I hope she's OK."

Like you care. "She's fine."

"I'm at home."

"Good. Stay there. Someone will be replacing me."

He hung up on Tarbell, dropped cash on the bar, and left. He waited until he was halfway to Tarbell's house before calling Gonzalez, who said he'd finish up the night shift.

Petersen was parked innocently in front of Tarbell's house when Gonzalez arrived. He recognized the handler's familiar Buick sedan when it pulled up on Tarbell's street. After a brief call from Gonzalez, he drove off to collect Lynette.

He found her waiting for him with her foot bandaged up and one shoe missing. Her hands were pretty grazed up from the fall. He stopped in front of her and smiled.

"Does Cinderella need a ride home?"

"Yes, she does."

He got into the car and drove her home. She hadn't been able to drive her own car. He'd have to pick that up from the mall in the morning. He put her in front of the TV and elevated her foot.

"Do you need anything?" he asked. "Coffee or anything? Ice?"

"No, I'm good."

He sat down next to her.

"You're not going back out?"

He slipped an arm around her shoulders. "No, Gonzalez has things covered for tonight. Tell me what happened."

"I just fell. I was riding the escalator with everyone, and I had my hands full. The escalator was packed. Someone bumped me and I fell."

"I can't let you go anywhere alone," he said with a smile.

J. Edgar, their black Lab, loped in from the backyard with his tail wagging. Petersen patted the dog on the head, and it settled down on the floor underneath Lynette's feet. Although it had only been days since Petersen had enjoyed this type of domestic bliss, it felt like an aeon ago.

"Is everything OK?" Lynette asked.

"Yeah." He didn't leave himself open to a follow-up. He was starting to act like a guilty suspect.

"You haven't seemed yourself."

"It's the nightshift. It's hard adjusting to the hours. I'm not a kid anymore."

Lynette nodded, processing the information.

"I heard a TV and voices playing when I called you. You were supposed to be on a stakeout."

He cursed himself. He should have taken the call outside. Life with him had rubbed off on Lynette. She was a good detective. "Yeah, I had to follow the suspect to a bar."

"And you complain about working the nightshift."

He smiled at her. When she smiled back, he noticed worry underneath it. She picked up the remote and silenced the TV.

"There's a problem, isn't there?"

She'd seen through him. He thought he'd done a good job shielding her from the mess he was in, but she knew him too well. He could deny there was a problem, but thirty-two years of marriage made it impossible to lie to her. She'd only believe the lie if she wanted to, and she didn't. All he could do was deflect.

"It's just the work. The guy's a scumbag. He's threatened a woman he works for."

He could tell from Lynette's expression and silence she wasn't buying it. He refrained from making the situation worse by talking even more.

"Are you sure it's just that? Nothing has happened, has it?"

"No, I'm fine. I just want to get this assignment out of the way. I'm going to tell Ingram I don't want these kinds of jobs anymore. If he wants me to interview witnesses or carry out background checks, I'll do it, but I'm not doing any more surveillance work. I don't want to spend my nights cooped up in my car when I could be spending them with you."

She frowned.

He took her face in his. Gray had crept into her hair and lines marked her mouth and around her eyes, but she was still the woman he fell in love with an age ago. When he kissed her, her lips were still as soft as they were when he kissed her after the birth of their first child, Lee. "Seriously, everything's OK. I've had a rough couple of days on this job, but I'm over the hump. Tomorrow's going to be better. If you can keep from falling down."

She smiled this time and meant it. He'd kept the problem from her, but he hadn't kept his true feelings from her. Tomorrow, he would explain himself to Ingram. She picked up the remote and unmuted the TV.

Later, when it was time for bed, he made her laugh by carrying her to bed, although it killed his back to do it. He slept well that night.

The next morning, she was up and walking, albeit with a limp and not well enough to drive yet. He wanted to see Ingram, but he needed to claim Lynette's car first. He arranged with an ex-police buddy living in Vallejo to drive her car back and he'd drive him home.

A few minutes before his buddy was scheduled to arrive, he went outside to wait. It was a beautiful sunny fall morning, crisp and clear. He found a flyer jammed under the windshield wiper of his Audi, which was parked in front of the garage. He yanked it free, cursing the jerk who'd put it under there, no doubt while he was in the sports bar last night. Just as he was about to screw it up and toss it in the trash, he remembered there'd been no flyer under his windshield when he'd rushed to the hospital to get Lynette. He opened up the twice-folded sheet of paper.

It wasn't a flyer. It was a printout of a digital photograph featuring Lynette sprawled out at the bottom of an escalator surrounded by her a tumble of shopping bags. There was nothing written or typed on the image. It wasn't needed. Petersen knew exactly who'd sent it and what it meant.

CHAPTER NINE

Fifteen years earlier

Brats catered to the college crowd with its buck-a-beer policy that went easy on student finances. It was a no-frills place with bare wooden floors and no real seating to speak of, but that didn't matter since the a plastic cup of beer only cost a buck. Everyone in Davis knew this place was a college hangout. Those over the age of twenty-five never bothered with the place, but there were always a few older guys who thought they could fit in with the young people and maybe pick up some pretty young thing. That fateful night had been no different.

He looked like an AC/DC refugee, with way too much denim for Davis in the May heat. He stood head and shoulders taller than most of the guys. He cut his way through the sea of bodies with a smile and gentle shove. Gwen made the mistake of making eye contact and groaned inside when he made a change in course toward her and Judy at the bar. Moments later, he'd squeezed into the bar alongside them.

"Can I buy you lovely ladies a drink?"

"Sure," Judy got in before Gwen could shut this guy down. Judy never turned down a free drink.

He peeled a twenty off a roll of bills and held it high for the bartender to see. It was supposed to impress, but Gwen fought the urge to roll her eyes. She was sure this crap worked with a lot of women, but he was paddling in the wrong pool.

The bartender came over and got their order in. Gwen stuck to beer, but Judy, being Judy, went with a Long Island Iced Tea that put a dent in the twenty. Mr. Denim went with a beer and a shot.

"I'm Desmond Parker, but my friends call me DP."

"Judy Brent."

"Gwen."

"No last name, Gwen?" he asked sipping his beer.

"Not yet, no."

"Don't be like that, Gwen. I'm just being friendly."

He was right. She wasn't being fair. She had no interest in Parker, but there was no reason to be rude.

"Litchfield."

"Gwen Litchfield," he said, sampling each word. "I like it."

"And my name?" Judy pitched in without malice. She just didn't want to be excluded from the fun.

"Equally as nice."

"Thank you."

Parker cast an appraising gaze over them. It picked their clothes off, long and slow. Gwen fought the urge to shiver.

"I'm guessing you go to school here."

"You guess right, DP," Judy said. "Seniors now."

"Seniors," Parker said, feigning shock. "It won't be long before you're taking the world by storm."

"You got that right," Judy said.

"What is your major, Gwen?"

"Genetics," she said curtly. The man's domineering conversational style was getting to her.

Parker put down his beer. "Wow, no one told me I was in the presence of genius."

"It sounds more impressive than it really is," Gwen said.

"You're being modest."

"She is," Judy said. "What about you? What do you do?"

Parker smirked. "A little of this. A little of that."

Gwen tried pounding down her beer to give her the excuse to lose Parker, but she couldn't choke it down. She didn't have a talent for it and wished she'd gone for a cocktail like Judy. Judy made her drink disappear with a few gulps. Parker paced himself after killing off the shot with a single swallow.

Gwen feared she and Judy were stuck with this guy for the night, until Zach came to the rescue. Parker was in the middle of a story intended to impress them when Zach called out, "Where's my girl?"

He waded through the throng toward Judy, Gwen, and Parker.

Zach sidled up behind Judy and looped his arms around her waist so they hung low across her belly. Judy turned her head and kissed him.

Zach's arrival forced Parker to take a step back. He was athletically built, possessing both power and speed.

"You're late, lover," Judy said.

"I'm in demand. What can I say?" Zach said. "Who's your friend?"

There was no malice in Zach's question. He'd stated his claim to Judy quite clearly. Sadly, Gwen didn't have the luxury of a boyfriend for protection.

"This is DP."

"Hey," Zach said to Parker.

Zach changed the mood. College life dominated their conversation, and Parker lost his dominance. It didn't take long before it became evident to everyone, including Parker, that he didn't belong. There was no opportunity for him to make himself seem important in their world. Gwen almost felt sorry for the guy. But Zach's arrival didn't dislodge him, it only forced him to couple up with her.

Brats' owner, Jason, leaned across the bar. "Gwen, it's zero hour. You ready to sing?"

She nodded.

"You're a singer?" Parker said.

"She's the best," Judy said.

"I'm OK."

The DJ cut the music and introduced Gwen and the band, giving her the chance to slip Parker's grip.

She climbed onto the stage to cheers and whistles. She wasn't with the band. They were a bunch of guys from the college who made some cash doing wedding gigs, but Fridays and Saturdays they played at Brats. She had a good voice, but not good enough to make a career out of it. She sang for the fun of it and the fifty bucks Brats paid her. She kicked off a five-song set of chart covers.

Gwen sang to the crowd, but periodically checked on Parker. Without her, he'd become a third wheel to Judy and Zach, and she watched him trawl the place for unattached girls. She noticed that each time he came up with nothing, his gaze returned to her. He latched on to a group of juniors she recognized. He slipped his arms around their shoulders, whispered something to the girls, then nodded at Gwen. His fascination with her left her cold in the sweltering room.

Partway through the third song, Judy waved at Gwen before she and Zach left, no doubt for a quiet place to indulge their desires. Gwen groaned inside. That left her alone with Parker. But when she finished the set, Parker was gone. It looked as if his act had run out of steam. His age and looks just paled against his male competition. Girls might go for older men, but they had to be the right kind, and Parker wasn't it. The tension bled from her as she stepped down from the stage.

Jason set her up with a glass of water for her throat and to put some fluids back into her body. With Parker gone, she loosened up for her second set. She called it a night at eleven and cut through the crowd to Jason.

"Beautiful work as usual," he said, closing fifty bucks in mixed bills into her fist and kissing the back of her hand. "Let's do it again tomorrow night."

She smiled. "Deal."

She walked out into the still warm night, but it was bracing compared to the heat of three hundred bodies pressed up against each other in a room with poor ventilation. The fresh air helped with the beer buzz she'd developed. The walk to her apartment would do the rest.

She hadn't gotten a block before an ancient blue and gray Chevy Suburban pulled alongside her. Parker leaned across the passenger seat to talk and drive at the same time. If the fresh air had killed her beer buzz, Parker buried it. She felt alert and nervous.

"You've got a great voice. I'm discovering you're definitely a woman of many talents."

Had he been waiting out here for her? She hoped not. He was probably waiting for any girl to leave in the hopes of netting her. Having failed with his wit and charm, he was pinning his hopes to his big truck. How lame. She carried on walking.

"Hold up a sec."

She shouldn't, but she needed to nip this in the bud. She stopped, and Parker parked at the curb and climbed down from his truck.

"I saw your friends leave."

I bet you did. "Yeah, they had somewhere else to hit tonight."

"But you didn't?"

"No. It's been a long week."

"Too much work and no play makes Gwen a dull girl."

"Well, this week, it's true."

Parker shook his head. "You know, I don't like to see a girl as smart and as good looking as you sleep through the best part of a Friday night."

Gwen guessed he'd used this line before, and it probably got him a grin nine times out of ten, but she only produced a polite smile. "Such is life."

"Can I persuade you to stay out?"

She smiled. "Not tonight. This girl has a date with her bed," she said and immediately cursed her poor choice of words.

"I'll give you a ride."

She debated his offer. Accepting it would get him off her back, but she could see him pushing for something else when he got her home. Besides, she didn't like the idea of this guy knowing where she lived. "No, I'm good. Thanks, though."

Gwen didn't give him the chance to try another avenue of questioning and said good night before walking away. She figured he would follow her in his truck, but she'd cut through the campus to lose him. It was a simple plan, but she didn't get the opportunity to try it.

Parker grabbed her wrist and spun her around. He bear-hugged her and smothered her scream with a kiss. He drove her backward into a shop front belonging to a real estate office and smacked her head off the brick facade. The impact left her woozy and her legs buckled, but Parker kept her upright. The move was seamless. To the outside world, they were drunken lovers getting a little ornery in public.

"Gwen, you're coming with me," he whispered and smacked her head even harder against the building.

This time, Gwen lost consciousness.

The present

Jerry Naylor had called Gwen on Sunday night with the go-ahead. Earlier in the week, he'd pulled some strings and had gotten her visitation rights to see Desmond Parker on Monday morning. But it hadn't been a sure thing because Parker himself had not yet agreed to the visit. His approval was required. On Sunday, Naylor had finally heard from Parker. The man didn't object, and Gwen was in.

Gwen stepped out of the shower with a towel wrapped around her. Paul stood in the bathroom doorway.

"I wish you'd let me go with you."

"I can't. This all happened before we even met. I need to do this myself. If I'm going to testify against him at his parole hearing, I need to look him in the eye."

"I wish you'd change your mind."

"I know," she said and kissed him.

He left her alone, and she breathed a little easier. The facade she put on for Paul was thin. Facing Parker was going to hurt, and having Paul at her side would be nice, but it wouldn't help her answer the questions she needed to ask.

She toweled off and blow-dried her hair. She tugged the towel free to slip into her clothes and caught sight of her naked body in the full-length wall mirror. She pretended she didn't see the scar, but she did. She approached the mirror gingerly, apprehensive of her own form. She didn't like mirrors. She saw too much in them. Today, she had to look. She had a pretty good figure for a woman entering her late thirties. Her belly was reasonably flat, her breasts possessed an eye-pleasing swell, and her legs remained toned. But she didn't focus on any of these attributes, just the scar. It wasn't much and few had seen it, but she always knew it existed and so did Desmond Parker.

It wasn't the scar itself that offended her but what it represented. Parker had severed one of her fallopian tubes when he stabbed her. A lucky strike according to him. The loss would have had little effect on her chances of getting pregnant, but she already had low egg production. Parker's knife wound halved a low percentage number. Because of his attack, she'd faced the grim reality that childbirth was a remote possibility. She and Paul had tried and tried to beat the odds and had all but given up hope when she became pregnant with Kirsten, their miracle baby.

She rubbed her fingers across the scar. It was smooth, silky compared to the rest of her skin.

"I think you should eat before you go," Paul said entering the room. Seeing Gwen, his words trailed off, and he stopped in the doorway.

SIMON WOOD

Embarrassed, Gwen grabbed the towel off the bed and covered herself.

"You don't have to hide it from me."

Gwen couldn't speak.

He closed the door and held her for a moment before pulling at the towel. She resisted, but for only a second. He tossed the towel on the bed. "You're beautiful, Gwen. You never have to hide yourself."

He sank to his knees and kissed the scar. She wanted to retreat but remained in place.

He looked up at her. Tears glistened in his eyes. "This isn't a wound. It's a scar. A scar is the product of repair. What happened to you is over. In the past. This scar proves it. It doesn't matter to me, and it shouldn't to you."

She pulled him to his feet and held him tight. "I love you so much."

"I know," he said. "I'll make you some breakfast."

She watched him leave and tears flowed the moment he closed the door. They were tears of happiness and of pain. She had to pull it together. She could let Paul see the affect Parker had on her, but God knows, she refused to let Parker know she still felt pain all these years later. She had to be battle tough. Anything less would only feed Parker's twisted ego.

She dressed swiftly, pulling on a blouse and slacks. Prison visitor's rules stated no showy or revealing clothes. She styled her hair and applied makeup. Nothing too heavy. Again, prison rules. When she was finished, she looked ready for a business meeting. She needed to treat her encounter with Parker this way. It helped her keep it together. She forced down an English muffin and a half a cup of coffee before kissing Paul and Kirsten good-bye.

The drive to San Quentin wasn't far and took less time than she thought. It was tough to think Parker was incarcerated within a forty-minute drive from her home. It was as if the legal system were taunting her.

As she crossed the Richmond–San Rafael Bridge to the Marin side, the prison loomed large to her left. An unimpressive off-ramp marked the prison's exit at the end of the bridge. Gwen had seen many vehicles take the exit over the years. She'd always assumed these people were family members or lawyers seeing their clients. It never occurred to her that they might be crime victims about to come face-to-face with their attackers.

She was the only one on the poorly kept road that ran along the coast out to the prison. A smattering of houses overlooked the road and the bay. The road dead-ended at the prison's outer gates.

She parked in the visitors' lot and checked in at the main gate. Her hands were unnaturally cold, and her breakfast churned in the pit of her stomach. She didn't have to go through with this. She could turn around and leave. It wouldn't matter that Parker knew she'd backed out. *No*, she thought. She'd come this far and she had to face her monster.

"I have an appointment with one of the prisoners."

"Inmates," the corrections officer said. "We don't call them prisoners."

It was a slice of political correctness she didn't let bother her.

The officer checked her name against the approved list of visitors and inspected her ID before letting her inside the prison. He quizzed her on any objects she was bringing in. "Nothing" was her answer. She owed Parker nothing, and he was getting exactly that, though she was expecting to leave with something. The officer handed her a visitor pass and she walked through an airport-style security checkpoint.

Another corrections officer introduced himself and escorted her to the visitor's area.

"Do you know Desmond Parker?" Gwen asked.

"Yes."

"Do you think he deserves parole?"

"I've been here all through his stay and he's kept his nose clean."

"Has he changed?"

"More than most."

The officer showed her into an empty, communal room filled with tables and chairs. It reminded Gwen of a drab, deserted cafeteria. There'd be no barrier between her and Parker. She picked out a table toward the middle of the room and sat down.

She was alone except for the guard. She sat waiting for Parker like he'd summoned her and not the other way around. The guard kept her pinned under his gaze. She fought the urge to strike up a conversation. She needed to focus.

A door opened and Parker entered, dressed in prison denim. Gwen's heart rate jumped into high gear, but she did her best to keep her fears internalized.

Parker smiled at her, but she didn't return the pleasantry.

Fifteen years of prison had changed him. The man who'd abducted her and stabbed her had been heavyset but strong. At first glance, she thought prison had eroded the latter quality, but then she noticed that even though he'd developed a paunch and lost some of his muscle, he still possessed the inherent strength that he'd used to overpower her all those years ago. Silver overran his chestnut-brown hair. He'd let it grow long, and it looked ratty. He'd entered prison a youthful thirty-nine years old, but time had etched deep lines into his face. He looked his age and then some. Gwen liked to think that prison had ravaged him.

He took the seat opposite her, and his smile broadened into a grin. Prison might have taken its toll on his body, but she doubted it had altered his soul. He was still the man he'd been all those years ago when he'd cursed her name and rammed the knife in her stomach.

"Gwen, you look great."

She felt the heat of his gaze appraising her before he'd sat down. She didn't reply to his comment.

"I have to admit that I'm a little surprised by you wanting to see me, but I guess it's about my upcoming parole hearing."

"They informed me about it."

"Do you still sing?"

Gwen kept a tight rein on her temper. "No. Too many bad memories."

"I hear you're married with a kid. Tell me about your family."

"They're none of your business."

Parker smirked. "Brr. A nasty windchill moves in from the east." His smirk dissolved into his lined face. "Keep it civil, Gwen. Just remember who requested this visit. I'm doing you a favor."

"There are some things you aren't entitled to know."

Parker snorted. "My lawyer advised against this meeting. He thinks this is some ploy to fuck up my parole hearing, but I told him you weren't like that. I told him you're one of the good ones, a Girl Scout. Tell me he's wrong."

"He's wrong."

He smiled, getting far too much pleasure from her reply. "So what do you want, Gwen? Don't tell me what your therapist thinks you want. Tell me what you really want."

"I don't have a therapist."

Parker grinned and leaned back in his seat. "Good. You're a strong one, Gwen. It was what drew me to you."

The man sounded like an ex-boyfriend instead of an attacker. They had shared a relationship. It wasn't a loving one, but it was one filled with strong emotions.

"Why have you come?"

"They tell me you've changed. I came to see if that's true."

Parker flung his arms out wide. "And have I?"

"You've gotten older and you've put on a few pounds, but that doesn't come close to answering my question."

She'd struck Parker's vanity, and he put away the bravado. Parker dropped his arms, and the gleam of enjoyment in his eyes dulled.

"You want to know if I've changed? Well, I have." He tapped an insistent finger on the table. "People change all the time. I'm sure you've been told about my behavior in here, and it's true.

I've kept out of trouble and kept a few kids from making their stay here worse. I've killed the boredom by keeping my mind entertained."

She wondered what kinds of things would keep Parker's mind entertained.

"You want to know if when I'm released, I'll come after you and finish what I started and take out your pretty little family in the process."

"Yes."

"You're in the past, Gwen. I'm not interested in you and your family."

His derisive tone of voice had been rising in volume and caught the guard's attention. "Is everything OK over there?" he called across the room.

"We're fine," Gwen said. She didn't want him breaking things up.

The guard nodded at her.

She was quiet for a long time. Parker had worked himself up. She wanted him calm. He couldn't hear her if his blood was up.

"This is upsetting you, isn't it?" she asked.

"What do you think?"

"Don't expect me to feel bad."

Parker exhaled.

"I'll be honest with you. Fifteen years doesn't even come close to repaying what you did to me. The DA told me you'd never see the light of day. That helped me sleep at night. Helped me heal. But now you may leave jail a free man. I need to know that if I happen to walk into you on the street, I can keep it together. I don't want to do to you what you did to me."

Gwen's deadly tone surprised even her. Parker paled. He'd expected a timid mouse to walk in and quake at the sight of the big scary monster. So had Gwen, but something had changed. Tarbell, she guessed. Another man believed he could intimidate her. It wouldn't happen. "Between us, I think I can cope with seeing you on the streets. And that's a good thing, as I don't want to throw my life away because of you. I have a great family, a good job, and way of life to protect. If I hurt you and take my revenge, I'll lose it all. I don't want that to happen, Desmond."

"Practice that little speech in front of the mirror?"

She smiled and shook her head. "You just bring the best out in me."

The remark released the tension that had built up in him. He leaned back in his seat. "You make it sound like it's a done deal. You can still destroy me during the hearing."

"I don't think so. If you've been the model prisoner I keep hearing about, the parole board will grant you parole and there won't be a thing you or I can do about it."

"So you think I'll get out?"

"I think so. The bigger question is what will you do when you get out?"

Parker's smile returned. "Worried I'll move into your neighborhood and get a job packing groceries at your local market?"

"No. I've told you I can cope with you being out."

"I've got some things lined up on the outside. Nothing grandiose. Felons don't get an easy ride."

"My bleeding liberal heart isn't bleeding."

Parker laughed. "I wouldn't expect it to. I want to start my own business. Classic motorcycle repairs. I love bikes and there are plenty of people out there who don't know how to maintain them. Pleased for me?"

Gwen wouldn't be drawn in. She realized he was trying to sell a line. It was the kind of stuff that would impress the parole board, not her.

"OK, you're going to leave me alone, but what about other women? Are you going to put in a repeat performance?"

The question was a low blow, but Gwen didn't care. So far, Parker had danced around her with smiles and banter. She hadn't seen the real him. She needed to provoke him. To his credit, he did a nice job of holding on to his temper.

"I have no intention of returning here."

"That doesn't answer the question. That tells me you don't intend leaving behind a witness to point the finger."

Parker sat forward in his seat, his hands bunched into fists under the table. "You may not like what you're hearing, but I've learned my lesson. If a woman tells me no, it means no. Got that?"

The guard walked past them in a passive-aggressive move to let everyone know he was still around, making sure nothing got out of hand.

"I have a question for you," said Parker. "Actually, it's from my lawyer, but I want to know too. Are you going to speak at my hearing?"

"That depends."

"On what?"

"On the answer to my last question."

Parker frowned, but said nothing.

"When you stabbed me and left, did you expect me to die?"

Parker didn't answer.

"Did you want me to die that day?"

"Yes," he replied without an ounce of remorse. "Yes, I did."

CHAPTER TEN

Gwen felt a change in air pressure as she left the prison, as if she could breathe more easily. She barely noticed the corrections officer who saw her out.

She reached her car and realized that she no longer felt nauseous and frightened. She'd faced Parker and come out the other side. She'd even managed to put a scare into him. She smiled at that one.

She pulled out her cell and called Paul.

"How'd it go?"

"OK. It was something I had to do."

"I'm proud of you. Celebrate isn't the right word, but let's go out somewhere. Just us. I'll get a sitter for Kirsten."

"OK. Sounds good. I'm going to work. See you tonight."

"I love you."

"Love you, too," she said and hung up.

The smile didn't last. She couldn't shake the feeling Parker would get his parole. He wouldn't hurt her. She believed that. Not physically anyway. But what stopped him from turning up on her doorstep, eating lunch outside her office, or sitting next to her when she took Kirsten to the movies? She'd robbed him of fifteen years of his life. He wasn't the kind of guy to forget that.

She could do without Parker adding to her troubles. Ingram said he'd have his investigation wrapped up in two weeks, and he'd have enough on Tarbell to fire him. Whatever damning evidence and strong-arm tactics he used on Tarbell, there'd still be issues. Ingram couldn't prevent Tarbell from suing Pace. No doubt she'd have to go to court and before that would happen, there'd be a war of words. She'd been there before when Parker went to trial. The idea of Parker being free to witness this debacle was too much. She dialed Jerry Naylor's number.

"I want to speak at Parker's parole hearing," she said.

"I heard you just finished up with him. Did something happen?"

"No. He was fine. He behaved. But fifteen years isn't enough for what he did to me. I don't want him getting out."

"I'll do what I can to make it happen."

She hung up on Naylor and looked over at San Quentin. It looked more like a castle perched at the edge of the bay to protect those inside from evils that lay outside its gates. She drove away from the prison, glad to put distance between her and Parker.

She pulled into Pace's parking lot just before lunch. The lot was close to full and all the spots close to the building were occupied. That meant a long and exposed walk to the building.

How long will this continue? she wondered. *How long will I keep viewing my environment in terms of threats?* It had taken her years to stop acting and thinking this way after Parker. She hoped it wouldn't be that long this time. She told herself that as soon as Tarbell was out of the way, she'd stop. It sounded like junkie thinking. She knew it wouldn't be that easy.

She went up to her office. A couple of people joked about her being a part-timer. She said her hellos to her staff and went into her office. She leaned down and flicked on her PC and when she sat up, Tarbell was standing in the doorway. He smiled.

"Yes, Steve?" Startled, she'd forgotten to use Tarbell's full name, but he made no objection.

"Everything OK, Gwen?" he said. "It's not like you to come in late. Anything wrong?"

"Everything's good. Something cropped up last night I had to take care of this morning." Did he think she had gone to the cops? "Nothing to do with anyone at work," she said with a meaningful look.

"That's good. I just wanted to make sure you and I didn't need to have a private talk." He knocked on the doorframe and left.

Tarbell unnerved her. If he was keeping tabs on her, she would have to be careful not to give herself away. Paul called Gwen late in the afternoon. He helped relieve the day's stress by putting Kirsten on the phone for a minute. Her daughter's excited voice put a smile on her face.

"Why don't you blow that pop stand early and come play with us?" Paul asked, taking the phone back from Kirsten.

"I can't. Too many alarm bells ringing. I think I'm going to be late again."

"Gwen, I thought we were going out. I've booked a table."

"I'll meet you there. When's the reservation?"

"Seven thirty at The Skyline."

"I'll be there."

"Just be sure you are, please."

She plowed on with her work. It was slow progress until five. The moment people began leaving, her work rate picked up. With no distractions, she'd pretty much caught up with her lost morning. Thoughts of a late night alone failed to unnerve her. Security guards now made sweeps of the building every hour. She put this new measure down to Ingram.

She eyed her watch. It was just after seven, and she was ready to finish up. She'd still make it to the restaurant if she left by seven fifteen.

A bank of lights went off on the far side of the building and a swatch of darkness fell across the floor. She guessed this was the guard's way of ushering her out of the building.

"Just a few more minutes," she murmured to herself.

Another bank of lights went out.

"Damn it," she murmured, then loudly for the guard to hear, "Give me a minute."

When a bank of lights the width of the building went out at once, Gwen looked up. Half the floor was in darkness. The stairwell and the elevators were lost to it. The next row of lights went out, then the next and the next. Darkness approached her office in a wave of solid blackness. Just the ceiling light in her office remained.

"Hey," she called out. "I'm still working in here, Mike."

No one answered.

She got up from her seat and went to the door. "Mike, I'm still here."

Still, no answer.

She remained silent and waited for Mike to appear. If he was making his final round of the floor before retiring to his seat in the lobby, he'd appear any second with a smile and an apology. He didn't because he wasn't there.

The hair stood up on the back of her neck. Something was wrong, and she knew exactly who was behind it. Tarbell.

Gwen grabbed her purse, leaving everything else. She bolted for the stairwell on the far side of the building, then stopped. The light switch panel for the floor was across from the stairs and elevators. She was running straight toward him. The emergency exit stairs were at the other end of the building. He couldn't be in two places at once, so she doubled back and bolted for the emergency exit, running into the darkness. She relied on the glow of screensavers and her familiarity with the floor plan to avoid running into the furniture.

Feet pounded the carpet to her left. She couldn't make out the exact location. Her eyes had yet to make the adjustment to the dark and the carpeted floor muffled any clues about where he was. She couldn't tell if Tarbell was gunning to intercept her or block the emergency stairwell.

She stopped. Tarbell stopped, too.

She strained to hear his breathing or movement and heard nothing. He couldn't be close, but he felt like the darkness, all encompassing.

She considered yanking out her cell and calling Ingram or grabbing a phone off the nearest desk and calling Mike, but if she reached for a phone, Tarbell would be on her before she had a chance to dial the number.

She cursed her stupidity. She should have locked herself in her office and called from there. It was no panic room, but it would have provided her the vital seconds she needed to make the call.

Any idea of returning to her office disappeared when her office lights went out, taking with them the last of the light on the floor. She whirled around to see a human form disappear into the total darkness. She didn't mourn the loss of the last vestige of light. He was behind her now. She had a head start. The emergency stairwell was dead ahead. She raced for the illuminated exit sign.

She slammed into the crash bar, but the door remained shut. He'd locked it or blocked it somehow. Of course he had. He wouldn't let her get away. The son of a bitch was always a step ahead of her. She wanted to scream in frustration, but there was no time. Feet pounded the floor behind her and a dark shape shifted in the darkness.

"I know it's you, Stephen."

Tarbell stopped with some hundred feet between them.

"Where do you think this is going to get you?" she asked. "Do you think you'll win if you hurt me or even kill me?"

She let the question hang in the darkness for him to embrace and answer. It was the perfect time to do it, in the dark. No one had to face anyone. They were just voices in the night, disembodied and belonging to no one.

"What is it you want?"

Her eyes began to adjust. She was no longer trapped inside a sightless void. The formless black turned into recognizable shapes and she could make out walls and desks. She picked out Tarbell's form. He stood motionless, seemingly deactivated by her words. It wouldn't last. Sooner or later, he'd make his move.

She wanted to tell him that people were on to him and Ingram was going to nail him. She'd love to turn the tables and put the fear of God in him for once. It was what she wanted to say, but couldn't. The situation wasn't desperate enough. If she tipped Ingram's hand, it ruined everything. Revealing PSI's presence was a one-time weapon to be used when she had no other option. Right now, she had an option and she took it.

She bolted for the main stairwell. She hoped she had the edge she needed to reach the lobby. She didn't have to get there, just be close enough to be heard.

"Help," she screamed.

Heavy footfalls thudded the floor behind her, then to the side of her. He was running a parallel path through the cubicles. She stopped screaming. This was no longer just a foot race. He was planning a move, no doubt to cut her off. She threw down her purse. Her car keys were in there, but it didn't matter. Getting to her car wasn't the plan. Finding a witness was.

She reached the back corridor, which was home to the legal department. At the end of the corridor were the stairwell and elevators. Fifty yards. Just fifty yards. A world of distance covered in seconds. Just as she reached the stairwell, a flashlight beam smashed her in the face. She lost her footing and hit the floor on her back, striking her head on the ground. It left her disoriented for a second, but a second was all Tarbell needed. He could stab her or bludgeon her to death with the flashlight. He had the advantage he needed.

"What the hell's going on?" Mike said. His face was lost in a blur of afterglow on her retinas.

Lights snapped on haphazardly as Mike ran his hand over the switch panel.

Gwen grabbed Mike's proffered hand and he hoisted her to her feet. Any remnants of Gwen's confusion dissolved. She had a witness and a protector.

"He's after me. Don't let him get away."

Mike was unarmed, but he now brandished his flashlight as a weapon. "Who?"

She dragged Mike into the office area. Even through her vision was dotted with afterimages, it was obvious there was no one else on the floor.

CHAPTER ELEVEN

Ingram and his people arrived in force, ten of them in all. Four men conducted a full sweep of the parking lot while another four cleared the building itself. Ingram and the woman Gwen remembered from her visit to his office stayed with her in Pace's reception area. It was a pointless precaution. Tarbell was long gone.

Two new people, a woman and a man, appeared at the entrance carrying tackle boxes. Ingram let them in. "Someone entered this building. I'm looking for prints on the exits and the light switch panel. Coordinate with Gonzalez. You'll find him on the second floor."

The technicians nodded and took the staircase.

"I'm hoping he didn't have time to cover his tracks," Ingram told Gwen.

Ingram's cell chirped and he keyed the two-way function. "Go ahead, Gonzalez."

"The place is clear."

"OK. Thanks." Ingram hung his cell on his belt. "Let's get you to a room to talk."

A banging on the glass door behind them startled them. Hands pressed against the glass and Paul called Gwen's name. She'd called him before calling Ingram, but it had taken him longer to get out of San Francisco.

"It's my husband."

"Let him in, Gloria," Ingram said to his associate.

Paul shoved Gloria aside and embraced Gwen. "You're OK. You're OK," he said, the words flitting between a statement and a question.

"I'm OK," she managed before breaking into tears.

"Let's go somewhere quiet," Ingram said.

Ingram ushered them into a meeting room. Gwen, Paul, Ingram, and Gloria filed into the cramped room. Four chairs surrounded a single table intended for two. Gwen felt instantly claustrophobic and it must have showed.

"Gloria, can you get the security guard's statement?" Ingram said.

"When is this going to end?" Paul asked after Gloria had closed the door.

"Very soon."

"I thought you people were supposed to prevent this from happening again," Paul demanded.

"Paul, please," Gwen said.

"No, Mr. Farris is right. It's obvious I need to step things up. I didn't want to go with a bodyguard because it'll raise questions here, but more importantly, people find it intrusive."

Gwen didn't like the idea of being watched over 24-7. Work might be awkward, but home life would be worse. How could she be herself with a bodyguard following her every move?

"I don't want that."

"I'm tempted to give you a driver. Someone who'll make sure you get to and from home unharmed."

"I can do that," Paul said.

Ingram thought it over. "It would keep the situation confidential. Would you prefer that?"

Gwen nodded.

"Let's go over what happened."

Ingram brought out his recorder, and Gwen went through events in detail. Just as she was getting to the end, Gloria poked her head inside.

"Got a minute?" she said to Ingram.

Ingram excused himself and left the room.

"I'm so glad you're OK," Paul said.

"Another ruined night. I'm sorry."

"It'll be a great one when that son of a bitch is out of our lives."

Gwen checked her watch. They'd eaten through their baby-sitting time. "What about Kirsten?"

"It's covered. I squared it with the sitter to stay longer."

Ingram reentered the room. He smiled at them, but it was a forced smile.

"What's wrong?" Gwen asked.

"Could I have a minute alone with your wife?"

Gwen went cold. Something bad was coming. Desperate and nasty notions came to mind. She tried to force them out, but one kept making it through—Kirsten.

"Has something happened at home?" Gwen's words came out quiet and fragile.

"No, nothing like that."

"I'm not leaving Gwen." Paul left no room for argument and Ingram conceded without a challenge and retook his seat.

"So far, we've found no signs of forced entry," Ingram said.

"He's got a cardkey."

Ingram nodded. "But he didn't come through the lobby. Video logs support that."

"The emergency exit. He used the emergency exit. It was locked when I tried escaping."

"Maybe so."

"Maybe so?" Paul said. "What's going on here? Are you saying Gwen made this up?"

Ingram failed to jump to an immediate denial. "At this point, there's nothing proving Stephen Tarbell was here tonight. There's no camera footage, no prints and no witnesses."

"I'm a witness."

"I need evidence beyond eyewitness testimony."

"What about the light switches? He had to have touched them."

"Yes, but if Tarbell did leave any prints, the security guard rubbed them off switching the lights back on."

"That's if he left any prints in the first place," Paul said. "This guy isn't stupid. If he knows how to dodge the security cameras, he knows to wear gloves."

Ingram nodded.

"You said you didn't find any prints on the doors," Gwen said. "Isn't that weird? Wouldn't you expect to find a bunch of prints belonging to half the people who work here?"

"Yes, but it doesn't help us prove he was here tonight."

Gwen hadn't eaten since breakfast. This mess combined with her hunger left her feeling nauseous and light-headed. The airless room only exacerbated the sensation.

"He was here tonight," Gwen said. "I don't know how he did it, but he was here."

Ingram frowned. "That's where the problem lies, Mrs. Farris. The reason I haven't put a bodyguard on you is that I had people tailing Tarbell every minute of the day and night. I checked in with my watcher. Tarbell has been home all night."

Gwen didn't have the words.

"An accomplice," Paul said. "The son of a bitch is using an accomplice. He's trying to discredit Gwen, and you're falling for it."

Paul's accusation bounced off Ingram. His focus was totally on Gwen. "Who did you see—Tarbell or someone else? You told me it was Tarbell, but I have one of my people contradicting you."

"Hey, I don't like your tone," Paul said.

"I just need to know the truth." Ingram turned to Gwen. "Are you certain you saw Stephen Tarbell here tonight?"

Gwen shook her head.

• • •

Tarbell surveyed the melee outside Pace Pharmaceuticals from a safe distance. His car was stashed several blocks away while he lay flat in the landscaping at the edge of the artificial lake across the street from Pace. The busy bees protecting Gwen were too concerned with ensuring their immediate perimeter was intact and the building was clear to bother looking farther afield.

Tonight's stunt was designed to test the strength of the protective shroud surrounding Gwen. The little scare he'd given her was nothing more than a bonus. The thought of her frightened voice kept him warm as he kept vigil in the rapidly cooling night.

What he'd seen hadn't impressed him that much. The rent-a-cop covering reception was next to useless. A blind and deaf mute would be more on the ball. And Private Security International's performance had done little to shake his resolve. Once Gwen had raised the alarm, it had taken them thirty-two minutes to respond. He could have easily killed Gwen and gotten away before these clowns arrived. But credit where credit was due, they weren't incompetent. They believed they had a twenty-four-hour watch on him. They had no idea that Petersen was in his pocket.

The interesting thing he noted was the distinct lack of cops. Neither Gwen nor the PSI people fell back on the infinitely more accessible police department. Local cops could have been dispatched to Pace within minutes. They would have shut it down and tossed out a dragnet, which would have been hard to avoid.

Pace was keeping this very much inside the family. It was a false economy in his opinion. He'd circumvented PSI's system quite easily. The cops would have taken him down within minutes with lots of messy publicity. That was it. Publicity. Pace was playing coy because it didn't want any publicity muddying its name.

PSI began leaving the building. They'd learned all they could tonight, which was nothing thanks to him. He didn't make the rookie mistake of leaving when they did. He could do without being spotted by Pace's people as he drove home. He waited until all of them left and the status quo was restored. Well, that was what he told himself. He actually waited to see Gwen leave. He needed to see that he was having an effect on her and he seemed to be. Gwen walked with her head down and shoulders hunched. The weight of the world rested on her. He almost felt sorry for her. Almost.

He waited until the last PSI car left before returning to his vehicle. He fired up the engine and dialed Tom Petersen's number. The watcher picked up on the first ring.

"I'm assuming you gave me an alibi," he said.

"Yes," came Petersen's terse reply. He'd been compliant since his wife's unfortunate tumble. "As far as everyone is concerned you've spent the night at home."

Tarbell smiled in the darkness. "Good. Is anyone coming over to check me out?"

"No. They trust me." Petersen sounded bitter at the admission. "I can't keep doing this."

"You don't have to, but if you don't, I'll take it as an insult and if I feel insulted, I know exactly where to go to relieve my frustration."

Tarbell let the threat trickle down the line and penetrate into Petersen. He waited for it to soak into that part of Petersen's brain that reacted to fear. He needed him. He could turn Petersen's replacement, but he didn't want to go through that. It would slow him down.

"I don't want you coming anywhere near my family," Petersen said. "Understand me?"

"Understood, as long as you keep your part of the bargain. Are you still on my team?"

Petersen cursed. "Yes. Yes, I am."

• • •

Gwen lay awake in bed. She'd watched the alarm clock pile on the minutes, then the hours. It was three in the morning. In four hours, the alarm would go off, kick-starting a new day in hell.

It wasn't working. Ingram had promised her protection. Tarbell was surrounded by Ingram's crack team of investigators, but he'd slipped through their defenses to get at her again. To make matters worse, she was losing Ingram's faith. He hadn't said it outright, but she could see that he doubted her story once he'd failed to find facts to back it up. She felt she still had the benefit of the doubt, but how long would it last?

She could understood Ingram's doubts. Tarbell hadn't just slipped Ingram's security; he'd managed to be in two places at once. Ingram had an eyewitness stating Tarbell hadn't left his home the entire time he'd been chasing her all over the building. How had he done it? He had to have an accomplice. It was the only explanation.

But which one had been where? God, she could have sworn it was Tarbell in the office. Even in the darkness, she recognized his gawky silhouette, but Ingram's investigator said he'd seen Tarbell himself in his front yard. What did he have—a double? None of it made sense.

She wished for the millionth time that Ingram's people had found a sliver of physical evidence tying him to tonight's stunt. Why was Tarbell still coming after her? That was the question no one was asking. As far as he knew, she'd complied with his request. His evaluation said he was a model employee. There was no need to persecute her.

Maybe her morning absence had triggered his suspicion. He could have read it as trouble and reacted with this incident to keep her docile. That made sense if she could work out his trick of being in two places at once.

It didn't matter how Tarbell did it. Tonight had proved one thing. When it came to the crunch, Ingram wasn't able to protect her. Tarbell had still managed to get to her. She couldn't rely on PSI being there to save her.

She could go to the cops, but how much could they do? They could arrest Tarbell, but he'd get bail. And arresting him would only antagonize him. There would be nothing preventing him from making good on his original threat. The police wouldn't give her around-the-clock protection, especially if they talked to Ingram and heard his side of the story.

She needed to protect herself. Cops never caught anyone in the act. They arrested people after the fact. That was what they had done with Desmond Parker. They couldn't prevent him from abducting her and stabbing her, and they couldn't stop Tarbell. There was only one way she knew how to defend herself against Tarbell.

She needed to buy a gun. Sleep came easy after that.

CHAPTER TWELVE

"C'mon, Kirsten," Paul called up the stairs to his daughter's bedroom. "We're driving Mommy to work today."

"No, it's OK," Gwen said. "I'll drive myself."

Paul frowned.

Gwen took this moment as a sign. If she could convince Paul to let her drive herself, then she'd do it. She'd buy a gun. If she couldn't, she'd forget all about it. She wasn't sure if she was up for this argument. She remembered last looking over at the alarm clock and it reading seven after five. As a result, her mind now dragged a fifty-pound weight behind it. But seeing Paul's disapproval ignited something inside her. Nervous panic drove her heart rate, and the sleep-deprived fog clouding her mind evaporated.

"Gwen, you're not going in by yourself. This psycho has gone after you twice."

"And he's missed both times."

"You want to give him another chance?"

"No, of course not."

"Then let me drive you. Let's send this asshole a message. We all know what happened last night, and it's not going to happen again."

"Do you honestly think you driving me to and from work is going to stop him?"

"Thanks. That really makes me feel good about protecting you."

"I didn't mean it like that," Gwen said.

"Then what did you mean?"

"There are going to be nine hours where you aren't going to be at my side. How does it really protect me to have you dropping me off and picking me?"

"I can't believe we're having this conversation." Paul grabbed the cereal off the table and shoved it back in the cupboard. "I don't care what you say. I'm driving you today and every day until Ingram disposes of him. Kirsten, come down here, sweetie. We've got to go."

It looked as if fate was making its decision for her. She wasn't going to buy a gun. It was almost a relief, but the one thing that kept her from accepting it as fact was something she'd said herself. Tarbell possessed the ingenuity to get to her at any time or place. So far, he'd gone the work route. It was an easy avenue to exploit. But going after her in her private life would be his next avenue. The office came with many limitations. The big, open world afforded him a wealth of opportunities. It left her cold to imagine what Tarbell would attempt next. All she knew was that he would try something. And no matter how good Ingram's people were and how many he put on the job, Tarbell would find a way to elude them.

Kirsten came trotting into the kitchen half dressed. Paul dropped to one knee and helped her pull her top on.

"So is that how it's going to be?" Gwen asked.

Paul looked over his shoulder. "How what's going to be?"

"Because you're the man, whatever you say is law."

"Oh, c'mon, Gwen. Don't pull that in front of Kirsten." He lifted Kirsten onto a kitchen counter and helped her on with her shoes. "This has nothing to do with equal rights and you know it."

She did and it was a stupid thing to say. She needed to break Paul's resolve, and playing the male chauvinist card wasn't going to work.

"Hey, baby girl, can you go back into your room for a minute?" Paul asked Kirsten.

"Sure."

"You're dynamite. That's why I call you Special K."

Paul lowered her to the floor, and she tottered back in the direction of her room. He waited until she disappeared before cornering Gwen against the dining table.

"Why don't you want me driving you to work? And I want the real reason. You've been shutting me out of this whole affair from the very beginning, so I need some justification, Gwen. It's not fair. You wouldn't accept it from me, so I won't accept it from you."

She hoped what she said next would persuade him. "I want to stand on my own two feet when it comes to Tarbell. I didn't with Desmond Parker. I let the police and the prosecutors run my life for me. I hid behind their protection because I believed they were bigger and badder than Parker. I was wrong. They didn't care about me. They cared about their careers and conviction rate. They traded his crimes against me for his compliance, and now Parker is getting out."

"There wasn't anything you could do about that."

"There was. I took a backseat to my injustice. If I do the same here, Pace will decide what happens to Stephen and not me."

Gwen felt her emotions race up from behind and try to sweep her away. Talking about Parker always did that to her. Judging from Paul's expression, this conversation was also upsetting to him. He pulled her to him and held her tight.

"I wish I could have been there to stop Parker," he said with a sigh. "But what has this got to do with me giving you a ride to work?"

"I'm taking a backseat again. Ingram is in charge of what happens to Stephen, and that means he's deciding what happens to me, and I can't let that happen. I don't want you driving me to work, because I don't want the son of a bitch thinking he's won.

I want him to see that no matter what he throws at me, I can withstand it."

Paul didn't say anything for several moments. He just held her. Then he said, "OK."

She pulled away from him. "Are you sure?"

"Yes. Go show the bastard who's in charge."

She smiled and kissed him. "Thanks."

She grabbed her purse and headed for the garage. On the way, she heard Paul say, "Kiddo, change of plan."

She drove off before Paul could change his mind. She checked her rearview mirror to see if he came out to call her back, but the sidewalk was empty. She released a pent-up breath.

She'd gotten what she wanted, but it failed to bring her the warmth of victory. She'd partially lied to Paul. She did feel Ingram and Pace Pharmaceuticals were sidelining her for the good of Pace's reputation. They didn't care about her. But none of this disguised the fact she'd lied to Paul. The only reason she'd wanted to be alone was to buy a gun. She knew Paul wouldn't approve, even if she never fired it. He couldn't know. He'd never forgive her for bringing a weapon into their home with Kirsten around.

"Gwen, what are you doing?" she asked herself.

Part of her said she was flushing good sense down the toilet, but another part of her, the part that had survived a violent crime, told her this was the right thing to do. There was only one person who could save her from the likes of Parker and Tarbell—herself.

She drove to the South Shore shopping center. It was a deserted wasteland at that time of the morning. She bought coffee and Googled gun store listings on her cell phone. She expected to see pages of places nearby, but her options ran to only a handful. Several of the listings scared her off with their austere descriptions. She went for West Coast Arms. In El Cerrito, it was the closest, and it also proclaimed to be the oldest gun store in the Bay Area.

She headed over there. On the way, she called in sick to the office. It would buy her a day. Her coworkers would believe the lie, and Tarbell would think he'd rattled her.

She felt distinctly out of place in the gun store. Being surrounded by all this firepower scared her. It wasn't her world, but this was where people came to protect themselves. A man wanted to hurt her, even kill her. If she deserved to be anyplace, it was here.

The owner, a bedraggled and bearded guy in his late fifties, noticed her hesitation and came out from behind the counter.

"I'm Charles Meyers. Can I help you with something?" he asked.

"I want a gun." Gwen blurted the request out. She sounded desperate. If she'd been in his shoes, she'd probably ask her to leave.

Meyers looked Gwen over before saying, "Well, you've come to the right place. What do you want it for?"

Stopping Tarbell, she thought, but said, "Personal protection. I work late nights."

Gwen expected Meyers to press her on the subject, but he took her answer at face value and nodded his understanding.

He quizzed her on her gun needs. He didn't hit her with the hard sell or come down on her hard and heavy with the second amendment rap that it was every American's duty to be packing heat. He approached her like a shoe salesman. He simply wanted to find the perfect fit. He handed her various automatics and revolvers for weight and feel. Eventually, they decided upon a 9mm Taurus. It was small and light and carried enough of a punch to make a dent in its target.

Gwen cradled the gun in the palm of both hands. She gazed at it. Did she want this? Was this the right way to go? She wasn't sure, but then she pictured Tarbell's silhouette chasing her through the office the night before. He'd chosen to play a phantom, never getting too close to her. The perfect time to catch him off guard would have been when he'd cornered her by the emergency exit. That would have given her the vital seconds to pull a gun. He wouldn't have had the time to disarm her before she fired. It made the decision easy for her.

"I'll take it," she said.

"Not quite yet, you won't." Meyers outlined California law. Gwen would have to obtain an official handgun safety certificate, which consisted of a written safety test and a hands-on safety demonstration, as well as provide fingerprints and proof of residency. Then there was the ten days for the background check before she could claim the gun.

Ten days. It might as well be a year. Tarbell would strike again before the waiting period was over. She had to believe she'd get lucky and survive the next ten days.

She looked at her gun one last time before handing it back to Meyers.

"Would you like to proceed?" Meyers asked, putting the weapon back under glass.

"Yes, I think so."

"Let's do it then."

Meyers instructed her on the handling of a handgun and put her on the range. She took and passed the state test and filed the paperwork for the background check.

"Thanks for all your help," she said. "This isn't an easy decision."

"It never is, but we do what we have to." Meyers put Gwen's paperwork into an envelope. "Have you been a victim?"

"Yes."

"That's a sad thing. I hope owning a weapon will remove the fear from your daily life."

She did too. "Thanks. I really appreciate that."

"It's my pleasure," he said. "I'm glad to have been of help. I sincerely hope you never have to use it."

• • •

Ingram called an emergency meeting at PSI's office. Petersen was the last to turn up. Ingram saw him and waved him into the conference room. The principal members of the Stephen Tarbell investigation team were assembled around the conference table. Petersen nodded a hello to Carlos Gonzalez, the lead investigator, who was responsible for the day-to-day management of the investigation. Reggie Glover, who took care of Tarbell's daytime surveillance, sat across the table. Also seated was Lorna Burchill, the records wiz in charge of the background checks. *And here I am*, thought Petersen. *Nighttime surveillance officer and traitor.*

Petersen took his seat facing Reggie. He was suffering from a nasty case of cottonmouth. The water decanter looked pretty good to him, but his hands were shaking.

"You look like shit, man," Reggie said.

"Working graveyard does that to an old guy. Remember, I should be sleeping."

Reggie laughed. "Ain't none of us getting younger."

Petersen squeezed out a smile. He liked Reggie. He'd been a Richmond cop for seventeen years before being shot on the job; he retired out on disability. He was a real mutt of a cop who'd worked everything from the streets to narcotics and everything in between. He'd caught a bullet working undercover. Petersen knew that unlike everyone else in the room, Reggie was a realist. The others had lived clean careers that allowed them to keep their ideologies. Reggie understood that a life of tracking down criminals wore you down and even compromised you from time to time. It made Reggie the one guy who might understand the shit he'd gotten himself into with Tarbell. An ally would feel real good about now.

Ingram closed the conference room door and sat at the head of the table. "I think everyone's aware of what transpired at Pace Pharmaceuticals last night, but just to clarify, our principal, Gwen Farris, claims that Stephen Tarbell made a second attack."

The word *claims* stuck in the air. It hung out with words like *unsubstantiated* and *allegedly* and other dirty words that cried disbelief. Petersen knew he could change all that but kept the truth to himself.

"I'm a little worried about where this investigation is going, so I'm after opinions. I want you to hear this."

Ingram placed a digital recorder in the middle of the table and pressed play. It contained Ingram's interview with Gwen and her statement. Petersen chewed on his lip as Gwen recounted Tarbell's game of cat and mouse. The panic in her voice plucked uncomfortable chords within him. He knew her fear. He knew the corner she'd been backed into. The recording reached its end, and Ingram snapped the recorder off.

"Carlos, you want to fill us in on the latest?"

Gonzalez consulted his notes. "OK. The security cameras didn't pick up an intruder, but we already know it's possible to enter the building and avoid camera detection. Mrs. Farris claims the second floor emergency exit was locked. No evidence of that was found. Fingerprints were found on the light switches, all belonging to the security guard who switched them back on. The second floor emergency exit is somewhat curious as no prints were found other than Mrs. Farris's. The door had been wiped clean."

"So what are we saying here?" Reggie asked.

"Nothing as yet," Ingram replied.

"C'mon, Bobby, don't turn coy. What's going on?"

"One possibility is that Gwen concocted events last night to reinforce her claim against Tarbell."

"I don't know. Her statement sounded genuine to me," Petersen said, hoping to inject an element of doubt. "Her answers sounded natural and unrehearsed."

Ingram nodded in agreement.

"The one problem is that we can't place Tarbell at the scene." Gonzalez pointed at Petersen. "We've got you to thank for that."

Don't I know it, Petersen thought.

"And you're sure he didn't duck out on you, Tom?" Reggie asked.

Petersen shook his head. "I had a visual on him when I got the call. He was there."

Reggie pointed at the recorder. "Like she says, we could be looking at an accomplice."

"Nothing to back that up," Ingram said. "I'm hoping Lorna can find us something."

"If he's got a partner, money will change hands at some point. If it does, I've got him," Lorna said.

"OK, we've got Gwen gilding the lily, or a possible accomplice," Reggie said. "Are we checking out the cleaning crew? What about B&E? We can't rule it out. Maybe some douche bag broke in for the petty cash or computers but wasn't expecting to find someone working late."

"It's possible but doubtful," Gonzalez said. "The whole thing was too calculated. The guy got in and out without getting his face on any of the cameras. The average thief isn't going to worry about that, especially if he's caught in the act."

"I don't like that Gwen's assailant never said a word," Lorna said. "If she was concocting a story, she'd tell us Tarbell threatened to cut her into pieces and feed her to his dog. Telling us he never said a word doesn't make sense. It lends itself to the accomplice theory. An accomplice can pretend to be Tarbell, but he can't sound like him."

Thank you, Lorna, Petersen thought, as her remark brought a nod of approval from Ingram.

"Lorna, what has your research kicked up?" Ingram asked.

"Stephen Tarbell is a pretty clean-living guy. Good credit report. No real debt beyond a mortgage. No outstanding warrants. A couple of parking tickets. Never been married. No dependents. Mother deceased. No siblings. His invalid father lives out in West Sacramento. Tarbell's been paying for caregivers for seven years."

"I can vouch for that," Reggie said. "He spends his Saturdays with his dad. Looks as if it's the caregiver's day off."

"All in all, the guy is a Boy Scout," Lorna said.

"Except for a violent side," Petersen tacked on.

"Do we know that?" Ingram asked. "Anger management issues for sure. Pace Pharmaceuticals provided documentary evidence supporting that."

"It's something that runs in the family," Lorna said. "The only dirt I struck was a couple of domestic calls back in the day alleging Dennis Tarbell was a wife beater. No charges were ever brought."

"What about you two?" Ingram asked. "You're with him 24-7. Thoughts on Tarbell?"

"I've got nothing," Reggie said. "He's goes to work, works, and comes home. He's a shut-in during the weekend."

"Same story," Petersen said.

Ingram sighed. "I thought this would be a simple case. At the moment, I've got nothing. I had the security video enhanced to see the hand gripping the trash enclosure the night Gwen was assaulted. It came back with nothing that gives us anything we can use. For all I could tell, it could have even been Gwen's hand."

"Obviously, there are doubts over the validity of Gwen's claim. Why don't we have her polygraphed? It'll clear this up," Petersen said.

Ingram shook his head. "I don't want to go that route unless I have to, but I inserted Amanda Norton inside Pace Pharmaceuticals this morning. Her primary assignment is to watch Tarbell, but I've told her to watch Gwen, too. I'm going to suggest to Pace that we put a team on Gwen. If she is fabricating anything, they'll catch it. Then I'll push for a polygraph."

"What's your gut feel here, Bobby?" Reggie asked. "Was she really assaulted the first time or is this a case of bad blood gone worse and she's playing the victim to oust Tarbell?"

Ingram took a long time answering. "I don't know. I believed her story originally, but now, I have to admit I have doubts. Pace didn't want to bring in the cops, and she didn't put up much of a fuss about it. I thought she was reluctant out of embarrassment, but now I'm wondering if it was because of what good police work might reveal."

It killed Petersen to sit there watching the investigation's tide turn against Gwen. Not only was Tarbell being given the benefit of the doubt, the focus of the team was turning to finding Gwen's guilty. But it was still a house of cards. It only took one word from him to bring Tarbell's shit crashing down. It was one word he couldn't give. Not yet.

"What's the aim here?" Petersen asked. "Say we catch Tarbell dead to rights. Then what? Do we turn him over to the police?"

"At this point, Pace would prefer we force him out."

Ingram broke the meeting up. Gonzalez said he'd be checking in on everyone.

Petersen walked out with Reggie. Reggie slung an arm over his shoulders. It felt like a slab of granite dumped on him.

"You OK? You really do look like shit."

This was his opportunity to chop Tarbell off at the ankles. He could bring Reggie in. They could work their own angle. Maybe they could trap Tarbell on tape. It wouldn't be hard. They'd have Tarbell, and he wouldn't lose face with Ingram. It was doable, but it wasn't good enough. No one had any intention of putting this guy away. There was nothing stopping Tarbell from coming back after him and his family. He knew what this psycho was capable of.

He forced out a strangled smile. "I'm just getting old. After this one, I'm hanging up my spurs."

• • •

Ingram returned to his office. A message from Amanda Norton waited for him on his voice mail. He called her back.

"How are you settling in?" he asked.

"Fine."

"Got a handle on our principal players?"

"Only one. Gwen's out sick today."

Understandable after last night, he thought. "OK. Stay on Tarbell. Call me if anything happens, and remember you have backup outside."

He said good-bye to Amanda and called Deborah Langan at Pace. He gave her an update on the investigation and their concerns. He asked to put a team on Gwen. Understandably, Deborah hesitated.

"I don't think I need to keep anyone on her for more than a few days," Ingram said sweetening the bitter pill. "I just want to be sure everything's straight. I don't want to railroad Tarbell if it isn't true."

"OK," Deborah conceded.

"Thanks. I'll let you know how it goes."

He hung up. He hesitated on dispatching a team to watch Gwen. Petersen had been right. Gwen's interview rang true. Nothing in her statement tipped him off as a lie. It was Tarbell's airtight alibi that screwed everything up. He needed to talk to Gwen. He'd push her hard. If he heard anything he didn't like, he'd send in a team.

He called Gwen's cell but got voice mail. He had told her to keep the cell on at all times, but she was out sick. The last thing she needed was calls coming in from the office. He looked up Gwen's home number and dialed it.

Paul answered.

"Hi, Mr. Farris. It's Robert Ingram from Private Security International. We met last night. Could I talk to Gwen?"

"She's at work."

The answer came as a sucker punch, catching him right under the jaw. "Paul, she called in sick this morning."

Silence came from the other end of the line. Ingram didn't like where this was going. His faith wasn't being repaid.

Paul's voice turned stern. "She went into work this morning. Are you sure about your facts?"

"No mistake. She called in sick. Do you know where your wife is, Mr. Farris?"

CHAPTER THIRTEEN

It was late and Tarbell had the Pace building to himself. He'd spent the day observing and noticed quite a bit. The things that were there and things that weren't seemed equally interesting to him. The familiar Durango belonging to his daytime watcher was parked in the neighboring parking lot. What bothered him most was the thing that wasn't there—Gwen. She'd left a phone message letting everyone know she was sick and wouldn't be coming into the office today. Obviously, last night's fun had proved too much for poor little Gwennie. Was she having a sick day or was she spilling her guts at PSI's offices? This was the second time she'd been out of the office since they'd gone into battle. It didn't worry him. Last night's exercise was supposed to be a reminder to Gwen that he hadn't gone away, but there'd been an unexpected bonus. His seemingly mystical ability to be in two places at once had sown the seeds of doubt at PSI. According to Petersen, feelings leaned toward him having choreographed the blackout games last night, but at the same time there was nothing to say Gwen hadn't masterminded the whole thing. It was her word versus the inconclusive evidence, and the evidence looked to be winning, tainted as it was. He liked having Petersen on tap, feeding him this intel. It made his campaign so much easier.

The other thing he'd been watching for was the mole. Petersen told him that PSI had inserted an investigator inside Pace to watch Gwen's back. He said he didn't know the identity of the investigator, but he was a bad liar. It didn't matter. Pace didn't have reams of people starting new jobs every day. PSI would have been smart to bring in three or four new hires to confuse him, but only one person had joined the company since last Wednesday. But then again, PSI was still under the impression he didn't know he was being investigated. No wonder they didn't bother to cover their tracks. So Amanda "Call Me Mandy" Norton had begun a new and illustrious career at Pace today. She was a temp working in the Inventory Control department.

He'd watched Mandy at work. She was good. She played at working very well without making it obvious what she was doing. He put that down to an easy first day. Gwen hadn't shown up so she didn't have anyone to protect. He'd noticed Mandy make a couple of sweeps through his department. She'd come to check the big bad wolf out in his lair under the guise that she was just introducing herself to everyone. She'd gone to Lauren to ask where Gwen was, and then introduced herself. It was a nice move not to engage him, but he wasn't going to let her get away with that maneuver. He jumped up, stuck out a hand, and inserted himself into the action.

"Stephen Tarbell."

"Amanda, but everyone calls me Mandy," she said, taking his hand. Hers was cool and dry. Not a hint of nervousness at meeting the great monster. She was first class in Tarbell's book.

"People call me Steve. Also, I'm the longest-serving inmate in this asylum, so if you need directions, feel free to turn to me. Isn't that right, Lauren?"

"He's not wrong. He knows this place inside and out."

Mandy smiled. "I'll remember that."

He and Lauren had quizzed her on her new arrival. She stuck to the cover story she'd been dealt, sounding clear and confident.

He watched her go and guessed she'd be straight on the phone to her boss to tell her she'd made first contact.

Well, if Mandy could visit him in his home territory, he could visit her in hers. She'd left at five with everyone else in Inventory Control. Bringing Mandy in as a temp was a mistake on PSI's part. Temps didn't work late, not without supervision, and that department never stayed late, leaving him to do as he pleased. He crossed the now quiet office space and sat at Mandy's desk. It was a typical spot for a temp. She was shoved in a cubicle with the worst office equipment available.

"Mandy, Mandy, Mandy," he said to himself, "and you were doing so well."

Clutter filled Mandy's little slice of Pace Pharmaceuticals. A couple of framed photographs of her, her husband, and two kids sat on the table while crudely painted pictures were push-pinned into the cubicle walls along with other little knick-knacks. It was way too much. She was a temp. Temps didn't bring all this crap to a place they weren't staying at. Even if she was full time, it took time to build up this level of junk. Everyone starts off conservative with a picture or two, then builds up to humanize their dull little corner of the working world. She'd overcompensated.

He picked up the family snapshot. It wasn't staged. It was her with her husband and two kids around the ages of six and eight. It surprised him Mandy had kids. She looked too young for that. She was blonde with a trim figure and a bland, round face. Very ordinary. This probably made her very good in these situations. She didn't come off as the cop or detective type. There was none of that arrogant and authoritarian vibe cops always give off.

All in all, Amanda "Call Me Mandy" Norton was a good investigator. It was going to be a shame when he ruined her. It had to be done. There was no avoiding it.

"Blame Gwen," he said to Mandy's photographed image, as he placed it back in its original spot.

Mandy could wait for now. He didn't have to rush. He'd stayed late to take care of Gwen.

He walked into her office and booted up her PC. While it ran through its start-up routines, he removed a CD from his jacket pocket and inserted it into the CD drive. The computer detected its presence and asked him if he'd like to install the software. He answered yes and let the program work its magic.

He'd bought the software off the Web during the weekend. He'd let his mind run free while at his dad's place. Inflicting terror on the old man had released something inside of him. A desire to inflict cruelty flowed through him like his own blood, feeding his mind and fueling new ideas for revenge. The more he concentrated on destroying Gwen's life, the more creative he became. He put off his need to harm Gwen physically. He would dismantle her world on a mental and spiritual level. Just like a virus, he'd pick away at her natural defenses until she was totally exposed. Then he'd go in for the kill.

Gwen needed taking down a peg or three. He'd already tarnished her reputation with PSI, but it was time to dirty up her image with the good people at Pace Pharmaceuticals.

A dialog box popped up on the screen telling him the program was installed. Now every keystroke, e-mail, and incoming and outgoing document was being recorded and the data copied and forwarded to his PC at home. And like a smile in the night, it was totally untraceable unless someone knew it existed. With the details the spyware would give him, destroying Gwen's reputation at work was going to be laughably easy.

"Done and done," he said with a smile.

• • •

Gwen waited at the park next to the Berkeley marina. It was four thirty, and the biting wind racing off the bay forced her to pull her coat around her tightly. A car horn tooted, and she watched

Paul pull up. Kirsten waved excitedly, and Gwen waved back before the girl hopped down from the car and rushed over to her. Gwen gathered her up and took sustenance from her daughter's embrace. Kirsten's simple hug reminded her of how alone she'd felt these last few days.

"Now will you tell me where you were all day?" Paul asked. "I've been worried sick since Ingram called me earlier."

There was no anger, just concern. It was more than she deserved. She'd switched off her phone when she'd played hooky from work to buy the gun. Among the repeated calls from Deborah Langan and Ingram wanting to know her whereabouts were Paul's. It had taken her hours before she'd had the courage to call him and tell him where they could meet. Now that they were face-to-face, she'd have to give a convincing explanation of her behavior.

"I'm sorry. I just wanted to be alone for a while."

"Can we go play?" Kirsten demanded.

"Sure we can," Gwen said.

Kirsten ran headlong into the park. The sun was fast falling toward the ocean beyond the bay. The day's warmth was still palpable, but the stiff breeze coming off the water chilled the air a little more than was comfortable.

Gwen took Paul's hand, and they followed Kirsten into the park. It was a popular spot, even on a weekday. People flew elaborate kites, joggers ran the winding paths, and dog owners called to their off-leash pets. Kirsten scampered over to a tan and white Australian shepherd dog. The owner told the dog to sit and OK'd Kirsten to pet it.

"He likes me," she called to her parents.

"Just don't upset him," Gwen called back before thanking the dog owner for indulging her daughter.

The owner called the dog to heel, leaving Kirsten momentarily disappointed before spotting two Jack Russell terriers roughhousing with each other.

"We should get her a dog," Paul said.

Gwen liked the idea of a dog. It would give Kirsten some responsibility and a playmate. "Maybe after Stephen is dealt with."

"Is that why you didn't go into work today, because of him?"

"Yes. I even drove there, but when I got close, I just couldn't do it." Every word of the lie burned her throat.

"Why didn't you come home then? With all the late nights you've pulled over the last few months, it would be nice to have you home for a change."

She didn't have to lie about this. She could have gone home or returned to work after buying the gun, but she wasn't ready to face either Tarbell or Paul. She just wanted to be alone. People were either fussing over her or frightening her. It felt good to be clear of anybody's reach.

"I don't know," she said. "I was a little embarrassed, I guess."

"You don't have to be embarrassed around me." He squeezed her hand. "If you don't want to face that moron, then don't. In fact, burn some of your vacation days and take yourself out of harm's way. Let Ingram and his crew worry about taking care of him. It'll do you good. We can go away somewhere while you recharge. You can put this behind you, and when you return to Pace, he'll be gone."

But she was already shaking her head. "We can't afford to go away anywhere."

"Yes, we can. We're struggling, but we're not desperate. We don't have to go far, just away." He smiled. "Visa can treat us. We can always file Chapter 11 later."

Goddamn him. He could always make her smile at the lowest of times. She leaned over and kissed him. "You're a butthead, do you know that?"

"Is that a yes?"

Her expression made it clear that it wasn't, and Paul's smile faded.

"Why?"

"It's running."

"You're not running. You're playing it safe. You're not the only one at risk here. What about Kirsten and me? He could be gunning to hurt us all."

Gunning. The word left her feeling sick. She'd been spending the afternoon trying to wash the idea of guns from her head.

Paul pointed at Kirsten. "Look at her. Do you want that freak laying his hands on her?"

Kirsten was oblivious to the threats surrounding her at every turn. Unknown predators prowled parks and playgrounds. Guys with too many drinks inside them climbed behind the wheel of their vehicles and drove down their street. No dire thoughts crossed her mind. She chased happiness in the form of crazy kites and excited dogs. It was an innocence Gwen would preserve at all costs.

"I'd die before I'd let him touch her."

"Then for her, if no one else, let's take off somewhere."

"You go, take Kirsten to your mom's, but I have to stay. None of this goes away until Tarbell is dealt with. Ingram is going to need me around."

"No way, Gwen. Talk about giving him what he wants. You home alone is his wet dream. If you're staying, we're all staying. But you have to make a deal with me."

She hoped she could agree to it. She knew she was pushing him, but she couldn't push him too much further. "What is it?"

"If you can't face him tomorrow, we go on vacation. No ifs or buts. We pack up the car and go."

"Deal. I even want you to drive me to work in the morning." She pulled him to her. "Thank you."

"C'mon, Special K, stop scaring the dogs," Paul called.

Kirsten stopped and frowned.

"Don't you want any dinner tonight?"

That got her moving.

They walked to the restaurant in the marina. It sat on stilts over the water. They'd come here often when they were both employed. Now the menu stretched their budget, but it made a welcome change. The hostess put the three of them in a prime window seat overlooking the bay. The lapping water and setting sun made for a romantic setting. Kirsten tracked the sun's descent and counted it down as it disappeared over the horizon.

With a bargain struck, Paul didn't hold a grudge about Gwen's disappearance. They talked and played with Kirsten. It was family life again. Their problems suddenly seemed small. Money troubles and Paul's unemployed status were minor irritations. Stephen Tarbell didn't even occur to her once during dinner. Gwen felt content.

She settled the bill, and they drove home. She and Paul swapped cars so she could get some girl time with Kirsten. Paul called Gwen on her cell and challenged 'the girls' to a race home. It wasn't a real race, as there wasn't much chance of one in the heavy traffic still heading home. They just went with the flow of traffic, picking the lanes that seemed to move the quickest. But traffic being traffic, they both pulled into the garage at virtually the same time. Paul held the edge on Gwen.

He opened Kirsten's door. "See, I told you I'd win."

"No, Daddy, we won," Kirsten said. "Mommy told me so."

"What?" Paul said, feigning indignation.

"Carry me, Daddy," said Kirsten.

Paul picked her up her from her car seat and carried her into the house while Gwen grabbed her purse off the backseat. He came straight back out with a fierce look on his face.

"What's wrong?"

"He trashed the house."

CHAPTER FOURTEEN

Gwen expected worse, but the invasion was no less of a violation. Someone had gone through their home. The house was in disarray—overturned furniture, drawers emptied out, and their possessions flung across the rooms. Despite the carnage, little looked to be broken, but it was impossible to tell if anything had been taken without a full inventory of their possessions.

Gwen followed Kirsten into her room. The girl cried when she saw the mess.

Paul appeared in Kirsten's doorway. "This was him, wasn't it?"

"Who else?" Gwen detected the note of defeat in her reply. She should have expected something like this. It was the natural progression in Tarbell's hate campaign.

"I'm calling the cops," Paul said. "I don't care what Pace or Ingram says. I'm telling them Tarbell did this."

Gwen didn't object. "Use your cell phone. I'm sure they don't want us touching anything."

Paul nodded, pulled out his cell, and left the room.

Gwen's cell rang, and she put Kirsten down to answer the call. It was Ingram. She'd called him after Paul had told her to stay in the car. She wanted to eradicate the doubt that had crept in after last night's incident.

"Gwen, it wasn't him."

"What do you mean? It had to be."

Paul poked his head through the door. He was still waiting for the cops to answer his call.

"I just checked in with my stakeout guy, and Tarbell is currently at home and has been since he left Pace tonight."

"That can't be true."

"It is."

"Then he's got an accomplice."

"That may be, but I can't prove that yet. Just hang tight, I'm on my way. Have you called the police?"

"We're on hold."

"OK, report the break-in, but don't mention Tarbell."

Gwen went to object but saw no point. She could point the finger, but no one would listen. She hung up on Ingram.

"It's not Tarbell," she said to Paul. "Don't mention him to the cops."

Paul shook his head and walked away.

Ingram arrived not long after the Alameda Police. He introduced himself as a friend and politely waited outside until Gwen gave her statement and came out to see him. The arrival of three police units drew the stares of neighbors, but no one ventured beyond their front lawns to lend their support. She leaned against the side of Ingram's car.

"Anything taken?" Ingram asked.

Gwen shook her head. "Just vandalism."

"This could be just that. A case of random vandalism."

She gave him a look he deserved.

"All I'm saying is we can't rule anything out. I know you want it to be him, but surveillance places him at home. That's solid. Yes, he could be using an accomplice but we've got no evidence of that yet. If we find it, I promise you, he will pay for this and everything else."

Paul came out of the house with an overnight bag. Kirsten trotted alongside him carrying her Blue's Clues backpack. Ingram said hello, but Paul ignored him.

"Look, you and Kirsten had better check into a motel or something," Paul said. "These guys are going to be here for some time. They want to talk to the neighbors and check for prints."

"OK." Gwen hugged him. "I'll call you when I've found a place."

"I know a hotel where you can stay," Ingram said to Paul. "I use it all the time."

"I'm keeping your secret," Paul told Ingram. "Just stop this psycho before something really bad happens, OK?"

Paul gave Kirsten a squeeze before she and Gwen got into Ingram's car. Ingram drove them to the Marriott in downtown Oakland. Gwen checked in, but Ingram registered the room with his credit card. Gwen didn't know whether or not to take this an apology for what had happened. He saw them up to their room and asked to come in. Kirsten was fading fast. Distress had burned up the last of her energy. Gwen told him to wait in the bar, and she'd see him after she'd put Kirsten to bed. She went down without a fight.

Gwen called Ingram up to the room the second Kirsten was asleep.

The room was a studio with a partition separating the bedroom from a lounge area. Gwen sat on the sofa, and Ingram sat kitty-corner in one of the armchairs. He leaned forward so he could speak in a low voice and not wake Kirsten.

"You ran out on us today."

"I just needed some time to myself."

"That's fine, but you need to inform me. I can't do my job if you don't."

"You told me I was done. That you and your team had it covered. You're watching Stephen every second of the day and night. How could I be in any danger?"

Ingram went to say something but smiled instead. "Because he has an accomplice."

"You said it."

"Look, I'm checking the accomplice angle. If he has one, he's going to have to make contact at some point. The guy is a loner. That means he's going to have to rent a partner. He's also going to have to pay and there's going to be a cash exchange."

"It's pretty obvious you don't believe in the accomplice theory, so if Stephen hasn't got one, what's going on?"

"One possibility is that last night's attack and tonight's break-in were random acts. A thief at Pace and vandals at your home."

"Oh, please, do you really believe that? Are you telling me that two random acts occurred and I happened to be a victim in both cases days after a man threatened to kill me? I don't know about you, but I don't believe in the coincidence fairy."

Ingram smiled. "I agree. It does seem unlikely, but it is possible."

"Ignoring coincidence, how else could he have done it? Could he slip out without your surveillance guy noticing?"

"I have confirmed sightings of him at the times of the attacks."

"So if we're ruling out a coincidence, an accomplice, and a rock-solid alibi, what else do we have?"

"That's the million-dollar question," he said rising to his feet.

It was a question he clearly didn't have an answer for. She'd hoped to force him into a corner, but she was the one who felt cornered.

"I'm going to check in with my watcher and pay a visit to Tarbell."

He went to the door and opened it. Gwen stopped him.

"What is it you're not saying?"

"Nothing, Gwen. Please don't concern yourself."

"Another option is that I faked the intruder at Pace. I can see why you'd believe that, but do you honestly believe I trashed my own home?"

"It's a possibility," he said and let himself out.

• • •

The moment Ingram called Petersen to tell him that he was on his way over, Petersen called Tarbell.

"My boss is coming to check you out. Make sure you're visible. Leave a drape open or something."

"I can do better than that. When's he expected?"

"In the next twenty to thirty."

"I'll put on a show."

The conversation was at an end, but Petersen kept it alive. "Look, you need to cool it with the hardcore shit. Two hits in two nights is too much. Be smart. Just back off."

His plea just bounced off Tarbell's thick ego.

"Don't lecture me. I can make it five nights in a row if I want. Are you worried someone will put two and two together?"

"You're pushing the limits of believability. Be smart is all I'm saying."

"Well, I'm pursuing a different but no less destructive line of action, which should please you. There'll be no physical or material damage for a while."

"This has nothing to do with pleasing me. Just do what you need to do and move on with your life."

"I'll take it under advisement."

Petersen released a breath when Tarbell hung up.

Silence reigned inside the car, but his thoughts kept making noise. He'd been a cop for a long time, so he knew the power of intimidation, but for the first time, he understood the courage it took to come forward as a witness, because he didn't possess it himself. He was an old guy with a pension trying to protect his family. He would have to rely on Tarbell making a mistake. Hopefully, he would. He knew Tarbell's type. Anger would get the better of the man eventually.

Ingram interrupted Petersen's thoughts by sliding into the passenger seat alongside him.

"Is he in there?"

"Yeah."

SIMON WOOD

Tarbell had listened and drawn back one of the drapes, but not all the way. It looked as if he'd been lazy about closing them. From where they were seated, they didn't have a clear view into the house, but it was easy to catch the flicker of the TV and movement from inside.

Ingram picked up Petersen's binoculars and tried to see inside Tarbell's house. "You're sure of that? I can't get a visual."

"I'm sure."

Then on cue, Tarbell appeared from his side yard wheeling out his trash cans to the street.

"Shit," Ingram murmured. "That ends that question."

It sure does, Petersen thought.

"And you haven't seen anyone go inside?"

"Nope."

"It would suit me fine if this son of a bitch has a partner, but I'm not seeing it." Ingram exhaled. "Even if he does have an accomplice, I don't understand why he's using one. It's not like he knows we're watching him."

Petersen went cold and fought to keep a shiver in. Ingram missed his panicked expression in the darkness. A part of him willed Ingram to make the connection and take the problem out of his hands. But the urge withered as he remembered Tarbell's photograph.

"He doesn't have to know he's being followed," Petersen said. "Him being at home could be for alibi purposes. He knows Gwen is itching to call the cops and that she'll point the finger at him.

"But who's going to corroborate that? You haven't seen anyone visit him."

"We're his alibi."

"I know. This asshole has us covering his butt. What a joke."

"Tell Gwen to drop the hammer on Tarbell. We could always say we weren't here and leave the prick high and dry."

"No." Ingram's answer was firm. "We do it right. PSI's rep is built on being better than the scum we nail."

It was a hard point to argue.

Petersen hoped Tarbell didn't get cocky. He believed he was smarter than everyone, and most likely he was, but he wasn't smart enough to acknowledge that other intelligent people existed. Petersen could envisage Tarbell cocking a look their way and tipping Ingram off, but to Petersen's relief, he acted as if no one was watching him. He positioned the cans in the gutter and returned to his house.

Ingram watched Tarbell intently. Petersen could tell that he still wanted to believe in Gwen.

Petersen needed to test the waters. "So if Tarbell was here when Gwen's home was tossed, what's going on?"

"I don't quite know. If we can't prove the existence of a partner and we cross out the chances of random bad luck, then I'm still looking at Gwen for possible involvement."

"You still believe she's making all this up?"

"Last night would have been easy to orchestrate. She switched the lights off, ran around the building screaming and claiming the emergency exit wouldn't open. It seemed like a good idea, but it backfired. You were on Tarbell all night, and we don't have any physical evidence tying him to the scene. So she trashed her own home today."

"Are you serious?"

"She went AWOL today. She told the office she was sick and her husband she went to work. It would be easy to work her own place over. She knows she's not being watched."

"But she knows we're watching Tarbell."

"I didn't say it made sense. She's frantic. She wants Tarbell taken care of quickly, so she's trying to help us along. This isn't the first time this has happened to her."

"What do you mean?"

"The background check kicked up that when she was a college senior at UC Davis, she was abducted by a guy who planned to rape her. She got away, but the guy, Desmond Parker, stabbed her. He's doing fifteen to life in San Quentin."

Petersen felt for Gwen. Life was dealing her a shitty hand of cards. At least Parker had been wrapped up and put away quickly. Tarbell had his hooks in and wasn't going anywhere.

"There could be some trauma driving her down this route," Ingram said. "Parker is up for parole."

"Christ," Petersen murmured. It was as if Tarbell was being gifted his own cover story. "Do you think she made up the initial attack?"

"I don't like to think so."

"So what happens now?"

"We keep on Tarbell and try to find a partner. In the meantime, I'm putting a tail on her. If she does try to implicate Tarbell in any crime that's her doing, then we have her."

Ingram stayed for a little while longer before leaving. He walked by Tarbell's house before picking up his car. As he drove into the distance, Tarbell put his face through the gap left by the undrawn drapes. Petersen squirmed as Tarbell looked his way, grinning. He had every reason to grin. Everything was going his way.

CHAPTER FIFTEEN

A cab with Gwen and Kirsten inside pulled up in front of the house. Paul waved at them from the front yard. He'd stayed the night at the house. Gwen had wanted him to come to the hotel, but he hadn't wanted to leave. She understood his need to protect their home. She was seeing her home with new eyes. The house looked no different from yesterday, unmarked, but it had changed. Normally, her home was a safe haven. If a storm came, it supplied shelter. If she needed love, two people there gave it. If she needed privacy, its walls provided it. Until yesterday, her home had provided protection.

She hugged and kissed Paul. He looked beaten from yet another blow dealt by life's complications. She wanted to tell him it was OK, but she didn't know if that was possible. He picked up Kirsten, and she followed them in.

Paul had cleaned up, and everything was pretty much back in its place. What couldn't be saved sat out on the patio in bulging trash bags. Gwen went from room to room. Although few things had been lost, the place seemed cold without them. It would take more than their replacement for the warmth to return.

Kirsten's weeping drew her from her thoughts. Her daughter was in her bedroom straining to tear open a trash bag. The bag suddenly split, spilling its contents of trash, a lamp broken to pieces, and damaged toys onto the floor. Kirsten picked up the head of her favorite teddy bear and tried to reunite it with its body. When it became obvious it wasn't going to happen, she burst into tears. Gwen dropped to her knees next to her daughter.

"I want Bo-Bo," Kirsten said.

To tell Kirsten the bear was of no consequence and easily replaced would be a harsh betrayal. Gwen took the two halves of the bear. "I can try to repair him, but I can't make him as good as new."

"But you can fix him?

"Yes."

The promise ended the tears.

They needed a change of scene. The three of them hit the stores to replace what needed replacing. They took a side trip to Toys "R" Us. As Kirsten ran through the store, Gwen had a chance to talk to Paul.

"I've been thinking about what you said last night, about going away until this has all blown over."

"And?"

"I won't be hounded out of my home as well as my job."

Gwen braced herself for Paul's objection, but instead he smiled. He took her hand. "Good. I don't want you to."

"Even after last night?"

"Even after last night. He won't force us out of our home."

Gwen pulled him to her and kissed him. "Thank you."

"Thank me by taking the rest of the week off. We can have some family time."

She shook her head. "I'm going into the office tomorrow. I want him to see he hasn't frightened me."

Gwen's appearance at Pace the next morning drew a hail of questions from concerned coworkers. News had gotten back about the break-in, and it took thirty minutes of telling and retelling the story before she made it to her office.

One of her coworkers remarked that things could only get better from now on. She wished that was true, but she knew nothing would improve until Tarbell had been dealt with. She resigned herself to the long day ahead. Ingram had been quite explicit. She wasn't to engage Tarbell. That was fine while PSI had her back, but Ingram had also made it clear that his faith in her was slipping. She couldn't rely on him to find out why Tarbell had vandalized her home. She had to do it herself.

Why trash her home? It wasn't necessary. Neither was chasing her through the office. As far as Tarbell knew, she'd played ball. She'd removed the black mark on his performance evaluation and had kept quiet about the assault.

She sat at her computer and pretended to work while she waited for Tarbell to leave his cubicle. Whether he'd figured this out or not, he remained glued to his desk.

Gwen's phone rang, and she answered it.

"Gwen, I heard about the break-in," Deborah Langan said. "From Robert Ingram."

Ingram's name changed the emphasis of this call.

"Why are you here today?"

"Just doing my job."

"Is that all?"

"Yes."

"Gwen, I realize how frustrating this must be for you, but I urge you to be patient. Don't do anything rash that could ruin the investigation."

The company seemed more interested in covering its butt than dealing with Tarbell.

Tarbell got up from his desk and walked past her office. He had to be dealt with now.

"I won't," Gwen said standing up. "Gotta go. Bye."

She followed Tarbell to the technical library. She lagged way behind so as not to spook him. The second she was sure he was alone, she followed him inside and locked the door.

He stiffened at the snap of the lock. Most people would have missed his fear unless they were watching for it. Gwen liked that he could be rattled like everyone else.

He turned around. "Gwen, did you need something?"

"Yeah, I need you to leave my family alone."

He shrugged his shoulders. "Sorry, I don't understand. Leave your family alone?"

The pretense infuriated her. She stormed over to him, cornering him. He backed up, even though he stood almost a foot taller than her.

"Don't play games with me. You pulled that stunt here the other night, cutting the lights and chasing me through the building, and you broke into my home last night."

Tarbell shook his head. "I don't know what you mean."

"No one's watching and no one's listening, so you can drop the act."

Suddenly, Tarbell changed. He shrugged off his facade and his feigned innocence gave way to the cruel expression she'd seen in the parking lot. It began in his eyes and spread through his entire body. His lanky frame seemed less awkward and more like that of a lean predator. Gwen took an involuntary step backward.

"Are you sure no one's listening?"

"It's just us."

"You'll forgive me if I don't believe you. Over the weekend, I realized something. As much as I hold something over you, you hold something over me, but it's all so ethereal. It's nothing either of us can touch. It would make sense if you decided to get something more solid." He paused and stared into her. She felt him trying to pick through her mind. "Are you wearing a wire, Gwen?"

"No."

"Do you mind if I check?"

Before she could object, he spun her around and yanked her jacket up. Her blouse was translucent under the harsh light. It was clear she wasn't wearing a wire or a recorder, but Tarbell ran his hands down her back.

She jerked away. She'd never let Tarbell touch her again. Not like that. She whirled around and stuck an accusing finger in his face, but he slapped it out of the way.

"I have to protect myself, Gwen." He felt inside the pockets of her jacket. "I can't take the chance that this is all a setup."

"I think you can see I'm not wearing a wire."

He cast his gaze over her, slow and methodical. "No, I can't. I can't see under your skirt. Lift it up."

At first, she thought he wanted to humiliate her again; push her down another level. But she didn't detect an ounce of lasciviousness in him. He needed to see because he really did believe she was wearing a wire. She needed him to acknowledge what he'd done to her. Ingram might not believe Tarbell had anything to do with the attack other night or the break-in, but she did and she needed to hear Tarbell admit it. She lifted her skirt up.

Tarbell came forward, but she held out a hand.

"You can look, but you don't touch me."

He nodded.

Gwen watched Tarbell's expression. The instant she saw any pleasure the skirt went down, but she saw none. All she saw was his need to protect himself from incrimination. He needed to make sure there was no wire that could record their conversation. She turned around for him so he could see everything.

He nodded his satisfaction, and she pulled her skirt down.

"What do you want, Gwen?"

"You got what you wanted from me, but you haven't left me alone. I thought we had a deal."

He moved in, pinning her into an alcove and positioning himself between her and the door. She tried to keep calm and show no fear, but her fast breathing betrayed her.

"Gwen, I need to make sure our deal remains intact. I can't afford for you to do something stupid like go to HR or the cops."

Does he know? He couldn't, but there was a telling edge in his voice, as if he was taunting her. She wouldn't be drawn in. If he knew something, let him say it.

"I'm not telling anyone about what you did."

"Sure, you can say that and I could go on faith that you'll do the right thing, but it's not good enough. Words are cheap. Actions are expensive commodities. They come with consequences. This is something we're both living with right now. I made a mistake, Gwen. I assaulted you. That action puts me in a dangerous position. You can turn me in at any time. That in itself is an act. If you sell me out, it changes my life irrevocably. Should you go down that route, I have no option but to retaliate. Escalation is such a nasty road to take. No one ever wins in that situation. So I protected myself against that possibility with a couple of preemptive strikes to remind you that should you decide to take action against me I can and will get to you first. I know where you live; I know what's important to you, and I have the skills and determination to follow through. Make no mistake, Gwen. You do anything to harm me and I'll destroy you and everyone and everything you hold dear. Is that clear?"

"Very clear, Stephen."

Gwen was breathing hard, sweating, and her extremities were cold. It was only natural. She'd been cornered by a predator far stronger than her. But her fear was an empowering emotion. So many people mistook it for weakness, but she knew better. So did Desmond Parker. He'd mistaken her fear for weakness and it had cost him. He'd almost killed her, but he didn't get his way. And neither would Tarbell.

"You haven't talked, have you?"

He was taunting her again. Did he know about Ingram and his people? She wanted so much to ask him, but that would only play into his hands. Her question would be her admission of guilt, and that was what he was fishing for. It didn't work that way. This wasn't his interrogation. It was hers. She'd come to get answers from him. She wasn't about to give any up.

"Your secret is safe as long as you don't come within a mile of my home or family."

"That's all I needed to hear." He smiled and backed away, letting her open the door. "Just keep it that way, Gwen. I can't be held responsible for my actions if you don't."

• • •

Amanda Norton almost missed it. Almost. She'd settled down quickly into her role at Pace Pharmaceuticals, getting a handle on the job and the people she was watching. It wasn't the first time she'd been inserted into a workplace under the guise of a temp. Usually the work was nothing more than photocopying and filing. Pace was a little different. The work required her to use her head, and that forced her to take her eye off her real job.

She'd missed Tarbell leaving his desk but spotted Gwen Farris stalking him across the building.

Until now, her two targets had behaved themselves pretty well. Tarbell was the more relaxed of the two. That wasn't to say she liked him. He gave off that creepy, too-clever-for-his-own-good vibe. Every office seemed to be issued one of these guys. Gwen was a harder proposition to read. The woman was wound tight. It wasn't surprising under the circumstances. If Gwen's move to follow Tarbell hadn't been so stiff and obvious, Amanda would have missed it. She grabbed a couple of files off her desk and trailed behind her.

Office surveillance law 101: Don't go anywhere without a piece of paper in your hand. Paper means you're working. No one questions you.

Amanda kept her distance. She'd lost Tarbell, but she didn't need to know where he'd gone. Gwen would lead her to him.

Gwen's pace outstripped Amanda's, but that was OK as long as she kept her in sight.

Gwen reached the end of a corridor and turned right. Amanda sped up. She turned right in time to see Gwen enter the library. Amanda hurried and caught the unmistakable snap of a door lock.

"Damn it," she cursed under her breath.

She couldn't see in or get in, but she did hear voices. They weren't clear enough to make out a conversation but certainly clear enough to pick up the mood, which was bad. She caught the harsh sound of Gwen's raised voice followed by Tarbell's angry baritone. It lasted only a moment before the level dropped to a calm note that failed to penetrate the walls.

Ingram warned her that this investigation wasn't as it seemed at first glance. The anchor pinning this one down had come away. No one liked drift in an investigation. It made it hard to control and direct. They were supposed to be investigating Tarbell. Now she was under instructions to watch the both of them. Little events like this one didn't help get the job done, of course.

The windows wrapping around the library were opaque. She couldn't see inside, and they couldn't see out. She made the pretense of dropping her files, spilling the contents over the floor.

It was a risky move. It was paper but it made a noise hitting the ground. It was loud enough for Gwen and Tarbell to hear, but she was banking on them being too wrapped up in their own world to be listening for others. The move could also draw the attention of some helpful passerby, and their voices might coerce Gwen and Tarbell into a speedy exit.

She dropped to one knee and slowly returned the paperwork to the file while she listened in. She still couldn't hear what was being said. It was a lost cause. She quickly gathered up her things.

All she could do was wait for them to leave. She crossed over to the water cooler halfway up the corridor with a view of the parking lot. She filled a Dixie cup and slowly drank while gazing at the jets climbing out of Oakland International and keeping an eye on the locked room.

Gwen left the room first. Blinded by her thoughts, she didn't notice Amanda. The mole checked her watch. Gwen had been in there a little over five minutes. Tarbell remained inside. She gave him five, then ten minutes, but he never emerged. Gwen had left the library door open. Amanda tossed the Dixie cup in the trash and walked past the room. Tarbell was working, but he instantly detected a stranger's presence. He turned and looked straight at her.

"Hi, Steve," Amanda tossed out on her way by.

"Amanda," he replied, coldly.

She hurried back to her desk, dumped the files, and headed out to the parking lot. She was careful not to come over as frantic. She got into her car and called Ingram on her cell.

"Just a heads-up, Robert. It looks as if Gwen Farris confronted Tarbell."

"Shit. When'd this happen?"

"Just now," she said and filled him in.

"OK. Keep a close eye on them. If there are any other closed-door antics, I want to know about them, ASAP."

"Will do. I'll e-mail you my daily report tonight."

"Thanks, Amanda."

She hung up and headed back to Pace's building. Behind her in the neighboring parking lot, Reggie Glover was getting a stiff back waiting for Tarbell to leave the building. He was probably tracking her progress across the parking lot. Knowing him, Reggie was checking out her butt, too. It was an old joke that had yet to wear out its welcome. Despite his fascination with her butt, he had her back. If anything happened, he'd come running. He'd be wondering about what she was doing out here. Casually, she put a hand behind her and made the OK sign for him. With his binoculars trained on her butt, he'd see the signal.

She smiled at the receptionist on her way in and returned to work. She kept a visual on Gwen and Tarbell, occasionally taking detours through their department. She watched for interaction and sudden excursions from their desks. They seemed to be behaving themselves now. They were doing their work and being professional around each other. It was a nice bit of restraint on their parts, especially Gwen's. If she was being terrorized as she claimed, God knew how the woman kept it all together day after day with the son of a bitch sitting outside her door. Amanda wasn't sure she could.

"Amanda?"

She turned around and met Priscilla Hunt, her supervisor for the duration. "Yes."

Priscilla held out a materials requisition form. "I need you to dispense these liquids and issue them to Manufacturing."

Amanda looked over the list. She was looking at an hour at least in the ambient storage room. It meant taking her eye off her two targets, but that was OK. She got the feeling that the day's hostilities were over. "Sure, I'll get on it right now."

She took the requisition and a cart into the storage room. If she wasn't an investigator, she could get used to this job. The money was good for what the work entailed. Her role in Inventory Control dealt with measuring out chemicals and distributing them to whomever needed them. Her chemistry knowledge was pretty poor, but she knew enough to be wary of the acids and bases listed. From what she read on the requisition, it was a pretty fearsome list of chemicals. She didn't have a clue what it all made. Half of it sounded like chemical warfare. Then again, sodium hydroxide was table salt. Who knew this stuff?

Pace's ambient storage room was spotless. It was another thing she liked about working in the pharmaceutical world. It was clean. Clean wasn't something that could be said of the majority of her assignments. The room was kept at a steady temperature. The bulk chemicals were stored in large containers kept on rows of gleaming stainless steel racks.

She set the requisition down on the measuring table, pulled on gloves, and put on her safety goggles before removing a five-gallon jug of isopropanol off its rack. She measured out the quantity needed and re-racked the jug.

She worked her way through the list. Sadly, not everything was as accessible as the isopropanol. She needed two liters of toluene and that was kept on the top shelf in large, collapsible rubber bags. The bags were a pain in the ass. They were practical but damn awkward to maneuver. Having them on the top shelf didn't help matters.

She wheeled a scissor lift over to the rack and raised it up. The lift didn't quite reach the top shelf, which meant hefting the bag over the lip of the rack. The bag was about three-quarters full, and it looked like a deflated balloon with a spout. She lifted the bag. It deformed around her hands. Lifting it wasn't the problem; hefting it over the steel rack's wire lip was. She balanced the bag on the lip to catch her breath, then jerked it hard to get it onto the scissor lift.

She felt the bag snag on the lip, but only for a second. Her momentum wrenched it free, but it also tore the thick, rubberized material. The chemical poured from the tear and the open spout.

Reflexively, Amanda closed her eyes and mouth as the chemical cascaded over her. The burning was immediate. Her screams could be heard clear across the building.

CHAPTER SIXTEEN

Tarbell sat at his laptop at home sifting through all the communications captured from Gwen's computer. While the spy software was an ingenious piece of technology, it wasn't an intelligent one. It caught everything entering and leaving Gwen's computer, every one of her keystrokes and every piece of spam that hit her in-box. It was tedious work, not helped by Gwen's phenomenal output. He'd hoped his tactics would have eaten away at her, affecting her concentration, but they hadn't slowed her down. Fed up with sifting through Gwen's crap, he shoved the computer away.

His agitation cooled when his thoughts turned to Amanda Norton.

He wished he could have been there when the toluene spilled all over her. He'd gotten there in time to see her being brought out of the storage room. The enormity of what had happened was etched into her face. It was like watching a porcelain sculpture dropped from a great height smash against the unforgiving sidewalk. The fall was graceful in its elegance and the destruction exquisite, considering the fragments of this unique construction could never be reassembled.

"That's the risk you run in your line of work," he said to himself.

To everyone involved, it appeared to be a terrible accident, but it was nothing of the kind. He'd orchestrated it, of course. His position within the QA department afforded him a godlike view of Pace's operations. He approved all requisitions coming out of Manufacturing before forwarding them on to Inventory Control. As the bottom rung in Inventory Control's ladder, Amanda would be the one stuck with retrieving the chemicals. After that, it was easy. Last night after everyone left, he went into the storage room with a pair of pliers and bent a wire back to make a hook to snag the bag of toluene. The collapsible bags were tough, but not that tough. Just in case the bag proved tougher than expected, he also forced the spout open. The solvent was coming out one way or another. Workers for the state's Occupational Safety and Health division would have questions and fingers would be pointed, but none of it would come his way.

It would have been fun to have infected Amanda with one of the many live viruses Pace had in inventory, but that would have raised too many questions and a full investigation. That would have been far too messy. No, he was content with what he'd done.

By all accounts, Amanda was in bad shape. She'd suffered chemical burns and some minor eye damage, but she was also looking at possible kidney and liver damage from the sizeable dose she'd been exposed to. She should be counting her blessings, though. It could have been a lot worse if she hadn't been put through decontamination procedures so swiftly.

At the end of the day, the extent of Mandy's injuries didn't matter. The important thing was she was gone. Another branch of Private Security International had been chopped off, no longer there to interfere with his work. He doubted PSI would replace Amanda. The kind of people they employed only wanted slam dunks, not risk. They wouldn't have any volunteers beating at the door to take Amanda's place.

All in all, it was an elegant piece of work. It was a shame he had no one to share this triumph with. He'd have to make do with entertaining himself. This elegance was something he needed to use on Gwen. Petersen was right. He needed to dispense with the intimidation stuff. It was incredibly satisfying, but it also maintained PSI's focus on him. There was no way he was going to get to Gwen with them on his back every step of the way. He needed to remove PSI from the equation. That way he'd be free and clear to do what he liked.

He found himself smiling. His sour mood had turned sweet again. He liked it when his dark moods didn't last.

He returned to his laptop and resumed combing through Gwen's correspondence. It didn't take long for him to fall upon something that caught his eye. Gwen's deleted e-mails folder contained an e-mail from Blackwell Biotech. They were a direct competitor to Pace Pharmaceuticals. They'd invited her to send her résumé for a position there. It was a very informal letter and obvious from the tone that the sender, Judy Brent, was a friend. It wasn't an unusual occurrence. Biotech was a pretty incestuous industry, and the Bay Area was a biotech haven with at least a dozen companies within a thirty-mile radius. She'd asked to meet Gwen for lunch, and Gwen had agreed in her reply.

Tarbell saw new possibilities as he read the brief e-mail. A plot was developing in his head. If he handled it right, he saw his way of ridding himself of PSI for good.

He went to the window and looked for Petersen. He didn't see his familiar Audi, so he called him on his cell.

"Where are you?"

"Around," Petersen answered.

"I'm going out. I need you to cover for me."

"What are you doing?"

"That's none of your concern."

"Leave that woman alone."

Tarbell hung up, then smiled. He admired Petersen's misplaced chivalry.

He liked how things were proceeding. The tide was turning. The grip PSI had on him was slipping. He just had to nudge it for them to fall away. He needed to strike again while events were in his favor, but for that he needed some inspiration. He knew just the place.

The drive to what he ironically termed his "ancestral home" was filled with bad memories. During the twenty minutes it took to get from El Cerrito to Vallejo, every turn of the odometer represented a new milestone in misery. He flinched at the sound of remembered slaps and punches. His mom had taken so many body blows that no doctor in the world could convince him that her decline in health in later years wasn't attributable to the violence dealt by his father. He'd once pissed blood for three days after a beating handed down by the man he hated calling dad. That was light compared to the punishment his mother took. He wondered if his years in this world would be truncated like his mother's. He had a lot of trouble with his guts these days. Some foods turned him inside out. Other times, he awoke with his kidneys screaming in pain. Yeah, he'd probably go the way of his mother, years before his time, while that son of a bitch sat in his chair sucking oxygen he didn't deserve.

Tarbell got out of the car and wandered over to the house. He had a flashlight in hand, but it remained off. Moonlight gave him all the illumination he needed. He stood before the house. He'd taken a lot of beatings here. He'd been young and could bounce back. He guessed that was why his dad had never backed off. He healed without leaving a mark. Had his dad wanted a lasting reminder of his skills? Was that why once the bruises faded and the cuts healed he needed to refresh them? Tarbell didn't know, and he doubted that son of a bitch knew either.

He climbed the steps, which were warped by time and exposure to the bay, and sat on the porch. He pictured Gwen at her desk telling him he didn't meet the company's expectations, and his disgust yielded a plan.

• • •

Petersen hoped he would be smarter the second time around and not get caught out by a cockeyed headlight. He'd borrowed his brother-in-law's Mazda. The car fit the bill. It was dark and anonymous. He parked on the cross street to Tarbell's home and waited for him to do something that would give him an opening to use against him. He just needed the slightest leverage to swing the faith back in Gwen's favor. Tarbell's garage door rolled up, and Petersen straightened in his seat.

"C'mon, asshole. Give me some rope to tie around your neck."

He let Tarbell get a little distance on him before pulling out after him. He expected Tarbell to go after Gwen, but instead of driving south to Alameda, Tarbell pointed the car north. The move ignited Petersen's curiosity.

He followed Tarbell to the outskirts of Vallejo. He wasn't sure what Tarbell had given him here. It was something, but it wasn't rope. The house sat perched on a hillside overlooking San Pablo Bay. It was in an unincorporated portion of the county with big undeveloped lots and few homes. The house itself was a wreck, decayed from years of neglect.

The winding road gave him the perfect opportunity to stash the car and find a good spot to watch Tarbell. At first he thought the house was Tarbell's base of operations, a retreat where he could hide incriminating evidence, but it didn't look that way. Tarbell just sat on the porch in the dark.

His heart stopped when the shouting began. For a terrifying moment, he thought Tarbell had spotted him skulking in the tall grass, but the shouting wasn't directed at him or anyone for that matter. Tarbell was nothing but a dog baying at the moon.

He moved in as far as his courage would allow him. Past encounters kept him from getting too close, and he lay flat on the ground, pressing himself into the dirt.

Tarbell laughed a big ugly laugh. "Yeah. I thought so. That was why, wasn't it? Just for kicks." He laughed again. "And for punches."

His laughs died and silence followed for the next ten minutes before he spoke again. There was no shouting this time. He kept his tone conversational.

Petersen strained to listen. He picked out chunks of the one-sided conversation. Tarbell bleated on about being screwed over and how he'd get back at the world for it. People would pay. The world would pay.

Petersen shook his head. It was easy to label Tarbell crazy, but he saw beyond the superficial label. He was listening to a middle-aged child unable to deal with his problems in an adult way. It was so weak for a man who prided himself on being the world's smartest man. In that moment, Petersen lost respect for Tarbell. Someone as emotionally stunted as he was could be taken down, and Petersen was more than capable of doing it.

But the moment didn't last. Tarbell's next outburst scared Petersen.

"That's what I'll do. I'll trap her." Tarbell's joyous laugh cut through the air. "She'll get caught up in her own netting."

Tarbell jumped up from the porch and ran back to his car. He turned it around and drove away.

Petersen scurried back to the Mazda. He didn't have to ask who the focus of the trap was. Panic drove his legs. Tarbell would use him for his alibi. He couldn't let that happen.

He followed Tarbell and picked him up on the freeway heading home. He wouldn't try anything tonight. If Petersen had learned anything about Tarbell, nothing he did was spontaneous. Everything needed planning. It gave Petersen time to do something.

He waited until Tarbell had been home ten minutes before calling him.

"What is it, Tom?"

"There's been a shakeup. I'm being reassigned."

"What?"

"PSI is putting me on Gwen's surveillance team. Someone else will take over for me tomorrow night."

"That doesn't work for me, Tom," he said in a singsong tone.

"I can't help that."

"I don't care what PSI says. You are going to continue watching my back at nights. I don't care how you do it, but do it. Do I have to push your wife down another set of stairs to get your cooperation?"

"No," Petersen said through gritted teeth. "I'll get back on this detail. You don't have to hurt Lynette. OK? OK?"

"You do your part and nothing will happen to her."

"I will."

Petersen hung up on Tarbell. It was a down-and-dirty attempt to chop Tarbell off at the ankles. It hadn't worked, but that was OK. He wasn't out of ideas.

"You won't hurt her, Tarbell," he said within the confines of the borrowed car. "I'll make sure of it. Not Gwen and not Lynette."

CHAPTER SEVENTEEN

Gwen left the office for lunch on Friday, as she'd done so many times before, but this time she felt vulnerable walking to her car. Nothing implied that Tarbell was following her, and Ingram's people were supposed to have that possibility covered, but they'd yet to prove themselves. She got behind the wheel and headed to a Thai restaurant on Alameda's main drag.

The constant stress she felt around her these days lifted when she entered the restaurant and Judy Brent popped up from her seat. She hadn't seen Judy since she'd left Roche to have Kirsten.

Judy hugged Gwen. "It's so good to see you. It seems like forever."

"I know."

The lunch crowd at the restaurant was light enough for them to get a window table. They ordered right away, to avoid having an ever-present waitress hover near their table.

"So how are things?" Judy asked.

"Good," Gwen answered, the word hard to say. It would have been so easy to let it pour out to Judy, but it was too much to load onto her.

Besides, Gwen knew that Judy had made the hour-plus drive from Vacaville to do more than eat lunch and catch up. She was hoping to entice Gwen away from Pace to Blackwell Biotech, the company she'd moved to after Roche. Even if they wanted Gwen to wash the floor, it was a tempting proposition at the moment.

"How's the family?" Judy asked.

It was an excuse to bring out the snapshots. Bragging about Kirsten took her mind off her problems. She told Judy some of her favorite parenting stories. Then, Judy returned the favor by bringing out her pictures. There were no children, but there was a new fiancé in her life. He was a handsome guy she'd met at the office.

"You'd think as the HR manager I would know all the risks about interoffice relationships, but in our case, it worked. We're looking at an April wedding."

The food came and the conversation changed from life to the real reason they were meeting. Judy's easygoing manner turned business professional. She sat up straighter, and her voice dropped a couple of octaves.

"Blackwell Biotech is looking for a new manager of QA."

"Like I said in the e-mail, I'm not really interested."

"I know, but please hear me out. If you don't, I can't write this off as a business expense."

Gwen smiled. "OK, then."

Judy outlined the position. The job was similar to the one Gwen held now. More staff and managerial decisions constituted the major differences. Right now, Gwen was still very much hands-on and found herself continuing with a number of pre-existing tasks she had before her promotion. The idea of more people to take that work away from her sounded pretty sweet when she considered what was sitting on her desk.

"It's still a no."

"Why? Is it the money?"

"No, it's good. It's better than what I'm getting now."

"Then what's the problem? The money's better. The house prices are better. You'd get a better bang for your buck. The benefits are just as good. And the best thing, no more Bay Area traffic."

"I just can't, Judy."

"What's holding you back?"

Tarbell was. With the mess their lives were in, it would be so easy to take Judy's offer, but Tarbell would win if Gwen ran away. He couldn't be allowed to get away with what he'd done. If Tarbell was gone and the job offer was still out there, then she might reconsider.

"Pace has been good to me. They promoted me after a year, and I haven't been in charge all that long. I don't want to be seen as jumping ship."

"No one is going to think that. We asked you."

"I know, but that's not what it's going to look like on my résumé. Others are going to think that I quit when the next job comes along."

"Not if you stick with us long-term. All that goes away."

Gwen smiled. "You're good at this."

"Guilty as charged."

Judy gave Gwen a couple of minutes of uninterrupted eating before starting up again.

"I don't get this, Gwen. I'm offering you a better job with better money and prospects, and you're saying no. There's got to be something behind it. Tell me what you need, and I'll do my best to make it happen."

Tarbell nailed inside a crate on a slow boat to China, she thought.

"Gwen? Is something wrong?"

"No, of course not."

"You could have fooled me. You're on the verge of tears."

Gwen's facade was slipping, and she could keep holding it in place, but she was too tired.

"There's a lot going on. I can't walk away from it. Not yet, anyway."

"Like what?"

"Paul's out of work. The construction trade is down and so are careers."

"Even more reason to come out to Vacaville. House prices are cheaper, and while the downturn is hitting everyone, Vacaville is going to keep on growing. They're going to need people like Paul more there than they do here."

"I know."

"Then what? Gwen, I can feel you holding back. We've known each other since college. Tell me."

"You're right. It's not just Paul. I have a lot of headaches at the moment."

Say it. Say Tarbell. Get it out before it eats you up. But she couldn't say it. Not yet. Judy was going to keep on digging until she got her answers. If Gwen didn't give her something, she would spill everything about Tarbell. She had to give her something else and she had it.

"Desmond Parker. He's up for parole."

Judy put a hand to her mouth. She understood more than anyone about Parker. She'd been there that night. Judy had broken down at Gwen's hospital bedside and evoked the one scenario that had haunted the both of them for years afterward. If she had stayed, would Parker have done what he'd done or would he have moved on to another girl? To Gwen, it now seemed a pointless question. If Parker hadn't abducted her, he would have abducted another girl, and that girl might not have been as lucky as her. Gwen's near death could have saved several other girls. That was the story she told herself.

"Oh, Gwen. How can they?"

"It was going to happen someday. It happens to be now."

"Just because he's up for parole doesn't mean he'll get it."

"It looks like he will."

"Is anyone doing anything about it?"

"I'm speaking at the hearing in a couple of weeks. It might sway the decision, but I'm not optimistic."

Gwen told Judy about her visit to San Quentin. Judy was in tears before Gwen reached the end. Parker dragged up a lot of old memories for both of them. Seeing Judy break down reminded Gwen of how far she'd come. As much of an influence as Parker was and would remain in Gwen's life, he was just a small part now. For Judy, it looked as if he represented more.

"I never should have left you that night."

"And I shouldn't have put myself in that situation. No one is to blame for what happened to me except for Parker."

The waitress came over and asked if there was a problem. Gwen said there wasn't and asked for the check. Judy paid and they left, their meals mostly uneaten. They walked up the street, ignoring the stores.

"Look, are you interested in the job?" There was no hard sell this time with Judy's question. It was heartfelt.

"Of course, but the circumstances aren't good."

Judy nodded. "I know, but I want you to really think about this. I'm going to hold the position open. Deal with Parker, then call me. If you want the job, it's yours. With everything in your life, it might make for the perfect fresh beginning. It'll be a chance for you and Paul to start over."

Gwen wondered if an element of guilt was playing into Judy's decision. She'd always held herself responsible in some way, and here was a chance to redeem herself. Gwen killed the thought dead. It was an unfair assumption. She put that down to Parker and to Tarbell's recent influence in her life. She took the offer for what it was.

Judy hugged Gwen. "Let's hope Parker's parole is denied and your problems end there."

Gwen wished they would.

• • •

Tarbell was finding it remarkably easy to frame Gwen. He put it down to his inside knowledge, his ease with handling electronic files, and the element of surprise. All he needed was a little privacy to make it work, and he was getting that moment now. It was five forty-five, and virtually everyone had had enough of another day in the salt mines. Gwen had gone, as had all his coworkers. A few managers and VPs were milling about, but they were used to seeing him plugging away. He needed them to leave so he could complete some final tweaks on Gwen's computer. In the meantime, he could get on with the real heavy lifting.

Each division of Pace Pharmaceuticals was assigned a particular mission. Here at the Alameda division, it was medical devices. The next big thing Pace Pharmaceuticals board members had nailed their bonuses on was a test for determining whether someone was likely to suffer from breast cancer. When they received FDA approval, Pace was looking at new business worth at least 200 million bucks. It was the hottest thing on Pace's books, and while it wasn't exactly an industry secret, no one else in the industry was close to coming up with their own version.

It went without saying that Pace would be pretty pissed if five years of research and development fell into a competitor's hands. Tarbell could barely contain his delight when he came up with the plan to discredit Gwen and switch the focus away from himself.

Pace had been going electronic for a number of years. All documentation was scanned and archived on network drives. Very little paper documentation was on hand unless it was only a few weeks old. The breast cancer research was kept on a protected drive that could only be viewed by staff with certain passwords. He wasn't one, but Gwen was and he knew her password.

That afternoon, he'd logged on as Gwen and copied the files to her computer. This simple act left an electronic trail with the IT people even though Gwen and the IT people weren't aware of it—yet.

When the last manager left, he went into Gwen's office, fired up her PC, and logged into her company e-mail account. He was pleased to see a couple of messages going back and forth between Gwen and Judy Brent. There was nothing too interesting in the correspondence, but beyond the banal banter there were a couple of juicy tidbits. Gwen had written, "Thanks for listening. It meant a lot opening up. You're one of the few people I can talk to about this."

What have you opened up about, Gwen? he thought. *Me?* He didn't think so, but it didn't really matter who Gwen told. There was nothing she could do to stop him now. His mood was buoyed again by Judy's final remark. "Please, think my offer over. You'd be a great asset here."

The nonspecific comment worked perfectly for Tarbell. He wrote a response to Judy's e-mail, attaching the breast cancer research files. He cc'ed the e-mail to one of Blackwell's senior VPs and made it very blatant what he was sending.

He reached around the back of Gwen's computer and jerked the network cable out, then hit send. With the cable disconnected, the e-mail with its career-ending payload went as far as the out-box, but not the sent folder. A dialog box popped up on the screen stating the message couldn't be sent and asked if he would like to try again. He clicked the no option and closed the e-mail program. Then he plugged the network cable back in.

He'd just done a very simple but clever thing. The message was unsent, trapped in Gwen's out-box. Nothing would happen until Monday when Gwen logged on and opened her e-mail program. As soon as she did, the program would send the message automatically. The e-mail would be date stamped with a Monday date and time that would put Gwen squarely at her desk and would override any record of the message having being stuck in the out-box. From there, the damage would be done. For all intents and purposes, Gwen would have sent the e-mail and there'd be a nice electronic log proving it.

That was it. Gwen was done. It was that simple.

He uninstalled the spy software. It wasn't needed anymore, and he couldn't afford for anyone to find it. He was already looking forward to replaying this moment of triumph at home. The spy software would have captured everything up until this moment and a copy would be waiting for him at home on his laptop.

"Done and done," he said and shut down Gwen's computer.

It had been a long week but one that had proved more than fruitful. Everything was in play. It was time to celebrate and enjoy his weekend. Next week promised to be one of fresh opportunities, all without Gwen Farris's interference.

CHAPTER EIGHTEEN

"Why'd you do it?" Deborah asked.

Deborah's accusing tone put Gwen's Tuesday morning into a downward spiral. Deborah had been all smiles when she called Gwen. She was still playing the close-friend role when she showed Gwen into her office and sat her down, but the pretense ended with that question.

The question threw Gwen. When Deborah had called her to her office, she thought there'd been a breakthrough with Tarbell. Maybe he'd tripped himself up and Ingram had been there to catch him, finally ending this mess.

"I'm not sure what you're talking about, Deborah. Why'd I do what?"

Deborah sighed. "How much of this run in with Stephen Tarbell is made up? Some of it? All of it? Now I know the man is insufferable and no one here would miss him, so I understand it, but I can't condone it."

Deborah pretended to sound understanding, but she was granite. There was nothing forgiving in her tone or demeanor. Gwen had never seen this side of her. She was usually the typical HR person, openly friendly and a company cheerleader. She didn't greet anyone without a smile and a thoughtful question about their family.

"What's going on?"

"PSI has yet to come up with a scrap of evidence supporting your claim."

"That's not what Robert Ingram said at his office."

"The benefit of the doubt was with you then," Deborah said.

Gwen pounced on the word. "*Then*?"

"Since then, there's been nothing. There's no evidence to support your claims."

Rising panic opened up a hole in the pit of Gwen's stomach. It left her nauseous. This wasn't the way it was supposed to happen. Ingram was supposed to find evidence on Tarbell and put him away for it. But the game plan had been failing all week, and Ingram had lost his faith in her.

But this meeting wasn't simply because PSI hadn't come up with any evidence exonerating Tarbell. If the investigation had simply not turned up any supporting evidence, Deborah's attitude would be different. She'd be consolatory, wrapping a comforting arm around Gwen's shoulders and telling her they'd done their best but there was nothing proving Tarbell had done anything. Instead, she was hostile and accusatory. Something had gone seriously wrong.

"Was Stephen supposed to be the scapegoat?" Deborah looked at Gwen with disgust.

"What?"

"Were you going to use his assault as a precursor to set him up?"

"Seriously, I don't know what you're talking about, so you're going to have to tell me."

Deborah opened a file in front of her. She removed a color photo and slid it across to Gwen. Gwen picked up the photo gingerly. It was a shot of her and Judy from the Thai restaurant. The photograph had been taken from across the street. It wasn't the greatest piece of photography in the world, the image was grainy and the sun shining down on the restaurant's window washed a lot of the detail away, but it was clearly her and Judy.

"Who is that?"

"Judy Brent. She's a friend of mine."

"Just a friend?"

"Just a friend."

"Who does she work for?"

Gwen could see how their meeting could be misconstrued. It was a misunderstanding that could be corrected with a simple phone call to Judy. But there was something wrong with this picture. Not with the picture itself, but with the existence of the picture at all.

"Have I been under surveillance?"

"You were in danger, Gwen. It was felt someone should be watching your back for your safety."

Gwen didn't believe that for a second. If Ingram had decided she needed a bodyguard, he would have told her, even introduced them. Not telling her she was under surveillance meant one thing. They weren't watching her back, they were watching her.

"Answer my question, Gwen. Who does Judy Brent work for?"

Gwen named Pace's competitor.

"At least you admit it. I didn't think you would under the circumstances."

"Under the circumstances? Look, this is getting out of hand. It's not what you think. We were college roommates. We were just catching up." She left out the job offer. She wasn't interested in taking it, and trying to explain it would only gum up this meeting.

"If you don't believe me, call Judy. She'll explain everything."

"We have called her."

Instead of this remark easing Gwen's tension, it served only to heighten it.

"What did she say?"

"Very little, once Blackwell's legal counsel got involved."

"Why are lawyers getting involved?"

Deborah looked disgusted by Gwen's näiveté. "Why do you think?"

Gwen shook her head.

"Drop the act, Gwen. It's over. You met with your friend to sell Blackwell the breast cancer research. We know all about it. I can't believe you were dumb enough to send the files through company e-mail."

The accusation hit that hole in the pit of Gwen's stomach. It made no sense. She jumped up. "I didn't send anything."

"Sit down, Gwen." It wasn't a request.

Gwen retook her seat.

"IT has a log of your e-mails. Not only that, there's a log of you copying the research files off the system drive. Why in God's name did you do it? You had to know we'd catch you."

"I didn't do it."

"Stop, Gwen. It's over. The best thing you can do is come clean."

"It's Stephen. He did this."

"Yes, it would be. Did you invent the assault to throw us off? Was it so you'd have our sympathy while you focused on stealing our research? Was that the idea?"

"It was Stephen." Gwen couldn't hide the desperate note from her voice. The falsely accused sounded desperate, but so did the guilty.

"Oh, please, Gwen. Give it up."

Gwen knew it was Tarbell. Fate and bad luck didn't have a hand in this. He did. He knew that inflicting physical harm would hurt him as much as her, so destroying her reputation was a far better solution. But for all his deviousness, he couldn't get away with any of this while she was in her office. He needed to do this while she was at a meeting or away from her desk. If she was at a meeting, she had witnesses to prove it. If she'd left the office for the day, she had PSI's surveillance to back her up. Tarbell had done a first class job of screwing her over, but it was as fragile and transparent as glass.

"When was the e-mail sent?"

"It's over, Gwen. See sense."

"When was the e-mail sent?" she insisted. "I guarantee I wasn't in my office when the e-mail was sent."

"It was sent at eight ten yesterday morning."

"That can't be." The words slipped out. She'd been at her desk from the moment she walked in until just before ten. There was no way Tarbell had gotten to her desk. He'd used the same magic to prove he was at home when he chased her through the office and trashed her home. Whatever it was, she couldn't see how the trick was done.

"Were you at your desk at eight ten?"

"Yes."

"It's over, Gwen. You were caught. Face up to it."

Gwen was facing up to it. She'd been trapped by something she didn't do.

"Why'd you do it, Gwen? Really."

Knowing she was beaten, Gwen said nothing.

Deborah slid a sheet of paper across the table. It was a print-out of an e-mail Gwen hadn't sent. It was a reply to Judy's last e-mail. It couldn't be any more incriminating if it wanted to be. It outlined that she was delivering the research she'd promised and that she was ready to accept the new job offer in return. The e-mail contained all the replies to their previous e-mails, including Judy's oblique offers to a position at Blackwell. It looked as if Judy had lured Gwen into selling out Pace. There was no point in telling Deborah the e-mail thread had only begun after Tarbell had assaulted her. Deborah was finished with Gwen. Decisions had been made. The guilty condemned.

"For a new job? More money? Hasn't Pace been good to you?"

"Does it matter?"

"Perhaps not, Gwen, but I thought we knew each other better than this." Deborah took back the photograph and the e-mail printout. "Did you take anything else?"

"If it's there to be found, you'll find it."

Deborah threw her hands up in surrender. "OK, Gwen, you win."

"What happens now?"

"You'll be escorted off the premises by security."

"I need to collect my things."

Deborah shook her head. "Security has already collected your purse and that will be given to you on the way out. Everything else will be forwarded to you at a later date."

"So, I've been terminated."

"You didn't leave us any choice."

"It wasn't my choice to give. If you look deeper, you'll find I had nothing to do with this."

But Deborah wasn't listening. "You will receive your final paycheck and medical benefits will extend until the end of the month, which I think is more than generous under the circumstances."

Deborah paused for a thank you that Gwen didn't supply.

"If you're wondering if there'll be any civil action for the industrial espionage, there won't be. The boards of both companies have decided they wouldn't welcome the unwanted publicity associated with this issue."

Gwen understood that. As unwitting dupes in this scam, they wouldn't want their name dragged through the mud. She wondered what assurances Blackwell Biotech had made to Pace about its innocence. Had they painted her as a lone agent trying to curry favor with a potential new employer? That seemed as good a guess as any.

"Blackwell assures us they haven't examined the documents. Seeing as the breach was discovered before anyone had a chance to benefit from the information, no real harm has been done to Pace."

"Who brought this to your attention? Stephen?" Gwen asked.

"I can't discuss the details, but Stephen had nothing to do with it."

Deborah made a call and two security guards appeared outside the door. They stood on either side of Gwen, neither one placing a hand on her. Deborah led Gwen on her walk of shame through the building and down the stairs to the lobby. The location of Deborah's office meant the walk was short and witnessed by very few, but it would be common knowledge before she reached her car. She pictured the shocked faces of her coworkers as they shared the news.

In the lobby, Deborah put out her hand and Gwen handed over her card key. It was an exercise in humiliation but for the wrong reasons. She wasn't ashamed of her behavior; she was ashamed of being tarred as a liar.

"I'm very disappointed, Gwen."

"So am I," Gwen said.

One of the guards pointed to the doors, and Gwen let herself out.

The moment she stepped outside, the enormity of being fired hit her. She'd lost her family's sole source of income. There were credit cards to pay, mortgage payments, utilities, and future medical bills. Their savings were down to the dregs. At best, they were good for a couple more months before it would get difficult. Her world was being driven onto the rocks, and none of it was her fault. She felt the hole in her stomach suck her in.

She missed her footing as she stepped off the sidewalk. She felt stupid and visible to the world. She glanced back at Pace's building. Faces pressed against windows watched her leave. She imagined the whispered exchanges as everyone tried to figure out what was transpiring. Some shook their heads. Shame should have forced her to look away, but she scanned the windows for Tarbell. She didn't see him.

"I didn't think you'd want to miss your moment of triumph," she said and got into her car.

• • •

Look surprised, you're clueless as to what's going on, Tarbell told himself as the vice president of Quality congregated what was left of the QA department in a conference room. Until then, everyone at Pace Pharmaceuticals who wasn't in the know had been left to speculate.

The panic had begun the moment Gwen left her office to see Deborah. The moment she was out of sight of her office, two of the geeks from IT rushed inside, closed the door, and pulled the blinds. They did what geeks do behind closed doors for ten minutes before emerging with Gwen's PC in hand. He guessed they could find remnants of the spy software if they looked, but they weren't looking for it. Nothing tracked back to him. Even if they did uncover an outside e-mail address where all Gwen's correspondence was being sent, all they'd find was a nameless Yahoo! account.

"What do you think's going on?" Lauren asked him.

He shook his head. "Damned if I know."

The second wave of hysteria hit when news of Gwen's supervised departure spread. No one had to be told Gwen had been fired. Everyone recognized the signs. The removal of her PC just confirmed everyone's suspicions.

Once Gwen had driven away, everyone descended on Quality Assurance. People wanted to know what was going on. How he would have loved to play professor to the students, answering all their questions, but he couldn't. All he could do was fend them off with clueless comments.

Managers and VPs prowling the area like big-game cats quelled the excitement. The masses returned to their posts. He fielded a few phone calls, eager for knowledge to pass on, but he had nothing for them.

Silence ensued. It left his coworkers edgy but not him. He understood the silence. Upper management needed to formulate a plan, including damage control and a successor to Gwen. Yes, Pace Pharmaceuticals was without a QA manager, but that would be temporary. A replacement would be installed before the day's end.

The QA manager is dead, long live the new QA manager, he thought.

Management kept everyone in suspense until the afternoon. Tarbell had noticed that all the managers had convened during lunch, where they were no doubt read the party line for mass consumption. As his department was called into a conference room, he noticed other managers calling their staff together and finding a sequestered spot to share the news.

This was it. The moment of truth.

He took his seat at the table. He wasn't presumptuous enough to take a seat at the head of the table. They hadn't made him Gwen's successor yet. It was a natural selection under the circumstances and one that should have been made six months ago. Gwen would be still employed if they had. Well, it was their loss, not his.

Besides himself, Lauren, and David—all that remained of Gwen's tarnished staff—Deborah from HR and Josh Hanson, the director of Regulatory Affairs, were in attendance. Greg Spencer, the vice president of Quality, presided over the meeting like a judge handing down a sentence.

"There's no point in pretending something serious didn't occur this morning," Spencer said. "It is with deep regret that I have to announce that Gwen Farris was terminated from Pace Pharmaceuticals for gross misconduct."

Lauren and David looked at each other, then at Tarbell for an explanation. He looked suitably shocked and shrugged in ignorance.

"That's crazy," David said. Tarbell always suspected he had a thing for Gwen.

Spencer nodded. "Sadly, it's true."

"What did she do?" Lauren asked.

Tarbell sat back. He wouldn't rush forward with a slew of questions. He'd only draw attention to himself. It was better if his two colleagues led the questions and he tossed in his own comments when it was suitable.

"For legal reasons, I can't reveal the nature of the misconduct, but rest assured there is no doubt over what she did. We were left with few options."

"I can't believe it," Lauren said.

"None of us can," Hanson said.

"This now brings up the matter of the department," Spencer said.

Tarbell straightened up in his seat. This was his big moment. This was where the planets realigned themselves and he assumed his rightful position in charge.

"It goes without saying, you three are more than competent to run day-to-day operations without supervision."

Flattery will get you everywhere, Tarbell thought.

"But someone is needed to make decisions that steer the department in the right direction."

Lauren and David both looked at Tarbell. Even they knew who should be running the department.

"That's why Josh will take over the department until a replacement is found for Gwen. He will make a great interim boss. Josh?"

Hanson took his cue to speak. "Like Greg said, I'll just be guiding the department. You'll be running it. I'll be coming by after the meeting to get a handle on what's going on in your areas."

Hanson's speech turned into white noise as the betrayal sunk in. They'd screwed him over again. No doubt Gwen had something to do with that. When she went down, she must have dragged him down with her. He could picture her grandstanding as they handed her a pink slip.

Bitch, he thought, the word spilling acid through his thoughts. Under the table, out of sight, his hands bit into his thighs. His fingernails cut deep into his flesh, but he felt no pain.

His pain was mental. He'd been screwed over by these idiots and Gwen again.

"Hopefully we can put the past behind us and move forward," Hanson said with a dumb-ass smile plastered over his face.

Not yet we can't, Tarbell thought.

CHAPTER NINETEEN

Petersen was getting ready to pretend to tail Tarbell again when the call came from Ingram. His normal routine consisted of driving over to Pace for the shift change with Reggie Glover. Once Glover left, he checked in with Tarbell to see if he needed him to watch his back. Each of these calls burned in his gut. If Tarbell told him to get lost, he found a bar somewhere and nursed a couple of beers punctuated by Cokes, watching the TV until they kicked him out with the barflies. Then he hung out on a street corner waiting for his shift to end. There was no way he could face Lynette at home. She'd see through him in a second. He was a traitor to a life dedicated to law enforcement, but slowly, he was working to make things right. He was building his own case against this prick. He had yet to exonerate himself, but he could look himself in the mirror. It was only a matter of time before he caught Tarbell.

"It's over, Tom."

A twinge told him he knew what was over, but he played along. This was the day he'd been waiting for. "What's over?"

"The Tarbell investigation. We caught Gwen Farris trying to smuggle company research to a competitor. She's out."

"What's that got to do with Tarbell?"

"Nothing, really. I don't really know if there was anything to the original claim, but it could have been a ploy to set Tarbell up as a fall guy. I think she may have been on a timetable, and things went awry when we didn't reel in Tarbell as quickly as she'd hoped."

"Do you believe that?"

"It's the prevailing theory. Either way, it doesn't matter. Pace pulled the plug. Gwen is no longer on the payroll, and we've got nothing concrete on Tarbell, so it's a job well done and back to the ranch for reassignment."

Ingram's tone was one of disappointment. Petersen knew him well enough to know he liked to finish his cases. The bad guys went to jail while the good guys and the oppressed rode off into the sunset. But Ingram wasn't a cop anymore. The days of seeing a case through no longer applied. Jobs got investigated until the client stopped paying.

"I would have liked to have seen this one through," Petersen said.

"Yeah, well, there's always next time."

"Not for me, Robert. I'm calling it a day."

"Why?"

"I'm not a kid anymore. My ass has gone flat from years spent on stakeouts. This job, working graveyard, has broken my butt for good. The money's nice, but I don't need it. I've put in my years and I want to spend the rest with my family."

"That's a shame, Tom. I'd hate to lose you. Is there anything I can do to change your mind?"

Petersen hemmed and hawed. "I don't think so."

"How about I take you off the surveillance jobs and put you on background checks and witness interviews?"

"Maybe. Give me six months away and ask me again. I might be stir-crazy by then and ready to bite your arm off to do anything." He finished the line off with a laugh.

"Will do and thanks. It's been good working with you, Tom. I'll get your final check out to you."

"Thanks."

"And don't be a stranger. Drop by now and again, and I'll buy you lunch."

"Will do, Robert. Take care."

Petersen hung up and dropped the jovial facade. Tarbell had gotten what he wanted. He had hung Gwen out to dry, and now he was free to do what he wanted. After witnessing his little rant outside the house in Vallejo, Petersen knew Tarbell wasn't the kind of guy to let this go. He'd keep hounding Gwen, and Petersen was counting on that. He wanted to be there when Tarbell did something that he couldn't worm his way out of.

He drove over to the Home Depot where his brother-in-law worked and swapped the Audi for the Mazda again.

"More UC work?" he asked.

UC. Christ, the guy watches far too much TV. "Yeah, I'm undercover again. Your part in the fight against crime has been noted."

The guy was as pleased as punch to have the Audi again.

Petersen checked his watch on the way to the freeway. It was after four. Tarbell would still be at the office, no doubt gloating over his success. *Live it up while you can*, he thought, *it won't last*. He called Tarbell's cell.

"The surveillance is off. You're in the clear."

"I guessed as much."

Tarbell didn't sound too happy about it. Petersen was surprised. He'd expected the douche bag to be turning handsprings.

"So we're all square now? You'll leave me and my wife alone?"

"You've got nothing to fear from me," his tone had hardened, "as long as you keep your word."

"I'm out. I don't work for PSI anymore. I'm retired."

"Good," Tarbell said and hung up.

Petersen joined the freeway and pointed the Mazda toward Alameda. He hadn't been able to protect Gwen while the investigation was ongoing, but now he could.

• • •

Gwen expected a fight when she dropped the bombshell that she'd lost her job, but she didn't get one. All Paul said was, "It's probably for the best."

An air of defeat had fallen over Paul, which she understood. After the assault, the break-in, and Desmond Parker's impending parole hearing, her wrongful dismissal seemed like the knockout punch. He hugged her and told her it would be OK. "These things have a way of sorting themselves out."

Gwen hoped that was true, because she wasn't seeing it yet. She did see one glimmer of light. She dug Judy Brent's business card out of her purse and called her cell number. It was after five and she'd probably be caught up in the evening commute. As Gwen called, she went outside onto the patio and walked a circle around the wreckage of their personal belongings. Judy picked up.

"What is it, Gwen?"

The frosty tone was unmistakable. Tarbell had drawn another innocent victim into his war.

"I just wanted to say sorry about this mess."

"You should be. What were you thinking, Gwen? I offered you a job. That was it. You didn't have to steal the company jewels for it. It was yours."

"Judy, it's not what you think."

"Do you know how much shit I'm in? The people here want to know what I was doing coercing you into a position. They want to know what other practices I've employed to bring people here. Christ, they're looking at sacrificing me to appease the gods at Pace, and I've got you to thank for it."

Gwen spotted her wedding photo among the rubble. It was still in its frame, but the frame had been split, shattering the glass. It had gouged the image. A diagonal slash cut across Paul and her. She bet Tarbell loved breaking this. She couldn't bear to look at it and turned the frame over.

"Judy, I didn't tell you something at lunch the other day."

"That you'd screw me over?"

"Just let me explain. Please."

"What?"

"Parker isn't the only problem in my life. One of the guys I work with assaulted me. He held a knife to my throat and threatened to cut me, then smashed up my home. I'm standing on my patio looking at the smashed remnants of half of our belongings. I'm betting he sent the e-mail to you, because I didn't. You have my word. He wanted to discredit me, and it worked. Sadly, you got caught in the crossfire. For that, I'm truly sorry."

Judy's tone softened. "Why's he doing this?"

"I don't know. He's not stable. I gave him a bad review and he snapped, and it hasn't let up."

Something resembling a disgusted laugh came down the line. "That's it? Some guy's pissed at a review and he's taking your life apart?"

"That's about the size of it."

"That's crazy."

"I didn't say it wasn't."

Gwen couldn't bear to look at her broken belongings anymore. She went over to the garden bench and sat with her back to the rubble.

"I'm wondering if the offer is still open."

"You've got to be joking, Gwen. You're Typhoid Mary. No one here wants a piece of you. I'll be lucky if I'm left with a job working reception here. No one is going to buy this persecution story. I'm not sure I do. No one trashes someone's life over a bad review. What happened? What did you do to him to cause this? Tell me. You owe me that much."

Gwen should have expected this reaction and in some ways, did. "Judy, I didn't do anything to this guy. I'm just in his way."

"Well, none of that helps me, does it?"

"I'm sorry, Judy. Really, I am."

"Look, I've got to go."

"Sure. I'll call you over the weekend. Maybe we can get together or something."

Judy didn't dignify Gwen with an answer and hung up.

Gwen didn't know whether to scream, cry, or throw the phone as far away from her as possible. Soon she wouldn't be able to afford to keep the damn thing anyway.

Paul poked his head out of the sliding door. "I've got dinner going. It's not much. Salad. You want to come in?"

She nodded. They ate under an oppressive cloud of silence with no one up for conversation. Dinner progressed into an equally quiet period of watching mindless TV. Gwen put Kirsten to bed around eight, then sat with Paul on the sofa watching a movie. The comedy failed to bring them a laugh, and they went to bed when it finished at ten. They took to their sides of the bed. Paul fell asleep swiftly.

Gwen lay there wondering how she was going to piece her life together. There were other jobs, but it would be tough finding one now. Biotech was a small world. Word would get around about this mess. No one in the industry would touch her. With the black mark from Pace Pharmaceuticals, no one would notice the career highlights on her résumé. It meant starting from the bottom again. A sob crept up on her and it got out before she could stifle it.

On the bright side, there was no more Tarbell. He'd won. He didn't deserve his victory, but his downfall awaited him. He'd trip himself up someday.

The crash of glass striking the floor followed a sudden bang. She sat up with a jerk. Her body tingled with fear.

"What the fuck was that?" Paul said. He stared across at her in the dark. The glow from the alarm clock illuminated his silhouette.

"Mommy. Daddy," Kirsten called.

Paul leaped from the bed. "Check on Kirsten."

Gwen chased after him. She flung the door to Kirsten's room open and flicked on the light. Her daughter was OK.

"Someone threw a damn rock through the window," Paul called from the living room.

"Stay here. Don't open the door to anyone," Gwen told Kirsten and shut the door.

She ran into the living room. Paul had jerked the drapes back. A golf ball–sized stone sat on the hardwood floor, and the picture window had a fist-sized hole in it. The tempered glass had fragmented into ten thousand pieces but held its shape in the window frame. Diamond-sized shards fell from the ruined window in slow succession like chunks of melting ice.

Gwen ripped the front door open.

"Where the hell are you going?" Paul shouted after her.

She pounded down the pathway in her bare feet and stopped at the sidewalk. A car was driving slowly away to her right. She chased after it. The car sped up the instant Gwen broke into a run. Paul yelled after her to stop, but she plowed on. She recognized the car. She just needed to see who was behind the wheel.

The Toyota was a long way ahead, but her street had plenty of four-way stops. She'd never catch him, but she just needed to get close enough to see the driver. She didn't want to leave room for doubt.

The car braked hard for the stop signs, but blew through each one. Gwen didn't gain on the car, but she kept up. The driver ramped up his speed, but he had to stop for the light. Traffic spilled across Hacienda Avenue without providing the driver a big enough gap to jerk out into traffic. Seeing him thwarted spurred her on. She ran hard, ignoring the abrasive concrete sidewalk shredding the soles of her feet.

The streetlight overhanging the intersection illuminated the car's interior. The driver turned around and she saw him. It was Tarbell.

The traffic light changed to green, and he roared away. It didn't matter that he'd gotten away because she'd seen him. Finally, he'd screwed up. He couldn't resist going after her one last time, and he'd blown it. This time, she had him.

She stopped running and a smile spread across her face. "Gotcha, Steve."

Paul came racing up behind her. "Are you crazy?"

"It was him."

"Who?"

"Tarbell." She grabbed Paul's hand. "We've got him. Let's get back."

When she reached home, she called Ingram.

Paul collected Kirsten from her room and brought her into the living room.

"Yes," Ingram answered sternly.

"Mr. Ingram, it's Gwen Farris."

"Gwen, why are you calling me?"

"Stephen Tarbell just threw a rock through my window. I saw his car, and I saw him driving. If you have one of your people go to his house, he won't be at home or wherever he says he is. It just happened. He won't have even made it out of Alameda yet. We've got him."

"You don't have him."

Ingram's stark reply killed her enthusiasm. "What are you talking about?"

Paul looked up at her questioning tone. She turned away from him.

"The investigation has been dropped."

A spike of rage ripped through Gwen. She wasn't going to be denied this time. Not when she had Tarbell cold. "What do you mean 'dropped'? He assaulted me, terrorized me at the office, ransacked my home, and framed me for this stupid espionage thing. Now he's just thrown a rock through my window. There's nothing to drop. You have to stop him now. You have a responsibility."

"Not to you."

"That's not what you said at your office."

"I said I would stop this man, but do you remember what Deborah Langan said?"

She did, but she didn't want to say it. She could barely admit it to herself.

"She said you were an asset to the company. Do you remember that?"

"Yes."

"While you were employed by Pace Pharmaceuticals, you were an asset. You aren't now. The investigation is over."

She steeled herself against this setback. "I'm innocent. We both know that. We have an opportunity to prove it, right now, and you're letting it get away."

"I'm not doing anything of the kind."

"You are. Pace sold me out, and you're turning your back."

Paul frowned. She knew he was disappointed in Ingram, not her. "C'mon, kiddo, let's get you to bed," he said to Kirsten and carried her back to her room.

Ingram was silent for a long moment. "I don't like being accused."

"I don't really care. You told me you'd protect me. You fell down on the job more than once. You left me and my family vulnerable. You owe me this courtesy."

"I don't owe you anything."

There was genuine disgust in Ingram's reply. She'd offended him, but she didn't care, as long as he did something. Tarbell had probably reached 880. At this time of night, he'd be thirty minutes from home. Ingram had less than thirty minutes to close the net on him.

"I'll go to the media. I'm sure they'd be interested in how you abdicated your responsibilities."

"I would advise against that course of action, Mrs. Farris. Pace Pharmaceuticals has already protected itself against any kind of trial, whether it be in court or by TV. If you cry foul, you'll be painted as a gold-digging opportunist who got caught with her hand in the cookie jar."

"You bastard."

"Don't blame me. I feel for you, Mrs. Farris. Truly, I do. But you were never my client. I wasn't hired to protect you. Pace hired me to protect their interests, and you aren't one of them anymore."

It was Gwen's turn to be silent. Pace had boxed her in. If she fought them, what remained of her reputation would be torn apart. She had no doubt about that. They'd promised to do that to Tarbell. Why wouldn't they do it to her? In the end, they wanted a productive workforce. It didn't matter who those people were.

"I'll be honest with you, Gwen." Ingram's tone had become almost gentle. "I believe Stephen Tarbell did assault you, but I can't prove it. I hope that means something."

"Under the circumstances, it doesn't."

Ingram sighed. "I'll talk to him and see about getting him to stop."

"See about getting him to stop? Wow, that's a great help. Please don't do me any favors."

Ingram ignored the insult and plowed on. "Call the police and report the broken window. Don't tell them about Tarbell. It won't help."

She hung up the phone in disbelief. She couldn't believe how naive she'd been. She thought if she could tie anything to Tarbell, it would make a difference.

Paul came back into the room and put his arms around her. "We don't need those people."

Paul was wrong. They needed someone. They were at Tarbell's mercy without anyone on their side.

CHAPTER TWENTY

Gwen awoke the next day feeling as if every nerve ending was exposed. It had been another night with little sleep. After Ingram had coldly given her the facts of life, the cops had arrived. A single officer to be exact. He had looked the mess and Gwen over with mild disaffection. Clearly, this broken window in the middle of the night was not inspiring him to go to the ends of the earth to bring the culprit to justice. He asked if she had any enemies. But his lazy demeanor only reinforced the fact that she had no intention of sharing. The cop handed her a report form to complete that could be mailed in and no doubt round-filed when it made it to the police department. Finally, he left, and cleanup began. They didn't have a board to cover the hole in the fragmented safety glass and had to make do with plastic sheeting and duct tape. They decided not to put a call into the insurance company, guessing that the thousand-dollar deductible would surpass the cost of replacing the window. Then it was back to bed.

The next morning, Gwen's internal body clock woke her in time for another day at the office. It took her a minute to realize that she could have slept in because there was no job to go to anymore.

She walked into the living room. The noise of the wind slapping and tugging at the plastic sheeting irritated her. She went from zero to pissed off in nothing flat. The noise reminded her that Tarbell had succeeded again at chipping away at her life.

Move on. Let it go. He's not worth it. Everyone involved in this mess had given her this advice in one form or another. It was a nice sentiment, but it was what people said when the bad thing wasn't happening to them. Well, she couldn't move on and she couldn't let go. She needed to give Tarbell a dose of his own medicine.

She dressed in jeans and a T-shirt, not bothering to shower or brush her teeth. Her hair was a tangle from a night spent tossing and turning. She pulled it back with a hair band, then grabbed her purse and keys.

Paul emerged from the bedroom, not quite awake. "Why up so early?"

"Couldn't sleep. What do you want for breakfast?"

He eyed the keys in her hand and the purse over her shoulder. She watched as a jolt of adrenaline woke him up.

"Where are you going?"

"To the store. I wanted to get some things."

"Give me a minute, and I'll come with you."

"You stay. You always go. Let me do it."

His expression said he wasn't buying what she was selling.

"I just want to be alone for a few. OK?"

It wasn't, but he said, "I'll get Kirsten up and call a glass place."

"Thanks. I won't be long."

She cut across Alameda. She didn't have much time. She had to reach Pace before Tarbell got there. There was no way she'd get past reception. She had to catch him on his way in.

She bullied her way through traffic and parked on the service road. The parking lot was partially filled with early arrivals. She scanned for Tarbell's Toyota but didn't see it. She went to pull into the parking lot, then decided against it. Her parking there could be viewed as trespassing. She wouldn't give them the satisfaction. She parked down the street and walked back. Remembering the security cameras, she kept to the trees lining the property.

She waited patiently, watching vehicles file into the parking lot. These people had been friends and coworkers yesterday. They were strangers now. None of them spotted her skulking behind a tree.

Tarbell pulled into the parking lot at exactly eight a.m. The sight of him returning to a job he didn't deserve inflamed her rage. It should be him out of a job, not her. On top of that, he should be in a jail cell, sharing quality time with the likes of Desmond Parker. Then he'd see how tough he was. She didn't wait for him to park. She cut across the parking lot, finding cover in the landscaping. She tracked his position, staying in his blind spot. He wasn't to have any warning. He'd never given her that courtesy, so why should she give it to him?

Tarbell had parked in her spot by the trash enclosure. The sick bastard probably chose it for sentimental reasons.

As he opened the door, she burst from her cover and raced up to him from behind. A jet climbing out of the airport covered the sound of her sneakers pounding the asphalt.

He turned and his eyes went wide. His shock spurred her on. He remained rooted to the spot.

She pushed out her arms and ran into him. The impact shoved him back.

She closed the space, putting her face in his. "I suppose you think you've won, don't you?"

The surprise drained from his face, and he shot her a derisive look. "I'm winning. Let's just call it that."

"Do you think you were clever last night, throwing stones at my window? I saw your car, and I saw you. Throwing stones? Really? Are you twelve?"

"Just testing the defenses, Gwen. I have more planned for you."

More? Why? What did he hope to achieve? Didn't he know he'd already won? "I thought you'd gotten what you wanted. You destroyed me."

She went to shove him again, but he caught her arms and held them outstretched. She tried to wrench them free but his strength kept her pinned.

"You're far from being destroyed, Gwen. You're bloodied and bruised, but I haven't even brought you to your knees yet. People like you—"

"People like me?"

"Yes, people like you, Gwen." His grip on her wrists intensified. She winced in pain. "You glide through life taking what isn't yours, while people like me give our all and lose every time."

She shook her head in disbelief. He'd held a knife to her throat and yet saw himself as the victim. It was unbelievable. "What did I ever take from you? When did I put a knife to your throat?"

He sneered. "People like you don't have to use knives. You have other weapons."

She was right about one thing. His perceived victimization was no more sophisticated than a child's. "If I'm a taker, then take note of this. This isn't over. Cling to your pathetic beliefs because that's all you're going to have left. You'll pay for what you did to me. I am going to make sure you do."

He jerked on her wrists, yanking her to him. "Do it, Gwen. I dare you, because you won't win. I'm rising up and pushing your kind down."

"You'll have to kill me."

He grinned. "So be it."

"Gwen," a voice called. "Gwen, what are you doing?"

Gwen snapped her head around. It was Lauren. Gwen watched as her former colleague took in the tableau before her. She knew Lauren would want an explanation. Tarbell supplied it first.

He shoved Gwen, releasing his hold on her. She stumbled back.

"Gwen, don't blame me for your mistakes. You did this to yourself."

Gwen almost smiled. Tarbell was good. She had to give him that. The scenario looked so damning. A distraught and acrimoniously fired woman returns to work the following morning looking for someone to blame and take out her frustrations on. Her ragged appearance surely didn't help matters.

"You son of a bitch," she said, disgust and admiration in her voice.

Her emotions surged out of control, but as she was swinging an arm to slap him, someone grabbed her from behind. She fought to shake herself free and a hat belonging to the security guard struck the ground at her feet. The battle was over, so she stopped fighting.

Lauren forced her way between them. Her face was filled with concern. "Gwen, stop it."

"This isn't over," Gwen said to Tarbell.

Tarbell embraced his new role as victim and backed away with his hands up. "You need help, Gwen. I'm sorry, but you do."

"Gwen, what are you doing?"

Gwen recognized Deborah's shrill voice calling across the parking lot.

Fantastic, she thought. Tarbell kept backing away, then headed for the office. Others had arrived and were gawking at the spectacle before them. They rushed to Tarbell's side to offer him support. They were finally seeing him as the victim he believed he was. *Could this get any worse?* She should retreat with what remained of her dignity, but she couldn't help herself.

"Stay away from my family, Stephen," she yelled as he retreated. "Do you hear me? Leave us alone."

Tarbell was heading into the building surrounded by a circus of newfound, protective friends. He didn't look back to acknowledge her.

Deborah blotted out Gwen's view of Tarbell. "Gwen, are you crazy? What are you doing here?" Realizing Lauren was still standing there, she said, "Can you leave us?"

This jolted Lauren out of her trance. "Oh, sure. Of course." She headed into the building. "Take it easy, Gwen. Call me. We'll go somewhere for lunch."

"If Mike releases you, are you going to be calm?" Deborah asked.

She was calm now, but saw no point in saying it and just nodded.

The security guard let go of her. Deborah asked him to give them a little space. He picked up his hat and stood a discreet distance from them but stayed close enough to wade in if trouble broke out again.

"Gwen, what were you thinking?"

"Stephen threw a rock through my window."

"I know. Robert Ingram called me last night."

Deborah knew. It looked as if everyone knew but wasn't interested in doing anything about it. She decided to cut her story short. She was playing the victim, the same card Tarbell was playing. It wasn't effective. Besides, she was finished with being the victim. Victims surrendered to their fate. She wouldn't.

"Then you know what I'm thinking," said Gwen. "You know why I'm here. I'm trying to finish what you failed to do. He just threatened to kill me."

"Enough." Deborah's command split the air. "It's over."

"It's not."

"It is as far as we're concerned." Gwen went to object, but Deborah held up her hand. "I don't want to hear it. Take your fight elsewhere. We don't want it here. At the moment, Pace plans no legal action. It's been decided to forget the incident and move on. But, if you keep this up, we will press charges."

"You're protecting him now."

"We're protecting ourselves."

Deborah waved Mike over and told him to see Gwen back to her car.

"For everybody's sake, including your own, go and don't come back."

• • •

Petersen watched the rent-a-cop walk Gwen back to her Subaru. He would have liked to have stepped in to help her when she confronted Tarbell, but Tarbell wasn't supposed to know he still had a tail, as unofficial as it was. He felt for this poor woman. His inaction had helped Tarbell dismantle her life, but he was changing that today. The shackles were off. He was free to help her nail that bastard. There was only one problem. The shackles no longer bound Tarbell either.

Gwen started her car, and he followed her to the main road. It was time to let her know someone was on her side. Together, they could construct a trap for Tarbell. It would probably involve her playing the bait, but that couldn't be helped. Tarbell wouldn't be able to resist Gwen as the bait.

He couldn't flag her down on the road. That was a limitation of not having a badge like a cop. He'd follow her to her destination, then introduce himself. He expected her to head home, but she picked up 880, then connected to I-80 East, heading for Berkeley.

He was interested to see where she was going. It could be nothing, but the unsettled feeling in his stomach told him otherwise. She headed to El Cerrito, and for an awkward second, he thought she was going to Tarbell's house; he felt relieved to see she wasn't. His relief didn't last when she pulled into the parking lot belonging to West Coast Arms.

Tarbell had pushed this woman too far and the idiot didn't see it. Both of them would get hurt if Petersen didn't step in. He parked on the street and waited until she entered the gun store before leaving his car and following her in. He arrived in time to see Gwen entering the indoor range carrying an automatic, a box of shells, and ear protection. His stomach burned again. It was obvious this wasn't Gwen's first trip to a gun range.

A bearded man behind the counter wandered toward him. "How can I help you?"

"Can I rent a weapon for some target practice?"

"Sure you can."

Petersen rented a .38 revolver and ear defenders and bought a hundred rounds and a couple of paper targets.

Besides Gwen, there was only one other person on the range. He was an athletic-looking guy shooting a competition .22 pistol. He'd tucked himself into the end booth against the wall, and his demeanor said he didn't want to be disturbed, which was fine with Petersen.

Gwen was stationed in the middle booth where the light was strongest over her head. He slipped into a booth two over from her. He didn't want to spook her by getting too close. At this point, he just wanted to observe.

He attached a paper target and sent it down to the end of the range. The target looked like a Halloween ghost flying along on its cable. He loaded the revolver with six rounds. The gun was well maintained, if unspectacular. He squeezed off six shots, taking his time, getting a feel for the weapon and letting the target settle after having each bullet hole punched through it. He was a pretty decent shot, but it took him a little time to adjust to an unfamiliar weapon. Once he had the gun's measure, he hit the mark every time. He liked the grouping he'd gotten after his first six. He popped the cylinder open and dumped the brass into the bucket next to him.

While he loaded another six into the .38, he watched Gwen. She was shooting a 9mm, from the looks of it. She was hitting the target, but there was far too much emotion going on, which under the circumstances, made a lot of sense. She aimed, fired, and fired again. She didn't steady her body, control her breathing, or wait for the recoil to pass out of her body before refiring. But despite Gwen's hurried style, emptying a ten-shot magazine faster than he shot six, she hit the target. When she brought her target back, he glanced at it. She'd hit it, but her grouping was scattered. If the target represented Tarbell, she'd hit him where it counted, but she'd more than likely hit something or someone else along the way.

He continued shooting, refining his skill with a weapon he'd never handle again, while he watched Gwen shred three more paper targets. When he noticed her packing up, he hurriedly emptied the .38 and retrieved his target, tossing it in the trash on the way out. He settled up and returned the unused rounds and equipment. He was out the door before Gwen left the range, and waited for her outside.

She emerged from the building with her head down and her mind preoccupied. He moved in and called her name. The sound of her name spooked her. She spun around, panic consuming her expression. He'd expected this reaction. There was no easy way of introducing himself. She didn't know him. He wasn't Tarbell, but he wasn't a familiar face either. He put up his hands in surrender.

"Gwen, we need to talk."

She bolted for her Subaru.

He withheld the desire to chase her. Instead, he called out, "I'm a friend of Robert Ingram's."

Ingram's name stopped her, but it didn't dislodge the hostility in her eyes. "Under the circumstances, I wouldn't call Robert Ingram a friend."

"Neither would I." He lowered his hands and slowly approached. "That's why I don't work for him anymore."

The remark helped unwind the tightly coiled spring inside Gwen.

"Gwen, can we talk? I want to help you."

Gwen unlocked her car and opened the door. "A lot of people offer their help but don't do anything for me. I'm better off without the help I've been getting recently."

"Would a picture of Stephen Tarbell busting your window last night help?"

She stopped. "You have it?"

"I've got it in my pocket. Can we go somewhere where I can show it to you?"

Gwen locked up her car, and they went to a Peet's Coffee that was housed in the mini mall. He handed her a picture he'd taken last night with his digital camera, then got the coffees. When he returned with the drinks, she wasn't quite smiling, but the weight of the world on her shoulders seemed to be gone.

"We can take this to Pace."

"You can, but it won't do you much good. It shows Tarbell breaking a window. Big deal. It's a misdemeanor." Judging from her expression, he'd punctured her good mood, but that was OK. She needed to be aware of the realities. He tapped the picture. "This represents a start. We build a case from here."

Gwen didn't look convinced.

"Who are you?"

"I'm a retired San Francisco police inspector. I used to worked for Private Security International on a contract basis. I don't anymore."

"Why?"

"I was part of the Tarbell investigation team, and I didn't like how it turned from Tarbell to you."

He'd planned on telling her how Tarbell had used him to compromise the investigation, threatened him, and gone after Lynette, but these were hardly the credentials to inspire confidence in him. He needed her to believe in him. Full disclosure could wait until this debacle was over.

"Thank you. It's nice to hear someone actually cares." Gwen looked relieved. "What are we going to do?"

"First, we're going to forget all about guns. They aren't the answer."

"Who's going to protect me—you?"

"Yes."

"Great, I had a whole security team watching over me and my family. Now I've got just you. Can you really make a difference?"

Her petulance failed to make an impact on Petersen. "Yes, I can. Do you have a gun?"

"I bought one, but I'm still waiting for clearance on the background check."

"When did you apply?"

"A week ago."

That meant she'd be a gun owner in a few days. "I'll have dealt with Tarbell before you get your gun."

"How?"

"That depends. Tell me the circumstances behind your firing and everything since he held a knife to your throat. I need to know everything."

She outlined it all in great detail. He wrote it all down in his notebook.

"Tarbell might think he's smart, but he can't avoid leaving a trail. He might not think he's left a trace, but there are footprints leading to his door. If he planted the files on your computer, he needed to have access to plant them. He's probably still got them. When he broke into your home, he probably took something. He'd want to have a trophy to remind him of his success. I just have to find it."

"So how do we find it?"

"We don't. I will."

She shot him a dubious look. "I can't pay you."

He couldn't take Gwen's money even if she offered it. He'd earned money he didn't deserve while living in the shadow of Tarbell's threats. "I'm not interested in that. It's for your own protection. I'm going to break into his home. I don't want you to be a party to that. You need an airtight alibi should there be any finger-pointing."

Gwen frowned. "If you break in and find something, is that going to be enough?"

"It'll give us a footing, but that's all."

Gwen sat back. He watched her consider everything he'd said.

"Finding evidence is one thing. But we need to catch him in the act. What are our other options?"

"Bait and trap."

A sour little smile appeared on Gwen's face. She'd connected the dots. "I guess I'm the bait."

"Yes, you are."

• • •

The call came just after lunch. "Hi Steve, it's Deborah. Could you come to Conference Room Two? I wanted to talk about the incident with Gwen this morning."

Tarbell had been expecting this call. It came a little later than he'd expected, but that was fine. "Sure, Deborah. When?"

"Now."

"Be right there."

He walked over to the conference room and let himself in without knocking. Deborah wasn't alone. That, he wasn't expecting, but he kept his surprise to himself.

"I'm sorry, Deborah. I didn't realize you were with someone."

Deborah smiled. "No, my mistake. I should have told you someone was joining us. This is Robert Ingram. He's a security consultant."

Tarbell pretended he didn't know who Ingram was. He shook hands with the man who'd unsuccessfully tried to ruin his life.

He sat down, and Deborah stood up. "Actually, I'm only here for introductions. This is a private meeting between the two of you."

Tarbell found this meeting a little disconcerting, but he showed the right level of concern to Ingram, while feeling quite confident.

"Nothing to worry about," Ingram said after Deborah left. "This is routine procedure. I get involved whenever a current or ex-employee threatens another employee."

Tarbell wondered if Gwen had received this same speech. "If you're talking about this morning, I don't think what Gwen did in the parking lot was a direct threat against me."

"Deborah told me you had to hold her off."

"Yes, but I wasn't fighting for my life or anything."

"Doesn't matter. You had to defend yourself. That's serious enough."

"Wow."

Tarbell thought he was doing a great job at playing the understanding nice guy. He hoped Ingram felt destabilized and uncertain about his motives now that he was acting like he wanted to protect a backstabbing bitch like Gwen.

Ingram broke out a notebook and poised a pen over a fresh page. "Can you tell me what happened this morning?"

"Not a lot to tell. Gwen came rushing up to me and started ranting and raving about getting fired."

"Why'd she pick on you?"

"She thinks I had something to do with it."

Ingram looked up from his note taking and smiled. "Which you didn't?"

Tarbell smiled back. He had to play it careful. "No. She's just looking for someone to blame, I guess."

"I can tell you the one person who was responsible for Gwen's termination, and that's Gwen."

It was music to Tarbell's ears. He almost asked Ingram to repeat himself just so he could enjoy the moment again.

"That's sad."

"It is. I hear there's been some animosity between you and Gwen. Can you tell me about that?"

Hmm, I wonder where you heard that little tidbit from, he thought. "Well, I can't say we were the best of buds, but I wouldn't call it animosity. I didn't always agree with her, but we did our jobs."

Ingram nodded and noted the response in his notebook. "So you didn't throw a rock through the window of Mrs. Farris's home last night?"

"Wow. Um, no. I didn't break her window. Why would I?"

Breaking Gwen's window was a petty thing to do, but it had been necessary to test PSI's interest level. After Gwen's termination, Petersen said the surveillance on him had been dropped. Before he tried anything serious, he had to know for sure. If he broke Gwen's window, who would come running? He'd even made sure Gwen saw him leaving. If PSI was still after him, all they had on him was destruction of private property—a misdemeanor. At worst, they'd force him to pay for the window. It was a small price to pay to know where he stood.

He felt Ingram appraising him.

"Mrs. Farris claims she saw you drive away from her home last night."

"Well, it wasn't me. I can't believe she said that."

"Can anyone verify your whereabouts last night?"

"Not really. I was at home, but I live alone."

"That's OK. A case of sour grapes." Ingram closed his notebook. "Because of today, I'm recommending that Pace obtain a restraining order against Gwen covering this building, its employees, and specifically you. She won't be able to come within a hundred feet of you."

While the idea of a restraining order against Gwen was an exquisite twist, Tarbell worried it might work against his plans. He shook his head. "Is that necessary?"

"I think so. That would also mean that you or anyone else listed in the restraining order cannot encounter or contact Mrs. Farris. The judge wouldn't like it."

Tarbell held back a smile. It was a shrewd move on Ingram's part, but it wouldn't stop him. "Why would I want to contact Gwen?"

"Why would you?" Ingram rose to his feet. "That concludes our business, Mr. Tarbell."

Tarbell shook Ingram's hand. The investigator gripped his hand harder than necessary. "This has been an unfortunate turn of events. By all accounts, Gwen Farris was a good and hard-working employee."

"Yes, it's very sad."

Tarbell went to release Ingram's hand, but the investigator tightened his grip.

"I consider this case closed, Mr. Tarbell. I don't want to receive any further reports of damage to Mrs. Farris's property. Do I make myself clear?"

"I don't know what you're talking about."

"Let's keep it that way, Mr. Tarbell."

It was pretty easy to read between the lines. Stay away from Gwen and nothing would happen. Ingram's veiled threat told him he was now free to do as he wished. He smiled.

"That won't be a problem."

CHAPTER TWENTY-ONE

"No," Lynette said vehemently. "I'm not going anywhere."

Petersen's attempt to sit Lynette down over breakfast and calmly tell her she needed to leave town for a few days had crashed and burned. Now that he was going after Tarbell, he was leaving himself open to retaliation, and Tarbell might do more than shove Lynette down an escalator.

"All the years you were on the job, you never asked me to leave town, so don't tell me it doesn't mean anything now. I knew something was wrong. Tell me what this is about."

He'd tried not to wear his heart on his sleeve, but Lynette's fall down the escalator had scared him, and it showed. No one had ever come after him before. It frightened him how easily it had been done.

There was no way he was going to get Lynette out of the kitchen, let alone out of town, without cluing her in on what happened.

"Is it this job you've been working?"

"Yes, it is."

His admission took the hard edge off of Lynette's expression. "But I thought it was over."

"Officially, it is."

She reached across the table and laid a hand on his. It was warm from holding her coffee cup. "What's gone wrong?"

"The subject I was following learned who I was."

"What do you mean 'learned'? Who is this man?"

"It doesn't matter how he did it or who he is. All that matters is that he knows who I am and where I live."

"And me?"

"Yes."

Her hand lost its heat against his. He'd scared her. That was good. Feeling scared would keep her vigilant.

"That's why I need you to go away."

"Will he come after me?"

"He's after me, but if he can't get to me, he might go after you to get to me. You know how these things work."

She nodded.

He'd yet to tell her the truth about her fall down the escalator. He would, but only after Tarbell was in jail. He needed her scared enough to be cautious, not panicked.

"What are you going to do?"

He grinned. "I'll do what I always do, catch the son of a bitch."

She forced a smile. "How long will all this take?"

"Not long. Today, we're putting an operation together to hook this fish. It won't take long after that. No more than a week."

She frowned. "If he's the fish, does that make you the bait?"

"No, it makes me the fisherman."

Her smile was warmer this time around.

"What do you need me to do?"

"Go to Tahoe. Take your sister. She doesn't need much of an excuse to go gamble." Lynette frowned at him, but he steamrolled over her disapproval. "Check in under her name. Don't call me. I'll call you. OK?"

She nodded.

"Good girl." He leaned in and kissed her.

He helped her pack while she called her sister and loaded her bags into the car with J. Edgar. The dog made for a good early-warning system should Tarbell come for him, but he wasn't about to put his dog at risk.

He watched Lynette drive off, and as soon as she disappeared from sight, he checked his watch. He was behind schedule, but he could make up the time.

He drove over to Eric Biden's place. Biden was the whiz Ingram used when it came to electronic surveillance. They'd worked a few jobs together and got along well. The day before, Biden had agreed to lend Petersen everything needed to wire up Gwen's house. Biden offered to do the install, but Petersen turned his offer down.

Loading the equipment into Petersen's car, Biden asked, "Is this a PSI job?"

"No, private. I don't want word getting back, so keep it to yourself."

"Sure. No problem."

"Thanks. I'll get all this stuff back to you in a week."

"Just remember, you break it, you buy it."

Petersen thanked Biden and headed over to Gwen's home. Paul had been resistant to his involvement when they'd met yesterday, but he was far more accommodating when Petersen arrived with Biden's equipment. He and Paul worked together installing the cameras in the main rooms, the yard and over the entrance to the house. Gwen and Kirsten acted as models to help set up the cameras. Should Tarbell approach or enter the house, he'd be caught on tape. Petersen set up the recording equipment in the garage and hid it under the usual garage bric-a-brac. It was a good setup. Tarbell wouldn't know what hit him until he was in jail.

There was a buoyant mood in the house. Petersen understood it. It was a long time since any of them had something to smile about. Tarbell would walk into this trap, and it was going to be sweet when it happened.

He was in the kitchen packing his tools into a sports bag when Gwen came in with Kirsten in her arms and Paul behind her.

"Now what?" Gwen asked

"I want the cameras running 24-7. Don't turn them off when you're in the house. If Tarbell strikes, we want him on tape. Swap the tapes out. Watch them if you like. If you don't see Tarbell, then record over them. OK?"

Gwen looked over at Paul. He nodded. "Sure," she said.

"Good. I'm going to Tarbell's to see what I can find. Hopefully, I'll find something that connects him either to the break-in or the computer files."

"Do you have someone watching your back?" Paul asked.

Petersen thought of Reggie Glover. He'd almost called him last night for backup, but he couldn't do that to Reggie. The guy still worked for PSI. He needed the paychecks to put his youngest through UC Berkeley. If they caught him breaking into Tarbell's, his kid could kiss a college education good-bye.

"Not on this one, but I'm fine." "Fine" came in the guise of a .45 from his days on the SFPD. Whenever he was primary through a door, he wanted the stopping power at his trigger finger.

"Let me come with you," Paul said.

"No. I need you guys to have an alibi. The moment I leave here, you should go somewhere public. Take in a movie, eat out somewhere, go to the zoo."

"Can we really go to the zoo?" Kirsten asked. "The one with the choo-choo?"

"Sure, sweetie, we can go there."

"Keep any receipts. They'll be time coded. Make sure you're remembered. I don't want anything coming back on you. Got it?"

"It makes sense, but I don't like it," Paul said.

"None of us do, I'm afraid," Petersen conceded. He saw himself out. Gwen followed him out to his car, alone. He put his sports bag in the back of his brother-in-law's Mazda.

"You be careful."

He smiled. "I will. Now get out of here, and keep your cell on. If I find something, I'll want to ask you about it."

She smiled back. "OK."

Petersen headed over to Tarbell's house in El Cerrito and parked a block away. He didn't want any neighbors seeing him walk up to the house. He grabbed the dog leash off the passenger seat for cover. If anyone asked what he was doing in their neighborhood, he was looking for his dog. It was a cheap trick, but it had worked for him before. He walked past Tarbell's home, scanning his surroundings for ways to gain safe entry to his property. An alley would have made access easy, but no such luck. He needed to find a way into the backyard.

Petersen liked the look of the house next door. There was a fence separating the two homes but no side gate, so there was a clear path to the backyard. And judging from the empty driveway and lights off in the house, Tarbell's neighbors weren't home.

He went up to the front door and rang the doorbell. While he waited for someone to answer, he studied the houses across the street. A car was parked in the driveway of one, but the other driveways were empty. He watched for curtain movement, but didn't see any. Things were looking good.

No one answered the door, and he wandered into the backyard. A tree in the corner of the yard made it easy for Petersen to clamber over the fence. He landed on all fours in Tarbell's yard, feeling the impact through his joints. He paused for a moment before getting to his feet.

He used a lock pick gun to open the patio door and let himself in. He checked his watch. It was a little after three. Tarbell liked working late. Even if he left at five on the dot, he wouldn't be home until six, but Tarbell wasn't who he had to worry about. He had to be away before the neighbors came home. He decided to leave by four thirty, whether he'd completed his search or not. He could always come back tomorrow.

He pulled on a pair of latex gloves before he touched anything in the house. Tarbell kept a neat home. He even made the bed before he left for work in the morning. The living room was a little stark—just a sofa, a lounger, a couple of bookshelves, a rolltop desk, and a TV. He seemed to eat well, judging from the ingredients in the fridge. There were no TV dinners in the freezer. Despite having three bedrooms and living alone, there was no guest room. One room had been converted into an office, and a home gym occupied the other.

He went to the office first. He switched on a laptop sitting on a desk. While he waited for the machine to boot up, he picked through the contents of the drawer and found a CD holder. From the cover artwork, it was easy to see it was spy software.

He called Gwen's cell. "Hey, where are you?"

"San Francisco Zoo."

He heard Kirsten's excited voice in the background.

"I'm at Tarbell's. I've found spy software. I don't know much about this stuff, but I do know it could be used to intercept e-mail and even send e-mails from your machine remotely."

"God, there's no stopping him."

"Yes, there is. These files Pace claimed you'd sent from your machine. What are some of the file names?"

He noted the file names down in his notebook. "Great. I'll get back to you."

He trawled the contents of Tarbell's laptop and for what-ever files the spy software had retrieved from Gwen's computer. He wasn't bad when it came to technology, but he was slow. He knew there was gold on the hard drive, but like gold, it was hard to extract. Finally, he found a directory entitled "GFarris." It looked as if the software had recorded every keystroke of Gwen's computer. It had captured a mind-boggling amount of data, especially considering the short period time it had been in opera-tion. The date stamps tracked back to days after Gwen's assault. Tarbell possessed a complete record of e-mail, visited Web sites, and every opened and saved file.

"Gotcha," Petersen growled. Listed among the files in the directory were the research files Gwen had supposedly stolen.

He called Gwen to tell her the news. "I found the files. They're on his laptop. We've got him, Gwen. We've got him."

"Are you taking the computer?"

"No. These need to be found legally. I'll talk to Ingram and get him over here."

"Thanks, Tom. I don't know how to thank you."

"We're a long way from the champagne stage, but we're getting there. I'm going to finish my search. I'll come by later tonight, hopefully by nine."

"OK."

He hung up, then printed off screen dumps of the file directories and snapped pictures of the spy software in the desk drawer. After he'd taken his pictures and pocketed his printouts, he replaced everything exactly where he'd found it and shut down the computer.

He checked his watch. His deadline to leave was closing in.

He searched for keepsakes. This guy was bound to have a trophy or two as a reminder of his triumph. He went from room to room but found nothing.

"Don't be the exception," he murmured. He checked his watch. He was running out of time. "Composure, Tom," he told himself. "Think like him."

There'd be a shrine for his mementos. It might be a safe-deposit box, but Petersen didn't think so. Tarbell would want to keep his prizes close so he had access to them at any time.

He'd come across a couple of shrines kept by criminals in his time. He'd uncovered one in a basement and another in a storage unit. These displays were often hidden away. He grabbed the stepladder from the garage and peered inside the attic space. The roof's shallow pitch made access impossible for anyone over two feet tall. His flashlight picked up nothing but fiberglass insulation.

It occurred to him that Tarbell didn't need a private place for his shrine. He wasn't a married guy hiding his dark secret from his family and friends. Tarbell didn't have any. This house was his fortress. Nobody was welcome. Because of that, he didn't have to hide his goodies away. He could keep them handy.

He'd searched every room except the living room. He went to the rolltop desk. It was a beautiful piece of antique furniture, but an odd thing to have in the room. He tugged on the brass handhold. The rolltop wasn't locked, and he slid the top back.

He didn't find a shrine, but he did find something. He put it down to Tarbell being new at this. Given time and confidence, a sick, twisted guy like Tarbell would surely create a display bigger than the rolltop could contain. For now, he possessed just one item—a large photo of the Farris family. Their faces had been crossed out with a thick Sharpie. Gwen's face had been crossed out time and time again. Petersen felt cold in the warm room.

He didn't touch the picture. Fingerprints marred the photo's glossy finish and he didn't want to contaminate this perfect piece of evidence. Tarbell was toast.

He brought out his digital camera. He snapped three shots of the photo in situ, then called Gwen again. She answered on the first ring.

"Have you got something?" Gwen asked, the screeching of birds loud in the background.

"You said nothing was taken from the break-in. Are you sure?"

"Yes."

"I found a photograph of you, Paul, and Kirsten. It's the three of you on the beach. It looks recent judging from Kirsten's age." He left the part out about their faces being crossed out. "Where did you keep the picture—at work or at home?"

He prayed she'd say at home. If Tarbell had stolen the photo from Gwen's home, it put him in the house during the break-in.

"Oh my God," Gwen said. "It hung in our home office. It was taken this summer."

Petersen grinned. He had the prick. "Great. We've got him. I'll meet you back at your house at nine to go over what I've got."

He hung up. "Gotcha, dickhead."

His delight lasted only a second. He sensed movement behind him and spun around in time to be smacked across the temple with a wine bottle. The bottle remained intact, but the searing impact put him on his back.

The left side of his face ballooned in seconds, forcing his eye shut. His vision in his right eye was reduced to a blur, but he could still make out Tarbell standing over him, holding the bottle at his side.

Tarbell raised the weapon. Petersen crossed his arms in front of his face to protect himself, but Tarbell hurled it away and dropped on top of him. Petersen, his senses in shambles, tried to hold Tarbell off, but he lacked the coordination and the strength to fight.

Tarbell slapped Petersen's arms aside and grabbed him by the throat. His long, spindly fingers dug deep into Petersen's neck, and his thumbs cut deep into his Adam's apple. The effect was immediate. Petersen wretched, choking on air going stale in his lungs.

Petersen snatched Tarbell's wrists and wrenched at them, but his grip was too strong to dislodge.

"Lies," Tarbell snarled. "You people keep lying to me. Everyone wants to deceive me. Everyone wants to ruin me. That's not going to happen, Tom. It has to stop, and it has to stop with you."

Petersen didn't know what the hell Tarbell was ranting about and he didn't care. The guy was on a rampage, and he was in his way.

Tarbell squeezed harder. A frightening noise escaped Petersen's throat. People didn't make that kind of noise and live. Panic electrified him and a burst of strength flooded his limbs.

He kicked out to buck Tarbell off and gouged at Tarbell's wrists with his fingers.

They were valiant but futile attempts. His efforts only served to spur Tarbell on. His grip never wavered. Petersen's view of the world turned black.

CHAPTER TWENTY-TWO

Tarbell stared at Petersen's dead, battered face. He was calm now. He didn't even have the strength to stand. His anger had bled out as the enormity of what he'd done started sinking in. He'd killed someone. He hadn't meant to kill Petersen, but he couldn't help himself. Fury had blinded him, and he'd literally gotten swept up in the moment. It was a weak defense, but it was the truth. This wasn't supposed to have happened.

"What were you doing here, Tom?"

He'd come so close to missing this invasion. After his meeting with Ingram, he hadn't been able to focus on his work. The man's limp-wristed attempt to warn him off Gwen needled him. It told him so much. Despite his attempts to exonerate himself and condemn Gwen, Ingram still believed some part of her original story. He'd wondered how much and left early. He bought himself a pass by telling Josh Hanson, his new boss, that he wanted to avoid any unpleasantness should Gwen return. Hanson folded to his lie like a cardboard box in the rain.

He wouldn't have suspected anything if it hadn't been for the camera flashes inside the darkened house. He was just about to hit the garage door opener when he saw them. The whir of the motor would have given whomever was inside advanced warning, so he pulled up on the street, entered the house through the kitchen, and grabbed the wine bottle off the countertop. Petersen was too busy talking on the phone to hear him creep up.

Tarbell gazed at Petersen's unmoving form on the floor. He guessed he should have expected something like this. Petersen spied on people. How could someone like that be trusted? Plus, Ingram made a living from people's mistrust of one another. So of course they'd tried to sell him a dummy. It was insulting to think he was that stupid.

His disgust waned suddenly. Why had Ingram warned him off if he'd planted Petersen for a second round of surveillance? It didn't make sense. It was a dumb move on Ingram's part, and he wasn't dumb.

He looked at Petersen's still form. *Was the investigation still active?* Tarbell wondered. For the first time, he regretted killing Petersen. Having to piece things together from a corpse made things harder but not impossible.

He jumped to his feet and rushed for the window. He'd taken his eye off the ball. He hadn't been watching for Ingram's people since Gwen had been fired. He looked for the familiar Durango or some other vehicle new to his street and saw only his neighbors' vehicles.

He went through Petersen's pockets for answers and found a set of keys belonging to a Mazda. It was a devious move on Petersen's part, dumping his Audi. He tried to remember if he'd noticed a Mazda following him of late and didn't remember one. He'd look for it later. It wouldn't be far away, and he needed to get rid of it before it got towed.

He separated the personal items from the impersonal. Along with the gun, he would keep Petersen's cash and the lock pick gun. The driver's license, credit cards, and everything that led directly to Petersen he would discard. He hoped to find a notebook or some other record, but the digital camera served as the only explanation for Petersen's visit. He scanned through the pictures, deleting them before tossing it on the pile for destruction.

He picked up the cell phone. It had ended up under the sofa after flying from Petersen's hand. He liked cell phones. They left an easily traceable trail of information. He sifted through Petersen's recent calls. He'd been calling one number a lot. He hit redial.

Gwen answered. "What is it, Tom?"

Betrayal yet again. His hand tightened around the phone until his knuckles shone white.

"Tom? Are you there?"

He hurled the phone across the room, and it smashed against the wall.

He didn't have to ask what had happened. It was obvious. Birds of a feather, he thought. Two people living under the same oppression flocked together to survive.

He felt somewhat safe. Ingram and company weren't seconds away from busting down his door. They'd written him off. They had a result for their client, and their client was happy enough to take no further action. Gwen, as usual, proved to be the problem. She might run to the cops if she suspected this kind of foul play. It wouldn't be a bright move on her part, since she'd have to explain the breaking and entering, but he could see her doing it. He blamed himself for that. He'd robbed her of a lot, so what did she have to lose?

Petersen had to disappear. Gwen could claim a lot of things, but without a body, all claims lost their foundation. Tarbell had the perfect spot for him.

He went out to his car on the street, drove it into the garage and closed the door. He popped the trunk and left it open before grabbing a roll of duct tape on his way back into the house.

He wrapped Petersen in the rug he'd fallen on and taped it in place.

More by luck than design, it was a pretty clean kill. Strangulation was a smart move. It left no blood behind. The rug was the only thing with traces of Petersen's presence and that was going. Petersen had even worn gloves, leaving no prints behind. The lack of cops on Tarbell's doorstep proved Petersen hadn't been seen entering his home. The guy had never been here.

He dragged Petersen's body through the living room and kitchen into the garage. The rug moved effortlessly over the hardwood and tile floors. Things got harder in the garage. Petersen was heavy for his size, an old guy who carried excess weight. The rug complicated matters. It made maneuvering and manhandling the body difficult and lifting the corpse into the trunk of the car nearly impossible.

Unease set in as the idea of being caught trying to manhandle Petersen's corpse into his trunk. Adrenaline flowed, giving him the strength to lift Petersen into the car. He was forced to cut the duct tape and fold Petersen's body differently inside the thick rug to fit the bundle inside the trunk, but he managed. He slammed the lid with a satisfying thud.

He bagged up Petersen's items for destruction and slung them in the passenger foot well. He threw a shovel on the backseat and reversed out of his garage. The second his wheels touched the street, Petersen was no longer a problem.

He picked up the freeway and joined the rush hour traffic. Trickling along with the vehicles on their way home, he felt conspicuous, since the car sat low on its springs at the back, but the feeling didn't last. He just looked like someone with the trunk loaded up. Progress was slow, but that was fine. He wasn't in a rush.

It was well after six when he turned into the driveway of the Vallejo house. He parked behind the house so his activities wouldn't be visible from the street.

The back of the property dropped away toward the water in the far distance. The property line didn't stretch all the way to the water, but it went far enough. He grabbed a shovel from the backseat and walked out toward the water. When he lost sight of the road, he dug. He hammered away at the dry earth. It came up, but it took its toll on his hands. Even through his gloves, he felt his hands blister.

The grave took time to dig. He felt the sun's heat at his back disappear as it disappeared over the horizon. He watched the orange and purple sunset turn to night before the hole was deep enough. It wasn't graveyard depth, but it was deep enough for Petersen. He climbed out of the grave and drove the car to the hole. Even though his hands had forced themselves into claws and his back screamed in agony every time he bent over, it was easy to pull Petersen from the trunk.

The body hit the ground with a thud. Tarbell unrolled him from his rug cocoon. He stripped off Petersen's shoes, belt, and anything else that would take time to decompose before shoving him into the hole.

The color had bled from his face. He was no longer a freshly dead man. His change was hypnotic. Tarbell felt he could watch Petersen's metamorphosis for hours, but he snapped himself out of his reverie.

He filled the grave. It stood out no matter how he disguised it, but that didn't worry him too much. No one came to this property, and the freshly turned earth couldn't be seen from the street. He put his faith in the elements. Fall would bring rain that would wash his tracks away. The sun would bake the ground dry in no time; and wild grasses would grow over it.

He loaded up his car and drove it back to the house. He sat on the back porch, watching the movement of the water and the ships cutting through it. Sweat covered his body. He let it cool against his skin. The hard physical labor had worked the shock of what he'd done out of his system.

Killer, he thought. He let the word work its way through his head. He'd joined a select group of people. It wasn't a group he'd wished to join. He had no problem intimidating people or inflicting a little pain, like he had with Gwen and Amanda Norton. It was the only way to get things done these days. To survive in this world, you had to be tough, and to get ahead you had to be tougher than the next guy. It was a speech his father had trotted out time and time again to explain his bruised knuckles. It hadn't impressed Tarbell back then, but he'd learned to believe it over time. But killing was a different thing. It far exceeded shoving someone aside to achieve a goal.

He'd crossed a legal and moral line and there was no going back. He was a killer. It was a title that would forever be attached to him. As his shock subsided, he expected guilt to fill the emotional gap, but it didn't. A void was being left. He'd killed, but killing came a lot easier than he might have expected. He could do it again if he had to. If he wanted to.

And oddly, he did.

He blamed Gwen for this fresh need. She'd turned him into a killer. She hadn't put his hands around Petersen's neck, but if it weren't for her, Petersen would be alive. He wouldn't pay for Petersen's death. Gwen would. It was only fair. Killing her would make things right.

The thought stopped him. There it was. The need to kill. Only a few hours after taking his first life, he wanted to take another. The odd thing was the need didn't bother him. He'd reached a place where rules and laws no longer applied. He would do what he needed to do. He could almost hear his father's approval. At last, he'd attained the kind of manhood his father had beaten into him inside this house. It would have given him an emotional boost twenty years ago. Now it didn't matter. He didn't give a damn about his father's approval anymore.

So Gwen was to suffer and die. It would happen, but not just yet. Some other scores had to be settled first.

• • •

Gwen sat on the sofa with Kirsten asleep at her side. The TV was playing footage from the surveillance cameras, but she wasn't taking it in. Petersen was late. He said he'd come by the house at nine, but it was after ten. Gwen had called his cell twice, but the calls went straight to voice mail. She had a bad feeling about his no show.

She grabbed her cell to call yet again, because Paul had the phone tied up. A headhunter had called while they'd been out at the zoo. Paul had been on the phone for ten minutes. She took it as a good sign, but Petersen's absence was sapping any potential good news.

She hung up on her call to Petersen when Paul came out of the office with a smile on his face. She tried to match it but came up short.

"What they'd say?" she asked.

"I have an interview Monday."

"That's great."

"You don't sound too happy for me."

She had to stop dwelling on the negative. Lord knew they needed something to be positive about. She stood up and embraced him.

"I'm sorry. You're right. I'm just a bit drained. It's great news."

"What's the great news?" Kirsten asked. Gwen had awoken her from her doze.

"Daddy has a job interview"

Kirsten squealed and jumped up and down. "Daddy's got a job."

He picked her up. "No, not a job, just the interview."

"But you'll get it."

"You know what, I think I will get it. I talked to the architect. We hit it off. I have a good feeling about it."

Gwen smiled. She liked seeing Paul's enthusiasm. It had been a while since she'd seen him that confident. "It's about time something went our way."

Paul pulled Gwen to him for a three-way hug. It felt good, but she couldn't relax. She slipped away and picked up the phone. She called Petersen's number and got voice mail again.

Paul put Kirsten down. "Petersen?"

Gwen nodded. "I've called his cell and his home number. There's no answer."

"Leave it for tonight. He's probably tied up with something or went home to be with his family."

"But wouldn't he have called if he was changing plans?"

Paul shrugged. "You don't know the guy that well. Maybe he isn't very reliable."

Gwen didn't, but she knew how dedicated he was. He didn't want Tarbell getting away with his crimes any more than she did. He would have called if he couldn't make the appointment.

"It's the picture, isn't it?"

Petersen had scared her when he told her Tarbell had a photo of them. She knew the photo he'd described, and there was no way Tarbell could have come into possession of it without stealing it. The second she'd gotten home from the zoo, she searched for the photo. It was missing. It was nice to have the validation that she wasn't going out of her mind and to prove that Tarbell had broken into her home, but it came at a chilling price.

"It's not just that."

"Then what is it?"

"What if something's happened?"

Paul frowned and put Kirsten down. "Nothing's happened. The guy knows what he's doing. He went there while Tarbell was at work, and he said he was leaving after he called about the photo."

It all made sense, but the last call she'd gotten didn't. Petersen's name had come up on the caller ID, but he didn't speak before hanging up. It hadn't meant much at the time, but his missing their meeting had changed that. What if he'd hung up on her because he spotted Tarbell coming his way?

"So what do you want to do?" Paul asked.

"Check on him."

"What does that mean?"

Paul had a hard edge to his voice. She didn't let it put her off. "Go by Tarbell's house."

Paul shook his head. "I should say no, but I'm not going to because you're not going to let this go."

She smiled. "Thank you. I won't be long."

"No way. If you go, we all go." Gwen went to object, but he cut her off. "I've let you cut me out of this long enough. We know what Tarbell is capable of, so you don't run off alone anymore."

She couldn't deter him. Not this time. Too much had happened to brush him aside anymore. "OK," she said.

There was no time for a babysitter, so Kirsten had to come with them. Gwen was hesitant about bringing her, but Paul was insistent. It wasn't hard for Gwen to read between the lines. He wanted her to see the risks she was taking. It worked. Strapping her daughter into the car seat left her queasy.

They took Paul's car as a precaution. Tarbell knew her Subaru too well, and she didn't want to tip him off in any way. Paul drove. The poor kid was dog tired and was asleep within minutes.

They traveled in silence. Gwen yearned for conversation to take her mind off her thoughts.

Paul slowed to a halt across from Tarbell's house. They were close enough to see the home but hopefully not to be seen by Tarbell. The lights were on inside, but it was difficult to see anything beyond that.

Gwen searched for the Mazda Petersen had been driving. "I don't see his car."

"I can't see him parking it close."

Paul put the car in drive and circled the neighboring blocks. Gwen still didn't see Petersen's Mazda. Paul returned to the spot across from Tarbell's house.

"Well, that tells you something," Paul said.

It does, but what? she thought. She'd gone into this venture with Petersen more than a little blind.

"OK, it looks like Tarbell is home, and Petersen isn't around," Paul said. "Now what? Do we knock on Tarbell's door?"

Paul's sarcasm struck the wrong nerve with her. "I can do without the attitude. We don't know where Petersen is and that's not a good thing. Not with Tarbell's track record."

Gwen's sharp tone roused Kirsten but only for a second. She asked where she was but was asleep again before either of them could answer her.

"OK, sorry," Paul said. "But the question of 'now what?' still stands. There's no way we can knock on the door."

"I know. I can't shake the feeling that something's happened."

"We can't sit out here all night. That means we're going to have to be a little sneaky. Give me the recorder from the glove compartment."

Paul kept a digital recorder he used when he was working. He recorded to-do lists and downloaded them when he got home. Gwen removed the recorder he hadn't had to use for over a year. The batteries had long since gone flat inside. She didn't understand why he needed it, but he took it from her and removed a legal pad he kept between the seat and the center console.

"What are you doing?"

He grinned. "Do I look like a member of the media?"

"No."

He grinned even wider. "I'll be back in a minute."

He walked to a house near Tarbell's; it still had its lights on. He knocked on the door and when someone answered, he went inside. Gwen's heart pounded. He was taking this risk for her. She became suddenly aware of how he must have felt during this entire ordeal. She'd been trying to protect him by keeping him in the dark. But he wasn't going to let her get away with it.

He emerged from the house a minute later. He smiled and waved at the woman who'd answered the door. The second she closed the door on him, he jogged back to the car.

"What did you do?" she asked.

"You said Petersen might have been caught, but that didn't mean Tarbell caught him. I went to that house and told them I was a reporter for the *Contra Costa Times* and I heard there was a break-in on the street, but I didn't know where."

"That's brilliant. What did she say?"

"That it hadn't happened. If the cops had lifted Petersen for breaking into Tarbell's place, there would have been plenty of attention."

It was a good point. They'd picked up plenty of spectators when Tarbell burglarized their home.

"Petersen doesn't seem to have run into any trouble here."

The news failed to bring Gwen any comfort. It still didn't explain why Petersen wasn't answering his phone. Not when he'd seemed so committed to calling her with every fresh discovery.

"Let's stay here for a while. I want to see what Tarbell does."

Paul was silent for a moment. "I'm going to say something you're not going to like."

Gwen didn't say anything.

"We're out here, stalking Tarbell. Tell me, what's the difference between this and what he's been doing to us?"

Gwen didn't have an answer.

After waiting thirty minutes with nothing happening, they drove over to Petersen's house. It sat in darkness.

"Doesn't look like anyone's home," Paul said.

"No," Gwen said and slipped from the car.

Paul followed her to the front door, and he rang the doorbell. No one stirred inside.

"I hate to say it, but I think your guy flaked out on you."

CHAPTER TWENTY-THREE

"Hey, it must be Saturday because you're here to screw up my day," Dennis Tarbell said when his son entered the living room.

Lupe had warned Tarbell that his father was in one of his moods before she left. Normally, it would have parked a black cloud over his head, but not today. Nothing his father had to say would make a dent. He was feeling too good about life. His father's bitching was just an annoying buzzing—a fly that needed swatting.

Killing Petersen had been the best thing he'd ever done. Taking a person's life had filled him with a confidence he'd never known. He should have killed someone sooner. It could have changed his life. Bosses complained he never exhibited the kind of confidence that they needed. They described him as antisocial. Since killing Petersen, he'd become more friendly and tolerant. If someone screwed up at work or cut him off on the freeway, he let it go. Their shortcomings weren't his.

Petersen helped his mood, too. Well, not Petersen per se, but Petersen's insignificance. The man had been murdered, and it didn't seem to matter. No one had come knocking on his door to complain or throw out accusations. He put it down to his first-class character assassination of Gwen. They were more likely to point fingers at her than him these days.

"You want something to drink, Dad?"

"I'd kill for a smoke."

He took that as a no and sat on the sofa. His dad wheeled his chair in his direction. His eyes sparkled with a disdain that amazed Tarbell. Didn't he ever take a mirror to himself? He could no longer sit up upright. His pallor turned the stomach of anyone looking his way. His breathing was labored even with the oxygen tubes trailing from his nose, and he was in a wheelchair. He wasn't the unstoppable figure pictured in the yellowed photographs on the wall. *How did this man ever frighten me?* Tarbell wondered.

"What do you think of me, Dad?"

Dennis snorted. "Do you really want to know?"

"Yes, I do."

"You're a disappointment. Not a small disappointment but a big fucking disappointment. The kind that makes me wish I'd never fathered a child."

It was a performance for the cheap seats. That was just what Tarbell was in the mood for.

"How am I a disappointment?"

"What the fuck is wrong with you? Do you want to be humiliated? Because if you do, I can do that for you. That's how much you sicken me with your presence."

Tarbell enjoyed needling his father with simple questions. It stood to reason that a Luddite like him couldn't handle conversation.

"I just want to know how I've disappointed you."

"Why?"

"It's important to me."

Dennis shook his head. "If you want to know, I'll tell you. Just get me a drink first, and make it a real drink."

Tarbell saw no point in denying the man booze. It wasn't like it could make his quality of life any worse. He got up and fixed his dad a whiskey. It was some Jack Daniel's knockoff, cheap and nasty, just like his father. He put the half-filled tumbler on the lap tray crossing Dennis's wheelchair.

He retook his seat while his dad gulped down half the cheap booze in one shot. His father's expression was close to rapture even though the drink forced a coughing fit.

"You're still a disappointment, but more acts of kindness like that and I might just forgive you your problems."

"What problems?"

"You're weak. You let people walk all over you. Hell, you let me, a fucking invalid, walk all over you."

"Anything else?"

"Sure. I've got a million of them." He swigged the whiskey. "You don't drink. I never trust anyone who doesn't drink."

It was a piece of homespun wisdom that made no sense. For all his father's so-called strength, he couldn't handle anyone who could abstain from drink. It was a twisted point of view.

"What else?"

"You don't do man's work. Men build things. They leave their mark on the world. They don't fuck around in labs with test tubes and white rats like some kind of Frankenstein. I bet you get a kick out of killing the small animals. Yeah, I bet you do."

Tarbell saw more of his father's insecurities. He was poorly educated. Tarbell was the first of his family to go to college. Dennis made it clear when the college acceptance came through that if Tarbell went, he'd receive no financial support. Tarbell had put himself through. It was his first act of defiance. How it must have stuck in the old man's throat.

"You're not married. Are you queer? I know I've asked you, but you never give me a straight answer." He laughed at the use of the word *straight* when asking if Tarbell was gay or not.

"Would it matter if I was gay?"

"Sure it would. It would make bringing you up a waste of time, not that it hasn't been already."

"I'm not gay."

"Then why don't you have a woman?"

"Because I don't want one."

"Yeah, right." He picked up his glass and finished off the whiskey. "You don't want one because you don't like them."

"I like women as much as you do, Dad."

Dennis's hand tightened around the glass. "What's that supposed to mean?"

"You slapped Mom around a lot for a guy who loved women."

Dennis hurled the glass at him. There was little heat behind the throw. It missed its target by six inches and bounced off the wall without breaking. Twenty years ago that glass would have hit him square between the eyes at sixty miles an hour.

"You watch your mouth, boy. Are you trying to piss me off? If you are, it isn't working."

Watching his father breathe heavily, Tarbell begged to differ.

"When your mother got out of line, it took a slap to put her back in her place."

Tarbell found it hard to disagree with this point. His mother did step out of line a lot, a line his father was forever redefining, making it impossible for anyone to stay on the right side of it. The beatings had sickened Tarbell, not only because of the violence inflicted upon someone he loved, but because of his mother's reaction. As soon as Dennis drew back a fist to strike, the lights went out in his mother's eyes. She retreated to a place within herself where Dennis couldn't touch her. It was how the weak survived but not how they triumphed. The bigger fist always won.

"So how else do I disappoint you?"

"You're nothing like me."

His father made it so easy for him. "That makes me very happy."

"You fucking piece of shit," Dennis said and tried to wheel himself forward. Despite his excited state, he didn't have the strength to move, and he gave up.

"I'm glad I've disappointed you, Dad. I would hate to think I brought you any feelings of pride."

"Well, you didn't."

"I have no desire to be like a man who covered his inadequacies with violence and intimidation."

"You ungrateful—"

"Shut up." Tarbell watched his father boil behind his silence. "You're disappointed in me because I wasn't afraid to follow my dreams and desires, unlike you. You worked the shipyards because it was easy. The work suited you, but you never stepped outside of your comfort zone. You had opportunities to move up, but you were too much of a coward to try. It was easier to fire cheap shots at management. You wanted to be revered, but all you did was fix broken things. And because you couldn't be revered, you decided to be feared. Hey, don't fuck with Dennis because he'll fuck you up. Pretty weak, don't you think?"

His father was silent for a long time. "Finished?"

"No. There are some things you need to know about me."

"Spit it out, then get out."

Tarbell ignored the attitude. It was all his father had to throw around these days.

"It pains me to say, we aren't too different. Like you, I've discovered that force wins the day."

"Yeah, right. What force have you used on someone?"

"My boss gave me a negative evaluation, so I held a knife to her throat and told her I'd cut her if she didn't change the review."

"Bullshit."

Tarbell didn't care if his father believed him or not. He would in time.

"I thought it had worked, but it hadn't. She pretended to go along with the plan but she sold me out to the company."

"Is this your way of telling me you got canned and now you can't afford that bitch, Lupe? Christ, trust you to screw up putting the strong arm to a chick."

"No, I've still got my job. I used the system against my boss. They fired her but that wasn't enough. Not only did she give me a bad review, she broke our bargain. That wasn't acceptable."

"What did you do?"

Tarbell had gotten his father's attention. There was a gleam of perverse pleasure in his eyes. He could no longer do these things himself, but he could live them out through others.

"I trashed her home."

Dennis clapped his hands together. "Maybe we are alike after all. There was this time—"

"I'm not interested."

His father's face dropped at not being able to relive a past glory.

"I'm not finished with this woman. She needs to be taught a lesson. I've finally weeded out the people surrounding her and killed the guy that was protecting her. She's vulnerable now. I'm free to do what I want to her."

"Bullshit. You didn't kill anyone." Dennis tried to inject bravado into his words, but it wasn't there.

"Have you ever killed a man, Dad?"

His father said nothing. Panic shone in his watery eyes.

"Come on, Dad. You threw plenty of punches, but did you ever take it to the next level?"

Tarbell felt his father's gaze examine him, picking away at him for the truth and finding it. It felt good to see his father frightened of him.

Dennis shook his head.

Tarbell got to his feet and approached his father. Dennis wheeled his chair backward but not fast enough to escape his son. Tarbell brought his father's escape to an end by jamming his foot behind the big wheel.

"But you've thought about killing someone, haven't you? Sure you have, but you never went through with it because you're a coward. Isn't that true?"

Tarbell leaned in toward his father. His father flinched. How he wished his mom could be here to witness this turn of events.

Dennis trembled but said nothing. Tarbell let his hand trail to the oxygen tube. It was a little reminder of their previous encounter. It had been pleasurable and disappointing to see his father the bully fold under so little pressure, but then that was how bullies operated.

Dennis's gaze fell to Tarbell's hand grazing the clear, plastic tubing. "You're right. I'm a coward."

"When you beat the shit out of some guy at the shipyard or a bar, did you ever feel bad afterwards?"

"Yeah, sure I did."

"How about when you hit Mom?" Tarbell gripped the tube and tugged it gently.

His father swallowed hard. "Every time."

"But you kept on hitting her. In fact, I remember you smiling when you hit her. Do you remember that?"

"It's not what you think. I might have looked like I was enjoying it, but when it was over, I felt like shit."

It was a nice sentiment, but his father would say anything to save his skin, Tarbell guessed. It was so typical of him to be this way. His mother knew her weaknesses, but at least she had known how to take the blows without bitching about it.

"We're not that different," Dennis said. "When you killed that guy, you felt bad, right?"

"No, I didn't. It was the best thing I ever did."

Tarbell took his father's big hand, a hand that despite its size, no longer possessed the strength to fight back, and guided it to the regulator on the oxygen bottle.

"Don't. Please, don't."

Tarbell rolled his eyes at the plea. How many times had his father ignored the pleas of others? It was about time the favor was returned. "Don't what, Dad? I'm not doing anything. You are."

Using his father's fingers he turned up the oxygen flow. The needle on the gauge climbed swiftly from the prescribed two liters per minute until it read ten liters per minute.

"Dad, what are you doing? You know what the doctor said. Don't mess with the regulator. Too much oxygen is lethal. What are you trying to do, kill yourself?"

Tarbell's father tried to turn the regulator back, but Tarbell jerked his hand away and pinned it to the arm of the wheelchair. Dennis went to yank the tubing from his nose, but Tarbell snatched his other arm and held that against the wheelchair arm also.

"Dad, why are you doing this to yourself?" Tarbell said. "You've got so much to live for. I don't know why you think you're such a burden. You're not. Please stop."

Raw animal panic burned in Dennis's eyes. His panic forced him to breathe harder and faster, sucking in more and more over-oxygenated air, each breath more destructive than the last.

The panicked look didn't last. Within a few minutes, lethargy set in from the overdose of oxygen. His father's eyelids slid down to half-mast, the tension went out of his body, and his rapid breathing ceased. Tarbell released his grip on his father's arms. Dennis didn't move. Tarbell smiled and sat back from his father.

"Do you know what's going to happen to you?"

Dennis Tarbell's gaze slowly turned to his son.

"Too much oxygen doesn't mix well with emphysema. It depresses the respiratory center of the brain, which leads to coma and ultimately, death. It's a pretty painless way to die and more than you deserve."

Dennis struggled in his seat, but he lacked the strength to do anything about his condition. His left foot popped out from its footrest and dangled an inch from the floor.

"I would prefer something more violent, but that's just not an option. Instead, I'm going to sit here and watch you suffocate. What have you got to say about that, Dad?"

A sob escaped Dennis's lips. Tarbell considered that the highlight of his life.

Silence between them followed. The only sound that pierced the silence was the hiss of oxygen flowing into Dennis.

It took twenty minutes before Dennis Tarbell lapsed into a coma. Tarbell rose from his seat and examined his father. He was under, and he wasn't coming back. He sorely wanted to stick around and witness his father choke out his last breath, but his alibi wouldn't allow it.

"You see, my father has been unhappy for so long. You might not think it from looking at him, but he was once a vibrant man. His illnesses have been tough on him." Tarbell came around the chair to face his father and peered into his thousand-yard stare. "I should have seen this coming when he sent me out to get him a cigar. I know I shouldn't have, but he missed having a smoke. It was one of the last joys left open to him."

He patted his father on the shoulder and left the house in search of a smoke shop. When he returned, he called 911 and told them the whole sorry story. He squeezed out a few sobs for appearances, but inside he'd never felt better.

CHAPTER TWENTY-FOUR

Monday. A new day and the beginning of a new week. Things would change this week. Paul could feel it. He checked himself out in the mirror. It felt good to be in a suit again instead of sweats. He might have been out of work for over a year, but it didn't show in his demeanor. He was confident, sharp—employable. He put it all down to the suit.

Gwen watched him from the bathroom doorway. "You look great."

"I feel great."

She sidled over to him and draped her hands over his neck. "You're going to knock 'em dead today."

He kissed her. "I think so, too."

Paul hit the road with the rest of the morning commuters for the first time in a long time. While his fellow drivers were no doubt bitching about the Monday morning crush, he couldn't stop smiling. He was part of the rat race again and he wanted his bit of cheese. If he got this job, he'd no doubt complain about the shitty traffic and the idiot who cut him off at the on-ramp just like everyone else, but he'd still be happy to be back.

He drove on autopilot while he went over his talking points. He'd been to enough interviews over recent months to know what he'd get asked today. Anything skill and experience related, he had down pat and he had enough references to sink a battle-ship. Where things got sticky was answering why he'd been out of work for thirteen months. It was one of those stick-it-in-and-break-it-off questions. He could claim bad economics, the war in Iraq or sun spots, but those arguments became harder to defend with every week he was without a job. Long-term unemployment came with a stigma all its own.

"Please give me the job," he murmured to himself.

He needed this position. He knew how touchy he'd become over time. Gwen had been an absolute star putting up with his shit. He knew it would have been a lot worse for him without Kirsten. His daughter kept him sane.

This job opportunity wasn't just for him. The good ship Farris was leaking on all fronts now that Gwen had been fired. Their money was just about gone. They wouldn't last long with both of them out of work.

They were still both reeling from her firing. Tarbell should be in jail for what he'd done. Paul could be bitter, but it did him no good. Gwen was better off working somewhere else. Pace had put her in danger when their hired detectives had played at trying to catch Tarbell. Despite the bad timing, losing her job was for the best.

"Concentrate," he told himself. He couldn't afford to be dis-tracted. Impressing Greg Solis was all that counted today. The Farrises needed to end their losing streak.

Paul followed the directions to the project site in Fremont. He knew the site already. It was a commercial building project that had hit the rocks when the investment fell apart. The building had remained half built and had looked destined for demolishment, but new investors had popped up. Construction would be kick-started when the permits were transferred to the new owners.

Nothing had hit the news about the project. According to Solis, the project architect, the investors were having a press con-ference in two weeks to announce the job was up and running again. By then, they wanted a crew onsite and working. It was tight, but it was doable.

Paul spotted the nine-story concrete and structural steel skeleton jutting into the air as he came up to his exit. He took the off-ramp and followed the roads to the site entrance. The chain-link fencing surrounding the site had long since been torn down, and many of the concrete surfaces had been tagged with colorful graffiti. That was going to be the rough part with this job—making sure the damage to the structure was taken care of after months of neglect.

As he bumped his car over the rough driveway, he came face-to-face with a tall, skinny man in a suit holding a pipe wrench in one hand. Paul tensed, but relaxed when the man with the wrench smiled and waved at him.

Paul stopped the car and swung the door open. He was slow about getting out, just in case this wasn't his interviewer.

"Greg?" Paul said.

"Yes. Paul Farris?"

Paul slipped from the car with his file containing his references and some notes he'd worked up on the project. He'd spent all of Sunday putting a work program together. It was overkill, but he needed to land this job.

Solis trotted over to Paul with his hand out. He noticed Paul gazing at the pipe wrench.

"Sorry about the hardware," he said, holding the wrench up. "With no security onsite until the papers are signed on this place, I need a little something for protection." He jerked a thumb at the graffiti. "We get a lot of homeless and vandals hanging out here. You can't be too sure."

Site security was always a problem. Copper cable got jacked for the salvage value. Tools got stolen for resale. Anything that was too heavy to lift or too complicated to operate got trashed. Security would be his first order of business—if they gave him the job.

Solis slung the wrench on the backseat of his Honda and locked the car. "I thought I'd make this a practical interview.

We've got to get this place up and running fast. I'm looking for someone who can do that."

Paul smiled. His preparation had been worth every minute of the Sunday he'd burned up putting his package together.

Solis walked Paul over to the building. "OK, we're bringing this project out of mothballs. You're the construction supervisor. What do you do?"

Although Paul hadn't seen the project plans, Solis was playing to his strengths. He knew how to assess a jobsite and break it down into functions and tasks. He led Solis through the building, outlining his plans for putting the building back on track and getting it finished within a reasonable timeline. At first he was a little stiff with his ideas, but the rust that had built up over the last year quickly fell away.

He watched Solis for his reaction. The man was lapping up everything he said. He reined in his enthusiasm before it got away from him. If everything was on the up and up, he was in a good position for this job. But he'd been in this position before only to have the job snatched away from him.

Solis pointed to the stairwell, and they climbed to the fourth floor. It had been partially framed in, but that was the extent of the work. If there'd been any utility lines put in, they'd been ripped out by scavengers.

"What would you do with this?" Solis asked as they wandered through the floor's skeletal layout.

Paul examined the studs for damage and rot. "Leave it as is until the floor plan changed."

Solis nodded his approval. He pointed to the far wall over Paul's shoulder. "And that?"

Paul turned and took an exploratory step toward the wall but didn't see what he could do with it. It was a wall. Just as he was about to turn back to Solis, pain exploded in his back. It spread out through his body, driving him to his knees. He tried to suck in a breath, but he'd lost the ability. Another blow, this time across his shoulders, sent him onto all fours.

He tried calling out to Solis, but the words didn't come, just a noise. He choked with the effort and tears filled his eyes. Whoever had gotten to him must have taken Solis out first. It had to be vandals, thugs, or the homeless. Someone had claimed this place as their own and as de facto owners, treated trespassers with brute force. Nothing else made sense.

"Greg," he said, the word burning his throat. He made himself rise to his feet before his attacker got in another blow. He scrabbled forward. His back burned where he'd been hit. Everything hurt too much to tell if anything had been broken.

"Where do you think you're going?"

Paul searched for an escape route. The stairway seemed like a world away and the unfinished building left him nowhere to hide. The studs running from floor to ceiling like wooden jail bars gave him some protection. He lurched between two studs. It was hard for Solis to swing the pipe with them in the way. He wrapped his arms tightly around the studs to hold himself up.

Now he came face-to-face with his attacker. Solis moved in toward him with a two-foot length of scaffold pipe. The sight of Solis coming at him sent his mind reeling. What had he missed? He felt as though five minutes of his life had been removed and spliced back together. The resulting confusion hurt his already dizzied mind.

"Nowhere to run, Paul."

Solis stood between him and the only functioning stairwell. He could simply jump out the unfinished side of the building where the floor-to-ceiling windows would go in, but he was looking at a three-story fall to the rubble-strewn ground. It was an escape, just not a good one.

"What's going on?"

"What's it look like?"

Paul didn't have an answer. Confusion kept getting in the way.

Solis slipped closer to him, and Paul backed up. Each step took him closer toward the windowless edge of the building. There were three or four more skeletal rooms to pass through before he was left with nowhere else to go.

He looked among the trash on the floor for a weapon—a length of stud, a piece of scaffold, a discarded hammer, an old saw blade, anything to fight back with. He'd even take a section of drywall for protection. But he saw nothing but dropped screws and spent nail gun magazines.

The second Paul took his eyes off Solis, the architect pounced. He sprang forward with the pipe raised above his head. Paul scurried back, slipped on something, and sat down hard on his backside. He snapped back onto his feet, but the damage had been done. Solis slipped between the studs separating them. Paul tried running, but Solis had the momentum and was on Paul before he could escape. Solis swung the pipe. Paul put up his arm to protect himself, and the pipe smashed down on his forearm, breaking it. Paul felt the bones shatter and almost puked from the pain.

Paul bottled the pain and jerked right to sidestep Solis and make for the stairwell. Solis spotted the move a second too late. He tried to cut Paul off, but Paul rushed through the framed doorway. A corridor of doorways stretched ahead of him toward the stairwell.

Paul held his arm tight to his side to dull the agony of broken bones grinding against each other. The stairs would hurt, but he could deal with that as long as he got away from this son of a bitch.

But Solis robbed Paul of that chance. He hurled the scaffold pipe at him, and it struck the concrete floor before bouncing up and entangling itself in his ankles. Paul's legs went out from under him, and he came down hard on his right hip and broken right arm. The agony drove a scream out of him he didn't think he had left in him.

Solis's footfalls echoed off the concrete.

Paul wanted to give up, surrender, but he couldn't. He wouldn't die at Solis's hands. The pipe was still knotted up between his legs. He grabbed it and brandished it to stave off Solis. He swung it back and forth, slicing the air.

But Solis ignored the weapon that had worked so well on Paul. He led with his foot and kicked Paul in the elbow of the arm holding the pipe. The kick struck Paul's funny bone. The explosion in his now numb arm forced the pipe out of his grasp. Solis followed up his first kick with a second to Paul's stomach. His foot connected with something that forced Paul to curl up into a ball.

Solis stepped back to appreciate his handiwork. Paul looked up at him through tear-blurred vision.

"Why are you doing this?"

Solis snorted. "Why don't you ask Gwen?"

Confusion became horrifying clarity. Paul knew who this man was. He'd finally met Tarbell.

Tarbell went over to reclaim the scaffold pipe. The significance of that simple act struck fear into Paul. He squirmed to get up, but his body failed him. He was only beginning to get the feeling back in his left arm. His fingers tingled to the point of burning, and there was no real strength in his arm to support his body.

Tarbell returned with the pipe loose in his grip and a sneer tight on his face. The soulless expression in his eyes forced Paul to push himself to his knees. Tarbell backhanded Paul savagely. Paul's balance wasn't with him, and he went down on his back. Tarbell raised the pipe above his head.

"Please, don't," Paul said.

Tarbell didn't listen. Paul didn't have an escape plan this time. He closed his eyes and waited for the final blow. Finding a job was the furthest thing from his thoughts when Tarbell brought the pipe down.

• • •

It was deep into the afternoon when her cell rang. It was Paul, at last. She'd expected him home hours ago, but she knew how these interviews went sometimes. They could drag on forever, especially if the interviewer liked you. She hoped that was the case and that it had not gone so badly that Paul had decided to slink off somewhere to be alone. She answered the phone as cheerfully as possible. "Who's this?" said an unfamiliar male voice.

That should have been her question and it struck a chord of irritation in her. "Can I speak to Paul?"

Gwen became suddenly aware of the background noise making it down the line. There were voices—not like those belonging to guys in a bar. Orders were being issued. Besides the voices, she heard vehicles, their engines sounding angry and urgent. Her stomach dropped when she heard the sound of a siren.

"Who's calling?" the man insisted.

"Gwen Farris. You have my husband's phone."

"Mrs. Farris, do you know where your husband was this morning?"

Panic took over. Gwen started to shake. Kirsten picked up on Gwen's mood change and trotted into the kitchen. "He went to a job interview in Fremont. Now, tell me who you are and why you have Paul's phone."

"I'm Detective Braga from the Fremont Police Department. Your husband's been severely injured."

"What do you mean severely injured?"

"He was beaten. He's in very bad shape."

Gwen fought to keep a grip. "How bad?"

"I'm no doctor, but someone worked him over and didn't expect him to be found alive."

"Oh God." Gwen slapped a hand over her mouth.

Kirsten held her hands out to Gwen. She picked her daughter up and held her tight to her. Her world was falling apart, and she needed to keep a hold on everything she had left.

"Where is he?"

"Paramedics have him en route to Eden Medical Center in Castro Valley."

"I have to see him."

"Mrs. Farris, he's in good hands. Right now, I need some information from you to help track down the perpetrator."

"If you have any questions, you can find me there." Gwen tossed the phone on the counter and grabbed her purse.

"Where are we going?" Kirsten asked.

"Daddy's been hurt, honey. We're going to see him."

Gwen strapped Kirsten into the car seat, ignoring the girl's questions. She peeled out of the garage and drove hard to the hospital. What had happened? He was just going to an interview. How had it turned into a beating? It just didn't make sense.

After a drive she didn't remember, she parked in the hospital's lot, straddling two parking spots. She jerked Kirsten free of her car seat. At first, she tried walking. But people walked when they had nothing to fear. So Gwen broke into an awkward run with Kirsten in her arms.

"It's going to be OK, baby. It's going to be OK," she told Kirsten, but the mantra was just as much for herself as her daughter.

She rushed up to an admittance desk, ignoring the line of people waiting to be seen. "I'm looking for my husband, Paul Farris."

"There's a line, lady."

"The police brought him in, I think," Gwen said, ignoring the protests. "He was a victim of a crime. The police just called me. Paul Farris. Where can I find him?"

The admitting nurse looked at her blank faced.

"Please, I need to find my husband."

Someone bitched about her cutting in line, but Gwen stopped it with a cutting look.

Gwen's frantic behavior ignited Kirsten's fear, and she began crying.

A supervisor intervened. She removed Gwen and Kirsten from the line. The woman spoke in soothing tones. She smiled at Kirsten and told them not to worry. She sat them down and said she'd find out what happened to Paul.

Gwen felt the heat of everyone's gazes on her. Kirsten's crying slowed to hiccupping sobs. She kept Kirsten on her lap and told her it was all going to be OK and prayed it was true.

The supervisor returned after a couple of minutes. Her expression was muted, but pleasant. "He's here."

She walked Gwen and Kirsten down a series of corridors and sat them down in a lounge. "Paul was brought in about forty minutes ago in critical condition. He's in surgery right now."

The phrase "critical condition" struck fear into Gwen. It raised too many frightening possibilities. "Can I speak to a doctor?"

"Not right now. They're working on Paul. I'll let them know you're here. A doctor will be out to see you as soon as they're done."

Kirsten broke into tears and Gwen pulled her daughter close to her. The supervisor saw that her words had failed to bring any comfort. She sat down next to Gwen and took her hand in hers.

"I can't imagine how you're feeling, but you're not the first person in this position. I can't tell you not to worry, but worrying isn't going to bring you or your little girl any comfort. All I can say is that we're doing everything we can for Paul. Just hang in there, OK?"

"Thanks," Gwen said.

The supervisor smiled. "OK. I'll drop by when I can."

Gwen watched the supervisor leave. Patients, nurses, and doctors wandered by, but she'd never felt so alone in her life. She pulled Kirsten to her.

"Daddy's going to be OK, baby."

A police officer appeared in the corridor. The moment he set eyes on Gwen, he made a beeline for her.

"Mrs. Farris?"

"Yes."

"I'm Detective Braga. We spoke earlier. Can I ask you a few questions?"

Braga was a heavyset guy in his late forties with big hands and a sensitive face.

"Sure."

"Is my daddy in trouble?" Kirsten asked.

"No, honey. The person who hurt him is."

Gwen shifted Kirsten to her lap and Braga took her seat.

"Can you tell me what happened?" Gwen asked.

"Your husband was found on the fourth floor of the Hogan Building in Fremont. He'd been severely beaten. He was found by some kids using the site as a jungle gym. They called it in."

"What has Paul said?"

"Nothing yet. He's still unconscious."

Gwen's stomach clenched, and she held Kirsten even tighter.

"That building was abandoned. Can you tell me what he was doing out there?"

"Job interview. He's a construction supervisor. He was meeting with someone from the construction company that had taken over the building."

Braga gave her a sideways look. "No one's taken that building over. The city is hoping someone will finish the project, but there's been no interest."

"That can't be right. He spoke to the architect several times. A headhunter set up the interview."

The mention of a headhunter caught the officer's attention. "Do you have the headhunter's contact info?"

"Not here, but I know the name of the recruiter and the firm. They're out of San Francisco."

"That's fine. I can track it down from there."

"What do you think happened?"

"I don't know. It could be a matter of being at the wrong place at the wrong time. We have problems with drug dealers using the building for deals. Maybe your husband got between a dealer and his stash. I want to check on this interview. I could be wrong about the building not being under new ownership. Can I get some contact details?"

Gwen gave him everything he needed to track down the recruiting firm, and he promised to be in touch and left.

With Braga gone, the waiting game began. Hours dragged by with Paul still in surgery. Patients and loved ones left and were replaced by others. The faces of the medical staff changed as their shifts changed. Kirsten fell asleep as the tedium kicked in, which was something Gwen wished she could do. Every hour that Paul was in surgery only underlined the severity of his injuries. The vague updates didn't help calm her either. She didn't dare leave her spot to eat or drink or even stretch her legs in case something happened.

It was after five when a doctor in medical scrubs emerged from a doorway. Gwen had wanted someone to talk to her, but now that the moment was here, a sense of dread crept up on her and threatened to crush her.

"I'm Dr. Korn. Mrs. Farris, could we talk for a moment?"

The supervisor they'd met earlier walked up behind the doctor. "You look hungry, Kirsten. Want to get something to eat?"

Gwen's dread intensified. They didn't want Kirsten here for the news. It had to be bad.

Kirsten looked over at Gwen for permission and Gwen nodded at her. The supervisor led her away.

Dr. Korn showed Gwen into a small room. His expression was grave. "I know you've been waiting a long time, but your husband needed a lot of care. He suffered some serious injuries—he broke his arm, collarbone, and four ribs. These have been taken care of, along with the internal bleeding."

The sense of relief left Gwen weak. She leaned against the wall to support herself.

"That's the good news. There's some bad news, too."

"Oh, God."

"Your husband also suffered a fractured skull."

Gwen feared the question she had to ask. "Is there brain damage?"

"I don't know, but there's a possibility."

She felt nauseous. The idea of losing the man she loved punched a hole through her chest where her heart was.

"Please don't alarm yourself. Currently, Paul's brain has swollen. We've relieved the pressure on it, and that's good, but he's currently comatose. We won't know the extent of the damage until he comes out of the coma. That said, I'm encouraged by what I've seen so far."

Coma. The word came with jagged edges. There was no way of hearing it without it hurting.

"Your husband is in very bad shape, but we've done everything we can to counteract that. I expect him to make a recovery, but he has a long road ahead of him."

Gwen hoped to God that the doctor wasn't trying to pacify her fears and that Paul would be OK. She couldn't bear it if he wasn't. "Can I see him?"

"Of course."

She thought she'd prepared herself for the worst. She expected Paul to have wires trailing from him and to have bandages, bruising, casts, and dressings. She hadn't anticipated a monster in place of her husband. Paul's face was deformed by heavy eggplant-colored bruises. The swelling was so horrific, his features were lost. She was going on trust that this was Paul. She didn't see one thing that reminded her of her husband. Shock got the better of her, and she broke into sobs. Dr. Korn led her to his office.

It took her a few minutes to gather herself. Dr. Korn gave her the time and space to recover, never interrupting her with trite assurances.

"When do you expect Paul to be out of his coma?"

"I can't say. These things are very unpredictable."

"You'll call me if anything changes? Day or night?"

"Of course."

Gwen found Kirsten in the hospital restaurant eating things she shouldn't be eating, but it hardly mattered. Kirsten wanted to see her dad. Despite her protests, Gwen couldn't let her. Images of Paul's disfigured face would never leave her. She couldn't do that to her daughter.

"Later, baby," she said. "Daddy's sleeping and can't have visitors."

She thanked the supervisor and carried Kirsten out to the car. Backing out of the parking lot, she felt uncoordinated. She guessed she shouldn't be driving, but who was there to turn to right now? Everyone seemed a world away with her sister in New York, her parents in Ohio, and Paul's parents in Florida. It would be so easy to have them come out, but she'd only be putting them in danger. She couldn't even turn to her friends, since they were giving her a wide berth these days. She realized she'd become quite isolated as the events with Tarbell had unfolded. Yet she'd never felt it until now, without Paul.

She joined the evening traffic, letting it sweep her along.

Her cell phone flashed at her. Messages had been stacking up. She'd been ignoring them while she was in the hospital. She was only interested in hearing from the police or the hospital. Everyone else could wait.

The phone burst into song. The ring tone was Rihanna's "Umbrella." It was a fun song Kirsten couldn't stop singing. It jarred her now.

She picked up the phone. Jerry Naylor's name appeared on the caller ID. She answered his call.

"Hi, Jerry."

"Hey, Gwen. Are you OK? Have I caught you at a bad time?"

When wasn't it? she thought.

• • •

Paul preoccupied Gwen's mind on the drive home. She couldn't imagine what she'd do if he didn't pull through. Naylor had called to tell her Parker's parole hearing was on Friday. Parker seemed insignificant right now, but she agreed to be there just to give her some control over her life.

She parked in the garage and walked Kirsten inside. The house felt empty without Paul. She felt it the moment she stepped inside. It was silent. Even when everyone was home and doing their own thing in their own rooms, the place buzzed with their energy. Without Paul, the house was a little quieter, a little colder, and a little darker.

Whether Kirsten felt the same or not, the moment she entered the house, she went straight to her room. Gwen tucked her into bed. As she went downstairs, she hoped tomorrow would bring some optimism.

She flipped on the TV for the noise but switched it back off when the phone rang. Thoughts of the hospital sprang to mind. She grabbed the cordless phone off the charger.

"Hello?"

"Hey, Gwen."

It was Tarbell. He hadn't featured in Gwen's thoughts all day and this was an unwelcome reminder.

"What do you want?"

"I caught the news. Paul's in bad shape."

"And why do you care?"

"Because he wasn't supposed to be found alive. I thought I'd done enough to kill him."

Tarbell. She should have known it was him. The attack was filled with his brand of hate. Gwen lowered herself onto the coffee table as the strength bled from her.

"Why'd you do it? Paul hasn't done anything to you."

"But he's important to you. That's all that matters. You still haven't gotten it, have you? I'm not finished with you. I won't be satisfied until you've lost everything you hold dear."

"All this because I gave you a bad review?"

"No, we're long past bad reviews. If you'd simply done as I'd told you, we'd be fine, but you tried to set me up. Yes, I know about them. How do you think I evaded their surveillance?"

It was all there. Gwen couldn't believe how easily he'd slipped every obstacle placed in front of him. No wonder her life was in the mess it was.

"You're strangely quiet, Gwen. Keep it that way. No one will help you."

Gwen could hear the enjoyment in Tarbell's voice. He was loving every second of her pain. Tears streaked her face, but she refused to give him the satisfaction of hearing her cry.

"Is that all you've got to say?"

"Just one more thing. Kirsten is next."

CHAPTER TWENTY-FIVE

"Gwen, what are you doing here?" Ingram asked.

One of Ingram's people had his hands out, blocking Gwen from getting any farther than the doorway to PSI's offices. The rest of Ingram's staff watched her, ready to get involved if she didn't back down. Ingram stepped in front of his investigator and told the guy blocking Gwen's access that it was OK but made no move to let her enter. The investigator returned to his desk.

"You shouldn't be here."

"I need to talk to you."

"Gwen, we don't have any business. Not anymore."

These weren't the words Gwen needed to hear. She had to get someone to listen. "Please."

Ingram hesitated, then nodded. He led her into his office and closed the door. She knew he was sympathetic to her plight; it was why she'd come, but his expression was stony.

"Gwen, you're making this situation worse for yourself."

How could she make it any worse? It was a joke under the circumstances. "My husband is in a coma right now."

"I'm sorry to hear that. What happened?"

"He was lured to a bogus job interview, beaten, and left for dead."

Ingram lost the faux concern and genuine worry entered his expression. "That's terrible."

"It is, especially as the person responsible is free."

Ingram's expression tightened. "Stephen Tarbell."

"Who else would it have been?"

"Gwen, please. You can't keep pointing the finger every time something bad happens."

"I'm not. He called me, told me he'd attacked Paul, and that Kirsten was next."

Ingram was silent. It was a good sign. Gwen hoped she was penetrating his thick layer of professional loyalty. He was a good guy, not some gun for hire. He cared about right and wrong. She'd known it from the moment she'd met him. She just needed him to believe in her, her situation, and Tarbell's boundless hate. Once she had Ingram back on her side, Kirsten would be safe. Her hopes grew with every minute he remained silent. He knew what Tarbell was like. He'd come around.

"I'm sorry, Gwen, it's not enough."

Days ago, a remark like this would have wounded her, but not mortally. Today, it was a stake through her heart. Her life was in shreds. She had nothing to cling on to. She dropped her head in her hands. "When is it going to be enough? When he sends you a videotape of him killing me?"

"Gwen, you're being ridiculous."

She shot him a look. "Oh please. You can't be ignorant enough to believe Stephen Tarbell is innocent in all this and that I made everything up. Way too much has happened."

Ingram's expression tightened at being called ignorant. Gwen didn't care. She needed him emotional. He'd act if he was angry.

"Gwen, I've shown you every courtesy. I've helped you where I can, but you're testing my patience."

"Mr. Ingram, I'm begging you to do something."

"Is this what it's going to be like from now on? Every time something happens to you, you're going to point the finger at Stephen?"

"Only when I know he's done something."

Ingram shook his head. "I should tell you that Pace Pharmaceuticals filed for a restraining order against you yesterday. Expect to be summoned for a court hearing in forty-five days. Let this be a wake-up call. You're heading down a destructive road, but you can turn back."

A restraining order, she thought. *It was obscene.* Suddenly, Tarbell's comment on the phone that nobody would help her made sense. Nobody would help her because she was no longer seen as the victim. "When did I become the enemy?"

"When you accosted Tarbell in the parking lot."

"The man held a knife against my throat, and you didn't take that sort of action."

"That was different. We were investigating a case against an employee. You aren't employed by Pace anymore. They're protecting themselves."

Gwen shook her head. "This is unbelievable."

"Gwen, you brought this upon yourself. You accosted Tarbell in public. What did you expect?"

"Some support. You promised to protect me."

The remark hit home. Ingram sank back into his chair. "You're right. I did promise you. The investigation didn't run true to procedure. I'll talk to Deborah and see if I can't get them to drop the restraining order, but I need you to promise you're going to stay away from Pace and Tarbell."

"None of that helps me. It doesn't keep Tarbell away."

Ingram shook his head. "You're not making this easy on yourself."

Easy. She couldn't remember what that felt like. She went to the window and stared outside just to avoid Ingram's disapproving look. "I'm just trying to get someone to stop Tarbell from hurting me and my family."

Ingram frowned.

"Did you ever believe me?"

"I believe something happened between you and Stephen and it escalated."

"That's not what I asked."

Ingram was silent for a second. "Yes. I believed you. In the beginning."

"And now?"

"The evidence doesn't back up what has happened to you recently."

The truth hung heavy in the air between them.

"Gwen, put this behind you. Your family needs you right now. It won't do any of them any good if you're in jail, and that's where you're going to end up if you don't forget about Stephen."

"So you're not going to help me?"

"No."

There was a finality in Ingram's one-word answer that left no room for misinterpretation. It was the closing of a door, the severing of a lifeline, the death of a relationship. Gwen could expect no further assistance from him regardless of what Tarbell did next. It left her cold and unsteady. She stood and walked out of Ingram's office. Ingram followed her out and stopped her in the corridor.

"As a friend to a friend, you should seek some help, Gwen."

"That was why I came to you."

• • •

Gwen was thankful she'd found a sitter to take Kirsten for the day as she watched Detective Braga appear from behind a door marked "Authorized Personnel Only" carrying a folder.

Gwen had gone to him after leaving Ingram's office. She'd given Ingram his chance to do the right thing, and he'd failed. It was time to turn to the police, which she should have done earlier. Screw Pace Pharmaceuticals' need for privacy. Doors were closing around her, but one remained ajar. Tarbell had made a mistake. Every one of his attacks had been self-contained except for the attack on Paul. Paul's beating was public. The police wanted the person responsible caught. She'd set them on him, and when they brought him in, it would reveal everything he'd done. She got up from her seat, where she'd been waiting for the last twenty minutes. Braga looked pleased to see her. It made a nice change for someone to feel that way.

"Thanks for coming in, Mrs. Farris. You beat me to the punch. I was going to call you this afternoon to see if we could talk."

She hoped this was a sign of good news. "Have there been any developments?"

"Yes. Let's go somewhere more private."

Braga got Gwen a visitor's badge and escorted her to an interview room. He closed the door and put the folder on the desk between them. It was slim, but it would be a lot thicker by the time she left.

"OK." Braga opened the folder. "I spoke to the recruiter who set up the interview for your husband. The information about the man your husband met with, Greg Solis, was bogus. Solis doesn't exist. Neither does the architectural firm Solis claimed he worked for. The phone number he provided tracked back to a prepaid cell phone. Whoever lured your husband to the building site attacked him and made off with his wallet, but that was all. That aspect worries me."

"Why?"

"This guy went to a lot of trouble for your husband's wallet. No, this situation is far too elaborate and a pretty flawed scheme for a plain mugging. You can only get away with it once before it raises the alarm."

"Was anyone else scheduled to meet with this Greg Solis?"

"The recruiter said Paul was the first of five scheduled interviews. I'll be blunt, Mrs. Farris; this looks personal. Does your husband have any enemies holding a grudge?"

This was where she would stick it to Tarbell and let him know what it feels like to be under the microscope. "No, but I do. A coworker attacked me in the staff parking lot. His name is Stephen Tarbell, and I believe he did this to Paul."

"Do you have anything to back that up?"

She was about to tell the detective about Tarbell's call last night when she noticed the subtle difference in his tone. The friendliness had been replaced by a disbelieving element. The shift threw her a second and her words dried up. Before she could say anything, Braga plowed over her.

"Did you ever file a complaint with the police?"

"No, my employer wanted to deal with it internally."

"Hmm," Braga said. "You're attacked by a coworker and your employer tells you not to go to the police."

"Yes."

"OK. And this would be the same employer and coworker who now have filed for a restraining order against you?"

Gwen groaned inside. She couldn't have this get in the way. "It's not how it seems."

"I spoke to your *ex*-employer, and they weren't very complimentary about your recent behavior."

Bad news traveled fast, and it had tainted her in Braga's eyes. He'd made up his mind about her and there was no changing it. Suddenly, the interview room felt small. Braga seemed to loom over her, and the wall pressed up against her back with no room for her escape.

"Stephen Tarbell attacked my husband. He called me on the phone to tell me about it last night."

The words just bounced off Braga. He had his facts, as screwed up as they were, and he was going with them.

"Do you think I did this to my husband?"

"No. Your alibi holds up, but I want this meeting to be somewhat of a warning to you, Mrs. Farris. I won't put up with any falsified statements concerning Stephen Tarbell in connection with your husband's attack."

"I haven't falsified anything."

Braga held up a hand. "If the investigation leads to Stephen Tarbell, then make no mistake, I will arrest him and hit him with the full force of the law, but the same applies to you. If I find you've crossed any lines, I will come down on you. Is that clear?"

Gwen saw no point in arguing. The damage had been done. "Yes."

"Then I need to get back to finding the person who hurt your husband."

Braga saw her out and watched her from the doorway. She felt his gaze on her as she crossed the parking lot to her car. She pretended she didn't notice him as she drove away.

As she pulled into traffic, the tears flowed. She thumped the steering wheel with a fist. How had it gone so wrong? How had Tarbell managed to twist the world into believing he was an angel and she was a demon? It wasn't fair. It wasn't right.

Looking back on it all, she saw how he'd done it. His demolition job was immaculate. No one stood in her corner. She could imagine him sitting in his home, gloating over his achievements. He'd ruined her, left Paul clinging to life, and it wasn't enough. Now he wanted to take it out on Kirsten, and when he'd finished, he'd finally turn his attention back to her.

She had one thing to be thankful about. Ingram and Braga had proved no one would raise a finger to help her. It left her with two choices—surrender to Tarbell, or fight back. She palmed away her tears. She knew which choice to make.

CHAPTER TWENTY-SIX

Tarbell found the padded envelope on his stoop when he checked for packages left by the mailman. No mailman had left this package. It hadn't been stamped, and there was no return address. It just bore his name written in black marker. But he knew who'd sent this mystery package from the block printing on the envelope. He smiled and picked it up. He'd play along.

He looked at the street and saw nothing unfamiliar or out of place. He closed the door and ripped the envelope open. Out fell a cell phone with a note attached. The note was simple, just a phone number with the words, "Call me, please." The writing matched that on the padded envelope.

A part of him wanted to be angry by this development. He hadn't seen it coming. But because he hadn't seen it coming, it pleased him. His actions had forced someone to act out of character. It didn't matter what the significance of this move meant. The simple act itself proved that he was having a profound affect. It was a compliment in a lot of ways, which was no reason to lose his temper. This ploy was a sign of her desperation. That pleased him and far outweighed any angry feelings.

He stretched out on the sofa, switched on the cell, and punched in the number. "Hi, Gwen," he said when she answered. "You've intrigued me. What do you want?"

"I want to make you an offer."

"If I want something from you, I'll take it. There's nothing you can offer that I can't take."

"You're wrong."

Gwen said this with such conviction it forced him to sit up. "Am I?"

"I have a proposal you can't turn down."

Gwen was fishing, but she had him hooked. He wanted to know more, but he was far from being yanked from the water.

"Why don't you tell me, then?"

"No. Not over the phone. This has to be done in person."

Tarbell saw through her and smiled. She wanted to lure him somewhere that would turn out to be some kind of police sting operation, or an excuse to turn his place over, or even where she could get the jump on him. It was a real shame. He'd hoped for so much more from her. Her desperation was so transparent.

"Have you forgotten about the restraining order?"

"I don't care. I need to talk to you in person."

"I don't think so, Gwen. This has bullshit written all over it."

"No, it doesn't. I want to make you a unique offer. We're well beyond cops and Pace Pharmaceuticals and anyone else you'd care to name. No one believes me. If they did, you'd be in jail right now for what you did to Paul, but you're not. That's because you've won, and nothing I can do will change that."

"Then you have nothing to offer me."

"But I do."

"And you'll only tell me in person."

"Yes."

Gwen made a persuasive case. He felt himself being tempted. This woman had nothing. He'd seen to that. Yet it wasn't enough to know she was ruined. He was curious what she might have in store for him. Did it have to do with the cops?

He couldn't be certain. But something dug at him. The cell phone. If Gwen was in league with the cops, she would have wanted their call to be recorded and traced back to his phone. She didn't gain anything by speaking to him on a cell that wasn't registered to him.

He thought it over. If he met with Gwen and she tried to hurt him, he'd have the upper hand physically. If the cops were waiting, they had nothing on him. Gwen could make all the crazy claims she liked. He didn't have to agree with them. Besides, he had that restraining order on his side to undermine her case.

"OK, Gwen. You win. When and where?"

• • •

The when was immediately. The where was The Overlook in Rodeo. It was a glorified bar that wanted to be a cutesy bistro on account of its view of the bay. The place was off the beaten track, literally. The Overlook sat where Rodeo abutted the water's edge. He was forced to drive on a dirt track when the city's roads ended. As he parked, he couldn't help but notice the view was not so much of the bay as of a huge oil refinery leaking smoke from its vent stacks. It looked to be a hangout for the local Harley Davidson club, judging by the bikes parked outside. It definitely wasn't a place frequented by Gwen and her family.

He parked in the dirt lot and walked in. The hostess, a blonde trying to live her life like a Tammy Wynette song from the looks of her, approached him. He waved her off when Gwen waved from a corner table by the window overlooking the mudflats and the refinery. He didn't have to worry about being overheard. They were the only ones in the dining area. The half a dozen or so patrons kept to the bar. None of them looked like undercover cops. They were far too rough-and-ready. And the location was far too secluded for anyone to be hanging around outside keeping tabs. So far, Gwen was being a good girl.

He slid into a seat opposite Gwen and turned it sideways so that he had a clear view of everyone's movements.

"Suspicious?" Gwen asked.

"Always."

She looked haggard and drawn. She usually had a sun-kissed complexion, but not now. Even in the dimly lit restaurant, dark circles ringed her eyes. It was good to know he was having an effect on her.

The hostess turned out to be their waitress, too. He ordered a Coke and an appetizer so that she'd leave them alone. After she'd delivered the drink, he asked to see Gwen's purse. She handed over the bag, and he rummaged through it without finding a recorder but removed her cell, in case she was thinking about leaving an open line to someone.

"Wearing a wire?"

She laughed and shook her head.

"Open up your blouse."

She did so without complaint. She unbuttoned her blouse past where her bra crossed her chest. He ignored the swell of her breasts and lifted his eyes when he found no sign of a microphone.

"Now we can talk," he said. "What's the offer?"

She buttoned her blouse. "Are you really going to kill my daughter?"

"Yes."

His stark answer hit Gwen hard. Cracks formed in her stiff resolve, but she did a good job of keeping her emotions restrained.

"Why? She hasn't done anything to you."

"Doesn't matter. It isn't about her. It's about you. She's important to you, and it's important to me that I hurt you; ergo, I hurt her to hurt you. It's simple math, Gwen. You have to see that."

"Haven't you had your fill?"

"I would have if you'd stuck to our bargain and just changed my evaluation, but you had to go back on your word. You had to tell someone. Believe me, I didn't want this to go this far, but you couldn't leave well enough alone. You had to keep betraying me. Everything that has happened is a direct result of what you've done to me."

Gwen was shaking her head in disagreement. He saw the disgust in her eyes.

"You reap what you sow, Gwen. And you keep sowing."

"My husband may never recover from his injuries."

Tarbell shrugged.

"You don't have any kind of remorse, do you?"

"No, the world is a cold place, Gwen. It took me a long time to realize that. Nobody really cares about me, so why should I care about them? That's something you haven't learned yet. It surprises me because you should have. Look at your life. Your husband was laid off not because he was a bad worker but because money was more important to his employers than his welfare. Pace didn't stand by you in your weakest hour. They turned on you and fired you without a second thought. Your husband is in the hospital in need of special care, but that care will end when the insurance stops paying. Then who will care? Tell me that, Gwen."

Tarbell realized his voice had risen. It wasn't enough to draw the attention of the barflies across the room yet, but he needed to keep himself in check. He sipped his Coke to calm himself. "These things have nothing to do with your offer, so why don't we talk about that and forget everything else."

"My daughter's life."

"That's not an offer. If you've brought me here simply to ask for mercy, you're wasting your time."

Gwen's smile was humorless. "I know that. I want to know if you'll spare her life if I give you something bigger and better instead."

"Like what?"

"Me."

It was Tarbell's turn to laugh. "Gwen, I'm coming for you after I'm finished with Kirsten. I thought I'd made that clear."

"You did."

"Then what are we doing here?"

The waitress checked in with them. These people always picked the wrong time. He sent her on her way with a look.

"Because I want to make it simple for you," Gwen said. "You kill Kirsten, then you kill me. Great. You'll have achieved everything you set out to do, but you'll also leave a whole pile of shit behind you. Even the dumbest cop in the world isn't going to walk away from Kirsten and my deaths, especially after Paul's near murder. It's going to spawn a messy investigation. You won't like messy. People will come knocking on your door and poke about in your life. Even if they can't prove anything, doubt will follow you like a shadow for the rest of your life. Trust me, I know from firsthand experience. Some dirt can't be washed away. That isn't what you want. You want a nice clean kill so you can move on with your life. That won't happen if you kill my daughter and me."

That wouldn't happen. He was smarter than that. He'd killed his father and Petersen and no one had come looking for him. No one was after him for Paul Farris's attempted murder. It stood to reason that no one would come after him for Kirsten's and Gwen's deaths if he did everything right. But there it was in glowing neon lights ten feet high for everyone to see—*if*. But he felt the *if* growing in size like a cancer. People like Petersen and his father were easy meat, but Gwen was different. He'd given her too many warnings. He was learning fast. Whoever he went after next wouldn't get a heads-up like Gwen had gotten. Their life had to fall apart around them without them knowing why. Gwen had probably talked to the cops after Paul's beating and mentioned his name, so he could see her point. They were linked, and while she couldn't do anything about that in life, she could in death. Fuck. He'd screwed himself on this point.

"So what's your offer?"

"Me for Kirsten. You skip her and you can do whatever you want to me. I'll guarantee you get your clean kill."

"Forgive me, Gwen, I don't see how you can make that guarantee."

"I know a place. It's on the coast close to the Oregon border. I grew up there. It's quiet. You can do whatever you want. No one will ever find me, and no one will ever suspect you. I'll just simply go missing. That'll make perfect sense. After all the black clouds surrounding me lately, no one will give it a second thought if I run out on my family after I drove them onto the rocks."

Tarbell saw the appeal. He knew he was giving up a kill, but he had no real interest in Gwen's daughter or husband. It was a beef just between them. Shouldn't it end with just them? It sounded right, but it also sounded too good. Gwen wouldn't sacrifice herself without a little fuck-you along the way, but he'd take care of that. He'd outsmarted her so far and would continue to do so.

"How can I trust you?" he asked.

"How can I trust that you'll leave Kirsten alone?"

It was a fair point. It had already crossed his mind to come after Kirsten once the dust had settled. It could be done, and he'd make it work.

"Trust is a tricky thing, Gwen. Tell me more about this quiet place."

"North of Crescent City, there's a place called Fort Richardson. It's an island that used to be a coastal defense outpost. It's a national park, but the tourist season ends next week, so it gets mothballed until the spring. Anything that happens there doesn't get found until the tourists come back at Easter."

Gwen stopped talking, and he just sat back soaking up the information and coming up with ideas for how to kill her. The concept of having Gwen to himself to do with as he pleased was spawning a host of ideas.

"Do we have a deal?"

"Can it happen tomorrow?"

"No. I need to tie up affairs and put Kirsten with someone. Also, we should go the last day the island is open. Tomorrow there'll be tourists and witnesses, and you don't want that. So, do we have a deal?"

Tarbell picked up his Coke and sipped it. "I think we do."

• • •

Gwen was still shaking when the phone in the living room rang. She'd managed to keep it together in front of Tarbell but had fallen apart the moment she reached home. Collecting Kirsten from the sitter had done it. Her daughter was the reason for what she'd done. The deal she'd struck with Tarbell was her only way out. Answering the phone came as a welcome relief. It took her mind off what she'd done.

"Gwen Farris?"

Gwen didn't recognize the woman's voice on the telephone line. "Yes."

"I'm Lynette Petersen," she said and after a short pause followed up with, "Tom Petersen's wife. You left a message on our machine."

She was long past worrying about Petersen, but maybe he could help her with the action she was planning to take. "Yes. Can I speak to him?"

"No. He's not here. Can I ask why you're calling him?"

"He's been helping me with a problem."

"Would this problem have anything to do with a man trying to hurt you?"

Gwen sat up in her seat. Petersen had talked to his wife about her. "Yes."

"We need to talk. Now, if possible."

Gwen wanted to tell Lynette to call back later, but the woman's urgency worried her. "I have a young child. Do you mind coming here?"

"No."

As soon as Gwen heard a car pull up, she went outside. Lynette was an attractive woman for her age, but worry was etched into her features. She ushered Lynette into the kitchen and sat her down.

"Thanks for seeing me."

"Not a problem."

"When did you last speak to Tom?"

"Last Thursday."

Lynette was silent for a moment. "That was the last time I heard from him, too."

"He hasn't been home?"

"I don't know; I've been gone. Tom said the person he was staking out had found out about him and knew where he lived. He sent me out of town for a few days for my safety. Is this related to you?"

It sure sounded like Tarbell. "I think so. Tom never mentioned it to me, though."

"What is all this about?"

"It's about a man called Stephen Tarbell," Gwen said and outlined the events of the last few weeks, from his first attack through to her firing. "Tom believed I was a victim. He offered to help without PSI's support. He installed security cameras here in case Tarbell breaks in again."

Lynette smiled, looking up at the cameras. "Just like Tom not to let things go."

"The last I heard from him he'd broken into Stephen Tarbell's house to find evidence. He called me to say he'd found proof, but I never heard from him again. I thought he'd been arrested for breaking in, but I guess he wasn't."

Lynnette looked down at the table. Gwen wasn't giving her the answers she'd been hoping for. Gwen also felt defeated. Lynette hadn't given her anything to go on.

"Mrs. Petersen, can I get you something to drink?"

"Water, please."

Gwen filled a glass and brought it back to the table.

"Did you talk to Robert Ingram at PSI?" Lynette asked.

"I've tried, but PSI has no interest in anything I have to say since I've been fired. They helped my employer take out a restraining order out against me. That's what Stephen Tarbell has done to my life."

"Why didn't you go the police when you didn't hear from Tom?"

"Considering what Tom was doing at the time, it wasn't a good idea. Besides, I thought he'd abandoned me. Everybody else has."

"Do you think this Stephen Tarbell could have hurt Tom?"

"Yes, I do."

"I'm going to report this to the police."

Gwen couldn't let that happen, not when she had everything so delicately poised. Police involvement would cast scrutiny on her she couldn't afford, but worse, the police would interview Tarbell. It would prevent him from striking back at her and keep Kirsten safe, but it was a short-term fix. Once he'd dealt with the police, he'd come after her again. She'd barely managed to keep a grip on her courage to follow through with her plan for dealing with Tarbell. In a month, it might not be there. She couldn't let Lynette involve the police.

"Lynette, I'm going to tell you something. I'm trusting you that what I tell you doesn't leave this room."

Lynette was silent. Gwen took her silence as a yes.

"My husband is in a coma. He was beaten and left for dead. Stephen Tarbell called me to tell me he'd done it. He's also sworn to kill my daughter."

Each piece of information seemed to put another crushing burden on Lynette. Gwen knew she should spare this woman the details. She was living in a state of fear, a fear that would be magnified by knowing what Tarbell was capable of. Lynette's husband had been missing for a week. It wasn't fair that Gwen should burden her, but she had to make her understand what was at stake.

"I can't let that happen, Lynette. Stephen Tarbell can destroy my career and my life, but I can't let him kill my daughter."

Lynette reached across the table and took Gwen's hand. "Come with me to the police."

"I've tried that. They aren't interested. Tarbell has made me into the monster. Everyone is protecting him. It has forced me to take matters into my own hands."

Lynette pulled her hand back. "Gwen, what are you talking about?"

"I've made a deal. I offered my life for Kirsten's."

"You're crazy. You can't."

"But I don't have a choice. I have to. Now I need your help."

Lynette pulled her hand away. "I'm sorry. I can't. I need to find Tom." She rose to her feet. "I have to go."

Gwen followed her to the front door. "Lynette, please, don't go to the police. I don't have anyone to help me. I'm desperate. I wouldn't be doing this if I wasn't."

"I'm sorry, but I can't help."

"He's going to kill my daughter. If you go to the police, it will guarantee her death."

That stopped Lynette. It was cruel of her to put this on Lynette, but she was way beyond being fair. Things had to be done her way from now on.

Lynette picked up a framed photograph off the mantel. It was a picture of Kirsten taken only the month before their lives had been hurled into free fall.

"Is this her?"

Gwen nodded.

Lynette brushed a caring hand over Kirsten's image before replacing the frame on the mantel. "I need a question answered before I can help you."

Gwen hoped it was a question she could answer. "OK."

"Do you think Tom is dead?"

Gwen closed her eyes. She didn't want to answer this question, but it was the only way to get what she wanted. She had to answer honestly. Lynette would see through anything else. "Yes, I do."

CHAPTER TWENTY-SEVEN

Fifteen years earlier

Parker's Suburban bounced over a pothole and Gwen jerked back into consciousness. A fog still clouded her thoughts from where he'd slammed her head against the wall, but rising panic soon cleared her mind. This guy had her and God only knew what he had planned for her.

He hadn't noticed her come to. She wanted to keep it that way and remained slumped against the passenger door.

She couldn't escape if she didn't know where she was. A sign flashed by for Woodland. She knew the farm community well, but she didn't recognize the road they were on. Woodland was small. She'd find a way to a road she knew. That was the easy part. Escaping was the problem.

Parker had been lazy. He hadn't bound her. He'd put his faith in his strength and her frailty. His focus wasn't even on her. He was singing along with the softly playing radio. She had an edge.

Not only had he not bound her, he hadn't even belted her into her seat. How fast were they traveling? She couldn't see the speedometer without moving and giving herself away. Judging by the world speeding by her window and the engine noise, she estimated they were doing about forty miles an hour. Forty didn't sound fast unless you were contemplating hurling yourself out of a vehicle. She was looking at some serious injuries if she jumped, but something worse if she didn't. She didn't have a choice.

She psyched herself up and focused on everything she needed to do. Grab the door handle and yank. Her body weight would force the door open and she'd tumble out. She wouldn't fight the fall. She'd just go with it, curl into a tight ball, protect her head and hope for the best.

Parker slowed for a bend. Gwen wouldn't get a better chance, and she yanked on the handle. The door didn't budge.

Parker grabbed her by the hair and jerked her across the bench seat over to him. "What do you take me for, an idiot?"

Gwen said nothing.

He put his mouth to her ear. "But you did. That's why you weren't very nice to me back there. I was just some redneck who you thought didn't deserved the time of day, let alone any common courtesy. Now you're going to find out what being rude gets you."

The panic Gwen had managed to quash earlier reemerged with a vengeance. Plotting her escape had quelled her fears, but now any chance of escape was gone.

"Lesson learned. Let me go, and I won't say anything to anyone."

Parker laughed a dirty laugh filled with cruelty. "You're a long way from learning a lesson, but I'll teach you. Yeah, I'll teach you real good."

He pulled off the road onto a dirt and gravel drive. The Suburban's headlights lit up a sorry-looking double-wide. He stopped the truck in front of it and cut the engine. "Home, sweet home."

He entwined his hand deep inside Gwen's hair and made a fist. Gwen yelped. He chuckled, then dragged her across the bench seat and out of the vehicle. "Scream if you like. No one will hear you."

It wasn't an empty boast. Fields stretched in all directions. Gwen didn't see any lights or houses. "Please don't do this. You don't want to do this."

"But I do."

Gwen broke into sobs. She'd done her best not to. She hadn't wanted to feed his ego or show any fear. Her legs went out from under her.

"C'mon, Gwen, don't embarrass yourself."

Parker dragged her to her feet. She struck out at him, but he grabbed her and shoved her through the door into the trailer. "Welcome to Casa Parker."

It smelled of old food and damp. He pushed her at the sofa, and she fell onto it.

She expected him to pounce, but he opened a cupboard and brought out a pair of tumblers and a bottle of Jack Daniel's. He smiled and poured two generous measures. The scene jarred. He couldn't seriously be trying to make a date out of this abduction. It was beyond ridiculous. He held out a glass to Gwen, and she took it, too afraid to turn down his hospitality.

He remained standing, putting a barrier between her and the door behind him.

"Gwen, you have to learn that you can't be a snob. You can't treat people like shit just because you think you're better than them."

"I didn't. I wasn't."

"Don't give me that. You and your friends thought you could treat me like shit because you're clever little college things and I'm some knuckle dragger."

"It wasn't like that. I just didn't know you."

"Well, here's our chance to get acquainted."

"I don't want to."

He slammed his glass down on the table. Gwen jumped. "See, Gwen, there you go again with that holier-than-thou attitude. You're giving me the brush-off before you've had a chance to get to know me."

"I have the right to decide who I get to know."

Parker snorted. "I guess you do. I suppose you want to leave."

Was this some kind of trick? He wasn't going to let her go after all he'd done. Or maybe he would. Perhaps this was an elaborate act to put the fear of God in her. Well, it was mission accomplished. "Yes. I want to go."

"Sing me a song and you can go."

"What?"

"It's quite simple. Sing me a song and you can go."

"I don't want to sing."

"Gwen, give me something here. You don't want to be with me, and now you won't sing for me. Am I that horrible?"

It was a question she didn't dare answer. "What do you want to hear?"

"Anything. I don't care. I just like hearing your voice. Sing me something from tonight. Your choice."

She ran through the songs from her set tonight in her head. She knew them but the words were smudged in her mind. "I don't think I can."

"Sure you can. You just need some encouragement."

He came over, took the glass from her hand, lifted her from the sofa, and pushed her to the center of room. Through the open doorway, an unmade bed showed her the alternative.

Parker took Gwen's seat on the sofa and sipped her whiskey. "C'mon, Gwen, give me your best."

She closed her eyes and pictured the words. The lyrics to a song appeared. She sang the first line. A tremor killed her normally clear voice.

"Oh, Gwen, you've got to do better than that if you expect to leave here."

Gwen opened her eyes. She looked from Parker to the door. It sat ajar. She zeroed in on that. She pictured herself leaving through that door and made herself believe that the door would remain open if she sang a song.

She turned her gaze on Parker and sang to him. Her voice wasn't as crisp as it had been back at Brats, but there was no tremor.

When she finished the song, Parker applauded. "That was very nice."

"Thanks."

She headed toward the door. Parker jumped up to block her path. "Sorry, I don't think I can let you leave."

She didn't argue or complain or even attempt to reason with him. She just bolted for the door.

He grabbed Gwen and drove her into a wall. The trailer rocked, and she buckled. He scooped her up and dragged her toward the bedroom.

She kicked. She wouldn't let him take her in there. If she went into that room with him, she'd die. She kicked again and tried to punch him, but failed to land a blow that had any effect on Parker. He was too big and too strong.

He threw her down on the bed so hard she bit her tongue. Blood trickled between her lips. The sight of it excited him. He fell on top of her and kissed her, forcing his tongue in her mouth. She tasted the alcohol on his breath and snapped her face away.

"Don't deny me now, Gwen," he snarled.

He pinned her down by the throat while he hitched up her skirt and jerked down his pants.

This can't be happening, Gwen thought. Her brain burned with fear. She couldn't let this happen.

She struck out at him and her nails gored his cheek.

He slapped her hard across the face. Fire-like bursts crossed her vision, but she also saw the bedside lamp. She grabbed it and smashed it across Parker's head. It made a hollow thud against his skull and dropped him to his knees.

She shoved him aside and raced for the door, but he hooked her ankle and brought her smashing down on her face. She didn't let that faze her, and she was back on her feet, running.

So was Parker. He grabbed her hair and snapped her head back. Gwen crashed into the dining table, breaking the flimsy thing. She went down with the table, and his dishes and the open bottle of Jack landed on top of her. She went for the bottle and swung it at Parker. It connected with his temple. His eyes rolled up in his head, and for a second, Gwen thought she had him, but he clung on to consciousness and slapped the bottle out of her hand.

"Bitch," he barked.

Hatred, thick and black, consumed his expression. It scared Gwen. She had only angered him, and she knew she'd pay the price now.

He pinned her to the floor by the throat with one hand while his hand grabbed something from among the table's wreckage. She didn't see what it was until he'd driven the steak knife into her midsection.

Gwen couldn't say it hurt. Pain ignited through her entire body, but it was immediately scattered by too many competing sensations fighting for prominence. All she knew was she couldn't move.

Parker stared at his handiwork. His overwhelming fury dissolved into panic.

"Oh, Christ," he murmured.

"Help me." The words came hard for Gwen.

He looked at her face, then at the knife, then back to her face again.

"Help me," she repeated.

Parker staggered back from what he'd done, then shouldered his way out of the trailer. Gwen knew he wouldn't be returning.

The present

Gwen lined up with the rest of the visitors entering San Quentin. She didn't receive special treatment this time. There'd be no one-on-one with Parker. That was because Naylor hadn't pulled any strings to get her inside. Naylor wasn't to know of this meeting. No one was. She'd submitted a formal request and hoped Parker would agree. She thought he would. Even blind to her reasons for visiting, he wouldn't be able to resist.

It hadn't been an easy decision for her to make. In a lot of ways, she hadn't made a decision. Her choices had been peeled away one by one until a single course of action remained.

Gwen passed all the security checks and was escorted into the same visiting area as before. This time, she wasn't alone. The room was packed with visitors and inmates.

Parker spotted her first. He put up a hand, and she weaved her way over to him. He smiled and put out a hand for her to shake. She hesitated for a second before shaking it. She didn't want her refusal to return the gesture to draw any attention. Taking his broad, strong hand cast her back in time. She remembered those hands pawing at her, trying to worm their way into her underwear. It was the same hand she saw in nightmares grabbing a knife and plunging it into her stomach.

"Good to see you, Gwen," he said, smiling. "I've got to admit, I wasn't expecting to see you before Friday. Can't get enough of me, eh?"

His little joke made her recoil, like she was hearing fingers drawn down a chalkboard. His smile broadened at seeing her discomfort.

He dropped the smile. "What do you want, Gwen?"

"I wanted to talk."

"And talk without Naylor's knowledge. I find that strange. My lawyer would find it even stranger."

Gwen felt a spike of fear. "Have you told him?"

"No. The son of a bitch would bill me. You're safe. I imagine that's what you were counting on."

Gwen said nothing and waited for Parker to stop playing. She needed him to be in a listening mood.

"Something you want to get off your delightful chest?"

"There's something."

Parker sucked in a breath. "So hard. So strong. Who would have thought that college girl I met all those years ago would become such a tough cookie. I like it. Really, I do. I like to think I had something to do with that change in character."

"You can think what you like."

"I can and do, even within walls. That's one thing they can't take away from me. So, what do you want?"

"I want to make you an offer."

Parker lost his playfulness and narrowed his eyes. "What kind of offer?"

"I need something done, and I think you can do it for me."

Parker flung his arms wide. "From in here?"

"No."

She let the significance of that remark sink in.

"Is this some stunt Naylor put you up to?"

"No."

"Yeah, right. If you're wearing a wire, anything you get in here isn't legal."

Gwen pulled her jacket open. "No wire. No Naylor. No anyone. This is just about you and me."

Parker wavered, his suspicion melting, but he didn't let it drain away completely. He'd been inside too long for that.

"What's the offer?"

She leaned forward. This was the part no one else was meant to hear. "Do you want to get out of here?"

"I'm going to. I just have to say my piece Friday and it's done."

"But you've got me in the way."

A crooked smile spread across his face. "I don't think so. You said it yourself last time. I'm the model prisoner and there are plenty waiting to take my place. I'll get my parole."

"Don't be so sure. I'll be a compelling witness. My life hasn't been going well the last few weeks. My career is in the toilet. My husband is in the hospital with a coma. My medical insurance runs out at the end of the month, and I don't have the money to renew it. So, I'm feeling vindictive, and I want some payback. Come Friday, I'm going to make you look like the devil incarnate, and no matter how squeaky-clean your record is inside, the parole board won't let you out. Ever."

Parker's hands curled into fists. "You bitch."

"Watch the tone. You don't want to draw any unnecessary attention."

"Neither do you."

Gwen shrugged. "Even if I do, I get to leave. You don't. So keep your cool. If you take a swing, I don't even have to turn up on Friday. Your parole will be done."

Parker uncurled his hands, but he was breathing hard. His chest swelled with each breath, stretching his T-shirt tight. He was still a man to be reckoned with. Despite the model-prisoner act, he was a brutal monster capable of despicable acts. He was the man she needed.

"I don't have to be so mean-spirited on Friday. After all, you're my past, not my present."

"But you'd like to see me rot in here forever."

"I would. I won't lie. But as much as I want that, you're not my boogeyman anymore."

Parker eyed her quizzically. "There's someone else out there."

Gwen nodded. "He makes you look like a choirboy."

Parker laughed. It drew a couple of glances but was nothing that caused anyone any real concern.

"I doubt that."

"Believe it. His cruelty is nothing you can match. I'm not belittling you. It's just a fact."

The remark brought Parker's humor to a short-lived end. Gwen's intent was sinking in. He knew he was being asked something. But for any bargain to be struck, it had to be said out loud.

"What are you saying?"

"I'll be supportive of your parole at the hearing."

SIMON WOOD

Parker's expression remained stony. "In exchange for what?"

Gwen took a breath to steady herself. Now was the time. The communal room where they sat was a good place to ask this question. There were so many conversations happening, there was no way the patrolling officers would zero in on theirs.

"A coworker of mine," she laughed, "an ex-coworker now, has been terrorizing my life. He threatened to kill me, he put my husband in a coma, and he's threatened to kill my daughter. I can't have that."

"What are you asking me to do?"

"I want you to prevent him from hurting my family."

Gwen expected one of two reactions. Parker would either laugh in her face, or he'd play it cool. She couldn't go to jail and leave Kirsten exposed to Tarbell. She willed him to play it cool—and he did.

"Do you know what you're asking?"

"Yes."

"Really?"

"More than you know."

"You think my parole is worth this?"

"Tell me you don't want to get out of here."

"I do, but not at any cost. If I get parole, I get a second chance. You've just given me that chance. I can go to Naylor right now and tell him what you just said to me. Your ass will be in jail faster than you can scream my name the way you did all those years ago."

It was time to use a Tarbell tactic against Parker. "Call who you like. You don't have anything on me. OK, I'll have a few hard minutes explaining why I'm here today, but if you say I tried to buy your parole, I'll deny it. It'll be your word against mine—and who do you think will win that little battle?" She let the facts of life sink in. "What's it going to be?"

Parker said nothing. He was weighing up his options. It played across his face. A month ago his parole looked solid, but not anymore. If Gwen spoke against him at his hearing, he wasn't going anywhere. She would put on the performance of her life to do it. He knew it. Gwen knew it. If he wanted out this time around, he didn't have a choice.

Parker took a breath and released it. "Kind words at my hearing aren't enough."

"I didn't think they would be. I know the risk you're taking and the position I'm putting you in. I'll pay you ten thousand."

Gwen watched Parker's resistance crack. He was counting the money and imagining his freedom.

"Are you in?"

Parker didn't answer.

"There's no time for thinking it over. Friday is only two days away. It's either yes or no. I need the answer now."

"Yes," said Parker.

CHAPTER TWENTY-EIGHT

The detective was coming, but Tarbell was ready for him.

It would have been nice if his father's death could have been boxed up and forgotten. It was the least the son of a bitch could have done for him after a lifetime of misery, but his father being his father, it didn't work out that way. He thought he'd done a good job of making the old man's death look innocent enough. The paramedics hadn't given the death a second thought, but procedure got in the way. He'd made one mistake. When they asked him if he'd been with his father when he passed, he said no. He wanted the official record to show he was nowhere near his father when he died. The second he'd suffocated the old man, he'd driven to Elk Grove, bought cigars, and driven back before calling 911. That way he could safely say he'd been away from the house for over an hour. It was a story the paramedics and the coroner accepted, but since his father had died alone, the county policy required an autopsy. The mention of an autopsy didn't scare him, but the mention of a detective did.

He'd laid low after that. He was a grieving son. He did all the things he was supposed to do. He arranged the funeral and the service. He was cremating the old bastard. His dad hadn't wanted that, but Tarbell didn't care. The old man deserved to burn, and it also prevented anyone from reexamining the body should they have second thoughts. He contacted everyone who needed to be contacted, which in his father's case, wasn't a long list. He'd alienated almost everyone during his lifetime.

Pace Pharmaceuticals had shown their support. They made a donation to a charity of Tarbell's choosing and granted him bereavement leave. Deborah Langan had been so gracious to him. It was two-faced, considering she'd brought in Private Security International to investigate him. When this was all over, he should pay her a visit in some form or another. He kept the idea in the back of his mind on a low simmer. He couldn't let that anger boil over right now or it might get in the way of the problem at hand.

The death certificate was the problem. The autopsy had been done, but the coroner wouldn't release the certificate or even give him the unofficial findings. The fact that they wouldn't tell him anything made the detective's interest all the more obvious. Maybe they wanted him on the defensive. It was a dumb move on their part. Had they never heard the phrase "forewarned is forearmed?"

The detective arrived at ten thirty. Tarbell saw the unmarked Crown Victoria pull up in front of his house, but he didn't acknowledge the detective until he rang the doorbell. He didn't want to look eager—or possibly desperate.

"Detective Wilhoit, Yolo County Sherriff's Department. Thanks for seeing me under these circumstances."

Tarbell smiled and showed the detective into the house.

Detective Wilhoit was younger than Tarbell expected. He was no more than thirty. Either he was a highflier or this investigation was a simple one.

Detective Wilhoit sat in a lounger but leaned forward in his seat. He pulled out a notebook and turned to a page. "I just have a few questions about your father's death. Is that OK?"

"Sure."

"I understand your father was in poor health, correct?"

Tarbell nodded.

"Would you say your father was a happy man?"

It was an odd question, but Tarbell took it in stride. It was better if he didn't think about the questions he was being asked, just answered them. "No, he wasn't happy. My father had been an active man, and for him to end up in a wheelchair was hard for him."

Detective Wilhoit nodded his understanding but made no notation of Tarbell's answer in his book.

"It must have been a burden for you—having to get a caregiver and all?"

Tarbell wondered if that question was as loaded as the gun on the young detective's hip.

"Not really. My parents raised me. It was the least I could do, all things considered." Tarbell hoped his answer wasn't too saccharine. It wouldn't take much digging to find out what a son of a bitch his father was.

"But your father was aware of the burden he was to you, financially and personally?"

"I guess so."

Had his dear old dad left a note behind in case of this eventuality? Had he said something to Lupe? Tarbell didn't think so. His dad never credited him with any balls. The last thing he would have suspected was that he'd kill him.

"Did you ever tell him how much his caregiver was costing you?"

"No, but I'm sure he had an idea."

Detective Wilhoit nodded and smiled. His pen remained poised over virgin paper. Irritation spread over Tarbell like prickly heat.

"Could you afford to keep paying your father's medical expenses?"

"Luckily, yes. I don't have any dependents other than Dad. I live simply, and I have a pretty good salary."

"But your father's condition kept you close to home. The caregiver told me you gave up your Saturdays to be with him."

"I'm not a big traveler. My vacations are spent in my home or nearby. I won't lie. I missed having my Saturdays to myself, but my dad was my dad."

Tarbell saw where this was going. Son tired of supporting his father lashes out and kills him. It was a desperate crime that Tarbell wasn't guilty of, and he felt confident he'd outrun any such accusation. Nevertheless, he had to tread carefully with Detective Wilhoit. He hadn't become a detective at a young age by being dumb.

"Your father's condition was never going to get better, was it?"

"No."

"He still had years ahead of him in theory, but they wouldn't have been fun ones, would they?"

"No, they wouldn't." Tarbell felt it was time to get to the point. "Look, I don't mean to be rude, but why all the questions?"

Detective Wilhoit frowned. "I have some difficult questions that I need your full cooperation with. Is that OK?"

"Sure, I guess," Tarbell said. He tried to relax, but playing his part in this drama made him irritable.

"Your father wasn't supposed to drink, but the autopsy turned up alcohol in his system. Do you know how that happened?"

"I gave it to him. I know he shouldn't drink, but he asks every time I visit. Usually, I'm more resistant to his requests, but he kept asking, and I gave in. It was something he did a lot when he was healthier. At this point in his life, I couldn't see what harm a shot would do him. He was already hurting. I'm sorry I did it now."

"No, that's OK. I think I would have done the same thing in your position. So he used to bust your chops over a drink every time you came?"

"Pretty much."

"Why did you give in this time?"

"This Saturday, he seemed more depressed than usual."

"His caregiver said he'd seemed preoccupied."

"Yeah, that's what she told me, and I saw it. So when he kept asking for a drink, I gave in. Did the drink contribute to his death? Please, tell me it didn't. I would hate for it to be my fault."

Detective Wilhoit held a hand up. "It didn't. Don't let it concern you. Many things contributed to your father's death."

Tarbell pondered the significance of "many things."

"The coroner who collected your father's body remarked in his statement that you went to Elk Grove to buy cigars."

"Yes, I did."

"Who were the cigars for?"

For effect, Tarbell took his time answering. "They were for him. He wanted a drink and a smoke. He'd gone without for a long time, and like I said, I didn't see the harm in this one occasion."

"I'm sure there are closer smoke shops you could have gone to than one in Elk Grove."

"Yeah, there are, but Pop went to the one in Elk Grove, and he wanted me to get him a cigar from there. I didn't see any reason not to."

"So your father sent you out to Elk Grove, even though he'd be at home at least an hour without any supervision?"

"Yeah, but it was only an hour. He was sick, but he wasn't that sick. It was OK to leave him that long. Well, that was what I thought at the time."

Detective Wilhoit had begun taking notes. Tarbell knew that this line of questioning was important to him.

"So your father asked for a drink and for a cigar and you gave them to him."

"Yes. Well, the drink anyway. I never had the chance to give him his cigar."

"Any life insurance on your father?"

Tarbell shook his head.

"But he owned the house in West Sacramento?"

"Yes. Look, tell me what's going on. My sick father died. I don't see the need for a detective."

"Your father's oxygen supply had been turned up high and as odd as it sounds, it caused asphyxia. This led to his death. We aren't looking at natural causes."

Tarbell's pulse quickened, pumping panic through his veins. He couldn't go to jail for his father's death. It wasn't fair. He had so many other things to do. He hoped it wouldn't mean he'd have to kill the young detective. Detective Wilhoit was armed, but he wouldn't expect a surprise attack. His gaze locked on the vase on the coffee table. It would be enough to immobilize the detective. It would be messy, and there'd be no way of covering it up, but there was no way he was leaving his home in cuffs.

"What do you mean? If it wasn't natural causes, what was it?" Tarbell shifted forward in his seat on the sofa, bringing the vase within arm's reach.

"Suicide."

The word pushed Tarbell off balance, and all the thoughts of grabbing the vase flew out of his mind.

"Suicide?"

"Yes, I'm sorry to say. Your father saw an unenviable future ahead of him, and it depressed him. He knew he was a burden to you and everyone around him. It must have preyed on him, and it finally became too much to bear. He sent you miles out of your way to buy him a cigar when you could have easily gotten one down the street. It left him plenty of time to turn up his oxygen."

Tarbell fought to keep a grin buried deep. He wanted to hug the detective for his stupidity.

"I'm sorry to be the one to break the news to you."

"That's OK, I guess."

Detective Wilhoit rose to his feet, pocketing his notebook. Tarbell followed him to the door as he saw himself out. He held out his hand, and Tarbell took it.

"I do have one last question for you, Mr. Tarbell. I don't like asking it, but I have to."

"It's OK. Go ahead."

"Did you know about your father's suicidal tendencies?"

"No."

"I understand if you took that drive to leave your father alone. I've known loved ones to do that. It's a kindness, I guess. It's something I can't condone as an officer of the law, but as a son, I can take an answer at face value."

Tarbell smiled. Detective Wilhoit was a nice guy. He was glad he didn't have to kill him.

"I hear what you're saying, but I didn't know my father was planning to kill himself." It was an honest answer that would pass any polygraph.

Detective Wilhoit said his good-byes and left. Tarbell closed the door, bristling with euphoria. Nothing stood in his way now. If he ever needed a sign of that, this was it. The world believed his father's death was suicide. Fantastic. It set him up for what he had to do next.

CHAPTER TWENTY-NINE

Fifteen years earlier

Blood poured out at a steady stream around the knife blade. Gwen was transfixed by it. She felt the blade move inside her with every breath. She wanted to rip the knife out, but she kept a grip on her fear. The knife was a plug. If she yanked it out, she'd bleed to death. The knife was killing her, but at the same time, it was keeping her alive.

She spotted the phone on the dining table. She was a 911 call away from surviving this nightmare.

She tried to stand, but the knife in her stomach had robbed her of her ability to walk. She rolled onto her side to avoid impaling herself any further. She clawed at the mangy carpet and dug her heels in for traction. She slid forward, screaming, as the blade shifted in her stomach. She wanted to hold the knife in place when she moved, but she needed both hands to drag her useless body across the floor. Tears poured down her face as she bit back the pain.

Progress was slow. The carpet clung on to her like hundreds of tiny hooks, snagging her torn clothes. Twenty feet seemed an impossible distance. Her progress was counted in inches, not feet. She'd die here in this trailer all because she couldn't drag her sorry ass twenty feet to a lifeline. It was funny and infuriating. She channeled her fury and pulled herself along. The table came closer and closer into view.

"Thank you, God," she said when she reached the table. She yanked on the phone cord and jerked the phone onto the floor. She didn't bother with the handset. She just punched in 911. She picked up the phone expecting to hear the sweetest voice she'd ever heard and heard nothing. Parker's phone wasn't connected. The bastard didn't keep up with his bill.

"Son of a bitch," she screamed and tossed the useless phone away.

Not only had she wasted precious minutes and spilled more blood she couldn't afford to lose, she was now twenty feet farther away from the door.

Her only hope was to stop a passing car. If twenty feet seemed like a transcontinental journey, dragging herself the hundred or so feet to the roadside was a voyage around the world.

She couldn't give up.

She turned around and dragged her way back to the door. She stared out at the quiet roadway. Not a single car cut a hole in the night. She could haul herself out to the side of the road and it was possible no one would drive by until it was too late. It was cruel and incredible.

She couldn't put her fate in luck's hands. She had to bring people to her. She just needed something to do it. A grease-stained stove with a squat propane tank underneath sat across from her. Parker didn't look like a guy who cooked much, and she realized that might just be enough to save her.

She pulled herself over to the stove and hauled herself onto her knees. The simple task forced a scream from her. She clung on to the stove and twisted all the knobs. The hiss of gas pouring from the burners had never sounded better, and the sickly stink of propane never smelled sweeter.

Parker's pilot light must have been broken because a gas lighter sat on top of the stove. Gwen grabbed it with the last of her strength and fell back. She hit the floor hard on her back and didn't move for a minute. The knife rang a note through her body like a tuning fork.

Propane was filling the trailer. She rolled onto her side and hauled herself to the door. She pulled her body through the door and down the step, then leaned through the doorway and ignited the lighter. She touched the naked flame to the carpet and the walls and anything else that would burn. The cheap materials ignited. It didn't take long for flames to spread. She dropped the lighter and dragged her limp body across the dirt and gravel toward the road. She ignored the sharp gravel cutting her palms and feet. She put the knife sticking out of her stomach out of her mind. These things couldn't slow her down if she was to survive. She had to get to the road and away from the trailer.

"Come on, Gwen," she snarled. "Keep going. Don't give up. You're nearly there."

She ignored the fiery crackling coming from the trailer behind her and focused on the road ahead lit by the moon.

A car sped by. It didn't see her. She was too far from the road, and the fire had yet to grow beyond a glow from within. It was heartbreaking to see the car speed into the night, but it didn't matter. There'd be others. She truly believed that. She had to.

She was less than ten yards from the roadside when the flames ignited the propane. The resulting explosion wasn't spectacular, but it made its presence felt. It blew the trailer's windows and door out, and the concussive boom carried across the flat fields. Gwen felt it wash over her. Anyone within a mile radius would have heard it, and with their inquisitiveness piqued, they would see orange flames climbing into the night's sky.

Gwen turned back to watch the blaze. Her work was done. She rolled onto her back and waited for someone to find her.

The present

Gwen drove to San Quentin aware that she held all the power. She could liberate or bury Parker. She might have made a bargain with him, but she could go back on it. If Parker balked, he had nothing on her. It was nice to have the power over someone, but it wasn't a feeling she enjoyed. It reminded her too much of the power Tarbell had over her, and in no way did she want to be anything like him. But she knew that in order to stop him, she'd have to act like him. She'd spent hours next to Paul's comatose body thinking about this moment and its consequences. Yes, this one act would change her forever, but it had to be done. Tarbell had ruined her. She had two options, succumb or overcome. Given Paul's condition, she knew which one she had to choose. Surrender wasn't an option. It wasn't right, and it wasn't fair. Paul would need a lot of care and attention, and Kirsten had her whole life ahead of her. When it came to Parker, Gwen had the power. And she was going to use it.

She parked in the visitors' lot and checked in at the security gate. Jerry Naylor wasn't there waiting for her, but she received the VIP treatment. A corrections officer walked her to the room where the parole hearing would be taking place. On the way, the officer chatted about the weather and whether Gwen had any weekend plans. Gwen didn't get the feeling that the officer was trying to plaster over the obvious difficulty of the situation, just that she was eager to chat about something that had nothing to do with life in a prison.

The officer told Gwen to wait outside the meeting room while she went in search of Naylor. He emerged from the meeting room with a polite smile and a sidekick. He introduced the sidekick as an assistant DA who'd be speaking on behalf of Yolo County.

"I'm glad you came today," he said, shaking Gwen's hand. "I know this isn't easy, but it's for the best."

Naylor's sincerity irritated Gwen. There was no falseness about his remarks, but he was the guardian of a faulted system.

Justice didn't count. The legal system was about bartering—getting the best possible deal for society instead of the right one. She knew how bitter her thoughts were, but it was hard to be forgiving, all things considered.

Naylor ran through the day's events. The parole board would hear from Parker, examine his prison history, and discuss his parole plans. Then they would hear objections and ask Gwen her feelings about Parker's potential release. Proceedings would start at the top of the hour.

"Can I get you coffee or anything?" Naylor asked. "It's pretty good, considering this is a prison."

Gwen shook her head.

When the time came, he guided her into the room and to a seat, as if she didn't know how to do these things herself. The room was set up like a boardroom with a single table where all parties sat. She, Naylor, and his assistant DA sat across from the two-person parole board. Parker's lawyer sat alongside Naylor. A tape recorder sat on the table to record every word uttered.

When everyone was comfortable, a corrections officer led Parker in. He was in his prison blues and uncuffed. He shook hands with his lawyer and took a seat. The officer sat behind Parker. The inmate made eye contact with the parole board, Naylor, and Gwen, albeit briefly. Gwen wondered if his choice to avoid eye contact with her was a nice piece of acting or a fear that he might give away their agreement. Either way, it proved that he was the right man for the job.

The chairman for the parole board kicked things off. After calling the proceedings to order, he, along with his partner, quizzed Parker. They discussed his crime and his feelings about what he'd done. Gwen tensed as she heard the dispassionate way they discussed the crimes committed upon her. It was a relief when they turned to Parker's prison history and his plans if released. The inevitable questions came. Was he sorry? Would he be a rehabilitated member of society if released? The questions sounded trite and childish. She paraphrased in her head. *So, Mr. Bad Man, are you sorry for attempting to rape and kill this woman?* Parker didn't seem to mind and jumped through all the hoops. It was his opportunity to show contrition and win the hearts of the parole board.

Parker sat up in his seat. "I wish I could say my crime that put me here was a one-time event, but it wasn't. I wasn't a good person. I used threats and violence to get my way and it put me here. Fifteen years is a long time to live with the errors I've made. I can't undo what I've done, but if I'm paroled, I won't be falling into my old ways. I want to do something new with my life. Prison has taught me what's important, and forcing my will on people isn't it. I have some goals and ambitions I want to achieve, and I hope you decide to give me the chance to do that.

"I'm glad Mrs. Farris is here today." Parker turned to face Gwen. "I know 'sorry' doesn't come anywhere near to making up for what I did to you, but I am truly sorry. I'm not after your forgiveness, because I don't deserve it, but please accept my apology."

Parker's gaze was intense and unflinching. Gwen didn't flinch either. She examined his stare for some hidden reference to their pact but saw nothing. Parker was not a novice when it came to lying and crime. He knew better than to share some private message with his eyes or his voice that could be noticed by others. Parker waited for her acceptance of his apology, but he turned away when she said nothing.

The chairman turned to Naylor's assistant DA for comment. He made an impassioned appeal to keep Parker incarcerated. His crime had been heinous and, despite his rehabilitation, the fifteen years served paled against the crimes he'd been convicted of. Gwen's stomach ached, and she shut out the man's statement.

When the assistant DA was finished, the chairman turned to Gwen. She was glad to be sitting. She wasn't sure she could have stood up without fainting. She interlaced her fingers to make a tight fist. To them, she must look like a frightened woman coming face-to-face with the man who'd left her to die. Only Parker knew different.

From the corner of her eye, she felt the heat of Naylor's gaze willing her to stick it to Parker. At the same time, she felt Parker's cool gaze on her, still wondering if she was going to be true to her word. A similar question passed through her mind. Then she thought of Paul, still lying in a hospital bed in a coma while Tarbell circled, waiting to pick off Kirsten, then her. She needed someone like Parker to do what Private Security International and the legal system wouldn't do.

"How do you feel about Mr. Parker receiving parole?" the chairman asked.

This was it. This was where she could be true to herself or give in to her needs. It was time to decide.

"I won't lie," she said. "I had hoped this day would never come. I don't think it's right or fair that Desmond Parker be released for his crimes against me."

She felt Naylor's approval radiate toward her. She felt nothing from Parker's end of the table.

"Don't you believe in rehabilitation?" the cochair asked.

"Don't you believe in the protection of victims?"

It was a gunshot-fast remark that shook the chairman's composure. She guessed she'd just painted herself as a hostile personality and her remark probably played in Parker's favor and not Naylor's.

"So, you would be upset if Mr. Parker was granted parole?"

"No."

Naylor gasped. Gwen didn't look at him.

"No?" the chairman said.

"Ten years ago, to know that Desmond Parker would be released would have done more than upset me. The man shoved a knife in my stomach and left me for dead. I had to drag myself forty yards across grass and dirt to the side of the road with a knife in my stomach. It's something you don't forgive in a hurry."

It was a remark that silenced the chairman again.

"That was ten years ago," Gwen said. "Ten years ago, I couldn't see this day. Physically, I was healing. Mentally, I was struggling. Today, it's not like that. I have a wonderful husband. He's truly a kind and gentle man. We have a child together who'll be going to kindergarten next year. I worked hard in my career and it has taken off. All in all, my life is good."

Gwen was talking about a time before Tarbell. Her life was in tatters now. It had all crumbled in a matter of weeks. Still, she could remember that life and imagine returning to it once more. Was she optimistic or delusional? She didn't think so. Parker had come close to robbing her of everything she held dear, but he'd failed and she'd moved on. She could and would do the same thing again.

"Ten years ago, I saw no life ahead of me, but one found me. Desmond Parker deserved to be punished for what he did, and he has been punished, both by the legal system and by his own guilt. I can't say I'll be ecstatic if Mr. Parker is granted parole, but I won't be upset. He is a man who tried to kill me and failed. He's a part of my past, not my present or my future. I love my life and my family. Desmond Parker has nothing to do with it. He has his life, and I have mine."

"So you wouldn't be upset if you encountered Mr. Parker in the course of your daily life?" the chairman asked.

"He'd be just another face in the crowd. Don't get me wrong, I have no desire to be friends. I just want to continue with my life as I'm sure Mr. Parker wishes to continue with his. His parole isn't my decision. It's yours. It's your conscience you have to live with. Not mine."

"Thank you," the chairman said.

The chairman asked her a couple more questions before adjourning so the board could make a ruling. Everyone would be called back in the next thirty to forty minutes. Gwen didn't wait around for the decision. She'd done all she could do and hoped it was enough. On the way out, Naylor chased after her, calling her name. She heard irritation in his voice. She kept on walking toward the exit and managed to get outside the building before he caught up with her and grabbed her arm.

"What the hell was that?"

She stared at his hand gripping her arm, and he released his hold.

"You know you screwed us in there." He fought hard to keep his voice civil. "Parker's going to be granted parole now and with no special conditions after what you said. Is that what you want?"

"It's not important."

"It's not important? That's not what you said two weeks ago."

"I lost my job last week, and my husband is in a coma after a near fatal beating. Desmond Parker is no longer an important issue. He can trawl the streets for more college girls for all I care. I have bigger problems to worry about."

"You don't mean that. I know you, Gwen. You wouldn't want him doing to someone else what he did to you."

Naylor was right. The idea of Parker repeating his crime on another woman left her feeling sick. It was an idea she shoved into the far corners of her mind. She didn't believe he would, and she hoped helping him get parole wouldn't give him the freedom to revert to his old ways. Anyway, it didn't matter now. Parker was a means to an end, and that was all she could think about.

"You're right. I pray to God he never assaults another woman. But if he does, it's your fault. You should have made sure he never got out. That was what you promised me, but that wasn't what you did."

Naylor tried to object, but Gwen talked over him.

"When you met me in the hospital after he stabbed me, you promised me you'd get him life, but you bargained with his lawyer. Parker tried to rape me, but you reduced it to assault to get a faster conviction. If anyone is responsible for Parker's parole, it's you. You sold me out back then, and you thought you'd ease your conscience by trying to kill his parole. Well, it has backfired, and you're going to live with the consequences."

Naylor was silent. She'd hit a mark. She was sorry she'd said it. It was something she should have said back then, not now. She wanted to apologize, but she had bigger problems, ones he couldn't help her with.

"I'm sorry you feel that way, Gwen."

"Can I go?"

Naylor nodded. "I'm sorry to hear about your husband."

Gwen didn't respond. She turned away before the guilt of what she'd just done got the better of her.

CHAPTER THIRTY

Gwen let Parker choose the place to meet. She guessed he'd have more experience than her at this kind of thing. He picked a park in Antioch. It was a good location, if "good" meant completely isolated. The place closed at twilight and was deserted by the time she arrived at nine. She parked and followed the trail with a flashlight into the park as arranged.

She glanced back over her shoulder at the parking lot barely illuminated by a couple of streetlights. Besides her own vehicle, there were no others. Either Parker was on foot or hadn't arrived. Uncertainty crept up on her. She was trusting Parker to behave. She believed he was interested in her money and grateful for her hand in getting him paroled. But all that might turn out to be wishful thinking. This park was a great place to finish what he started back in Davis. She cursed herself for not bringing protection. Even a can of pepper spray would have been something. She stopped. It wasn't too late. She could stand him up and rearrange the meet on her terms.

Listen to yourself, Gwen. You're getting paranoid. She shook her head. Leaving wasn't an option. She didn't have the time for rescheduling. She'd gotten Tarbell hooked, and he'd only wriggle on the line for so long before she lost him. She had to trust that Parker would be true to his word. But just in case, she brought out her key chain, slipped a key between each of her fingers, and closed her hand around the fob. It wasn't much of a weapon, but she'd escaped Parker once before with less.

The trail led her to the meeting place—the entrance of a closed mine that was now the park gift shop. The moment she reached the barred and gated shop, Parker emerged from behind a nearby tree.

A bolt of panic struck her. This was the first time since he'd stabbed her that she was face-to-face with him alone. It brought memories of her abduction flooding back. She hadn't expected the wave of emotion, and she couldn't control it. Instinctively, her grip on her keys tightened.

Parker's gaze flicked to her spiked fist. He stopped a safe distance from her and tried on a smile for size. It didn't quite fit.

"Forgiveness is not easy, is it?" he said.

"No." She didn't know if he was trying to pacify her, but she didn't like it. This had to be weird for him too, but she didn't want empathy between them. Not after what he'd done to her. This was just business.

"How's freedom?" she asked.

"Different, but I'm getting used to it."

After Gwen's star performance at the parole hearing, Parker's release had come swiftly. She'd left Naylor no option but to request the minimum conditions for Parker's parole. He'd been released on Monday. It was now Friday. Tomorrow, he would help her kill someone. It was going to be an eventful week for him.

"Did you bring the money?"

The cash came from Gwen's sister. It was a lot of money to most people but not to Lucy. She worked on Wall Street. She wasn't Forbes 400 material, but ten thousand was a sum she had on tap. The money request had raised suspicions, but Gwen had allayed them with a story about car problems. Lucy had FedExed the cash over right away. Gwen reached inside her purse and pulled out an envelope containing half of Parker's agreed payment. She tossed the money to him.

He caught the envelope but didn't bother checking it. "Gwen, I'm not going to hurt you."

Gwen said nothing, and Parker didn't make a move.

"If you're looking for an apology, I gave it already. I meant what I said at the parole hearing. I'm sorry. I promise you that you're not in any danger, and it has nothing to do with the ten grand you're paying me. OK?"

Still Gwen said nothing, but Parker took an exploratory step forward. When she held her ground, he moved within arm's reach. Her grip on her keys remained tight.

"OK, I've got my money. Now tell me exactly what you want done for this money."

"Stephen Tarbell was my coworker. He threatened to kill me. I want you to kill him."

"Why?"

"You don't need to know why. What you do need to know is that he attacked my husband, leaving him in a coma, and he's threatening to kill my daughter before he comes after me. He'll make good on his threat. I think he killed a private investigator. You'll be working hard for your ten thousand."

"Jesus."

Gwen noticed that genuine shock marked Parker's face. He might have thought he'd brought carnage to Gwen's life, but it paled against what Tarbell had achieved.

"I've offered myself as bait. I'll let him do what he wants to me as long as he doesn't lay a hand on my daughter."

"So you're going to be a part of this."

"Yes. It's the only way it will work."

Parker raised an eyebrow, but she ignored it and outlined her plan to lure Tarbell to Fort Richardson. She handed him a prepaid cell phone, just like the one she'd given Tarbell and the one in her pocket. She'd programmed her number into it. She also gave him an envelope containing five pages of notes with locations, directions, times, and dates. It was all handwritten, making it easy to get rid of. She couldn't take the chance of anything being found on her computer if anyone came asking when Tarbell didn't surface. She'd gone to three different libraries in two different counties to look up the information. She'd even gone to the extent of burning the legal pad she'd made her notes on in case anyone read her impressions on the clean sheets underneath. Extreme paranoia? Maybe. But she wouldn't go to prison, not for Tarbell.

"How closely is your parole monitored?"

"Not very, thanks to you. I have to check in with my parole officer Monday."

"Good. You'll be back before Monday. Don't forget to use cash. I don't want you leaving a credit trail."

He smiled. "I'm a felon. Credit cards don't come easy."

Gwen's next question was the big one. "Do you have a weapon?"

"I have what I need."

Gwen didn't ask for more details. She didn't want to hear it was a knife.

"This all takes place tomorrow. We'll stay in touch by phone, but that's it. We don't meet other than when it's done. Just go to the places and times you have in your notes. You'll find me there as arranged. Wherever I am, he won't be far behind. You shouldn't have any problem finding him."

Parker nodded. "What about disposal?"

"The Pacific."

"I never expected this of you, Gwen."

"Is that why you picked me out all those years ago? Because I wasn't the kind to fight back?"

"Jesus Christ," Parker said and backed up a step. "Don't go there."

"Why not? I think you owe me an answer. It's the least you could do."

"Isn't killing a man for you answer enough?"

"Not even close."

Parker was quiet for a long time. "OK, I went for you because you were a hot little number, and I thought you'd be a quick lay. That was all I was after, but I wasn't good enough for you. I thought if I got you away from your friends, you'd come around, but you didn't. That pissed me off. I took it too far; I admit that, and what happened, happened. OK? That's your answer. Happy now?"

She wasn't. There were no magic answers. It was an answer she'd always known. It didn't take any genius to work it out. Shitty luck put them together in Davis, and it had hurt both of them, changing both their lives.

"I don't like the position you're putting me in, Gwen. I'm many things, but I'm not a killer."

Gwen wondered if she'd misjudged Parker. Fifteen years ago, he was filled with hate and contempt. She didn't know if prison had rehabilitated him, but it had certainly mellowed him.

She felt the itch of a nervousness creep up on her. She prayed she hadn't made a mistake. "I didn't get you paroled for you to back out."

Parker remained stoic. "Gwen, you have no hold on me. I don't have to be here. I can take your money and leave and there's nothing you can do about it. You tell someone, and you'll only be incriminating yourself."

Gwen bristled. "So you are backing out."

"No. I want to prevent you from making a mistake you'll regret."

"There's no mistake to make. I've tried the alternatives, and they didn't work. If there was another way, I would take it, but there isn't. This has to be done."

"Gwen, killing this guy won't be the end of your problems. His death will stick to you for the rest of your life. Killing someone leaves behind an indelible mark. Trust me, I know. Driving a knife into your stomach is something I wake up to every morning. Some mornings my hands are curled around that knife even though it has been sitting in an evidence bag for fifteen years. Do you want to live your life like that? Do you want your daughter knowing what you've done?"

Parker's words hung in the air as heavy as gun smoke.

"I don't have a choice." Her voice sounded small and vulnerable in the night.

"You do. It might not seem like it, but you do. You always have a choice." He pulled back the flap on the envelope containing the five thousand dollars and ran his thumb over the bills before pocketing the cash. "OK, I'll help you. I made a bargain with you. Ten grand isn't much, but it's a start for me. I can get that bike business off the ground with it. And I feel I owe you something more than an apology."

She nodded and turned to leave.

"Gwen, what if he kills you first?"

The same question had rattled around her head. It should have scared her, but it didn't. "It doesn't matter. As long as you do your job, you'll get the rest of the money. Stopping Tarbell before he can get to my daughter is all that counts."

• • •

Ingram sat alone in his office. Everyone had long since left for the evening. The occasional hum of a car passing by was the only thing to penetrate the silence of his thoughts.

He hadn't liked how the Gwen Farris/Stephen Tarbell case ended. The client was satisfied, but that wasn't good enough for him. The investigation had ended in a shambles with one of their own severely injured. The person he'd initially protected had turned out to be the instigator. That did happen sometimes. But in his experience, on such occasions, there was a common thread that ran through the investigation that made sense of the chaos. This one didn't have one. It still wasn't clear to him who was guilty and of what, exactly.

Even with a slew of new assignments preoccupying his time, Gwen's impassioned visit last week kept bothering him. He tried putting it out of his head and moving on, but he couldn't any longer. Gwen had triggered the investigator in him. Just because he had a result, it didn't mean it was the right result.

He struggled with the idea that Gwen Farris had concocted the whole story that Stephen Tarbell was out to get her as cover for her theft of Pace's breast cancer research. Why would she do it? Playing the victim bought her sympathy, sure, but it also bought her attention, which is the last thing she would have wanted. Industrial espionage required anonymity. Instead of keeping her head down, she'd made a big deal about the incidents when Tarbell had assaulted her in the parking lot and the office building. She'd also reported the break-in at her home, the busted window, and the attack on her husband. The whole thing seemed way too elaborate for someone trying to build a sympathy case.

"Shit," he murmured. "What am I saying? That I sided with the wrong person?"

Feelings meant nothing. He needed proof.

Once again, he pulled up the digitally enhanced video on his computer of Gwen's alleged attack near the parking lot's trash enclosure. He forwarded through until he reached the only piece of action, the fingers gripping the wall. He watched and rewatched those few seconds of video, then froze the image, blew it up, and printed it. Even using a magnifying glass he couldn't tell if he was staring at a man or a woman's hand. His gut told him it was a man's. Gwen's hands were small and slender. These fingers were much too big to be hers. But he'd pushed magnification to the point where pixilation distorted the image. He threw the printout and magnifying glass down. He needed something solid that would support the weight of his reputation.

He pulled out the case file, which was thick in comparison to the usual slim folder created by a normal two-week investigation, just a handful of papers that consisted of a background check, surveillance logs, and a statement from the claimant. The Farris/Tarbell case file had spilled into three folders. He was going to be here awhile sifting through it all. He took the case file into the conference room, told his wife not to wait up, and ordered dinner in.

After rereading the incident reports, he decided Tarbell wasn't an innocent party in Gwen's deception. Amanda Norton's verbal report convinced him of that. She'd seen Gwen corner Tarbell in Pace's technical library after she claimed the man had trashed her home. If Tarbell was a clueless party in all of this, the confrontation shouldn't have happened. There'd be no reason for it. What had they been talking about? If Tarbell had truly been innocent, he would have simply walked away from her.

He pictured his encounters with Gwen, including her latest visit. She was a woman driven to the edge, not a guilty woman trying to save her ass. Combined with Amanda's account, it made for a compelling piece of circumstantial evidence.

As he went over Amanda's reports, he thought about his injured investigator. He wondered whether Amanda's accident was really an accident. It seemed like it, but with the twists and turns this investigation had taken, he was having his doubts.

He dragged his now cold takeout food over. He tried eating, but it tasted like ashes. Food wouldn't taste good until he'd gotten to the bottom of Gwen's case. He pushed the food away and returned to the case files.

Removing Tarbell from the equation, the string of calamities to strike Gwen and her family pushed the limits of bad luck. Paul's near-fatal beating pushed it one step too far. He wasn't convinced of Tarbell's involvement, but he needed to know whether the incident belonged in the world of coincidence or something more sinister. He called a contact in the Fremont Police Department for information. His contact told him that until Paul came out of his coma, they had no active leads.

It was midnight by the time he'd gone through the case file, and his brain had turned to pudding. He needed some air. He pushed his chair out from the conference table, rode the elevator to the lobby, and told the security guards on the front desk that he'd be back in ten.

The night air felt good on his skin. With the exception of a handful of homeless guys bedded down in shadowy corners, the financial district was deserted at this time of night. Walking the blocks surrounding his building, he pinned his tentative theory together. Gwen Farris had a falling out with Stephen Tarbell, and he retaliated. Ingram decided that he believed her about the incident in the parking lot and the rock thrown through her window. That left the break-in and lights-out chase at the office. For those incidents, Tarbell had an alibi, thanks to his nighttime surveillance guy.

He kicked around the accomplice theory again. It seemed reasonable, but one thing punched holes in it. Try as they might, his investigators had discovered no signs of Tarbell working with anyone. Yet the only way Tarbell could have had a hand in all the incidents was with an accomplice. There had to be one.

He turned around and returned to his office. He pored through the surveillance reports looking for a crack in the investigation to support the accomplice theory. He listed down the time of all the attacks on Gwen, hoping for some commonality or linkage. He examined his list. It wasn't much, but he saw something he hadn't noticed before, and he didn't like it.

Everything had happened at night. That wasn't uncommon in itself. It would be hard to go after Gwen during the day, especially when she was at the office with so many witnesses around. But at night was when Tarbell's alibi was at its weakest. The man was a shut-in with no friends or social life. His alibi only worked because someone from Ingram's surveillance had said he was at home.

Ingram's thoughts snagged on a fact. PSI, his own people, had provided Tarbell with his alibi. But that wasn't strictly true. Only one person had covered Tarbell during the night. He removed all the surveillance reports for all the attacks. Every one of them had Tom Petersen's name at the top. The possibility of an accomplice stopped being just a possibility.

CHAPTER THIRTY-ONE

"Kirsten, don't be a pain this morning," Gwen said, fighting to put her daughter's sweater on her.

"I don't want to go."

Gwen pulled the sweater off Kirsten for the second time. "I know you don't want to. I don't want to either, but it's something I have to do."

"Then don't do it."

It was that simple to a three-year-old. Gwen wished the whole world operated with the same simplicity. She knelt down in front of her daughter.

"I won't be gone long. Just a couple of days."

The significance of what she'd said hit her hard. If all went right, she'd be back in a couple of days. If it didn't, then…. She pushed the idea from her mind before it bedded in.

"But why?" Kirsten moaned.

"I have to go away. Daddy's still in the hospital, so you need to stay with someone."

"Can't I come?"

"No, babe. Lynette is going to look after you. She's nice. You'll like her. She has a dog."

That caught Kirsten's attention.

"It's a big, black Lab."

Gwen held out Kirsten's sweater again. This time, she put it on without trouble.

She packed an overnight bag, then bundled Kirsten into the car and drove her over to Lynette Petersen's home.

Lynette came out while Gwen was lifting Kirsten from the car. Kirsten went quiet at the sight of the unfamiliar, older woman but warmed to her when she greeted her by name. They went inside the house, Lynette carrying Kirsten's backpack filled with clothes.

"You have a dog?"

"Yes, J. Edgar. He's in the yard."

Kirsten looked to Gwen, and she nodded. Kirsten went scampering off in the direction of the yard.

"We can talk now," Lynette said.

She took Gwen into the kitchen. From there they could see Kirsten playing with the big dog. Lynnette poured Gwen coffee she didn't want and they sat at the table. Hanging on the wall was a picture of Tom Petersen holding a marlin as big as he was.

What happened to you, Tom? Gwen thought. The likely answer scared her.

"You're going through with it," Lynette said.

Gwen brought out Parker's second payment and held it out to Lynette. "Should anything go wrong, I need you to get this to a man called Desmond Parker. All his information is in the envelope."

Lynette pushed Gwen's hand away. "You have to think positively. You can't have failure in your mind. You need to kill this man, and that's what you're going to do."

Gwen put the money away but held out the second envelope with the notes she'd written for Lynette. "The risks are too high for me not to take precautions, Lynette. If it goes wrong, I need you to get Kirsten to my sister in New York. These papers will tell you how to contact her."

Lynette smiled. "I promise to take care of it. But it won't come to that. You are going to succeed, and Kirsten will be waiting for you when you return. You have to believe that. OK?"

Gwen wasn't sure she shared Lynette's confidence, but could tell she had to respond. "OK."

"Good."

Lynette was strong. Gwen didn't know how she did it. She guessed it had something to do with having a husband who had spent his life in law enforcement. She'd spent decades living with the idea that one night he might not come home.

"I have a request, Gwen."

"Anything."

"If you can, get him to tell you what he did to Tom."

"I will." It was a tough promise, but she'd keep it if she could.

Kirsten, squealing with delight from making J. Edgar bark, drew their attention. They went out in the yard and played with Kirsten and the dog. Gwen waited until Kirsten seemed comfortable with Lynette before she knelt down and said good-bye, holding back her own tears. Gwen left her daughter in the backyard with the dog. Lynette walked her out, but before they reached the door, Lynette guided her into a home office. This time, it was impossible to avoid reminders of Petersen. This was his office. It was a cop's room, filled with statutes and codes and too many mementos.

"I want you to take this."

She slid back a closet door and removed a metal cashbox. The key was in the lock. She twisted the key and removed a heavy-looking, short-barreled revolver, as well as a small box of ammunition.

"Tom told me guns weren't the answer."

"That was when you were under his protection. You're not now. No one is protecting you. You need this."

Gwen didn't argue and reached for the weapon, but Lynette maintained her grip on it. "You have to follow through now. Don't give him a second chance. Got that?"

"Yes."

Gwen left with the gun and got behind the wheel of her Subaru. She started the engine, but she couldn't leave, not without doing one more thing. She had to see Paul before she left. Despite Lynette telling her to think positively, she knew this could be the last time she'd see her husband. She couldn't leave without saying good-bye.

At the hospital, she checked in with Dr. Korn. He escorted her to Paul's room. Somehow, he saw improvement under the layers of trauma. She just hoped he was right.

"Trust me, things are getting better," he said before leaving.

The second she was alone with Paul, she broke down. This was her fault, yet at the same time it wasn't. It tore her in two. She'd set Tarbell off; she was guilty of that, but Tarbell's skewed view of the world and cruelty were really to blame. All she was guilty of was doing her job. It never should have come to this, but that didn't matter. It was hers to finish now.

She picked up Paul's hand and held it close to her face. A clip covered his thumb and registered his pulse on a monitor.

"I'm going to get Tarbell now," she said. As she talked to him, she hoped the words would penetrate the deep sleep he was lost in. She liked to think her plan would go her way. It was two against one after all, but she wasn't confident. Tarbell was unstoppable. He'd dismantled her life piece by piece. He said he was going to kill Kirsten, and she believed him. Anything he set his mind to he achieved.

At the same time, Parker was an animal. Her hope was that he'd cancel Tarbell out, and she'd be there to tip the balance. In theory, it could work. Yet while she could succeed, she could also fail. Then Tarbell would win and win big at the expense of her family.

"Someone is looking after Kirsten while I'm gone," she said, still holding her husband's hand. "Should anything happen, she'll get in contact with my sister. I know Lucy will take Kirsten until you're back on your feet. Kirsten will be totally safe. Tarbell might think he can get to her, but he can't. He won't. I've made sure of it."

She squeezed Paul's hand in the hope he would squeeze back, but it remained limp in her grasp. She didn't let it depress her.

The doctors had made her feel confident that he would grip her hand again. Whether she would be in any condition to hold his was another question entirely.

"I don't want to think negatively, but we both know it's a possibility that he'll win. He seems to get stronger every day. But I want you to know that I did my best for us and Kirsten." She laughed. "God, I'm glad you're not conscious. You'd be so pissed at me right now. You'd be telling me how crazy I am, then grabbing my hand and insisting to come along. No wonder I love you, you're a demonstration in contradictions."

Tears were streaming down her face. She palmed them away. "I'm going now, and if all goes well, I'll be back. Just don't be too angry at me, OK?"

She kissed his cheek and left.

• • •

Ingram drove over to Petersen's home unannounced. Frustration had set in. He'd left three voice mails on Petersen's cell, and he hadn't called back. He didn't like to think his investigator had been guilty of any impropriety. Petersen had always been a sharp investigator with a wealth of experience from his law enforcement career. Still, Ingram couldn't ignore what he'd unearthed in black and white.

He drew up in front of Petersen's home. He didn't care if Petersen saw him. He wanted answers. If he had to spook the ex-cop to find out the truth, so be it.

Lynette Petersen opened the door to him.

"Can I speak to Tom?"

"He's not here."

He should have known. Ingram's voice mails had sent him running. It was a dumb move on his part. He should have just confronted Petersen. "When will he be back?"

"I don't know."

"Where has he gone? I need to get in contact with him."

"I don't know."

He went to say, "How can you not know?" but stopped himself. He'd been in so much of a hurry to confront Petersen, he'd missed the obvious. He didn't know Lynette Petersen well, but every time they'd met she'd been warm and friendly. That wasn't true on this occasion. She was cold and uninviting. Pushing her wasn't the way to go.

"Can I come in for a moment? It's important."

Lynette paused for a second before letting him in. She ushered him into the family room and closed the door.

He didn't like the feeling he was getting and waited for Lynette to sit before sitting next to her.

"Lynette, I'm worried about Tom. He hasn't been himself recently. Is everything OK?"

"He's fine. What makes you say that?"

"The work we do is stressful, and it gets to the best of us." He smiled. "That's all."

"He's fine."

Lynette's tone was way too defensive. She was protecting Petersen, but Ingram nodded like he understood.

"So everything's good?" he said smiling.

She smiled back. There was a waver to it. "Yes. Everything's good."

"It's odd that he's gone away and you don't know where he is or when he's coming back."

Her smile crumbled and fell away. She stammered out a protest, but he bulldozed over her.

"Did you know he resigned?"

Her expression said his question was a news flash. He wondered what else was news to her. It was clear she didn't know what her husband had gotten involved in.

"Lynette, do you want to tell me what's going on?"

She was silent. He pressed the silence by not speaking. He wouldn't speak until she spoke the truth. He'd let the silence do the work until it became an uncomfortable wedge that forced her to open her up.

The everyday quiet noises of the average family room became loud. The tick, tick ticking of a wall clock. The roar of a passing car. The hum of the DVD player underneath the TV. These sounds were momentarily drowned out by the barking of a dog and the delighted squeals from a child from outside the house that followed. Lynette's eyes widened as the pounding of a child's feet and the noise of a dog's scrabbling paws echoed through the house. Ingram looked at Lynette, and she looked away.

He went to the door and opened it. Kirsten Farris stood on the other side of the door, hugging Tom Petersen's black Lab.

"Kirsten?"

"Hello," Kirsten said, tucking her chin into her shoulder and looking shy.

Ingram was lost for words. He'd thought he'd prepared himself for any eventuality, but he was wrong. He turned to Lynette. "You need to tell me what's going on. Now."

CHAPTER THIRTY-TWO

G wen put miles between herself and home, unsure whether she'd be returning. Two suitcases sat in the trunk filled with clothes and personal items. If she never returned, she wanted to seem like a woman unable to cope, who'd ditched her family in an effort to escape life's problems. It hurt to think that if she was killed, everyone would see her as a coward, but maybe that would give her the edge of desperation she needed for survival. It was too late to worry about it now. The die had been cast.

She drove hard, pushing the speed limit all the way. She only stopped for gas. She needed to eat, but the idea of it turned her stomach. The junk food she'd bought when she filled up for gas remained unopened on her passenger seat.

A hundred miles south of Fort Richardson, her legs developed a shake. She didn't know whether to put it down to low blood sugar or fear. The shaking wasn't a good sign either way. She pushed the problem from her mind and kept driving.

Road signs for Fort Richardson counted down the final miles, but she ignored them. She had to visit somewhere else first. She drove out to the home she'd grown up in. It had been painted green in her day. It was a pleasing shade of red now. The detour had a calming effect. As she stepped out of the car to stretch her legs and get a closer look, she found she was smiling. This place was filled with so many happy memories, but it wouldn't be for long. This place would become synonymous with Stephen Tarbell. She'd never be able to return here. The stain would be too indelible. Her smile fell away.

She went back to her car and picked up the main highway running through the area. She pulled out her cell and called Parker's number.

"Where are you?" she asked.

"In position."

"How is everything?"

"Busy. There are more people here than I would like. Rangers are hanging around."

"It's early yet. Nothing happens until the park closes."

"I hope you're right."

"If I'm wrong, it doesn't matter. If Tarbell kills me and there are witnesses, he's screwed. He'll go to prison and your work is done for you."

"You want me to walk away if he gets picked up?"

"Yes."

She could hear Parker's mind working. A way out was presenting itself where he didn't have to kill Tarbell.

"But he has to be picked up at the park, smoking gun in hand," she said.

"Christ, Gwen, are you really going to let this guy kill you?"

"Not if I can help it."

"But you're willing to die for this prick."

"Not for him. For my family. I won't let him hurt them any more than he has. I would die to protect them."

That silenced Parker. It was understandable. She doubted he had anyone in his life who would do the same for him. Parker looked out for Parker. No one fought for him, and he had no one to fight for. Selflessness was an alien concept to him.

"Have you seen Tarbell?" she asked.

"No. I'll call you if I do."

"I'll have the phone on, but I won't be taking any calls until this is over. He believes I have this phone solely for talking to him. If he catches me talking on it, he'll know I'm lying."

"OK. I'll hang up. Good luck, Gwen. I mean that. Just know I've got your back, OK?"

"Thanks."

She put the phone in the cupholder next to her and concentrated on her driving. Images of Paul lying in his hospital bed, tubes and wires spilling from him, and Kirsten playing with J. Edgar kept filling her head, but she squeezed them out. Her family was all that mattered to her, but they couldn't distract her. Not now. If she wanted to survive today, Tarbell had to be her focus. It was all about how to lure him into the shadows for Parker to do what he was being paid to do. It wouldn't be easy. The situation was tenuous. Tarbell's enthusiasm for punishing her might mean he got to her before Parker got his chance, but she didn't think this was likely. As much as Tarbell thought he was better than everyone, he was a product of his obsession. All his hate was focused on her. As long as it remained that way, he wouldn't see Parker until it was too late.

She wished she relished this moment, but killing Tarbell would bring her no pleasure or even closure, despite all he'd done to her and her family. Killing him was simply an act of survival. He was a virus that threatened to consume her if she didn't stamp him out. Parker had been right when he said that this act wouldn't leave her. She already knew it wouldn't. A dark cloud would follow her forever, but it was the price that came with being the object of Tarbell's twisted obsession.

She parked her car on the street half a mile from the park. She couldn't leave it in the park's parking lot. She would be leaving the park long after everyone else. Her car would draw attention after a while.

She got out and pulled on her waterproof jacket. Rain fell at a steady pace. The grim weather seemed to suit the occasion.

She emptied her pockets of her money, driver's license, and anything that could identify her onto the hood of the car, gathered them into a bundle, and leaned in through the passenger side to shove the bundle in the glove box. She needed only two things—her cell phone and Lynette's revolver. The gun was in the rain jacket with six rounds in the cylinder and another twelve loose in a pocket. She grabbed the cell and locked the car. Then she hit speed dial for Tarbell.

When he answered, she said, "I'm here. Where are you?"

• • •

"Still on my way," Tarbell lied. He watched Gwen through a pair of binoculars from a nice little hiding spot he'd carved out for himself in the trees opposite Fort Richardson's entrance. He'd staked out the park since early morning. He wasn't stupid. He would like to believe Gwen was telling the truth about sacrificing herself as part of some noble act, but he just didn't buy it.

He needed to see what she had planned, and more importantly, who she'd dragged into this game. He didn't know who would be her ally these days. He'd pretty much made sure she was alienated from everyone, but maybe there was someone he'd missed. The scheme was too elaborate for the cops. They wouldn't take a chance like this with a civilian. Now, Private Security International was a different matter. They weren't confined by rules and regulations, let alone the accountability of the police. It was a shame Petersen was dead. His knowledge would be very useful right now.

Tarbell waited to spot Gwen's knights in shining armor. The moment he saw them, he'd be gone. He wouldn't be drawn into a fight. He'd simply go home and take it out on Kirsten and Paul. It would make for a nice welcome-home present for Gwen. Of course, maybe it was just his paranoia driving him to believe she had a horde of supporters in the wings. She could still be a lone wolf, but a wolf, lone or otherwise, was a dangerous animal. He couldn't trust her. That was why he'd staked out the spot she named in her instructions.

"Where are you?" he asked as he watched her.

"I'm heading into the park."

"You're early. You wouldn't be screwing with me, Gwen, would you? I wouldn't like that. You know what I'll do if you cross me."

"I'm just here early, Stephen. There's no need to panic."

"I'm not panicking, just warning you."

He had watched as Gwen walked around to the front of her Subaru and, leaning against the hood, emptied her pockets of cash and credit cards. With that task finished, it looked as if she had nothing on her except what she stood in. It was an interesting move that got his attention. It definitely looked as though she was alone, stripping herself of adornments before she sacrificed herself for the greater good. Maybe Gwen was going to be true to her word. He didn't let the idea sweep him away. He maintained his healthy dose of skepticism for now.

"Stephen, I want this to go as smoothly as possible. I'm not going to cheat you. OK?"

"Sure, Gwen. Whatever you say. What are you going to do now?"

"Just wander around the park. I drove past it earlier, and it seems pretty busy."

"You said it wouldn't be."

"It won't be when it closes. Don't leave your car in the park's lot. It gets locked by the rangers."

He smiled. "Nice try, Gwen. Who says I have a car?"

"No one, Stephen. Don't make this so difficult for yourself. You've won. You've got what you wanted out of this."

"Thanks for the advice, Gwen. I'll be seeing you later," he said and hung up.

He waited for her to make contact with her cohorts, but she didn't. She didn't signal or call anyone. She simply put the phone away.

"Gwen, are you really going to do this?" he murmured.

Gwen headed back to the park. Tarbell tracked her progress from the safety of the tree line. No cars followed her. No people overtly or surreptitiously made contact with her. He let her enter the park and waited for someone to make a move on her before he followed her in.

He'd done his homework before coming here. Fort Richardson was an interesting place. It wasn't just a park but a relic of a bygone era. It had been a gunnery outpost as part of the coastal defense system to protect the US from an invading threat from the Pacific. Outposts like this littered the West Coast. It called itself an island, but in reality it was a spit of land, fifty acres in size, that sat two hundred yards out into the ocean. An artificial causeway sturdy enough to take foot traffic and wide enough for a ranger's pickup to access the island connected it to the mainland.

He guessed Gwen had chosen the park because of the causeway. At high tide, it became submerged. He saw the park for what it was—a trap. Once high tide cut it off, no one got on or off. But it was a trap that worked both ways. It trapped her as well as him. He smiled and followed a group of tourists across the causeway and onto the island.

Gwen had been right about the park being busy. He had no option but to encounter tourists. He played it cool and didn't avoid anyone's gaze. If someone greeted him, he greeted them back. Someone might remember him, but they'd have a hard job. He was a tourist, too. He was dressed like them. He looked like them. He was here to enjoy the park just like them. He did nothing to make anyone think otherwise. He'd slip from their minds before they reached their cars.

The island's topography afforded him a number of good hiding spots. It was a flattened-out dome covered in trees. The only clear-cut area belonged to the decommissioned gun battery, its accessory buildings, and a picnic area. Where the island sloped into the water, the battery rose up to create a concrete monolith to support the four large guns.

Gwen wandered from gun to gun in the bunker-like concrete structure, exchanging smiles with her fellow tourists and nothing else. She sat on a bench facing the water and stared out at it for half an hour. No one stopped to sit next to her. For the millionth time, Tarbell wondered if Ingram was playing some part in Gwen's plan. If his people were here, they were certainly playing it cool. None of the couples, families, or occasional loners seemed out of place. No one walked the perimeter or feigned interest in the park while keeping close to Gwen at all times. Either these people were the best of the best, surveillance operative–wise, or they were who they appeared to be—tourists.

Just watching Gwen irritated him. She was salt on a wound, itching and burning in a way that had to be dealt with. He couldn't believe he'd let her blight his existence. Well, it would all end soon. Not in days but hours.

He emerged from his hiding spot and went over to an events center perched on a ridge above the cannons. Gwen meandered from spot to spot, counting the time down.

He smiled and shook his head. He had to hand it to her. She was playing this straight. She really was going to sacrifice herself for her family. He would have admired her if she hadn't done what she'd done to him first.

Rangers passed through the crowd announcing over megaphones that the park was closing. People filed toward the exit. The rangers ushered those out that didn't. He retreated into the tree line for cover.

From his secluded spot, he watched for Gwen. She followed the main glut of tourists leaving but peeled off at the restrooms. She looked to be entering them but ducked down the side of the building. He waited for her to reemerge and she didn't. It looked as if they were on.

"It's time to reap what you sow," he murmured.

"You got that right, brother," an unfamiliar voice said.

Before Tarbell could react, a powerful arm snaked around his neck, drawing him up onto his toes.

It looked as if Gwen had found herself another ally. Tarbell smiled. He was right not to trust her.

A hunting knife filled his vision. It was a nice knife. He wondered how it compared to the one hidden in the depths of his jacket pocket. If Gwen's hired hand was going to show off his knife, it was only fair that Tarbell do the same, and in a swift movement he thrust his knife backward.

CHAPTER THIRTY-THREE

Gwen crouched down with her back against the restrooms to hide. The surrounding trees did a good job of putting her in shadow. The rain added another layer of protection. Nobody looked up as they scurried along trying not to get soaked, not even the rangers.

From her position, she watched people head out of the park and across the causeway. The tide was coming in. Water was already slopping across the causeway's low point, and it wouldn't be long before it was submerged. The flow of people dwindled to a trickle, but she remained still. The rangers stood at either end of the causeway making sure everyone was leaving. She knew they'd return for a final sweep of the park to ensure no one got stranded on the island. She hoped Parker and Tarbell had found themselves suitable hiding spots.

When the last people returned to the parking lot, two rangers lowered the barrier and stood guard, preventing anyone from entering the park. The rangers on the island side called for any remaining visitors to leave while performing their final sweep. Gwen held her breath as one ranger checked inside the restroom before locking it. The rain ensured their final inspection remained a cursory one.

Gwen watched the rangers hustle across the causeway and lock the barrier. She waited until they drove off before rising to her feet. She pulled out her cell and switched it off. If anything had gone wrong, it was too late to put it right. Fate would decide her future. There was no time to think, only act. If she kept to her plan, she'd survive this. The second her thoughts drifted, she was dead.

The rain was coming down hard now, and she pulled the hood of her rain jacket over her head. It obscured her peripheral vision, and the noise of raindrops striking the material drowned out the sound of footfalls. These were a couple of vulnerabilities for Tarbell to exploit, but it would hardly be more helpful to have the drenching rain driving straight into her eyes.

She knew this park well. This had been her and her sister's playground as kids. Imagination filled the gaps left by the decaying structures. To them, it was a fully functional gun battery capable of blasting pirate ships and sea monsters out of the water.

She kept in the open, following the gravel roadway behind the guns. It would draw Tarbell out for Parker to pounce. It was a simple approach, but simple was good. "C'mon," she murmured. "I'm here. Show yourself." She tightened her grip around Lynette's revolver.

She peered inside the empty rooms that were once the gunpowder room, shell room, and plotting room. When Tarbell made no move, she climbed the stairs to the observation level and crossed the top of the gun battery. The only way to reach the park below was a ladder set into the masonry structure.

She didn't see Tarbell until he grabbed her. She had no idea where he'd come from, but it didn't matter, he had her. He slipped an arm across her chest, keeping her pinned in place while the other cut into her throat. She gagged reflexively and yanked at his arm, but it was locked solid. Her racing heart and frightened brain demanded oxygen to fight back, but Tarbell's vicelike grip prevented her from breathing.

She hoped to God Parker was closing in. She wouldn't last long under this punishment. Tarbell's assault felt so much more violent now than when he'd assaulted her in Pace's parking lot. If she had ever doubted his intent to kill her, she didn't now. He meant it. He heaved back on his heels, hoisting her off her feet. Her weight put more pressure on her throat. A strangled yelp made it out as she choked against Tarbell's forearm. Her eyes watered, blurring her vision. She yanked even harder on Tarbell's arm with both hands. It had no effect.

"If you're hoping for your playmate to rush in to save you, it isn't happening. I took care of him, just like I took care of Tom Petersen."

The revelations smashed into her. Parker and Petersen were dead. Tarbell had overcome a hardened felon and outwitted a seasoned cop. How was she supposed to stop him?

She broke into a series of ragged coughs, but the pressure on her throat prevented them from getting out. Pressure was building up from within her body as well as from outside. She kicked out with her legs but failed to strike a crippling blow.

"You're dying, Gwen. How does it feel?"

She reached into her pocket and grabbed the revolver, but it snagged on her pocket. Panic overwhelmed her. Her vision had reduced to a smudge, and she yanked and yanked at the weapon to rip it free of its prison. It came away with a tear of material.

She didn't think about the placement of her shot or any of the things she'd been taught during firearms training. She swung her arm up past her head and aimed, hoping for a head shot or anything to get him to let go.

She got her wish without firing a round. Tarbell released his grip. A sick sensation filled her when her feet failed to contact with the structure and she plunged over the edge. Gravity snatched her and hurled her the fifteen feet to the ground. She clipped the wall on the way down. It tipped her before she slammed into the wet dirt. The shuddering impact drove the remaining air from her lungs and her head bounced off the earth, leaving her unable to breathe or think.

Tarbell clambered down the ladder. "I knew I couldn't trust you, Gwen. You can't trust anyone in this world."

She hardly heard Tarbell's taunts. Thoughts of survival swirled inside her head. She curled her hand tight around the revolver that wasn't there. It lay twenty feet ahead of her. She pushed herself to her knees, but her body vibrated like a bell struck too hard and she collapsed. She crawled toward the weapon. She grabbed the gun, slipping her finger through the trigger guard, just as Tarbell stood on her hand. She yelled out and Tarbell pressed down even harder.

"Screaming won't help."

She gritted her teeth as her index finger broke under the pressure.

Tarbell removed his foot and kicked her hard in the ribs. She rolled away from the weapon and he picked it up.

"I can't believe you brought a gun, but don't worry, I won't shoot you. I'm going to use my hands." He pocketed the weapon. "No quick exit for you."

"This isn't over," she said.

Tarbell grabbed Gwen by her jacket and dragged her across the ground toward the water. She tried to shake herself free, but her moves were uncoordinated. Tarbell simply slapped her feeble attempts aside. Just the act of being dragged made her dizzy and nauseous. It was as if her brain was slopping around inside her skull.

Rain splashed into Gwen's eyes, but it couldn't obscure the sight of Parker lumbering across the park, clutching his stomach. She almost cheered.

Parker disappeared from sight as Tarbell dragged her around the battery down to the shore. Small waves broke over the rocks. Never had such a comforting noise sounded so terrifying.

She wouldn't die like this. Not helpless. She didn't care if she died today, but she wouldn't die lying on her back like a stranded turtle. Tarbell might win, but he'd have to hide his battle scars when she was finished with him.

"I hear waterboarding is all the rage. You'll have to tell me what it's like."

"Try it for yourself," Gwen said defiantly.

Tarbell plunged her head into the water. Ice-cold, it acted as a slap to the face and snapped her senses back into place. The salt water invaded her nose and mouth. She choked on it and had no option but to breathe it in place of air. Tarbell's grinning face looked down at her, distorted through the water. She struck out at his shifting image and caught him across the jaw. It did nothing to dislodge his grin.

Just as it became too much for her, Tarbell jerked her from the water. She came up coughing and choking, water clogging her nose and throat.

"No holding your breath, Gwen. That's not how the game is played."

He plunged her back in. She snatched a lungful of air before she disappeared below the surface again. She grabbed his forearms. Panic turned her fingers into talons and they bit deep into his flesh.

Tarbell shook his head in disgust and punched her in the stomach. Instinctively, she opened her mouth and sucked in more water before he yanked her free.

"What did I say about holding your breath?"

He forced her back down, deep below the surface. Her head connected with one of the jagged rocks and rosy tendrils of blood snaked through the water.

There hadn't been a chance to grab a breath this time. She thrashed in an attempt to get above the surface. The world overhead turned white with froth. Tarbell pressed hard on her chest with his knee.

She didn't know how much water it took to drown a person, but she felt she couldn't take much more. As if reading her thoughts, Tarbell jerked her free once again. Her chest burned from sucking in air.

"Consider this a baptism, Gwen. It's the only way you're going to get into heaven."

"Heaven will have to wait," Parker said from behind Tarbell's shoulder. He put his weight behind a blow he drove into the side of Tarbell's head.

It was like watching a building being demolished. Parker's precision blow took Tarbell's foundation out. He collapsed from the impact, falling sideways into the water, but he maintained his grip on Gwen, dragging her with him. Parker snatched Tarbell's hand from her jacket and wrenched it free. She shoved herself clear of the water and sucked in the sweetest air she'd ever breathed. Her exhale turned into coughing, but she didn't care. She was breathing. She pushed herself onto her feet, but overexertion and the weight of her waterlogged clothes took her legs out from under her and she fell facedown. She clambered to her feet again, this time more carefully. The rain was coming down harder than ever and the sky was a smudged bruise, but the world had never looked so beautiful.

Parker wore a gray hooded sweatshirt. Rainwater had turned it dark, but blood from a stomach wound had turned it darker.

"If anyone is going to meet their maker, it's you, asshole," Parker snarled as he pushed Tarbell below the water and held him down, putting his full weight on his chest. Tarbell wrestled to break free, but Parker was too big for him. The water wasn't even knee deep but it was deep enough to drown Tarbell. He was finished.

This was the moment Gwen had thought would never come. It was a chance to revel in Tarbell's pain for a change after what he'd done to her and Paul. But seeing Parker, driven by animal rage, slowly drowning Tarbell disgusted her. The fight was such a mismatch. Parker was a brute compared to her gangly coworker. Tarbell's true, weak nature was reflected in the pathetic sight of his skinny arms and legs flailing in the water.

It was on the tip of her tongue to tell Parker to stop. This wasn't his fight. It was hers. Paying him to kill Tarbell felt like a huge weight on her gut. She closed her eyes, but the sounds of thrashing water and choking cries filled her ears. She steeled herself to stand by as he died. She'd been thrashing underwater moments ago, but Tarbell had taken no pity on her. In fact, he'd probably enjoyed it. She had to let the plan move ahead, but Parker was right. This day would leave a scar on her soul that would never heal. But as much as it would hurt, it was a worthy scar.

She opened her eyes, and her breath caught in her throat. A glint of steel flashed in the water. Tarbell thrust his hand out with a knife tight in his fist.

Gwen cried out, but it was too late. The knife disappeared into Parker just below his ribcage. A crimson bloom spread around the knife handle. It was far more severe than the existing wound. Parker went stiff as if frozen in the moment. He held on to Tarbell, keeping him pinned below the water, but then his legs buckled, and he dropped onto his knees into the rapidly reddening water.

Gwen went for the revolver before she remembered Tarbell still had it. He had it all now—the gun, the knife, and her last hope.

Tarbell emerged from the water, clothes soaked to the skin, and shoved Parker aside. His strength gone, Parker slumped into the water, facedown.

Tarbell spun around to face Gwen. His hate bordered on a physical presence.

Gwen raced back to the shore.

"You can run, Gwen, but you can't hide. Not from me. Not ever."

His words followed her across the shore and into the park.

CHAPTER THIRTY-FOUR

Ingram drove blind for the first hundred miles. He knew Fort Richardson was somewhere between Eureka and the Oregon state line, but that was it, because that was all Lynette Petersen knew. Gwen had been smart about keeping many of the details of the plan to herself to prevent anyone from stopping her. He called the office and got his PA to Google the place for directions.

Hundreds of miles lay ahead of him. He had no idea if he'd arrive in time, even driving at crazy speeds, but he had to try. How desperate must Gwen have felt to turn to Parker to help her, a man who'd brutalized her? She'd been driven to it by frustration. A frustration he now felt. He wanted to do something, and he was helpless to do so. He thumped the steering wheel.

"Stupid, stupid, stupid," he growled.

How had it gotten to this point? It was a question he knew the answer to. He'd let this woman down. Everyone charged with protecting her had failed. It was about time he rectified that error.

He could stop it all with a single phone call to the cops. His cell sat within easy reach. It would be so easy to make the call, but he couldn't do that. The cops wouldn't look upon Gwen's plan favorably. If he could stop her before anyone got hurt then he would have done something good for her. He didn't know if he could save her from the cops entirely, but he could sure minimize the damage. He owed her that much.

He wasn't just trying to save Gwen. He had to save Tarbell too, as much as Tarbell didn't deserve saving. No one owed that son of a bitch anything after he had put Paul Farris in a coma. But Petersen had been missing for days, and Ingram knew Tarbell had had a hand in it. He needed to know what happened to him. He hoped to God Tom was OK.

"Be safe, buddy. Please, be safe."

Ingram piled on the miles. Traffic thinned out the farther north he traveled. Towns became less frequent. He increased his speed until the weather stepped in. The temperature dropped, the sky darkened, and the rain lashed down. He saw his speed drop along with his chances of reaching Gwen in time.

His spirits lifted when he passed signs for Fort Richardson. They gave him hope.

He turned into the deserted parking lot and slithered to a halt. He jumped from his car in time to hear a woman scream.

"Christ," he murmured. He was too late.

He went to the car's trunk and grabbed his only weapon, a tire iron. He wished he had a gun, but this morning, he hadn't thought he needed one.

He hopped the barrier preventing people from crossing the causeway to the island fort, but the barrier was totally unnecessary. The tide provided a natural security. The causeway sat beneath several feet of water and would get deeper with the incoming tide. He didn't think. He just waded out into the water.

The water was bone-chillingly cold, but that wasn't the problem. A waist-high wall edged both sides of the causeway. Slots cut into the walls allowed the water to drain out. Water sluiced through the slots from the movement of the rising tide, effectively squirting jets of water at Ingram's ankles then sucking them back out. Each step was met by a blast of water that rocked his balance. He worked hard to stay on his feet, but it reduced his pace to a crawl. Two hundred yards to the island soon seemed like two hundred miles.

Another scream split the air.

Keep screaming, Gwen. If she was screaming, she was surviving. He had more to fear from silence.

A wave smashed into the causeway, kicking up a wall of water. It slammed into him, driving him onto his hands and knees, then below the surface of the water. With nothing to hang on to he was driven into the opposite causeway wall. He yelled out and seawater flooded his mouth. He forced his head above the surface and grabbed air before the undertow dragged him back across the causeway.

He flailed for something to grab on to, but it was impossible with only one free hand. The smart thing was to drop the tire iron he clung, to, but he couldn't rely on finding another weapon when he reached the other side.

A moment of calm water between waves gave him the opportunity he needed to push himself to his feet. He was breathing hard and fatigue doubled his body weight, and he'd yet to cover a quarter of the distance.

He was tiring fast, and it showed when a wave split around the island and smashed back together on the other side. It caught him in the swell, forcing him up, then sucking him down. The undertow bounced him off the causeway and dragged him back toward the shore. He'd be damned if he'd start all over again and fought the pull of the tide, but he was losing. He wanted to yell in frustration, but another thought preoccupied his mind. It had been a long time since he'd last heard Gwen scream out.

• • •

It had all gone wrong. This wasn't supposed to be happening. Parker was dead or dying, and it was her fault. She'd never thought for one second he'd die. She'd prepared for the possibility that he'd keep the money and leave her twisting in the wind but not that he'd end up dead.

"Gwen," Tarbell screamed her name.

She was running, not well, but running. Being dropped off the gun battery and half drowned had taken its toll. Her body no longer absorbed the shock of running. Every footfall rammed a spike into her brain. She wanted to be sick, but there was no time for that. If she stopped, she died.

Sprinting down the slope, she slipped on the wet grass and fell forward, striking the ground on all fours. Her head swam from the jarring impact. She staggered to her feet and felt instantly light-headed. The park turned into a Dalí painting.

"Gwen," Tarbell screamed again.

She'd never outrun him to her car, not in this condition. She needed a second. She staggered over to the battery, stumbled inside the doorless room marked "plotting room," and leaned against the wall before she fell down. She focused on a single spot, and the world slowly solidified and the nausea passed. The brick building held the cold and drew out her remaining body heat. She was suddenly aware of how cold and wet she was, and she broke into shivers.

"Where are you, Gwen?" Tarbell shouted. "I'm not going to let you leave."

And she couldn't leave. Running wouldn't stop Tarbell. Worse still, there was a mess left behind. Parker would be found. Whether anyone connected the dots between him and her was another thing, but it was a problem for her. Worse, she'd lost her element of surprise. Tarbell would never fall for a trap like this again. He'd follow through with his threats. She couldn't leave until she finished what she'd set out to do.

"Don't make this any worse than it is. Come out and I might spare your daughter."

She didn't believe him for one second. He'd go after Kirsten. This bungled ambush guaranteed it.

She looked for a weapon in the room. A shard of brick gouged from the wall sat on the floor. It wasn't much, but there was nothing else, and she snatched it up.

She peered outside the doorway. Tarbell was up on the top of the gun battery with Petersen's gun loose in his hand. He had a clear view of the park in all directions. She was a sitting duck.

She hid back inside the plotting room and scrabbled for an idea, but didn't come up with one. There was no way of her creeping up on Tarbell while he held the high ground. She had to get him down to her level. Even if she did, then what? She couldn't take him one-on-one, especially with the gun. The only way to end this was to give Tarbell what he wanted—her. But if she sacrificed herself, she had to take Tarbell with her. It was the only solution that would save her daughter.

The sudden realization that she wouldn't see her family again punched a hole in her chest. She'd never see Kirsten grow up. She'd never know if Paul recovered. But she had to do this for Kirsten's sake. She sank to her knees, and a sob escaped her lips.

"Come on out, Gwen. It's getting boring."

She stood up and palmed her tears away. No more tears. No more self pity. The future of two people she loved depended on what she did next. Sacrificing her life would mean nothing if she didn't engineer Tarbell's death.

She peered out of the doorway. She couldn't see him on the top of the battery. That was good. If she couldn't see him, he couldn't see her. She edged outside and pressed her back against the plotting room wall, then peered around the edge of the building. Tarbell stood next to an observation tower scanning the horizon for her. He'd crossed a catwalk from the gun battery to reach the tower.

It was the best seat in the house, but it did have its limitations. The observation tower was a blast-resistant box with slits for holes. Tarbell had to circle the walkway around the tower to see everything.

An iron staircase going up to the observation tower stood forty yards across from her. If she could sneak up on him, she could push him over the side. It was a solid idea, as long as she kept to his blind spot.

The second he disappeared from sight, she took a breath and darted over to the staircase. She didn't get five feet before a bullet struck the ground in front of her.

"Didn't think I'd see you? You really do take me for an idiot." Tarbell emerged from his hiding spot and raced back across the steel catwalk for a better shot.

Gwen was exposed, trapped in the middle of no-man's-land. To double back to her hiding spot would mean stopping to change direction, giving Tarbell more than enough time to line up an accurate shot. Instead, she kept running forward, heading for a recess in the gun battery's slab-sided structure. She slammed her body up tight against the wall. It was a hiding spot but no sanctuary. She had only seconds before Tarbell caught up to her and shot down at her from above like an angry god. She waited until she could hear his footfalls slapping the battery's concrete surface above her before breaking into a run.

The simple move bought Gwen vital seconds. The curving route across the top of the gun battery put Tarbell in a position with no clear shot at her.

She used the head start to pound along the gravel roadway behind the guns. From the corner of her eye, she caught Tarbell running parallel along the top of the battery. Only distance and a difficult angle kept him from taking his shot.

Tarbell cut back across the catwalk toward the observation tower and stopped mid-span. Now he had a straight shot at her. It would be very simple for him to put one in her back. In a panic,

Gwen looked at all the doorways to the buildings. Unlike the plotting room in the gun battery, each of the rooms had doors and the rangers had padlocked them all. She had nowhere to hide.

"Time to say good-bye, Gwen."

Tarbell fired. His bullet struck the ground off to her right. She didn't know if he missed by accident or was taunting her. She tensed for the next shot.

"Stephen Tarbell," a voice bellowed. "Put the gun down."

Gwen spun around. Ingram was staggering toward the gun battery, heading directly for Tarbell. He was soaked from head to foot and looked worse for it. He held a tire iron in his hand.

Tarbell whirled on Ingram. He aimed Petersen's gun at him.

Ingram kept moving forward as if a gun wasn't pointed at him. "It's over. Put the gun down."

Tarbell kept the gun trained on Ingram, and the investigator kept coming. Gwen felt panicked. If Ingram thought Tarbell wouldn't shoot, he was wrong. She couldn't have someone else die trying to protect her.

"Stephen, I thought you were here to shoot me," Gwen yelled out.

Ingram looked at her in shock. She didn't care about his reaction. Tarbell's was the only one that mattered.

Tarbell spun back around to look down at her from his vantage point on the catwalk. His expression chilled her. She saw nothing but hate. "Promise me you won't hurt Kirsten and you can still have me, Stephen." She spread her arms wide. "I won't fight."

Tarbell switched his aim to Gwen. She braced herself for the bullet.

"Promise me, Stephen. You have to promise."

Ingram ran forward. "Drop the gun. I won't give you another warning."

Tarbell didn't break his gaze on Gwen. "I promise."

Just as Tarbell pulled the trigger, Ingram hurled the tire iron. It smashed into the back of Tarbell's neck, sending his shot wild. The bullet struck the ground at her feet.

Gwen saw the light go out of Tarbell's eyes. He stumbled hard against the safety railing. It caught him across the waist, and he toppled over the edge. She caught his look of shock as he plunged to the roadway. He pointed the gun at Gwen on the way down but hit the roadway before he could fire a shot, snapping his neck upon impact.

Ingram rushed over to Tarbell and twisted the revolver from his grasp. Tarbell's gaze was fixed on Gwen. She walked over to the man who had tried to destroy her life and looked into his vacant expression.

"It's over, Gwen. He's dead."

Ingram's words sounded alien and the meaning of those words even more so. She was safe. Her family was safe. It didn't seem real. She'd been fighting so long, the idea of being safe seemed like something out of a fairy tale. But it was true. She no longer had to fear what a new day would bring. The truth was evident on Tarbell's face, deathly pale and unmoving.

It took her a moment to realize Ingram was still talking to her. "What?"

"I said, where's Parker?"

Gwen bolted and Ingram chased after her. She clambered onto the rocky shore expecting to find Parker face down in the water, but he was lying on his back at the water's edge, holding his stomach. She dropped down at his side.

"I thought you were dead," Gwen said.

Ingram barged past her and lifted up Parker's sweatshirt. It had turned red from where he'd been stabbed. Ingram examined the wounds.

"It looks bad, but it's not serious. Gwen, keep pressure applied." Ingram went for his cell phone off his belt. "We need to get you to a hospital."

Parker grabbed his wrist. "No hospitals. If they see a stab wound, I'm finished. I'm back in prison."

Ingram jerked his hand free. "That's not my problem."

"You call the cops, it's not just me who goes to prison, she does, too."

Ingram looked at Gwen. She said nothing. She let the weight of her fate press down on him. She believed he'd do the right thing.

Ingram flipped open his phone, but his fingers made no attempt to hit any of the buttons. He closed the phone. "You're in luck. It's fried from being wet."

He moved Gwen's hands from Parker's wounds and pressed them hard to stanch the bleeding. "I can patch you up and get you out of here. I'll give you the address of someone who can take care of this properly. No questions asked."

"Thank you," Gwen said.

Ingram looked grave. "Don't thank me yet. After we've got him out of the way, we're calling the police."

CHAPTER THIRTY-FIVE

Ingram's car pulled up outside. It had been a month since Gwen had last seen him in the days after Tarbell's death. He had been working hard with the police investigation to keep Gwen out of jail. Tarbell's death seemed like a lifetime ago. Gwen went to the door to let him in.

"You're in the clear, Gwen," Ingram said.

She smiled. "Come in."

She took him into the kitchen. Paul and Kirsten were waging a losing battle with Kirsten's puppy, Hugo, trying to teach obedience to the ten-week-old Jack Russell terrier mix.

"Paul looks good," Ingram remarked as Gwen handed him a cup of coffee.

"He's coming along."

Paul had emerged from his coma the week after she'd returned from Fort Richardson, and the hospital released him the following week. He still looked like Frankenstein's monster, but he would mend with time. The only lasting effect from his coma seemed to be amnesia. He'd forgotten certain things, and he had problems with his short-term memory, but the prognosis was that the amnesia would pass. He wouldn't necessarily make a full recovery, but he was expected to regain his short-term memory. Regardless, it was good to have him home.

"So what happened with the investigation?" Gwen asked.

"The overwhelming evidence points toward Stephen Tarbell, so the police are satisfied and won't be seeking any charges elsewhere."

She owed Ingram her life, although she felt it was his penance to help her. Together, over the last month, they'd bent the law, concocted stories, omitted facts, and changed details. Yet in the end, so many big things had played in Gwen's favor that they'd only falsified smaller details. The finding of Petersen's body on Tarbell's family property in Vallejo explained why the gun in Tarbell's hand belonged to Tom Petersen. Paul reinforced the case against Tarbell. He might have lost a lot of memory, but he hadn't forgotten who'd beat him almost to death. Some memories just couldn't be destroyed. Examination of Tarbell's laptop revealed the stolen breast cancer research from Pace. Phone records showed that Tarbell had called Gwen on repeated occasions. The only thing the police had on Gwen was going to Fort Richardson. She admitted it was her idea to lure Tarbell there to sacrifice herself to save her daughter. With no one else to dispute her claim, the police had nothing to charge her with.

"So it really is over."

Ingram smiled. "It is."

Now she could rebuild a broken life and move on. The idea of it excited her, but her joy lasted only a moment. She could move on, but that wasn't true of everyone else. Tom Petersen couldn't and neither could his wife. Gwen hadn't attended Petersen's funeral, but she and Lynette had seen each other once after she returned from Fort Richardson.

"How's Lynette?" she asked.

"Doing about as well as you'd expect. She's put the house up for sale. She's already moved out to live closer to her grandchildren."

Gwen wished she'd gotten to say good-bye, but maybe it was for the best they didn't speak. They only had tragedy in common. It wasn't the basis for a friendship.

"Have you seen Parker?" Ingram asked.

She hadn't seen him since she and Ingram had carried him across the causeway to his car. It had been hell getting across the submerged causeway. Ingram assured her it was a hell of a lot easier getting him across when the tide was in than when it was coming in. The real miracle was that he'd gotten himself patched up and back home before his next meeting with his parole officer. She'd gotten the remaining five thousand to him through a trusted intermediary. She'd attached a note: "All sins forgiven. Start fixing bikes and never look back."

"No, and I won't," said Gwen.

"I suppose you wouldn't under the circumstances."

She'd spent a couple of sleepless nights thinking about Parker and what he'd done to her in Davis and what he'd done for her in Fort Richardson. Forgiveness was a hard road to travel. Sometimes, she felt ready to forgive Parker. Other times, she wished Tarbell had finished the job and Parker had bled out on that beach. But as the weeks after Fort Richardson passed, she finally felt reconciled. Parker had served his time, and he'd tried to save her from another monster. It was penance enough. They would never have a relationship, but she could forgive him. Time served, she decided.

"I want to apologize to you," Ingram said.

"For what?"

"I should have done more."

"You came through at the end."

"That's not good enough. It never should have gotten to where it did. I should have seen how Tarbell manipulated the situation. I should have prevented it from escalating."

Yes, you should have, she thought, but if she could forgive Parker, she could forgive Ingram. If he hadn't seen the truth and come after her, she would be dead.

"I'm just glad that you did what you did. Let's leave it at that."

"OK."

They toasted with their coffee mugs.

"I do have one more piece of business, and that's bringing you a message from Pace Pharmaceuticals," Ingram said. "They understand that you were an innocent party, and they want to offer you your job back."

The job offer came as no surprise. Since the truth had come out, Pace had picked up Paul's medical expenses and indicated they would continue to do so until he was fully recovered. It was a slice of charity Gwen didn't turn down.

"Tell them thanks, but no thanks."

"There are no strings attached."

"I realize that, but I can't go back now. It will be a constant reminder of what Stephen Tarbell did to me. I want to move on and put everything to do with that man behind me. I already have a couple of interviews lined up."

"OK. I'll let them know. Just know the offer is always open to you. Also, should you have any expenses, Pace will cover them."

She saw Ingram out. They shook hands on the doorstep.

"Good luck, Gwen."

"Thank you."

She closed the door and joined her family on the patio. They meant everything to her, and Stephen Tarbell meant nothing.

The End

ACKNOWLEDGMENTS

My thanks goes, yet again, to my wife, Julie, for all her hard work and the help from her gang of poisoners. Special thanks goes to California Department of Corrections and Rehabilitation for their help and generosity, and please forgive me for any and all artistic license taken. And a big thank you to Judy Brent for outbidding everyone to win the right to have her name used as a character in the book.

ABOUT THE AUTHOR

Photograph by Barry Evans Studio, 2003

Anthony Award–winning author of a dozen books as well as over 150 published stories and articles, Simon Wood is an ex–race car driver, a licensed pilot, an animal rescuer, an endurance cyclist, and an occasional private investigator. Having dealt with dyslexia from an early age, Wood's ambition has been met with rave reviews for his previous publications, including *Accidents Waiting to Happen*, *Dragged into Darkness*, *Working Stiffs*, *Paying the Piper*, *We All Fall Down*, *Asking For Trouble*, *The Fall Guy*, and numerous others published under his horror pseudonym, Simon Janus. Originally from the UK, Wood moved to the US in '98 to share his world with his American wife, Julie—and a longhaired dachshund and four cats.

16127113R00198

Made in the USA
Charleston, SC
06 December 2012